Jennifer Haigh is the New York Times bestselling author of *Baker Towers*, which won the PEN/ Hemingway Prize. Her fiction has appeared in Granta, Ploughshares, Good Housekeeping and elsewhere. She lives in the Boston area.

www.jenniferhaigh.com

FAITH

Spring, 2002. Sheila McGann has been estranged from her relatives for years, but has remained close to her older brother Art, the popular pastor of a large suburban parish just outside Boston. When Art finds himself at the centre of a sex scandal involving the city's priesthood, Sheila returns to Boston, ready to fight for him and his reputation. What she discovers is more complicated than she imagined. Her strict, lace-curtain Irish mother is living in a state of angry denial. Sheila's younger brother, Mike, to her horror, has already convicted his brother in his heart. But most disturbing of all is Art himself, who persistently dodges Sheila's questions and refuses to defend himself.

Books by Jennifer Haigh
Published by The House of Ulverscroft:

BAKER TOWERS

JENNIFER HAIGH

FAITH

Complete and Unabridged

CHARNWOOD
Leicester

First published in Great Britain in 2011 by
Harper, an imprint of
HarperCollins*Publishers*, London

First Charnwood Edition
published 2012
by arrangement with
HarperCollins*Publishers*, London

British Library CIP Data

Haigh, Jennifer, *1968 –*
  Faith.
  1. Family secrets- -Fiction. 2. Brothers and sisters- -
  Fiction. 3. Irish Americans- -Massachusetts- -Boston- -
  Fiction. 4. Sexual misconduct by clergy- -Fiction.
  5. Domestic fiction. 6. Large type books.
  I. Title
  813.6–dc23

  ISBN 978–1–4448–1119–3

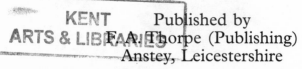
Published by
F. A. Thorpe (Publishing)
Anstey, Leicestershire

Set by Words & Graphics Ltd.
Anstey, Leicestershire
Printed and bound in Great Britain by
T. J. International Ltd., Padstow, Cornwall

This book is printed on acid-free paper

For Jimmy, my first friend

It's a fight you'll never win
And now you bow your head in shame
For a sin no one forgives
— DROPKICK MURPHYS, 'THIS IS YOUR LIFE'

He lives for God, who lives by the Rule.
— ST. BENEDICT

Here is a story my mother has never told me.

It is a day she's relived a thousand times, the twenty-first of June, 1951, the longest day of that or any year. A day that still hasn't ended, as some part of her still paces that dark apartment in Jamaica Plain, waiting. I imagine the curtains closed against the five o'clock sun, hot and bright as midday; her baby boy peacefully asleep; her young self with nothing to do but wander from room to room, still filled with her dead mother-in-law's things.

At the time she'd thought it a grand apartment, her from Roxbury where the children slept three to a bed. Even as a boy her husband had had his own bedroom, an unimaginable luxury. His mother had been injured somehow giving birth and there had been no more children. This fact alone made the Breens wealthier than most, though Harry's father had only worked at Filene's stacking crates in the warehouse. The entire apartment had come from Filene's, on the employee discount, the lamps and brocade divan and what she had learned were called Oriental rugs. Mary herself had never bought a thing at Filene's. Her own mother shopped at Sears.

In the bedroom the baby slept deeply. She parted the curtains and let the sun shine on his face. Harry, when he came home, would pull

1

them shut, worried someone might see him dressing or undressing through their third-floor windows. Sure, it was possible — the windows faced Pond Street, also lined with three-deckers — though why he cared was a puzzle. He was a man, after all. And there was nothing wrong with the sight of him. The first morning of their marriage, lying in the too-soft bed in the tourist cabin in Wellfleet, she had looked up at him in wonderment, her first time seeing him in daylight, his bare chest and shoulders, and her already four months along. Nothing wrong with him at all, her husband tall and blue-eyed, with shiny dark hair that fell into his eyes when he ducked his head, a habit left over from a bashful adolescence, though nobody, now, would call him shy. Harry Breen could talk to anyone. Behind the counter at Old Colony Hardware he had a way with the customers, got them going about their clogged pipes and screen doors and cabinets they were installing. He complimented their plans, suggested small improvements, sent them out the door with twice what they'd come in for. A natural salesman, never mind that he couldn't, himself, hit a nail with a hammer. When a fuse blew at the apartment it was Mary who ventured into the dark basement with a flashlight.

What did you do before? she'd asked, half astonished, when she returned to the lit apartment and found Harry and his mother sitting placidly in the kitchen, stirring sugar into teacups.

We didn't burn so many lights before, the old lady said.

It was a reminder among many others that Mary's presence was unwelcome, that Mrs. Breen, at least, had not invited her into their lives, this grimy interloper with her swollen belly and her skirts and blouses from Sears. As though her condition were a mystery on the order of the Virgin Birth, as though Harry Breen had had nothing to do with it.

She lifted Arthur from his crib and gave his bottom a pat. He wriggled, squealed, fumbled blindly for her breast. The sodden diaper would have to be changed, the baby fed. In this way minutes would pass, and finally an hour. The stubborn sun would begin its grudging descent. Across town, in Roxbury, girls would be dressing for the dances, Clare Boyle and her sister and whoever else they ran with now, setting out by twos and threes down the hill to Dudley Street.

She finished with the diaper, then sat at the window and unbuttoned her blouse, aware of the open curtains. If Harry came upon her like this, her swollen breast exposed, what would he do then? The thought was thrilling in a way she couldn't have explained. But it was after six, and still there was no sign of him. When his mother was alive he'd come straight home after work. You could set your watch by it, his footsteps on the stairs at five-thirty exactly, even on Fridays when the other men stopped at the pub for a taste. Lately, though, his habits had shifted. Mondays and Tuesdays he played cards at the Vets.

3

Once, leaving church, he'd nodded to some men she didn't recognize, a short one and a tall one sharing a cigarette on the sidewalk. *See you tomorrow, then*, Harry called in a friendly tone. The short man had muttered under his breath, and the tall one had guffawed loudly. To Mary it couldn't have been plainer that they were not Harry's friends.

★ ★ ★

They'd met the way everyone met, at the dances. Last summer the Intercolonial was the place to be; now it might be the Hibernian or the Winslow or the Rose Croix for all she knew. On a Saturday night, with Johnny Powell's band playing, a thousand or more would crowd upstairs at the Intercolonial, a mirrored globe hanging from the ceiling so that the walls shivered with light.

She was seventeen then, too young for such pleasures. But it had been easy enough to slip out on a Friday night with Ma dead asleep, exhausted by the work of getting three small ones bathed and in their beds. And it wasn't even a lie to go dancing on a Wednesday, when Mary really did attend the novena at nine o'clock as she was supposed to, the church packed with other overdressed girls and men who'd already had a drink or two, who'd meet up later across the street at Fontaine's Café and make their plans for the evening. *All right, then. See you at the hall.* The men were deep on Wednesdays; you could change partners all night long if you wanted. Thursdays were a different story, maids' night out, the halls packed with Irish girls. There was almost no point in going on a Thursday, the numbers were so against you. On a Thursday you were lucky to get a single dance.

Harry Breen hadn't chosen her, not at first. That first time they'd danced purely by chance. She knew all the dances — the reels and jigs, the wild *céill*. At the Intercolonial waltzes were the thing, though once each night Johnny Powell would force the dreamy couples apart. *Line up, everybody, for the Siege of Ennis.* A mad crush, then, as they formed two long lines, men and girls facing. You'd take your turn with every one, herself and Clare Boyle laughing the whole way through. Some of the men were clumsy, some so strong they'd nearly swing you off your feet.

She noticed Harry a moment before he reached for her. He was taller than the rest, his movements liquid; he swung her gracefully, smooth and controlled. And that thing she first felt, that swooning joy: maybe it was simple geometry, the relative size and shape of their bodies, his chest and shoulders just where they should be, their hips meeting, her eyes level with his mouth.

The plain fact was that she'd chased him, courted his attention. Gone to greater lengths than any girl should. There was no point, now, in being ashamed. She had a ring on her finger and it hardly mattered how. They were married fast by her uncle Fergus, who'd skipped, discreetly, the time-consuming step of publishing the banns. Fergus had guessed what everyone would soon know, that Mary had gotten exactly what she wanted, and a bit more besides.

She looked down at the baby at her breast.

In the kitchen she took her beads from the drawer and found the station in time. Missing the Archbishop's greeting was like coming late to a movie; she'd be unable to enter into the spirit of the thing. When Harry's mother was living, they had knelt in the parlor for the rosary. Now the old lady was gone and no one was looking, so Mary dragged a chair to the open window and settled herself there. *I believe in God the Father Almighty, Creator of Heaven and Earth.* Through the window a breeze came, carrying the Archbishop's voice from the two apartments below. Up and down the street, every radio was tuned to the same station. Through every open window came the same holy words.

It being Thursday, they started with the Joyful. As a girl she had studied the illustrations in her mother's missal. The Joyful Mysteries were the most straightforward, the pictures almost Protestant in their simplicity: the Blessed Virgin kneeling in prayer, waiting for the angel; the Virgin noticeably pregnant, embracing her cousin Elizabeth. The Sorrowful were haunting and in a way lovelier: Our Lord kneeling in the Garden of Gethsemane, glowing in His anguish, perspiring drops of blood. But it was the Glorious Mysteries she waited for, Our Lord lifted into heaven, clouds bubbling beneath His feet like a cauldron of spirits. The Resurrection, the Ascension, the Assumption of the Virgin: all these stirred her deeply, even though (or perhaps

6

because) she understood them the least. That was the beauty of it: contemplating the miracles, sublime and unknowable, and yet the words you repeated couldn't be simpler. *Hail Mary, full of grace.* A prayer you'd known since earliest childhood, familiar as your mother's voice.

She closed her eyes and enjoyed the breeze, the baby's warm weight, the Archbishop's familiar intonations. She had seen him once standing beside the carousel at Paragon Park, eating ice cream with a dozen beaming nuns. In photos, in full regalia, he was imposing, and yet you never forgot that he was from St. Eulalia's in South Boston, that his own father had worked in the repair pits at the Boston El. He never forgot it, either. You could tell this from the photographs: the Archbishop tossing around a football with the CYO boys, or raising a glass at a priest's golden jubilee. The Archbishop wouldn't say no to a drink, according to her uncle Fergus, who'd met him on several occasions. Cushing was God's own, and yet he was theirs, too, in every way a regular man.

She heard two sharp knocks at the front door.

'Coming,' she called, drying herself with a tea towel, noticing all at once the wet stains on her blouse.

She threw open the door. A strange man stood there smoking a cigarette. He wore a thin mustache and was her own height, though she was barefoot and he wore heeled boots. It took her a moment to place him: the short man from outside the church.

'Is your husband at home?' He looked over her

shoulder, his eyes darting around the room.

'I'm sorry, he's not.'

From the kitchen the Archbishop droned: *Glory be to the Father and to the Son and to the Holy Ghost.*

'Listening to the rosary, were you? My mum does that every night.' The man dropped his cigarette and crushed it with his heel. He stepped past her into the apartment. 'You're sure he isn't here?' He glanced into the kitchen as though Harry might be hiding and Mary felt a sudden urge to laugh, a nervous tic. She was forever laughing at the wrong times.

'He hasn't come home yet. Try the store, maybe?'

'I've been there. He left hours ago.'

'I don't know, then. He could have stopped off at the pub.'

The man frowned. 'Never seen him take a drink, myself. Likes to keep his wits about him, doesn't he?' He smiled then, and she saw that on both sides his teeth were missing. It made the front ones look suspect, like the vampire dentures children wore at Halloween.

In her arms the baby let out a loud hiccup. She raised him to her shoulder. 'Excuse me. I was in the middle of feeding him.' Patting him gently, waiting for him to burp. She was afraid to look down at her blouse.

The man stepped in close to her, smelling rankly of cigarette. 'Sorry to miss that,' he said, and to her horror his rough hand touched her face.

Arthur let out another hiccup and vomited in a great burst.

'Jaysus!' The man stepped back, shaking his sleeve. It was coated in yellow spew.

'Oh, no! I'm so sorry.' Mary took the towel from her shoulder and wiped uselessly at his sleeve. The smell was terrible, sour as vinegar. The man tore his hand away, eyeing the baby like a snake.

'That's a real charmer you've got there.' He turned to go. 'Tell your man Shorty wants to see him.'

She closed the door quickly behind him. The door, then the bolt, then the chain.

*　★　★

Tell your man Shorty wants to see him.

He had never, in her memory, stayed out after dark. Only for the card games, and then he always told her beforehand: *I've got the cards tonight, so don't hold supper. I'll have a sandwich or something at Taylor's.*

If he stayed out all night, would she sit up waiting? Brushing her teeth a hundred strokes, a hundred strokes to her long dark hair. Always the counting calmed her — brushstrokes, rosary beads. Half the reason she loved the dancing was the counting of the steps. It gave her mind something to do.

A strange fear gnawed at her stomach. For the first time she wished for a regular man, who'd go to a pub on a Friday. Then, at least, she'd know where to find him. But it was true what Shorty had said: Harry liked to keep a clear head. There was nothing to do but go to Old Colony Hardware. As detectives did in the radio serials: she would go to where Harry was last seen.

I've been there, Shorty had said. *He left hours ago.*

How many hours? she wondered. Where on earth could he have gone?

She went to the telephone. 'Is Father Egan in, please? This is his niece, Mary Breen.' The name new enough, still, to have an odd flavor on her tongue.

'Wedding tonight,' the housekeeper said. 'He'll be back late. I can have him call you tomorrow.'

'Yes, please,' Mary said.

Arthur was cranky and lethargic, his arms and legs moist. She coaxed him into his clothes. Downstairs Mrs. Ruocco was already in her housecoat. She looked startled when Mary came to the door.

'It's my father,' Mary said. 'I have to go see him in the hospital. Could you look after the baby, please?'

Her father was dead five years already, and couldn't be hurt by her lie.

How light she felt, walking up the street with no baby in her arms. She had done it her whole life and never realized. Old Colony Hardware was closed, of course, the metal grille pulled shut in front. Upstairs was an office and a storeroom. Both sets of windows were dark.

Around her the sidewalk was empty, the shops — a butcher, a shoe store — closed for the night. Above them, in apartments, people were living.

The open windows rained down cooking smells, the scrape of cutlery. From above the butcher's came strains of music — Tommy Shields's program, she'd know it anywhere.

Mary Breen stood staring up at the windows, understanding, slowly, that she was alone. The swing of her life had stopped short and sent her flying. She was eighteen on the longest day of the year; she had bet everything on Harry Breen, and had nothing left to lose. She, my mother, crossed the street to the El station, where a train would take her to Dudley Street, and the dancing.

Most of you have heard, by now, what happened to my brother, or a version of it: the alarming events of that spring and summer, the single, vile accusation, still unproven, that made a ruin of his life. In Philadelphia, where I live, his story was buried deep in the Nation section, a terse paragraph picked off one of the wire services, giving little more than his name, Arthur Breen; his age, fifty-one; and the name of his parish, Sacred Heart. The Boston papers paid more attention, delving into his years at seminary, his time in Rome, the three suburban parishes where he served without incident. As is typical in these cases, his accuser was not named.

You may not remember the particulars. In that year, 2002, it would have been easy to conflate the story with others. The sad truth is that such tales are no longer rare. As a girl I once went along with my mother, who cleaned, for no pay, the parish rectory every Saturday morning. I watched her take wastebaskets from the bedrooms and bathrooms and empty the used dental floss and crumpled Kleenex into a metal trash can she then dragged to the back door. I was very small, five or six, and flabbergasted by the discovery that priests blew their noses. The very idea gave me a jolt.

12

That isn't to say I considered priests superhuman. Despite his flash costumes and his one, peculiar superpower — the miracle of transubstantiation, performed seven days a week, twice on Sundays — old Father Cronin had little in common with the masked heroes in comic books. And yet I did see him as *other than human*, made of different stuff than the rest of us. It sounds fanciful now, but I truly believed it, and I suppose other children did, too.

I mention this because a child's ideas about priests seem relevant to the story, though the world has changed in thirty years, and for all I know children have, too. Though I never saw a priest do anything truly outrageous, I probably wouldn't have objected if I had. Honestly, I expected them to be strange. The rules allowed it, even required it: the lonely rectories, the long black dresses. At the same time, I understood that these men were not born priests. My brother had been a normal boy, a child like any other. It was at St. John's Seminary that he became something else. That he himself was transubstantiated.

How exactly that happened is a question I still ponder. I was a teenager when Art was ordained. It is a memory that still haunts me: nine young men in white robes lying facedown on the cathedral floor, receiving the blessing of Cardinal Medeiros, who ran the Boston Archdiocese at the time. When he had finished with them, the candidates were seated on the altar. An army of priests filed past to offer blessings, a hundred times the laying on of hands. Truly, it was

13

something to see. Yet I am a doubter, and I doubt that these rituals caused Art's transformation. At most, they simply marked it. Transubstantiation had begun years earlier. Art was not yet a man when he started becoming a priest.

He was fourteen, and I was too young to notice, when he left us for St. John's — its high school division, what was then called the minor seminary. It isn't called anything now. The Archdiocese no longer corrals together herds of parentless boys in the throes of hormonal upheaval. I'd like to say that Lake Street finally came to its senses, but the truth is that there are no longer any boys willing to be herded. It's hard to imagine now, but in the mid-sixties there was no shortage of volunteers. Every autumn, male teenagers from across the Archdiocese were packed off to Brighton, traveling home, as Art did, on holidays and occasional weekends. It sounds quaint, in an age when every teenager carries a cell phone, to say that he wrote weekly letters to my mother, but that is what he did. Ma read them aloud at family dinners, at church functions. Frankly, she bragged. To have a son at St. John's was a prestigious thing for a family like ours. I was an erratic student, and my younger brother Mike downright hopeless; but Art excelled in all subjects, not just the priestly ones. He had an ear for languages and music; his voice, before it changed, was fine and pure as the top register of a clarinet. As a boy he sang or whistled constantly, a habit that irked my father.

Cut it out, will you? he'd complain when he caught Art humming under his breath.

Art, who feared him, hushed instantly, only to start up again a few minutes later. He was not a defiant child; in fact, the exact opposite. But his singing was unconscious and irrepressible — an expression of his native exuberance, the dreamy, buoyant soundtrack running through his head.

Whatever his other sins, my father, Ted McGann, is not a dour man. He has been known, late in the evening, to croon a few bars of 'Mother Machree' in a manly tenor; in his young days he was considered to have quite a voice. It was Art's repertoire that rankled him. My brother was a small, slight boy; puberty came late to him, and the Rondelles and the Supremes were still an easy reach. I imagine the family sitting down to supper, an unseasonably heavy meal of beef stew or shepherd's pie. Imagine rather than remember, though technically I was there, in my high chair, eating mashed potatoes with a spoon. All five of us, in fact, were present, my mother eight months pregnant with a kicking, oversized male infant, Mike taking up as much space as possible even in the womb. The snug eat-in kitchen was stifling, filled with afternoon sun. Like most of our neighbors, we kept Raytheon hours. My mother put dinner on the table at five o'clock precisely. Dad's shift ended at four.

At dinnertime the radio played softly in the background — my mother kept it on all day, at low volume, as she cleaned or cooked or laundered. Marooned with a cranky toddler, she was profoundly lonely, yet she chose its staticky drone over the gossip of the neighborhood

15

women, whose company she both longed for and scorned. She was the first to notice when Art began humming, the first wisps of his sweet falsetto. Even now, in her older years, she hears like a bat. Her foot would seek his under the table, a nudge of warning. But Art could not be stopped.

She glanced nervously at my father. His anger was a mercurial thing, sometimes gathering slowly, sometimes bursting forth without warning, a fast-moving storm. He drank then, but not as much as he would later. He might have stopped off for a quick one after work, no more. Yet even sober he had a temper. I say this not to shame him, but because his anger was a factor in Art's choices: my brother's place in the family and the reasons he left us, the sad trajectory of his priesthood. A factor, even, in his recent actions, ending in the events I'll get to soon.

★ ★ ★

Grantham is a seaside town, battered by weather. It occupies a narrow finger of land jutting into Boston Harbor, the outermost reaches of a cluster of suburbs known as the South Shore. At its thickest the finger is a half-mile wide, so that no house is more than a quarter mile from the ocean. To the west of the finger lies Boston Harbor. A commuter ferry crosses it four times a day, from Long Wharf in Boston to Grantham's Berkeley Pier. On the east side of town, grand old houses occupy the Atlantic beachfront, built when the town was a vacation spot for the

16

wealthy. (You may have seen the famous photo of a future president, a blue-eyed urchin of three or four building a lopsided Camelot in Grantham sand.) Today the old Victorians are still standing, dark in winter, in season rented by the week. Year-round residents like my parents live in low Capes and ranches, covered in vinyl siding to cut down on the painting, though the salt air still takes a heavy toll on porches and windows and doors. The backyards are squared off by chain-link fences. The houses are tidy or ramshackle, depending on the street, but even the most derelict neighborhoods have a certain charm, gulls squawking, a seasmell I never noticed until I moved away. In stormy weather add the low moan of Grantham Light, the second oldest on the East Coast.

There are storms. It's impossible to describe Grantham without mentioning the wind. It is, I'm told, the windiest town in Massachusetts, no small distinction if you've witnessed Province-town or Gloucester or Marblehead in a gale. I heard this from an insurance agent who, after the blizzard of '78, spent half the eighties processing claims for Grantham homeowners. In most months the wind is omnipresent, a constant ruffling, scratching, snuffling, as though a large pet, a zoo animal perhaps, were sleeping at the back door.

My parents' house is three blocks from the seawall, so by local standards they live inland. Like many places in town, theirs started out a Cape. The prior owner had added a second floor, two snug bedrooms that would soon belong to

17

me and Mike. When I go back to visit, which isn't often, I am struck by the closeness of the place. Our living arrangements were so intimate that no cough or sneeze or bowel movement could go unnoticed. I fell asleep each night to the sound of my father's snoring, a low rumbling beneath the floorboards. Dad was the rhythm section, riffing along with the soprano gulls, the bass violin of Grantham Light, the percussive brush of the wild, wild wind.

In the eyes of the neighborhood we were a small family, made exotic by my mother's past. She had been married before, a brief teenage union that her uncle, also a priest, had used his influence to have annulled, though it had already produced a son. Her husband had disappeared into a bright Friday afternoon when Art was just a baby, for reasons that remain mysterious. According to Aunt Clare Boyle — not really my aunt, but a childhood friend of my mother's — he'd borrowed money from a South Boston shark only a fool would cross. It remains to this day a breaking story: fifty years on, the details are still subject to change. Clare, lonely in her old age, uses the information to attract visitors, serves it up a scrap at a time alongside the shortbread and milky tea.

The marriage itself was no secret — Art kept his father's surname, Breen — but it was a topic we didn't discuss. According to a raft of yellowed papers I found in Ma's attic, the Commonwealth granted her a divorce on grounds of abandonment, a fact never mentioned. She preferred the

18

Church's explanation: the marriage had simply never occurred.

And so my father, Ted McGann, became Art's stepfather. At the time nobody used the idiotic term *blended family*. Maybe such households exist, but in our case, the label did not apply. We were two distinct families, unblended, the one simply grafted on to the other. I felt, always, that Art belonged to Ma and to his lost father, Mike to my own father and what I think of as Dad's tribe, who are noisy and numerous and in their own way impressive. Like them Mike is blond, square in the shoulders and jaw. He has the McGann restlessness, stubbornness, and stamina. It says something about him, and the way he lives his life, that he has never solved a problem by mere reflection. This goes a long way toward explaining his role in Art's story. He so resembles Dad that he seems to have no other parent. His DNA is pure McGann.

I have always been fascinated by heredity, the traits passed on from mother and father, the two sets of genes whirred together in a blender. Art and I favor our mother. From the time I was thirteen or fourteen, people have noticed the resemblance: *Ah, Mary, she's the picture of you at that age.* Always Ma dismissed the idea — quickly, prophylactically, as if afraid of where the conversation might lead. Once she turned to study me intently, as a stranger might. *Really?* she asked, as though she were seriously considering the possibility. And then: *I don't see it, myself.*

Yet a few facts even Ma can't deny, such as

19

our common height, our dark hair and pale freckled skin, our eyes that are sometimes green, sometimes brown. Ma and I have long faces, thin lips, sharp noses. These are features a woman must grow into: homely in childhood, plain in adolescence, attractive in middle age. Well into her sixties, my mother was finally quite striking, though the overall effect was not beauty, but a fierce kind of astuteness. Art's more generous features, his dimples and full mouth, must have come from his father. Because I have no way to verify this, not even a wedding picture, I am free to fill in the details as I like; and I like to think that there was something sweet and expansive in that man, Ma's first love.

As a child I felt caught between these two families: on the one hand Ma and Art, who *looked* like my relations; on the other Dad and Mike. I switched allegiances as it suited me, depending on which way the wind was blowing.

The wind, of course, being Dad.

My father's drinking, and his anger. Each fueled the other, though in which direction? Did he drink because he was angry, and or did he get angry when he drank?

Art was twelve when my parents married, and I can imagine how that affected him. My father, as I've suggested, is not an easy man, and here was a boy used to having his mother to himself. Ted McGann was twenty-four when he met Ma, just out of the Navy and, by Clare Boyle's account, looking for a good time. Why he got mixed up with an older woman (four years, to Aunt Clare, was a significant age difference), a woman who already had a child, was a Sorrowful Mystery for the ages.

Of course, Clare Boyle knows nothing about men.

I have seen photos of my mother at the time, her skirts shorter than I have ever seen her wear, her black hair long and loose. Where's the mystery? My parents were handsome people; they dated a few short months and quickly became engaged. If I know my mother at all, she kept Art clear of my father until the deal was closed, a habit she maintained throughout my childhood, perhaps unconsciously. Even now (especially now) her firstborn is a subject she and Dad don't discuss.

Art remembered little of their engagement, a fact I have always found significant. Before the wedding he met Ted a handful of times: a few Sunday dinners, an afternoon at the beach. Then the man moved into their apartment — they lived in town then, the top floor of a three-decker in Jamaica Plain — and soon I was born. A year later my parents bought the house in Grantham, and the following year Art went off to St. John's, the first step in his long journey to become a priest.

★ ★ ★

If you aren't Catholic — or maybe especially if you are — you have wondered what possesses a young man to choose that life, with its elaborate privations. I have asked Art this question, expecting the boilerplate Church response, that

21

priests are called by God. His answer surprised me. It helps, he said, to be a child, with little understanding of what he is forfeiting. Love to marriage to home and family: connect those dots, and you get the approximate shape of most people's lives. Take them away, and you lose any hope for connection. You give up your place in the world.

His words startled me, the deep weariness in his voice. We were speaking by phone late one night, a few years back. I have tried to date the conversation, with no success. We are both nocturnal, and likely spoke after midnight. But was it five years ago, or four, or three? Had he already met Kath Conlon and her son?

We became close in adulthood, a fact my younger self would have found surprising. Art had been a fixture in my early life, a regular presence at family gatherings; but our child-hoods had scarcely overlapped; we never shared the noisy, grubby intimacy I had with Mike. My younger brother tells a story about his own fourth birthday. (Can he really remember that far back? Or is he merely conjuring up a photo from the family album, one I also recall: Mike sitting regally in his high chair, a chubby potentate; before him a decorated cake, a candle shaped like the number 4.) Art had brought him a toy, a stuffed giraffe with a ribbon round its neck, and Mike knew to say *thank you* even though it was nothing he wanted, a gift for a baby or, maybe, a girl. He had hesitated, unsure how to address the man in black. The aunts and uncles called him 'Father.' Yet Art was also his *brother*. None of it had made sense.

I felt a similar confusion. My deeper closeness with Art coincided with my move to Philadelphia and, not accidentally, the end of my churchgoing. It was easier to think of Art as a brother the less I thought about his work, and in Philly I had no contact with priests. I once phoned Art in mid-August and asked, innocently, how he'd spent his day. I'd forgotten it was the feast of the Assumption, though the Holy Days of Obligation had been drummed into my head from an early age. We both knew then that I had left the fold forever. Except for the one time, which I'll get to later, he never tried to coax me back.

It seems, now, that I should have seen trouble coming. But Art had been a priest for twenty-five years; moreover, he had never been anything else. I understood that his life lacked certain kinds of human closeness, but then so did mine. I'd recently placed a down payment on a studio apartment, a large sunny room at the top of an old row house. In Philadelphia it was all the space a high school teacher could afford, and all I could imagine needing, a concrete commitment to the path I'd been following quietly for years. I'd tried marriage — briefly, disastrously — and was divorced with a slice of wedding cake still in my freezer, awaiting our first anniversary. It had long appeared likely, and at last seemed decided, that I would always live alone.

Was it my own loneliness that made Art's invisible? I wouldn't have said he was unhappy being a priest. I was present the Sunday he gave his first homily and I can still remember his ease at the pulpit. Years of parochial schooling had overexposed me to sermons, but Art's were unlike any I'd heard. His style was gentle and humorous, slyly persuasive. He was so thoughtful and engaging that I might have listened to him anyway, even if he weren't my brother. His new life fit him. Singing the Kyrie, he seemed to glow with a deep contentment, his rich tenor filling the small chapel, his eyes closed in prayer. Unusual, and gratuitous, to sing it in Latin: I understood this was a private gift to my mother. I turned to look at her sitting behind me, her eyes full.

How alive he seemed to me then, how exhilarated by his first baptism, first wedding, first midnight Mass. But these are old memories. In recent years he scarcely spoke of his work. Our conversations revolved around family news, the aches and illnesses of our aging parents, Mike's marriage and the births of his three sons. Art never expressed regrets, not explicitly; but of course he had them. Show me a man of fifty who doesn't regret the lives he hasn't lived.

I read over what I've written — *of course he had them* — and am ashamed of myself, the words seem so smug and facile. How easily I dismiss his sorrows, the griefs and losses that haunted him. The truth is that I loved Art, and that I failed him, in ways that will become clear.

For the first few months I tracked the scandal. Soon the reports referred to Art's case only in passing, and I realized that the story was much larger than my brother. At minimum it involved the entire Boston Archdiocese, hundreds of victims, dozens of priests. Day after day, until I could swallow no more, I ingested the queasy details, nicely organized in timelines and bullet points. The reporters didn't strike me as biased, and one could hardly accuse them of laziness. One persistent fellow dogged my poor parents for months. I don't believe, as my mother still does, that the press set out to make Art a monster. The accusations themselves were monstrous. And the evidence either way — of his guilt or innocence — was very slim.

And whose fault is that? a small voice asks me. It isn't God's voice or my brother's, but the voice of my own conscience, which I have ignored successfully for some time. I have kept Art's secrets. My excuse until now has been loyalty. Art asked that I tell no one, and I have kept my word.

Two years have passed since the events of that spring — a calendar spring, equinox to solstice; three months that, in New England, can feel like summer or winter. My parents still live in Grantham. On the surface their lives are unchanged. But my mother no longer attends daily Mass, or cleans the church rectory or pours coffee at parish dinners. On Sundays she sits alone in a rear pew, her head bowed. (My father won't set foot in a church, but that's nothing to do with Art. He hasn't been to Mass in years.) Kneeling before the Blessed Sacrament, Ma prays only for her Arthur, that God in His mercy will forgive whatever he has done.

Lately I visit Grantham without seeing my parents. I've never done this before, but then I've never had any reason to go back beyond guilt and a vague sense of obligation. Now I sleep on the foldout couch in Mike's finished basement, waking at dawn when my three nephews clamber down the stairs to play video games at high volume. I pay visits to Art's former church and rectory, and to those who knew him at that time: the church council; the parish housekeeper; the few diocesan priests willing to talk to me, only one of whom Art might have called a friend. We meet away from their rectories, at Dunkin' Donuts outlets deep in the suburbs, at diners, at bars. It is a function of my upbringing that I find it unsettling to drink with a priest. Certainly my mother would be mortified at the thought. Recent events have done nothing to dim her admiration of these men, and yet her encounters with them — at Legion of Mary bake sales, the annual Christmas luncheon of the local Catholic Daughters of the Americas — are fraught with anxiety. Three years ago — just before Art's disgrace — she attended a celebration of his silver jubilee. She beamed with pride through the anniversary Mass. Yet according to Mike, who sat beside her, at the dinner afterward she was nervous as a cat. Introduced to a series of friendly men in clerical collars, she flushed and stammered, stricken with embarrassment.

What she fears — I know this — is exposure. Of her own sins, real or imagined; her and my father's secret shames. After I have told Art's story, it's possible, likely even, that she will never speak to me again. Foolishly maybe, I hope otherwise. In my fantasy we sit together in her

26

quiet kitchen, just us two. I open my heart to her and lay it on the table between us. I am still child enough to wish it were possible, adult enough to know it isn't. We are too much ourselves, the people we have always been.

★ ★ ★

The Bible offers four accounts of the life of Jesus, told by four different writers: Matthew, Mark, Luke and John. God's Beatles wrote in different languages, in different centuries. Each saw the story in his own terms. Matthew had a particular interest in Jesus's childhood. Mark cared mainly about the endgame, the betrayal, crucifixion and death. Only Luke — who never met Our Lord — mentions the two famous parables, the Good Samaritan and the Prodigal Son. John's gospel is full of miracles and revelations, the raising of Lazarus, its own charmed poetry. *I am the Light of the world. I am the true Vine. Abide in me.*

The story of my family likewise changes with the teller. Ma's version focuses on the early years. (Each year at our birthdays we were treated to our own nativity stories — Art the preemie, Mike the breech birth, myself the induced labor — as though she were trying to decide, once and for all, which child had caused her the greatest misery in coming into the world.) Mike's gospel is terse and action-packed; like the apostle Mark, he cuts to the chase. Clare Boyle's tale, if she'll tell it, is full of innuendo and hearsay. Like Luke, she

27

merely repeats what she's heard.

Art was our apostle John.

For most of my life, I have refused to take part in the telling. In some way this was an act of rebellion. I was eighteen when I moved away from Boston, and I'd had enough of the McGann family lore. But recent events have changed my thinking, and I offer here my own version of the story, a kind of fifth gospel. The early pages borrow heavily from other accounts. The miracles and revelations will come later, the stories never before told.

So, to those who remained loyal to my brother, and those who didn't: here is his story as far as I know it, what Art told me at the time and what I found out later, and what I still can't verify but know in my heart to be true. In many cases I have re-created events I did not witness. There was nothing sophisticated in my method. I simply worked out what certain people must have said or felt, a task made easier by the fact that the two leading men were my brothers — one who confided in me, if belatedly and selectively; the other so deeply familiar that I can nearly channel his thoughts. This isn't as extraordinary as it sounds. It's mainly a function of his consistent character that in any given situation, I can predict, with dependable accuracy, what Mike would say and do. As for the other actors in the story, I have done my best, relying occasionally on the memories of people who may have reason to mislead me. Where their recollections seem dubious, I have noted this. In the end I believe that I have reported events fairly. So much has been spoiled and lost that there is no longer any reason to prevaricate.

Why would anyone go to such lengths to tell this sorry tale? It's a fair question, and the answer is that no one would, unless she'd felt God's presence and then His absence; once believed, and later failed and doubted. A sister might tell it, a sister sick with regret.

Art's story is, to me, the story of my own family, with all its darts and dodges and mysterious omissions: the open secrets long unacknowledged, the dark relics never unearthed. I understand, now, that Art's life was ruined by secrecy, a familial failing; and that I played a part in his downfall — a minor role, to be sure, and a third-act entrance; but a role nonetheless. There is no healing my brother, not now; and Aidan Conlon is a child still; it's too soon to tell what his future holds. So maybe it's for myself that I make this public act of contrition. My penance is to tell this ragged truth as completely as I know it, fully aware that it is much too little, much too late.

The story begins on a bright afternoon many years ago, one I remember as though I'd seen it. (This is natural enough in a family like ours, with its canon of approved stories. They are told in the manner of repertory theater: hang around long enough and you'll hear them all.) Imagine the trees tinged with red, a sky so clear it seems contrived, the high blue heaven of tourist brochures. It is the first resplendent day of a New England fall, and Ma's new husband is driving from Grantham to Brighton, his hand on her thigh. They are dressed for a wedding or a funeral: she in Sunday hat and gloves, he grudgingly coaxed into a suit. In the backseat is a battered footlocker from his Navy days, packed with the few possessions a junior seminarian is allowed. Squeezed in beside it is Art, fourteen years old, staring out at a scene that will shape the rest of his life: the headquarters of the Boston Archdiocese and its famous seminary, St. John's.

The decision to come here had been his alone. From the age of ten he'd served as an altar boy. Two mornings a week he'd met Father Cronin in the vestry at St. Dymphna's, helped him into his chasuble and alb. At the altar Art genuflected, lit candles, carried cruets. At Consecration he rang the bells. The sound never failed to send him soaring, a feeling that was nearly indescribable: a sweet exhilaration, a spreading warmth. In those moments he'd sensed a transformation occurring, before him and inside him. Bread and wine into the Body and Blood. An ordinary boy into something else.

In the confessional Father Cronin posed the question. *Have you ever considered it?* They discussed at some length what a vocation felt like, how you could ever be sure. *Certainty will come later*, the priest promised. And one Sunday after Mass, he invited Ma to the rectory for a chat.

Now, washed and waxed for the occasion, Dad's car passed through the stone gates. A few others were already parked behind the dormitory, a cavernous brick building perched atop a hill. Ted hefted the trunk to his shoulder and with much grumbling hauled it up three flights of stairs, down a long corridor to the cell Art would share with a boy named Ray Cousins. (I do not invent this: in those days at least, seminarians, like prisoners, slept in cells.)

Like all others on the third floor, Art's cell was small and square. In it were two narrow beds, two wooden desks. The floors were bare; metal blinds hung at the one window. There were no rugs — a fact my mother emphasizes in the telling — and no curtains. No trace, anywhere, of anything soft.

Dad set down the trunk. Ma was uncharacteristically silent, her eyes welling. It was the moment Art had dreaded for months.

'I'll be fine,' he said, embracing her. 'I'll write you.' Briefly he shook Ted's hand.

★ ★ ★

I should say a few words about that campus, which figures so prominently in the life and ministry of my brother. How those buildings came to be is a story in itself. For the nearly forty years that William Cardinal O'Connell ran the Archdiocese, Boston was the capital of Catholic America, and in his eyes it deserved a *facciata* as grand as the Vatican. 'Little Rome,' the local papers called it, the hills of Brighton dotted with monuments: the seminary's neoclassic library and exquisite chapel, the elegant palazzo where the Cardinal slept and the ostentatious mausoleum where he sleeps now. At the entrance of each building was carved the Cardinal's own motto, *Vigor in Arduis*.

Strength Amid Difficulties.

It was, in every way, the house O'Connell had built.

Art was barely a teenager when he arrived there, and for twelve years it was — not his home, exactly, but as close to one as an aspiring priest was allowed. Later I would visit him there. Together we walked its landscaped hills, its winding footpaths. Art showed me a shady grove of cedars that hid a secret: a round swimming pool, long drained, its cement cracked. The pool was twelve feet across and five feet deep. Cardinal O'Connell had ordered it dug for the summertime refreshment of his dogs, two black poodles that, like the seminarians in their black cassocks, suffered from the heat.

32

*　　*　　*

In minor seminary, order was paramount. The boys lived according to an ancient template, a sixth-century invention. Benedict was not yet a saint when he fashioned it. Forever after, it was known as the Rule.

The Rule governed the boys' movements. The seminary day was punctuated by bells. There were bells for sleeping and waking and morning Mass, for meals and study and sports. Six classes a day, each an hour. Each opened and closed with a prayer.

At first bell the boys rose and dressed. An upperclassman hand-picked by the rector made his way down each corridor, singing out the morning greeting: *Benedicamus Domino.*

The boys sang in answer: *Deo Gratias.*

The day's first class was Latin. The teacher, Father Fleury, had studied in Rome. He was young and fair-haired and wished himself elsewhere — among the ruins at Ostia Antica; kneeling before the Sacrament at Santa Maria Maggiore; walking along the Tiber, breviary in hand. In a few short years the Latin Mass would be abandoned, but at St. John's at least, the fact would go unacknowledged. The curriculum would not change. Why learn Latin if the Mass was said in English? If the boys wondered, they gave no sign. They declined and conjugated and asked no questions. Father Fleury corrected them rigorously.

In nomine Patris, et Filii, et Spiritus Sancti.

A bell rang.

The boys processed to algebra, then history. The noon bell called them to chapel. In silence they walked to the refectory for lunch. A hot meal always, meat bathed in slick gravy — unappetizing fare, and yet they'd have killed for more of it; the invisible cooks, by ignorance or design, misjudged the hunger of growing boys. The priests sat up front at a long table, the rector at the center. At his elbow was a brass bell. If he rang the bell after the blessing, talking was forbidden. A seminarian would read aloud from scripture. A hundred boys chewed and swallowed.

A bell rang.

English came next; then biology. A bell rang for afternoon rec. The gymnasium had tall mullioned windows, as the dead Cardinal had ordered; they'd been covered in chicken wire to protect the fine glass. The boys suited up for basketball, a game Art had once avoided. (In Grantham it was a sport for tough boys. A Morrison or a Pawlowski might take out your eye.) But like everything at seminary, sport was mandatory; and Art was no longer the smallest or the shyest. Day after day the boys raced across the court, a crest painted at its center: *Seminarium Sancti Joannis Bostoniense 1884.*

A bell rang.

The boys showered and dressed, for dinner, Rosary, Spiritual Reading. At eight o'clock came the Grand Silence. Until breakfast the next morning, talking was forbidden. Not a word would be spoken in the corridors.

The routine was fixed; it deviated for no one.

Like those before him — *more majorum* — Art lived by the Rule.

★ ★ ★

He took to this new life with great enthusiasm, a sunflower turning its face to the sky. He loved the orderly days, the mornings in chapel. The silence nourished him; his soul expanded to fill it. Every moment of the day became a prayer. The buildings themselves thrilled him, their high vaulted ceilings — to draw the eye upward, said Father Dowd; the mind closer to God.

Father Dowd taught the boys music. He was the youngest of the faculty, a brand-new priest, only eight years older than the senior boys. The other priests treated pupils with a certain disregard, knowing that half would leave before graduation; that a scant 10 percent would eventually be ordained. But Father Dowd was not dismissive. He was known to have favorites. Those boys who sang out joyfully, who were not struck deaf when singing harmony: his work was made bearable by such pupils, the Arthur Breens and Gary Moriconis who could still hit the high notes. That first year, unspoiled by puberty, Art sang like an angel. In class, after his solo, Father Dowd had said as much. 'What I would give for a dozen Breens,' he told the boys, his eyes misting with pleasure. Arthur Breen could sing anything. His voice was God's gift.

'Such a pity,' Father Dowd told the class, 'that it has to change.'

He launched, then, into a history lesson.

Centuries ago, a voice like Arthur Breen's would have been preserved by castration. The *castrati* were the superstars of their day, the *primi uomi* of early opera. They sang with otherworldly range and power, the darlings of popes, cardinals and kings.

Listening, Art had blushed scarlet. From that day onward he avoided Father Dowd's confessional, a choice easily justified: Father Dowd's line was always the longest, his favorite boys — Ray Cousins, Gary Moriconi — at the head of the line.

Of Art's teachers, Father Fleury was the most inspiring. He spoke often of his travels to Rome. The splendors of Vatican City he called *our patrimony*. Every Catholic ought to visit as often as possible. To his pupils it was a stunning admonition; in their working-class neighborhoods, Rome might have been Neptune. Art listened in fascination. His Latin vocabulary doubled, then tripled, so desperate was he to please Father Fleury. It was a task that demanded considerable effort, the priest's attention was so clearly elsewhere.

Adult indifference, its power to motivate children, is old news in Catholic circles. My own mother practiced a version of this approach — by natural inclination, I suspect, more than by design. Father Fleury's disregard was, to Art, oddly reassuring. He was unused to flatterers like Father Dowd, confused by male attention of any kind. With his stepfather, indifference was the best you could hope for. If you did anything to attract his notice, there would be hell to pay. But unlike Ted McGann, Father Fleury wasn't volatile or angry, just preoccupied with other matters. Art lived to impress him. Years later he would recall the time he scored a 99 on a quarterly exam and was rewarded with a rare smile.

He had made no errors, but Father Fleury did not award 100s. He subtracted one point, always, for original sin.

Art had never had a father. When Ma's first marriage was annulled — literally *made into nothing* — Harry Breen was expunged from the record. Art was the awkward reminder of a union that had, officially, never been. Now, suddenly, he had more fathers than he knew what to do with: Father Fleury, Father Koval, Father Frontino, Father Dowd. They taught him more than Latin and history, algebra and music. By word and example they taught priestliness: ways of speaking and acting; of not speaking and not acting. Restraint and discipline, obedience and silence.

For a shy boy, these formulas were a help and a comfort. Art didn't miss his old school, the rough-and-tumble Grantham Junior High. St. John's was a haven from all that frightened him, the alarming interplay of male and female, that intricate and wild dance. Like many boys he feared the opposite sex. But even more intensely, he feared his own.

A certain kind of boy unnerved him, hale athletes, confident and aggressive. At seminary such specimens were blessedly few. From the first it was clear that a range existed: alpha males

37

at the one end; at the other, the distinctly effete. Both extremes were, to Art, alarming. Like Latin nouns, the boys came in three genders: masculine, feminine and neuter. He placed himself in the third category, undifferentiated. In the seminary at least, it seemed the safest place to be.

Matters of sex, of maleness and femaleness, were in this world peripheral. He felt protected by silence, grateful at all that was left unsaid. Once, at a Lenten retreat, Father Koval had delivered a steely sermon, exhorting the boys to keep their *vessels clean*. To Art, at fifteen, the words remained mysteriously figurative, vaguely connected to all that had distressed him in his old life: at home, the nighttime noises from Ma and Ted's bedroom; at school, the fragrant and fleshy presence of girls.

The life of a celibate priest. Father Koval had compared it to climbing Mount Everest: the outer limits of man's capacity, a daring test that few were brave enough to attempt. The rhetoric was aimed at the boys' nascent machismo; to Art, who had none, it rang false. A better comparison, he felt, was a journey on a spaceship. A priest was isolated and weightless. He existed outside gravity — the force that attracted bodies to other bodies, that tethered them to God's earth.

★ ★ ★

Art grew up in this atmosphere, outside gravity. Troubling questions were answered for him, and he accepted these answers in gratitude and relief. So when he graduated from high school and entered the seminary proper, he was unprepared for the sudden change in the weather. That September a new rector was brought over from Rome, a strapping, ursine priest named James Duke.

The previous rector had been mild and scholarly, a soft-spoken man with a distracted air. But *Il Duce* was another sort entirely. He exuded, by priestly standards, an air of raw masculinity; and surrounded himself with others — Father Noel Bearer, Father Stephen Hurley — of the same type.

The new regime seemed, at first, comically harmless. Their demeanor struck Art as clownish, a self-conscious parody of manliness. Then came the warnings — repeated with ominous frequency — against *particular friendships*. This injunction was not new. Close friendships violated the spirit of community; they were contrary to the Rule. Under the old rector, *particular friendships* had seldom been mentioned; now, suddenly, they seemed a matter of great concern. No suggestion was made, ever, of illicit affections between the men; but everyone was aware of the subtext. Art found himself avoiding his best friend Larry Person, who shared his interest in music. They no longer rode the T into Boston to hear Sunday concerts downtown. Smoking in the courtyard between classes, Art took notice of who else was standing at the ashtray. Groups of three or four were acceptable. Twosomes were inherently suspect.

Among the men paranoia blossomed — fears inflamed at the end of the school year, when a few were told by their confessors that the faculty harbored concerns. Art's old cellmate Ray Cousins was censured for his distinctive voice. The criticism was so vaguely worded that Ray didn't understand, at first, why he was being scolded. True, he admitted to Art, he wasn't much of a singer; still, many a parish priest had learned to fake his way through the Mass. But Ray's deficiency was not musical. His voice was high-pitched, with a discernible lisp. Suddenly Art no longer felt safe in the epicene middle. In the era of *Il Duce*, nobody was safe.

And yet somehow he came through unscathed; his own masculinity, however stunted and friable, was never questioned. At the time, and for years afterward, this fact astonished him. That spring he was chosen, at Father Fleury's recommendation, to spend his four years of theology study at the Gregorian University in Rome, a rare distinction. To Clement Fleury he owed his escape.

I was a little girl when Art left for the Greg, too young to understand much of his business there. I do recall impressing my fourth-grade class with the postcards he sent me: the Colosseum and Forum and Trevi Fountain; multiple views of St. Peter's, each bearing a florid stamp. *Poste Vaticane*.

One of these cards is still in my possession, a nighttime shot of the basilica Santa Maria Maggiore, an exquisite jewel box of a church. It is a glittering repository of Catholic treasure

— priceless sculptures by Bernini and Jacometti, every flat surface bedecked with frescoes and mosaics. The ceiling, legend has it, is gilded in Inca gold. In Art's opinion — inherited from Father Fleury — Santa Maria is more beautiful than St. Peter's. Judging from my postcards, I would have to agree.

★ ★ ★

Meanwhile, beyond the seminary walls, the world was changing. Art had been baptized into one Church, confirmed into another. A bold new pope, the astonishing Roncalli, had proclaimed an *aggiornamento*; a new day had dawned. The liturgy went from Latin to English. The altars were literally turned around backward, and priests said Mass while facing the congregation. In choir lofts, organs were joined by acoustic guitars.

It seemed inevitable that the changes would continue. True, Roncalli's successor, Cardinal Montini, was no reformer; but Montini was not young. The next pope, it was said, would bring the Church into the twentieth (or at least the nineteenth) century, and perhaps beyond.

Art was twenty-five when he left Rome. He had traveled widely across Europe, seen every major cathedral in France and Spain. He returned to Boston with a powerful sense of mission, ready for ordination and all that lay beyond. *Aggiornamento* had inspired a whole generation. In Rome he'd met priests from Central and South America who spoke movingly

41

of their people's struggles, the Church's power to effect social change. Activism was the Church's future, and Art itched to be a part of it. For the diaconate year, as his classmates dispersed to local parishes, he was sent to a shelter for homeless men in the city's South End. It was an unusual assignment, uniquely tailored to his tastes and aspirations. Once again, Father Fleury had worked his magic on Art's behalf.

The South End has since gentrified, filled with posh restaurants and pricy boutiques, but in those days it still belonged to the poor. Each morning Art rode the T deep into Boston. At the shelter he ministered to the maimed and broken, the sick and delusional. There were men back from Vietnam, scarred by combat; lost inmates from state psychiatric hospitals decimated by budget cuts. There were addicts and runaways, boys barely out of childhood who came on buses to South Station and sold themselves on Washington Street. It was a veritable army of the needy, and yet the Archdiocese paid little attention. When Art arrived there, only one priest was seen in the shelters and on the streets. Art knew him by reputation only: the Street Priest, young and long-haired, who walked the Combat Zone in vests and blue jeans, seeking out the lost. The Street Priest's apartment on Beacon Street was a gathering place for the desperate, the lonely and addicted. On Sunday mornings he said Mass there, with twenty or thirty runaways sitting Indian-style on the floor.

To Art it seemed the stuff of urban legend. He himself had handed out blankets and the

Eucharist; occasionally he heard a garbled confession; but certainly he was no Street Priest. In his first week he was mugged at knifepoint. At the shelter he was treated as a curiosity, when he was noticed at all. If the Street Priest was the clergy's future, Arthur Breen felt better qualified for the past.

In other ways, too, the future frightened him. The celibate priesthood — would it go the way of indulgences and Latin? — was a point of fierce controversy. He'd been a boy at St. John's when he first heard this debate. At the time it caused him considerable distress. The priesthood had seemed to him ancient and unchanging. That it might, in a few years, transubstantiate, he found deeply unsettling. He'd been prepared and willing, at the rash age of fourteen, to give himself over to it entirely, in exchange for certain protections. He'd marked it definitively as his safe passage through the world, the only life, perhaps, to which he was suited. It seemed impossible that his Church would betray him in this way, change so profoundly the rules of the game.

He needn't have worried. The changes never materialized. Amid much fanfare, the new Polish pope visited Boston. He flew directly from Ireland; at Holy Cross Cathedral he blessed the city's two thousand priests. Later he said an outdoor Mass on the Common. A hundred thousand Catholics prayed in the rain. But in the ensuing years he would move the Church backward, not forward. To Art — a grown man then, and no longer so fearful — this was less reassuring than expected. For the Church, and for him, it seemed a missed opportunity. He wondered for the first time if they'd both made a mistake.

★ ★ ★

After ordination he was assigned to a parish, Holy Redeemer in suburban West Roxbury. He became a priest — a good one, he felt, though where was the proof? His effect on the world, on the souls in his care, was frustratingly intangible. He felt keenly his own inadequacies. At first this awareness was constant, and nearly paralyzing. In later years it visited him periodically, a recognition of all he wasn't and would never be.

He felt it most acutely in the confessional, that chamber of secrets. He was twenty-seven years old, but in most ways that mattered he felt like a child. Ted McGann, at his age, had spent six years in the Navy, had fathered two children. He had married Art's mother at an age that seemed supernatural, and undoubtedly had women — perhaps many women — in the years before.

Art had known, always, that he was not like his stepfather. In the confessional he learned he wasn't like other men, either. Men his age had wives and families; addictions, criminal records, mistresses, debts. They lived double and even triple lives, a fact that astonished him. To Father Breen, even a single life seemed a towering accomplishment.

He lived like a teenager in the parish rectory. It was an imposing place, three rambling stories.

On the second floor lived a full-time director of music and the two young curates; Holy Redeemer was a large parish, wealthy enough to support a full staff. They lived in a warren of small bedrooms and shared a single bath. Upstairs was a plush suite of adjoining rooms, strictly off-limits. It was the exclusive domain of the pastor, Father Frank Lynch.

In every way Father Lynch lived above them. The whole house rang with his presence: his decisive step on the parquet floors, his manly laugh, his Old Spice cologne. To Art it was like suffering a second stepfather, only worse. Ted McGann's style had been gruff indifference, but Father Lynch took palpable glee in tormenting him. Father Lynch was Ted times ten. At the dinner table he kept up a steady stream of banter, at the expense of Art or the other young curate — a Filipino named Renaldo Calderon, who spoke halting English and had the advantage of not understanding the pastor's barbs. This left Art largely alone in his resentment of Father Lynch and his cronies, Father Bob DeSalvo and Father Marty Raab, local pastors who dined several times a week at Holy Redeemer. The three old boys had known each other for years; they'd developed a crude, jocular rapport more suited to a fraternity house than a rectory.

And yet a fraternity boy would enjoy far greater freedom than the young priests did. Ten o'clock was their unofficial curfew; at that hour Father Lynch locked the rectory door, and no one else was allowed a key. Mealtimes were sacrosanct, snacking forbidden. Art earned at that time a hundred dollars a week; he was saving up for a used car. On Monday mornings he took Communion to the local hospitals, driving the parish sedan. Every Sunday night he had to beg Father Lynch for the keys.

It was the old parish system — anachronistic in the late 1970s, a strange throwback. To Art, who still believed he was joining a progressive Church, the clerical pecking order came as a shock. But the Archdioceses of New York, Philadelphia and Boston — the hoary Irish axis — were notoriously conservative, still ruled by the old boys. For Frank Lynch and his ilk there had been no Roncalli, no aggiornamento. The Vatican Council had simply never taken place.

At the dinner table they lamented the liturgical changes: the jazzy new hymns, the hippy-dippy vestments; the ritual exchange of the Sign of Peace, in which the faithful shared greetings and handshakes and sometimes, to Frank Lynch's disgust, kisses and hugs. 'It's one big communal love-in,' he groused. Bob and Marty chimed in with their own complaints: the infants bawling through the Consecration, the communicants who, imagining themselves invisible, sneaked out the side door after receiving the Sacrament instead of returning to their pews. Not to be outdone, Frank spun a yarn about the teenagers he'd caught playing cards in the choir loft, oblivious to the Mass taking place down below. To Art it was like being trapped at the table with three aging comedians, each trying to upstage the others. It seemed an occupational hazard: priests were used to having an audience, unaccustomed to sharing the floor.

At the table he was like a well-behaved child, seen and not heard. Yet in the parish his responsibilities were ponderously adult. Every Saturday, before evening Mass, he heard confessions. For two hours his parishioners confided their faults and failings; their most intimate affairs awaited his review. That he was expected to furnish guidance seemed utterly laughable — Arthur Breen, who'd known no intimacy of any kind. Yet no one else saw it; the cassock hid all that was lacking in him. It was to the cassock that these good souls confessed. Art imagined sending it to the confessional with no priest inside it, a long black robe dangling on a hanger. In many cases, it would have just as much wisdom to impart.

He felt, most of the time, like an impostor. Over the years he'd had fleeting doubts about his vocation. Always he had pushed them aside. *Certainty will come later*, Father Cronin had promised; but certainty had not come. Would the Lord have called a man so clearly lacking? He could have chosen anybody. Why would He settle for Arthur Breen?

Of course, he wasn't entirely useless. Children adored him, lingering in his confessional. And the elderly asked little of him. Their expectations of the sacrament were largely ceremonial: a series of responses, a penance, a blessing. The problem was everyone in the middle, men and women in the jump of life, driven by human longings; *crawling over each other like puppies*

47

in a dogpile, as Frank Lynch once said.

Art had spent his whole life in the company of men, and yet he found them hardest to counsel. Hard, even, to talk with. With priests he could hold his own in conversation, but laymen were a different matter entirely. In their company he felt irrelevant, tolerated out of politeness like a spinster aunt. The men of Holy Redeemer were OFD — Originally From Dorchester: hardworking guys who'd made it out to this middle-class suburb, but still rough at the core. On the church steps after Mass he saw them talking. What, exactly, did they talk about? In the spirit of preparation he studied the sports page, until Father Lynch caught him at it. 'There will be a test later, Arthur,' he admonished in a simpering tone. The breakfast table erupted in laughter, and Art, mortified, abandoned his efforts. Who was he trying to fool?

With the parish women he had more success. About their concerns he understood even less, but their company was at least not adversarial. They mothered him. A cough or sniffle at the pulpit prompted a dozen worried inquiries. He was given hand-knitted scarves and sweaters, herbal teas and vitamins and once, an electric space heater. *It must get drafty in the rectory,* said the donor, one Mrs. Duddy, and in this she was not mistaken. The heater got him through a long Boston winter, until Frank Lynch discovered and confiscated it, grousing about the electric bills.

If all this feminine fussing was occasionally grating, Art never resisted. The parish women cared for him, and he was grateful for their affection. As human connection went, he was a beggar at the banquet, unable to refuse love of any kind.

Week after week they flocked to his confessional — *Breen's hen party*, Frank Lynch called it, a sneer in his voice. Younger hens might have won his grudging respect, but these were past the age, women so long married that their husbands rarely figured in their confessions. They spoke of squabbles with other women, harsh words exchanged with sisters and daughters. It seemed that women, in the end, were concerned mainly with each other. Husbands became mere accessories, barely noticed, like the gold wedding bands they wore on swollen fingers and couldn't take off if they'd tried.

It was a role that fit him comfortably: confessor to the matronly, the homely, the stout, the plain. Younger women confessed, too, though not as often; and with them Art was less easy. The prettier the woman, the more awkward he felt. This generation — his own generation — had a different understanding of the sacrament, whose name had been changed from Penance to Reconciliation. Some took the new name to heart, and pulled aside the grille for a face-to-face chat.

(Unless, of course, the revelations were of an intimate nature. Then the grille stayed closed.)

One such confessant he recalled distinctly. Cindy Clay was a Vietnam widow — Art's age, slender and fair-haired. Her flowery perfume lingered in his confessional. For the rest of the afternoon he'd know she'd been there.

One Advent she made a memorable confession: she had used birth control. For no good reason Art felt himself sweating. As confessions went it was hardly incendiary: he had his own private doubts about *Humanae Vitae*, as did many priests he knew. The problem here was more basic: Cindy Clay had admitted contracepting, but not the act that necessitated it. In the eyes of the Church she was an unmarried woman, and the act in question was *fornication*. The facts of the matter were clear.

Had she been less attractive, he might have been able to say it. Instead he found himself dumbstruck. Hastily he assigned her a penance, falling back with relief on the familiar words. *Go in peace and sin no more.* He pronounced the last words with particular emphasis, as though they exonerated him. As though in speaking them, he had discharged his duty.

On the other side of the screen the kneeler creaked. Cindy Clay rose to go, a cloud of lilacs in her wake.

★   ★   ★

Every parish had a Cindy Clay, or several. He was assigned next to St. Rose of Lima, on the North Shore. It was a parish of young families, its elementary school thriving. As the new assistant pastor, Father Breen functioned as a kind of youth minister, a duty that suited him perfectly. He trained altar boys and spoke to

Confirmation classes. He did sacrament preparation for the tiny First Communicants, and subbed for a religion teacher in the parish school. The young mothers were his own age, grateful for his involvement. More than once he heard the wistful compliment — *You would have been a wonderful father, Father* — in a tone that was nearly flirtatious. If there was a proper way, a priestly way, of responding, Art never found it. He blushed, stammered, mumbled. *Thank you. You're very kind.*

Holy Redeemer, St. Rose, Our Mother of Sorrows: Art's life as a priest divided into chapters. The newspaper accounts mention them only briefly. *Father Breen served without incident.*

In the spring of 1994 he was assigned to Sacred Heart.

2002

Holy Week, for a priest, is like the year's first snowfall: he knows it's coming, yet somehow it always catches him off guard. The crowded Masses, the hundreds of confessions, the sickbed visits; the extra hours of sermon preparation, in a vain attempt to avoid repeating what's been said a thousand times before. The hectic pace is shocking to a man who feels marginally useful most of the time. Art understood that to most of his flock, his services were not essential. At their baptisms, marriages and funerals his presence was expected, but in the intervening years they scarcely gave him a thought.

He had grown up in the priesthood, and grown tired. In his early fifties he'd begun to grow old. He was a slight, nervous man, prone to stomach upset and a yearly bout of bronchitis — ailments he blamed on his two vices, coffee and cigarettes, dissipations even a priest was allowed. Over the years he'd lost hair and weight, energy and stamina. He felt, increasingly, that he'd lost his way. That Lenten season — the season of repentance — had shaken him profoundly. This year he had a great deal to repent. And yet, as he prepared to celebrate the Resurrection and Ascension, he felt a glimmer of his old sense of purpose, like a dream remembered. The sensation was short-lived but potent. It seemed, however briefly, that *aggiornamento* was still possible. That a new life lay ahead.

The rituals of the season still touched him. The Palm Sunday gospel — Jesus riding into Jerusalem to cheering crowds, the shining moment of triumph before the looming betrayal — could move him nearly to tears.

Behold, thy King cometh unto thee.

That Holy Week was Art's ninth at Sacred Heart, and though he didn't yet know it, the final week of his ministry. Had he known, he might have skipped the endless parish council meeting that, due to a scheduling glitch, took place on Spy Wednesday, just four days before Easter.

The meetings were a chronic source of frustration. The council had been appointed by the pastor, Father Aloysius, just before a stroke landed him at Regina Cleri, the archdiocesan home for aging priests. The old man clung stubbornly to his title even as Father Breen took over his duties. Because Art was still, nominally, a mere assistant pastor, any decision involving money — as in the end they all did — required approval from the Archdiocese. It was a slow, cumbersome process that demeaned him in the eyes of the council, seven men and two women, most old enough to be his parents. They were pious souls, fiercely loyal to the parish (all but one had been baptized there, a fact often mentioned) and hostile to any suggestion of change.

Old themselves, they seemed not to notice the congregation shrinking and stooping around them, the young families leaving, the Communion lines shorter each year. At daily Mass the pews were mostly empty, dotted with gray heads. Unconcerned, the council reminisced about the old days, the elaborate church festivals, the parish high school so overenrolled that an entrance exam was needed to keep classes a manageable size.

It had been, at one time, the largest suburban parish south of Boston; its parishioners came, in equal parts, from the towns of Dunster and Braintree. The church, school, rectory and parish hall occupied an entire block, thanks to a diocesan building boom that started in the 1950s, the era of packed masses and heavy collection baskets. The church itself was vast and modern, with a central altar and pews on three sides — a design much maligned by the older parishioners, who still called it *the new church*. (Its predecessor, with its Communion rail and elaborate statuary, had been destroyed by fire in the early seventies.) The sleek new structure, in their eyes, looked suspiciously Protestant: the Sacred Heart nowhere in evidence, the altar marked by a looming crucifix.

That year Spy Wednesday was cold and rainy, like many nights in late March: the streets puddled, the storm grates loud with runoff. If the air were five degrees colder, Greater Boston would have been buried in snow. Art's winter cold had blossomed into bronchitis, and a deep cough had lingered. An evening in bed would have done him good. Instead he dosed up with cough syrup and wound a muffler around his throat.

That night's meeting was held in the church basement, the parish hall already in use by a local chapter of Alcoholics Anonymous. Art had offered them the building while the Unitarian hall was under renovation — sparking complaints from the council, who groused that the hall was for parishioners' use only. Art had refrained from speculating how many AA members likely belonged to Sacred Heart.

He was greeted outside by Flip Finn, who stood beneath an awning at the back door. His real name was Philip, but in the parish he was known by the childhood nickname. For Art it evoked visions of trained seals, an impression reinforced by Flip's short limbs and narrow shoulders and smooth bald head.

'Evening, Father. They're all here except Marilyn.' He nodded toward the church basement. 'Smells a little damp, if you ask me. You might want to get the dehumidifier running. You could grow mushrooms down there.' A former engineer for the MBTA transit line, he kept busy in retirement by delivering a constant stream of technical advice to those in need, women and priests especially. Like many competent men, Flip was genuinely alarmed by such people, with their minimal understanding of the physical world and, when its systems broke down, their limited ability to cope.

They walked together down the stairs, into a wide, low-ceilinged room lit by fluorescent tubes.

Used by the elementary school as a lunchroom, it retained a sandwich smell, peanut butter and tuna fish. At one of the long tables sat the council members, still wearing their coats.

'Father, it's freezing down here,' said Kay Cleary, rubbing her plump arms. 'Any chance we can turn up the heat?'

'I'm on it,' said Joe Veltri, springing to his feet. He was a small, spry man who worked part-time as the church custodian, a job Father Aloysius had created when Joe was laid off from Raytheon.

Art sat at one end of the table, Flip Finn at the other. Flip cleared his throat. 'We've got a lot of ground to cover, so I say we dive in. No sense waiting for anyone,' he said pointedly.

'I agree,' Kay said.

Just then Marilyn Burke swept into the room, shaking her wet raincoat. 'Sorry, sorry. Traffic was murder. The rain,' she said, taking the empty seat next to Art.

She was his lone ally on the council — its youngest member and an obvious outsider, the only one not baptized at Sacred Heart. Over Marilyn's objections, the council met at five-thirty precisely, which forced her to leave work early. She was a high-level administrator at South Shore Hospital; at least once during the meeting, a cell phone would ring inside her designer handbag — prompting frowns from the other members, all dressed for retirement in windbreakers and stretch pants. Kay Cleary favored seasonal sweatshirts: Easter bunnies, pumpkins in autumn, the Bruins or Celtics in winter. 'I like to be comfortable,' she often said, though Marilyn Burke looked just as comfortable in her high heels and sharp suits. Kay had once complained to Art that Marilyn's perfume gave her headaches.

(What am I, the hall monitor? he wondered. Am I supposed to tell her not to wear it?)

That night's agenda was a long one. The annual church festival was approaching, which meant a hundred small decisions — tent rentals, liquor license, ads in the local paper — that Art was required to approve. He glanced periodically at his watch, fearing that his housekeeper had left for the day. This hectic week they had scarcely spoken; they'd communicated through notes attached to the refrigerator. Art longed for a face-to-face conversation. There were urgent matters — one, anyway — they needed to discuss.

It was nearly eight o'clock when the meeting adjourned. Art was halfway out the door when Marilyn Burke flagged him down. 'Father, I have great news.' Her daughter Caitlin had settled on Notre Dame — this in defiance of her father, who'd lobbied for Boston College and offered bribes, a new car, to keep her in town. It was an ongoing tension in the marriage, Don Burke's overprotectiveness, which to his wife reeked of sexism. The older Burke boy had gone to Stanford; at eighteen he'd been practically kicked out the door. Art had written for Caitlin several letters of recommendation. *Don't go crazy for BC*, Marilyn had joked. *Save the glowing praise for Notre Dame.*

'The Fighting Irish,' Art said, grinning. 'Good for Cait.'

Marilyn opened her mouth to speak, but Art was already moving. He gave her a wave as he crossed the street to the rectory, a large, rambling Victorian that had once housed a half-dozen priests. By the time Art was assigned there in the early nineties, the parish was down to two.

In the kitchen he found Fran Conlon — a large, comfortable woman, sixty or thereabouts, in a lavender trench coat and matching fedora. (*It's uplifting*, she'd told him when he remarked on the color. He'd often seen her waiting at the bus stop on Atlantic Avenue, recognizable from down the street.)

'There you are. Weren't they chatty tonight?' she said. 'I was ready to bring you a sleeping bag.'

Art grinned, relaxing a little. For years now, his favorite part of council meetings had been grumbling to Fran afterward. There was no need to rush in, to pepper her with questions. He had the whole evening to steer the conversation around to Kath and Aidan. There would be plenty of time.

'They wasted twenty minutes complaining about the accommodations,' he said. 'Two months in a row meeting in the church basement! I've been ordered to tell the AA people to get lost.'

'Let me guess,' said Fran. 'It was Flip Finn leading the charge. Flip or Joe Veltri, one or the other.' She slipped off her coat. 'Wouldn't hurt

61

either one to dry out a little. It's the juicers who take it personal when anyone else shows some discipline.'

Art settled at the kitchen table and reached into his empty pocket for a cigarette. In the past year he'd quit, relapsed, and promptly come down with bronchitis. Now he'd quit again, but the reflex hadn't left him. In moments such as this, he reached automatically for a cigarette.

'You look tired, Father.' Fran took a casserole from the fridge. 'Have you seen the doctor?'

'I had to reschedule,' he said. 'Monday. I promise. That smells good.'

'Corned beef and cabbage. Let me heat it up for you.'

'Don't go to any trouble,' Art said.

She waved away his objections. 'The next bus isn't for forty minutes.'

'Don't be silly, Fran. Of course I'll drive you home.' His questions could wait until then, he decided. The conversation would flow more easily when his hands were busy, his eyes focused on the road.

'This is delicious,' he said. 'Please have some.'

Nearly every weeknight they shared, by unspoken arrangement, the dinner Fran cooked. Still she waited for his invitation.

'Don't mind if I do,' she said.

Fran's cooking, like the woman herself, was warm and heavy and comforting. Her repertoire — stews and chops, boiled dinner, fish on Fridays — was identical to his mother's, but there was no comparing the results. In his first months at Sacred Heart, Art, underweight his whole life, finally filled out a little. This was due as much to Fran's company as her cottage pie. Since Father Aloysius's departure, the dining room was never used. Art and Fran lingered at the kitchen table, talking sometimes late into the night.

On Spy Wednesday they covered their usual topics. Fran was an ardent Sox fan, a loyal reader of the *Boston Herald*, a cynical authority on misdoings at the State House. Finally Art could restrain himself no further, and did a little spying of his own.

'Heard anything from Kathleen?'

A shadow passed over Fran's face.

'We aren't speaking much these days, Father. I'm afraid she's up to her old ways.'

'Why do you say that?' Art said — careful, careful.

'That Kevin Vick is hanging around again. She denies it, but I have an inside source.'

'Aidan?' Art said, feeling his heart.

'He tells his granny everything.' Fran hesitated. 'This is what it's come to, pumping a child for information. But how else am I supposed to know what's going on over there? If Kath is using, she'll lie about the color of the sky.'

Is he all right? Art wanted to say but didn't. Does he like his new school? Does he ask about me?

In the last seven months he'd seen the boy only from a distance. Just before Christmas he'd left a gift on Kathleen's porch, a toboggan tied with a red ribbon. He'd waited nearly an hour that time, his car parked across the street, for Aidan to come home from school.

Later, after dropping Fran at her neat duplex, Art pondered what he'd learned. Kevin Vick was a recurring presence in Kathleen's life, a local hood who disappeared periodically for unsavory reasons: thirty days in a court-ordered rehab, brief jail terms for possession and driving under the influence. Art had met the guy only once, when Vick stopped by unannounced at Kath's apartment, something he was clearly accustomed to doing. Art and Kath were drinking coffee in the kitchen when Vick's battered Camaro squealed up to the curb. As was typical of the wayward young, he was dumbstruck in the presence of a priest. *I just need to get some stuff*, he'd mumbled, heading straight for Kath's bedroom. Kath was palpably embarrassed, while Aidan — who normally hovered like a hummingbird during Art's visits — seemed to be in hiding. Was he afraid of Kevin Vick? Fran had long maintained that the man was dangerous. Art suspected that the truth was subtler and more pernicious: that under his influence, Kath herself became dangerous.

At this thought, he made an illegal U-turn — in the local dialect, *banged a Uey* — on Atlantic Avenue and headed west to Dunster. A century ago it had been a village in its own right, with shops and a Congregational church and a pretty town green, until it was garroted by a state highway and absorbed into the noisy, traffic-strangled Boston suburbs. Kath Conlon lived on North Fenno, a side street at the far end of town,

64

in a three-decker Flip Finn had bought as an investment. Art had convinced him to take her on as a tenant, despite her lack of references or a steady paycheck. *I'll vouch for her*, he'd promised, sounding more confident than he felt. *If she's ever late with the rent, you can come to me.*

North Fenno was short and narrow, the houses set close to the curb. Aidan and Kath lived on the first floor, in a shotgun apartment with a kitchen at the rear. Art drove past slowly, noting lights in the windows, Aidan's yellow toboggan still lying on the front porch, though the snow had melted a month ago.

Kevin Vick's beat-up red Camaro was parked at the curb.

Well, now what? Art thought. At one time he would have knocked at the door, but those days were gone forever.

(And if he *had* gone to her door that night — would this have changed anything? It seems unlikely. The match had been struck, the fuse already lit.)

In the end he turned the car around and headed for the rectory. He would do as Fran had asked: he would remember Kath and Aidan in his prayers.

★ ★ ★

Back at the rectory, beside the old rotary phone, he found a stack of messages. It was the usual mix of parish business. Sister Ursula, the school principal, had set a rehearsal date for the

65

eighth-grade commencement. A young bride had called to schedule her wedding. (In all his years as a parish priest, Art had never received a phone call from a groom.) Only two of the messages could be called personal: one from his old friend Clem Fleury in Rome, another from Sheila, me, in Philadelphia. They were recorded faithfully in Fran's neat handwriting, indistinguishable from my own or my mother's or my aunt Clare's — evidence of our shared education, twelve years in the parochial schools. (My brother Mike, taught by the same nuns, writes illegible chicken scratch, as do my father and his brother and all their male children. I think back to those school papers corrected in red ink — *Penmanship!* — marked down half a grade if an *i* was left undotted, a *t* uncrossed. Maybe only the girls were penalized in this way.)

Messages in hand, Art retreated upstairs. With Father Aloysius gone, he had the run of the place; but from long habit — he had lived his whole life in shared housing — he avoided the common areas, the dark parlor and stiff sitting room. I would see these rooms a week later, when I came to help Art pack his few possessions before the Archdiocese changed the locks. Undoubtedly the circumstances influenced my perception; still, I pitied the engaged couples reporting for their mandatory Pre-Cana counseling, squirming for hours in those punishingly uncomfortable chairs. Art felt at ease only in the cluttered front room, which served as the parish office, and in Fran Conlon's kitchen, with its lingering smell of breakfast. He spent the rest of his time in his bedroom, which he'd outfitted with a stereo and portable TV. Also a cordless telephone, from which he returned my call.

He left a message I now know by heart. I have replayed it several times, analyzing the tone of his voice. *Sheila, it's me, Brother Father. The man in black. I've escaped from a hostage situation, three hours with the parish council. I'm slammed tomorrow, so I'll try you on Friday.* If he had any inkling of what was about to happen, he gave no indication. There was no hint of distress in his voice.

★ ★ ★

I have reconstructed his movements the next day, Holy Thursday. I have in my possession Art's desk planner, its black leather cover embossed with the numerals 2002. From long practice I decipher his cramped handwriting (he too, it seems, was given a pass on penmanship). At 9 A.M. he attended a fellowship breakfast at St. Thomas Presbyterian, sponsored by the local Ecumenical Council. In the afternoon he heard confessions and gave the sacrament at Mountain View nursing home. On the same page, I found a yellow Post-it note: *Drop by choir rehearsal.* He had doubts about the new director and feared a disaster on Sunday morning, her first Easter at Sacred Heart. Thursday evening he celebrated the annual Mass of the Lord's Supper, a ninety-minute extravaganza complete with full choir, trumpets from the eighth-grade orchestra and the ritual foot-washing, Art kneeling at the altar before twelve barefoot parishioners, like Christ bathing the feet of the Apostles. Afterward the Eucharist would be carried, in solemn procession, to the Repository. With luck he'd eat supper by midnight. Fran would be long gone, and he'd have no chance to question her about Kevin Vick. He would sit in the kitchen with the *Atlantic Monthly*, eating whatever she'd left in the refrigerator, then rush through his prayers and fall exhausted into bed.

Which brings us to Friday morning, the Friday in question. Good Friday, if you are raised Catholic, is something of a trial — an endless day to be loathed and dreaded, if you are the Catholic child of Mary McGann. Each year Mike and I suffered it together: a day of no school, no television, no loud playing; a day of rosaries and soggy fried fish. My mother took a certain pleasure in disparaging our flimsy modern devotions — put to shame, she claimed, by the extreme rites of her girlhood, Good Friday as it was meant to be observed, at her childhood parish in Roxbury. From noon to 3 P.M., the hours Our Lord spent hanging on the cross, young Mary Devine had knelt in prayer, with nothing but a piece of toast in her stomach. (Having strictly observed the Friday fast, one full meal per day, and that without meat.)

Off to church now, she'd conclude sourly. *What's left of it.* At this Mike would stare at me with mournful pious eyes and we would both fall out laughing, and Ma would bemoan the fate of our souls.

Though it was rough going for the faithful, a

priest's Good Friday duties were light. Mass could not be celebrated, which was itself a rare freedom. Years ago, when Art was a lowly cleric at Holy Redeemer, Frank Lynch had declared Holy Thursday an all-night poker game. Priests from the surrounding parishes drank until dawn and slept until noon, the one day of the year they were excused from morning Mass.

In Art's datebook, that morning is blank. At 2 P.M. he would lead the Solemn Commemoration of the Lord's Passion. In the evening he was expected at the newly concocted Family Service, led by parishioners, and the elementary school's performance of the Passion Play.

As it turned out, he did none of these things. His calendar makes no mention of what actually happened, the 10 A.M. phone call from Bishop John Gilman, an aide to the Cardinal.

At ten-fifteen Art got in his car and drove to Lake Street.

It takes nearly an hour to drive from Grantham to Brighton, where the Boston Archdiocese was then headquartered. Art traveled west on Commonwealth Avenue, the road climbing and dipping through the suburbs of Brookline and Allston. What was he thinking as he drove? He told me later that he'd had no idea why he'd been summoned, which seems incredible. For months the entire city had been reading about the scandal, priests from all over the Archdiocese accused, reprimanded, exposed.

'Okay, I had an idea,' he admitted when I pressed him. 'But my idea was completely wrong.'

To make sense of this, I've had to think about what it was like to be a priest in Boston that spring, when anyone in a collar was suspect. 'Maybe we were paranoid,' Father Fleury told me later, 'but it seemed that the whole world suddenly looked at us sideways.' One after another reputations were destroyed, careers ended, lives ruined. Among the first to fall was the Street Priest who'd walked the Combat Zone: at his apartment on Beacon Street, he'd apparently offered more than a weekly Mass. Amazingly, no one suspected it at the time. No one gave a thought to those lost children sitting cross-legged on his floor, the Street Priest looking down on them from a great height as they received the Eucharist from his hands.

To Art, one allegation was even more shocking. Ray Cousins, his old cellmate, had been accused of molesting a boy. Ray was a gentle soul — 'the last guy you'd ever suspect' — but the Archdiocese was making an example of him. The Cardinal had been widely vilified for covering up such allegations, so now he made a great show — just for appearances, Art insisted, *pro forma tantum* — of taking every accusation seriously. Anyone who'd ever known Ray was being interrogated. Naturally Art's name would be on the list.

So as my brother drove the final hill into Brighton, it was Ray Cousins he considered: could it possibly be true?

At the bottom of the hill he slammed on the brakes. Comm Ave. was clogged with traffic, vans and trucks parked on both sides of the road, some with engines idling, satellite dishes attached to their roofs. Well, of course: nearly every night the local news featured a dispatch from Lake Street, the Cardinal's response — or usually, his silence — at each new allegation of abuse. For these segments the Chancery was always the backdrop, a reporter standing before the building as though at any minute His Eminence might emerge.

Art drove past the news vans and took the long way around, through the back entrance. He parked behind the Chancery, where Church business was conducted. After the death of the great O'Connell, his successor — my mother's hero, Cardinal Cushing — had made this

71

addition to the campus. The Chancery is a square brick bunker, of a utilitarian ugliness so incongruous that it seems intentional, as though Cushing — a local boy, a famous populist — had been making a point.

As promised, Art's official escort was waiting at the rear door. Gary Moriconi stood with his back to the building — coatless, smoking, his cassock flapping in the wind. 'Of all people,' Art fumed to me later. I have since met Father Gary, a short, stocky man with a barrel chest and a memorable voice, nasal and high-pitched, that doesn't match his body. He was Art's age, fifty-one, yet his dark hair was suspiciously free of gray.

The two greeted each other with a wariness that went back many years. At seminary they'd been classmates, but not friends. Art saw at a glance that Gary knew exactly why he'd been summoned, which was not surprising. He had always been privy to secrets.

'They're waiting for you,' Gary said archly. He took a final drag and butted his cigarette — a large ash can had been placed at the door for this purpose. But instead of leading Art into the Chancery, he turned and started up the hill.

'I didn't understand, at first, where we were going,' Art explained to me later. But as he followed Gary up the wet footpath, the grass soaking his wingtips, it dawned on him that he would be seeing the Cardinal at home — in the mansion referred to, with audible capitals, as The Residence.

He was alarmed then, but only for a moment

— because as they climbed the hill, he saw that the change of venue had nothing to do with him. The Cardinal couldn't take *any* meeting in the Chancery. On the sidewalk below, a crowd had gathered: men and women milling about, drinking coffee, talking on cell phones. His Eminence wanted to avoid the long unprotected walk across the lawn, in full view of the TV cameras. 'The perp walk,' Art told me later, with a wincing smile.

Vigor in Arduis.

'Vultures,' said Gary. 'They're here every day.'

They entered The Residence through a porte cochere and headed down a long passageway, their wet shoes squeaking on the marble floors.

'I've never been inside before,' Art admitted.

'Never?' Gary sounded incredulous. 'It's a pity you couldn't see it in nicer weather. In summer the gardens are spectacular.'

'So I've heard.' Art knew — everyone did — about the Cardinal's annual Garden Party, where his favorite priests mingled with politicians and millionaires, the benefactors of Catholic Boston. Of course Gary Moriconi would be invited. It was just the sort of gathering he'd enjoy.

'Down the hall is the chapel, where they film the TV Mass on Sundays. Upstairs are meeting rooms and the Cardinal's quarters.' Gary seemed to enjoy playing tour guide. Certainly he knew his subject. He'd spent twenty-five years, his entire career, criss-crossing these grassy lawns. After ordination he'd stayed on at St. John's, in an administrative post created especially for him. He'd remained an amanuensis to the powerful, an eager mouthpiece.

'Have a seat.' Upholstered settees had been placed here and there against the walls. 'I'll let them know you're here.'

He continued down the corridor and knocked lightly at a closed door. Alone, Art paced the long hallway. On both walls, hung at ten-foot intervals, were portraits of the current Cardinal. Some were skillful; others might have been made by children. One in particular caught Art's eye: His Eminence as a young priest, rendered in oils. It reminded him of an old colorized photograph, the young man with a high flush in his cheeks, as though they'd been smeared with rouge.

A moment later Gary reappeared. 'This way.' He led Art into a large anteroom with more couches, backed against the walls as if to clear the floor for dancing. The thin gray carpeting could have used a cleaning. The walls were bare. The Residence, impressive as it was, lacked a single piece of art that did not depict the Cardinal. There was not even a nice reproduction of a Giotto. Art sat, watching a set of double doors.

In a moment the doors opened. 'Arthur.' Bishop John Gilman, the Vicar General, crossed the floor briskly, a small, spry man in a black suit. He gave Art's hand a cursory shake. The gold pectoral cross was hidden in his jacket pocket. Only its chain was visible, looped across his black rabat.

'Come in, come in. His Eminence has another appointment at noon.'

Art followed him into an inner office, a high, shadowy room crowded with furniture. The Cardinal sat at a hulking wooden desk, his back to a window. His face was familiar as a relative's: the shock of silver hair, the meaty jowls. His hooded eyes were furtive and intelligent, his heavy brows like eaves covered with snow.

He rose — a big man, hunched and imposing in his black cassock — and took Art's hand in both of his. It was a trademark of sorts, like the cassock's red piping and matching buttons: the Cardinal's famous two-handed shake.

'Arthur, thank you for coming,' he said, as though they were old friends. As though, in the Cardinal's eighteen years in Boston, they had ever exchanged a word.

Art followed him to a round table at the other end of the room. The Cardinal sat heavily. On the table was a single sheet of paper. He laid his hand upon it, as if to show off his massive gold ring.

'This arrived in yesterday's mail.'

From across the table Art peered at the document, a letter on law firm stationery. The text was brief, nearly covered by the Cardinal's hand.

The whole ordeal lasted fifteen minutes. After the initial revelation Bishop Gilman took over. His cheeks, Art noticed, were flushed; a patch of psoriasis bloomed beneath one ear. This made him look agitated, in the throes of some high anguish, yet his tone was matter-of-fact. Calmly he explained the particulars: Art would be placed on leave but would continue to receive his salary;

would be covered, as always, by the Archdiocese's health insurance. He was to vacate Church premises immediately, Gilman said with emphasis. That was the most important thing.

'Where do I go?' Art asked.

The bishop took a business card from his chest pocket. On the back of it he wrote an address. 'We took the liberty of renting you an apartment. Temporarily, of course. Until we get this straightened out.'

In the end they told him nothing: not the name of the accuser; not even what he was supposed to have done. Art had asked both questions immediately; both times Gilman looked expectantly at the Cardinal, who silently bowed his head.

'You'll be served with papers,' Gilman said briskly. 'I imagine they'll go to the rectory. Take care of that today, if you can. Have your mail forwarded to the new address.'

Art stared across the room at the man's empty desk, behind it an idyllic view of trees and lilac bushes and rolling lawn. How strange that His Eminence worked with his back to the window, as if he had no interest in the world beyond him. It was more than strange — it was somehow not quite human — that he preferred looking in.

'What about the parishioners?' Art asked. 'It's Easter, for God's sake. What on earth do I say to them?'

'Nothing,' said Gilman. 'I'm serious, Arthur: you don't say a word to anybody. You leave that to us.'

'And this afternoon? I'm supposed to do the Passion at two.'

'No worries. We'll send a substitute,' Gilman said.

At that moment His Eminence got to his feet. Bishop Gilman did the same, and Art understood that the interview had ended. He took a final look around the room, the walls hung with more portraits of the Cardinal.

Again His Eminence clasped Art's hand.

*   *   *

Art drove away from Lake Street, past the news vans on Commonwealth Avenue. His dusty gray Honda attracted no attention. For the moment anyway, he was alone with his shame.

Mindlessly, mechanically, he drove to Dover Court, a bank of brick buildings opposite the highway — the sort of apartment complex that, if you live in a North American city or suburb, you pass every day without noticing. The grounds were landscaped, the curving driveway studded with speed bumps. The property was larger than it appeared from the road — four identical structures, each three stories high, wide and deep enough to house dozens of apartments. The one closest to the road was hung with a bright green banner: NOW RENTING, SHORT OR LONG-TERM LEASE.

He parked behind a small outbuilding marked OFFICE. Inside, a young Indian woman sat behind a desk. Her hair was long enough to sit on. She wore thick glasses and a colorful blouse.

'Hello,' said Art. 'I think you have some keys for me.'

'Oh, yes. Mr. Breen.'

He blinked, startled by the *Mister*. The Roman collar was a symbol everyone recognized: Sikh cab drivers, Muslim women in headscarves. But the morning was cold and damp; he wore a trench coat over his clericals, a plaid muffler at his throat.

She reached into the desk drawer and handed him a bright green envelope, labeled *Welcome*. 'You're in the A building, the first on your left. The smaller key is for the mailbox. I left a copy of your lease there.' Her voice was low and soothing, with a musical lilt.

Art took the envelope. Outside a brisk wind had started. Rain blew across the parking lot in sheets. He crossed to the A building. The front door was propped open, the lobby piled with cardboard boxes marked BEDROOM, STUDY, KITCHEN. He spotted a hive of mailboxes and turned his key in the one marked 310. Inside was another green envelope.

As he stood waiting for the elevator, a man came through the door carrying another box. A young guy, big and red-haired, in a Boston College sweatshirt.

'Jesus,' he breathed, setting down the box. 'I picked a great day to move.' He eyed the green envelope in Art's hand. 'You too?'

Art nodded.

The man offered his hand. 'I guess we're neighbors. Chuck Farrell.'

'Art Breen. Let me give you a hand.'

The elevator doors opened. Together they piled the boxes inside.

'That's it, I guess,' said Chuck. 'I don't have much. I got kicked out of my house,' he said out the side of his mouth, like a comedian telling a secret.

'Me too,' said Art.

Chuck grinned sheepishly. 'Lot of that going on. They call this place Divorce Court.' Again he offered his hand. 'Thanks, man. I'll see you around.'

'Good luck to you,' said Art, heading for the stairs.

Apartment 310 was on the third floor, halfway down a long hallway. The corridor was very dark, the carpet and wallpaper navy blue. Art turned his key in the lock.

He stepped into a large, empty living room. The blinds were closed, the carpet and walls an identical shade of beige.

He tore open the envelope in his hands. A sheaf of stapled papers, legal sized. Stuck to the top sheet was a yellow Post-it note, inscribed with feminine cursive, the sort of round, buoyant letters the nuns had deplored.

Rent paid through Oct. 1.

Six *months?* Art thought.

It was the first clue he'd been given about his future.

★   ★   ★

That afternoon, desperate to escape the empty apartment, he drove around aimlessly. By habit or instinct he found himself in Grantham. To his relief, Ma's Escort was gone from the carport. Well, of course: on Good Friday she'd be in church. Her parish, St. Dymphna's, had a Passion service at three o'clock. Home alone, Ted McGann rarely answered the door.

He waited until dark before driving to the rectory. Upstairs in his bedroom, he unplugged the portable television, its screen the size of an index card. He filled a duffel bag with shaving gear, socks and underwear and a random selection of secular clothes: a few odd shirts, a single pair of blue jeans, a windbreaker emblazoned SACRED HEART BASKETBALL. He left behind a garish Hawaiian shirt and a closetful of black clericals, unsure when — or if — he'd wear them again.

It's time, now, to turn our attention to Aidan Conlon and his mother. It may seem strange that I have avoided speaking of them until now. I will admit that I find the subject difficult, as Art himself did. Three years ago, without warning, Art turned up on my doorstep in Philly; and late that night, over many glasses of wine, he spoke of them at length. His stammer, his flushed cheeks, unnerved me. He seemed uncomfortable and yet — I have to say it — strangely animated. It was an emotional state I had never sensed in him, a heated and fluttering excitement.

He'd met them in the spring, had been working in his office when Fran brought them by the rectory. Art described the scene so precisely, in such great detail, that I felt uneasy. I sensed that the particulars mattered tremendously, that this was a memory he had replayed many times.

It was a bright morning in April, unseasonably hot, the room filled with sunlight. He sat at his desk writing a letter to the regional school administrator, Monsignor Gerard Mooney — *Father Money*, as Art had come to think of him. In a few short weeks, the Confirmation class would be treated to a day at a local amusement park, a parish tradition. This year's class was unusually large, and the cost of admission had increased. Experience had taught him the proper way to frame such requests: the stilted diction, the supplicating tone. *To simplify matters on the day of the excursion, I ask that the funds be disbursed as soon as possible so that tickets might be purchased in advance,* he concluded, a sentence he quickly deleted. Father Money moved at his own glacial pace and would not be hurried. An insistent tone was never acceptable, not if the church itself were on fire.

Hunched over his desk, Art butted a cigarette and lit another. He was aware of the hot breeze through the open window, the green smell of cut grass. That, at least, was good news: Joe Veltri had managed to get the old mower running, and petty cash would cover the gas and parts. A new tractor would have meant more begging, a longer and far more obsequious letter that would have taken all morning to compose.

He stared out the window feeling like a restless schoolboy, trapped in the classroom on the first, long-awaited day of spring. Fran had filled the feeder in the courtyard, and a flock of small birds — robins? wrens? — had descended, trilling rapidly. In one corner stood a waist-high statue of St. Francis, arms outstretched in welcome. Birds lit briefly on its hands and head. Art closed his eyes, feeling pleasantly drowsy. For a minute or two he drifted. He was roused by a sudden brutal squawking, an airy rush of wings.

Blinking, he saw that the courtyard had been invaded by seagulls, gray and white and insistently cawing. They were a chronic nuisance, persistent as pigeons, large as cats. Every few weeks Joe Veltri cleaned their droppings from St. Francis's tonsured head.

'Fran?' Art called absently. 'They're back again.'

Then he went to the window and saw the cause of the commotion: a small, dark-haired boy stood in the courtyard with a bag of potato chips. He wore shorts and a Red Sox T-shirt and was, Art noted, the exact height of St. Francis. His expression was rapt, his eyes wide.

Art watched, fascinated, as the boy doled out the potato chips. The gulls swarmed around him, squawking madly: six, ten, a dozen, more. Finally the boy threw down his bag and backed away from the mass of shrieking birds. He looked both delighted and terrified.

Art was standing at the window when he heard a knock at the door.

'Father?' Fran opened the door a crack. 'Can I bother you a minute?'

He turned. She stood in the doorway, a young woman behind her. 'I'd like you to meet my daughter, Kathleen.'

Art blinked, confused. Fran had been at Sacred Heart longer than he had. He'd met her two sons, their wives and children; but she had never mentioned a daughter.

'Hey. Hi.' The girl was young and slight, half as wide as her mother. She wore tight blue jeans and an abbreviated pink T-shirt; a diamond stud twinkled in her navel. Her hair was dark at the roots, the ends streaked platinum blonde.

'She's back from California,' Fran said.

'For now.' Her eyes darted around the room. They were arresting eyes, pale gray, startled and startling, ringed with black liner. Her left foot tapped briskly in its high-heeled sandal. 'Hey, have you seen a kid running around?'

'He's out there.' Art put out his cigarette and nodded toward the courtyard, now a riot of seagulls. The boy stood with his back to the rectory wall.

'Oh, for heaven's sake. Excuse me, Father.' Fran rushed out of the room and down the hallway, her tread heavy on the wood floor.

'What's he doing, feeding the gulls?' Kath went to the window. 'Jesus, will you look? They're everywhere.' She let out a sharp laugh. 'He has a thing for birds.'

They stood watching as Fran appeared in the courtyard. 'Honey, don't feed them! They're dirty birds.' She stooped and knelt stiffly. 'Help your mimi pick up these chips.'

'Fran, don't worry about it,' Art called out the window. 'Joe can clean up later.'

'Thanks, Father, but he needs to learn. He can't be making a mess at other people's houses. Come on, Aidan.'

It was an awkward moment, Art and Kath standing at the window, watching the little boy and his grandmother, with her two knees that needed replacing, gathering Ruffles from the parish lawn.

'Fran, be careful,' Art called.

'Don't worry about her. She lives for this stuff.' Kath turned her back to the window. 'She's driving me crazy, I swear to God. Following me around the house with a broom.'

'How old is your son?' Art asked.

'Seven. Eight in August.'

'Is he enrolled in school yet?'

Kath shrugged. 'It's almost summer. What's the point?'

'There are six weeks left in the term. A month and a half.' And then, before he knew quite what he was saying, Art added: 'We can take him at Sacred Heart.'

The offer was totally irresponsible. Kath couldn't pay the tuition, hadn't applied for a scholarship. She wasn't even a member of the parish. All this would have to be explained in some future, groveling letter to Father Money. It's only a few weeks, Art told himself. I'll deal with that in the fall.

'It's almost lunchtime,' he said, glancing at his watch. 'Aidan can meet Sister Paula. She has the second-grade homeroom.'

'Now?' said Kath.

'Why not? I can take him over myself.' Art led the way into the kitchen, where Fran and Aidan were throwing the potato chips into the trash.

'Hello, Aidan,' he said. 'I'm Father Art.'

★   ★   ★

Recently, over coffee with her mother, I learned a few facts about Kath's history.

She was twenty-seven the spring she reappeared in Grantham. She'd been gone for eight years. In California she lived briefly with a Navy man named Jack Strecker, and got pregnant. Among Art's papers is a calligraphed Certificate of Christian Baptism from St. Sebastian Church in San Diego, dated June 1, 1994. It lists the boy's name, Aidan Andrew Conlon, and his mother's, Kathleen Marie. No father is named.

'We had no idea where she was,' Fran explained to me recently. We had drained the coffee pot and stood in the rectory kitchen drying dishes. The new priest had forbidden her to use the dishwasher, claiming it made too much noise. 'I was sure I'd never hear from her again. Then she called one Christmas sounding messed up, and said she'd had a baby.'

'Messed up how?'

'Talking in circles. Hyper. She was high, I guess.'

Fran's older son flew out to San Diego and found Kath broke and homeless, sleeping on a friend's couch. She wouldn't let him see the baby. She told him to get lost. By then Jack Strecker had shipped out and Kath was working in a nightclub — doing what exactly, she refused to say and Fran shuddered to imagine. It was information no mother wanted to hear.

It was in San Diego, according to her mother, that Kath acquired a drug habit. Fran blamed Jack Strecker, and loneliness; the stress of early, unplanned motherhood, evil influences far from home. I knew by this time that Kath had told Art a different story, that she'd smoked or snorted one thing or another since junior high, often under her parents' roof: pot, speed, crack cocaine. For a long time she had no preference; she took what was free and available. In high school, and afterward, she was always some-body's girlfriend. She explained with a certain pride that she'd never paid for drugs.

86

Fran had no more word from Kath for several years, until the day she appeared at the door with her seven-year-old son, looking for a place to stay. Fran said yes, of course, but a blind man could see that the arrangement wouldn't last. She and her daughter were oil and water, any peace between them tense and temporary. Kath had completed a court-ordered rehab in San Diego, but even sober she had an unpredictable temper. When she eventually flew into a rage and stormed out of Fran's duplex — as seemed inevitable — she and Aidan would end up on the street.

'Did Art know this?' I asked.

'Sure,' said Fran. 'I told him everything. That first day, when I brought them by the rectory . . . ' Her voice trailed off. 'Aidan took to him right away. And Father was so good with him. I blame myself, in a way.' She took the last cup from the drainer. 'What a mistake.'

★   ★   ★

And that's how it began. Aidan started school the following day. Each morning he rode the city bus to the rectory with his grandmother. At Art's suggestion the boy joined him for breakfast, though most mornings he left half his Cheerios floating in the bowl. Finally Fran came to her senses and served his cereal in a teacup. Art relayed these details to me by phone, amusement and tenderness in his voice. I found it all a bit mystifying, his delight in the daily routines of a second grader, but I chalked this up to my own inexperience. Art spoke of Aidan with the fawning interest of a new parent, an emotion I had never felt.

And yet, undeniably, my brother seemed well. Quietly, without fanfare, he kicked his thirty-year smoking habit. His annual spring cold failed to appear. For the first time in his adult life, he'd made it through the winter without taking antibiotics. He had never felt better in his life.

Each day at two-thirty, when the school day ended, Art would see the boy standing at the curb, waiting for his mother's car. When Kath was late, as often happened, Art invited him to the rectory for a snack, the milk and cookies he'd added to Fran's shopping list. On days when Aidan rode the school bus home, Art found himself oddly disappointed. For the rest of the afternoon he felt unsettled, as though he'd skipped some essential component of his day, a meal, a shower, his morning prayers.

I will admit that I found Art's behavior startling. Like him I am long single, accustomed to quiet and privacy, and it was hard to imagine rearranging my routines to accommodate a stranger's child. (I say this without pride or shame. It is simply a fact.) Yet my brother did this eagerly, without being asked. In some eyes, this alone incriminates him. In light of recent revelations, such enthusiasm for a child — a boy especially — by a grown man — a priest especially — is inherently suspect.

Yet it's worth noting that the adults closest to Aidan — his mother and grandmother — were not alarmed. 'I didn't give it a second thought,'

Fran told me later. 'I was more worried about that Kevin Vick, if you want to know the truth. I knew he was bad news.' Kath had dated Vick in high school, an angry delinquent who'd spent his sophomore year in juvie and had been in and out of trouble ever since. Now he had reappeared, and Kath saw him almost daily. 'He's been busted for drugs, Father,' Fran confided to Art. 'More than once, from what I gather. If Kathleen moves in with him, she won't stay sober another week.'

Hearing this, Art made inquiries. Flip Finn owned several buildings in Dunster, and a week later Art moved Kath and Aidan into the apartment on North Fenno Street. The St. Vincent de Paul Society provided used furniture, a kitchen table and chairs, a sturdy sofa that was almost like new. Art spent a Saturday afternoon driving back and forth to Dunster with Marilyn Burke's son, who helped him unload the furniture from the parish van.

And it seemed for a while that Kath had turned a corner. At an AA meeting she ran into an old schoolmate, Chris Winter, whose father owned a towing business in Dorchester. It was a family operation, with Chris and his brothers driving. Their sister, pregnant again, had been placed on bed rest; until she delivered, they needed a replacement to cover the phones.

Kath worked the day shift, eight to four. At four-thirty she rolled up to the rectory in the ancient Buick Regal that Chris Winter had sold her for cheap. She honked the horn until Aidan appeared on the front step, in the relaxed school uniform Sacred Heart had adopted, khakis and a navy polo shirt. Child care is expensive, and Aidan was too little to come home to an empty apartment, so I suppose this arrangement suited her. She would claim later that it was Art who'd proposed it, a fact he did not dispute. Certainly it pleased him to see Aidan on a regular basis. For Fran it may have been less than convenient to have a small child running around what is after all her workplace, but she is a doting grandmother and for all I know enjoyed every minute.

Which leaves only Aidan to consider. Later, as I wandered through the sitting room and parlor — rooms hardly conducive to playing — I had to wonder: how did he occupy himself in the rectory for two hours a day?

When I asked Fran this question, she gave a cautious reply. Most days Art helped him with his schoolwork. Aidan was behind in all subjects; he'd had pneumonia that winter and had missed most of the second grade. After Art checked his arithmetic, they took turns reading aloud, books Art borrowed from the school library. Fran recalled two titles in particular, *Homer Price* and *The Big Red Balloon*. I read them both as a child. Parochial school libraries are notoriously underfunded. In thirty years their catalogs change hardly at all.

'Where did Aidan do his homework?' I asked.

'In Father's office,' Fran said.

His schoolwork finished, Aidan was allowed to play outside. His favorite spot, Fran told me, was the stone bench in the courtyard. Some days he

90

sat there for an hour or more, drawing the birds who came to the feeder. She had never seen a child so rapt.

But in April, in Massachusetts, dry days are the exception. How did Aidan occupy himself on rainy afternoons?

Sometimes, to get him out of her hair, Fran let him watch television. Educational shows only, she insisted.

The only television set was in Art's bedroom.

*   *   *

School let out the third week in June. After that Art and Aidan were inseparable. With Kath at work, he took the boy on excursions to the Children's Museum and the Museum of Science. They picnicked at Houghton's Pond and Wompatuck State Park. Fireworks were watched; parades, a puppet show. Planning these excursions, I am sure, required time and research. Art had no experience in arranging amusements for children. To his own nephews — our brother Mike's boys — he was nearly a stranger. At family gatherings he greeted them awkwardly, asked the usual adult questions about teachers and Little League. The boys answered in monosyllables and tore off in the opposite direction, eager to escape.

Aidan's birthday was the last week in August. When Art asked what he'd like to do, the boy clamored to go to the beach.

They set out on a Thursday afternoon, Art, Aidan and Kath. Had Fran Conlon gone along, the day, the rest of Art's life, might have unfolded differently. He might be in his rectory still, squabbling with the parish council, growing fat on her cooking, and I would have no story to tell. But Fran declined Art's invitation. Two brushes with skin cancer had convinced her, finally, that her freckled skin was not made for the sun.

I have in my possession a packet of photos taken that day at Nantasket Beach, a place I recognize from my own childhood. Back in those days, Paragon Park was a mecca for children; its roller coaster and carousel drew families from all over Boston and the South Shore. The park has since closed, but a few landmarks remain. Rifling through Art's photos, I recognize the old carousel, now restored; Funland, the beachfront arcade. In one shot, Kath Conlon stands hunched over a pinball machine, frowning in concentration; in another she lies stretched out on a beach towel in a striped bikini, smoking a cigarette. Her body is a teenager's, small breasts, sharp hipbones. Tattooed on her forearm is the dark shape of a cross. There are several photos of a sand castle in progress, Aidan in yellow swim trunks, digging with a plastic shovel. A candid shot of my brother standing at the water's edge, his thin bare legs and sunken chest, his arms surprisingly muscled. It's the only time I've ever seen him without a shirt.

Of all the photos taken that day, only one disturbed me: a close shot of Aidan stretched out on a beach towel, wet and shivering. He

lies on his back, gazing up at the camera
— held, apparently, by some adult standing
close above him. He looks confused, yet
pleased by all the attention. He wears a shy
smile.

The day Art was summoned to Lake Street, I was at home in Philadelphia, absorbed in my own concerns. To my surprise I'd been asked to chair the English department the following September, out from under a fierce old girl named Gail Hunter who refused to retire though everyone agreed it was time. I don't know what it means to chair a department at other public high schools, but at George Washington Carver it involves a small pay raise in return for countless hours of administrative work; weekly meetings with the principal; mediating disputes among a cantankerous staff which, in my case, would include the deposed Gail Hunter. I felt, in short, that I'd been asked to host a brain tumor. In addition, I was distracted — again and always — by a situation with a man.

The week before, after a long night of quarterly parent-teacher conferences, the younger faculty had set out for some serious drinking at the bar down the street. It's a place I've always disliked — its shiny brass gantry, its canned Irishness — but it's close to school and to a subway stop, handy since a few of us will inevitably overimbibe. That night, I am sorry to say, I was among the guilty, and Danny Yeager, the new guidance counselor I knew only slightly, offered me a ride home. He is a local boy and a physical type common here, blond and husky, with clear blue

94

eyes and a broad intelligent face. I had watched him nurse a single beer all evening, his usual habit, and though this made me distrust him as a person it gave me confidence in his driving. One thing led to another, as people say, the result being that I avoided Danny Yeager in the school corridors and was both depressed and relieved that he hadn't called.

I was eager to discuss both matters with Art. I hadn't seen him in six months, since his impromptu visit to Philly; but we'd stayed in close touch by phone. He was never any help with my love troubles, but twenty-five years in the Boston Archdiocese had made him a master diplomat, expert at identifying hopeless situations and extricating himself without alienating anyone, skills that would have come in handy in the Philadelphia public schools. I called him several times that Friday, but neither he nor Fran answered the phone. Not for the first time, I was irked by my brother's refusal of modern technology: no cell phone, no e-mail, not even an answering machine. What if I'd been a dying parishioner awaiting the Last Rites? If his employer were any other than the Catholic Church, Art's quaint attitudes would not have been tolerated. But as I would soon learn, he wasn't the only priest in the Boston Archdiocese — far from it — who preferred living in the past.

I had a rough idea of his Easter schedule — I knew, for example, that on Saturday afternoon he might hear a hundred confessions — and so wasn't alarmed when he didn't call. But after Easter morning came and went, I actually considered phoning my mother, who spoke with Art daily. Not unusually, I couldn't face that prospect. Instead I called my brother Mike.

It's easy enough to sum up a stranger. The people closest to us are harder to define. As I have said, Mike is a person of consistent character. Since childhood he has changed hardly at all. As a boy he exuded energy; he excelled in all sports and hated school, its rules and constraints, the constant enjoinders to sit still. Though he often misbehaved, the nuns warmed to his ready smile, his cheerful way of owning up to his sins. By nature he is honorable and straightforward, or maybe it's just that he lies so ineptly that he decided early on it wasn't worth the trouble. In this way and others, he is a pragmatist. When faced with our father's anger, Mike took the expedient path. After puberty he was a head taller than Dad, and though both are natural athletes, twenty or thirty years of alcoholism will slow a man's reflexes. My father is one kind of fool, but he's always had an instinct for self-preservation. He figured correctly that much past the age of fourteen, Mike couldn't be safely provoked.

He had a young man's temper, and it got him into the usual troubles. He won and lost an athletic scholarship to Boston College High School: he got into fights, and his grades were poor. A year later he was caught breaking into an empty summer house in Grantham, but the arresting officer, Dick Brady, was a drinking buddy of our father's, and the charges were mysteriously dropped. After high school Mike worked as a security guard, a bouncer — the jobs a young man takes if he is unambitious and strong. At Dick Brady's urging he enrolled at the community college, got a certificate in law enforcement and was hired as a town cop. This was the Mike I knew when I left Grantham. Later — after the Navy, after meeting Abby — his life took a different turn. He has matured into a responsible husband and father, and made my parents proud.

That Easter Sunday I imagined the phone ringing in Mike's house in Quincy. It's a big place, handsome and solid, with four large bedrooms and a fenced yard framed with tall trees. Mike sold it to himself eight years before with his brand-new realtor's license — paying himself a huge commission, I have heard him joke. Since then it had doubled in value and filled with children: my nephews Ryan, who had just turned seven; and Michael and Jamie, the five-year-old twins. As the phone rang and rang, I recalled that Mike had invited our parents for Easter dinner, so I would have to speak with my mother after all.

Mike's wife answered the phone.

'Oh, Sheila. Hi.' That flat midwestern voice, with its shortened vowels: *Hiy, hiy.* Abby doesn't make small talk, not with me. She has her reasons, though they are old ones and don't seem worth hanging on to all these years. We are a small family and see each other little enough; I'd be willing to fake a little warmth if she would. Isn't that what family is all about?

'Honey, it's your sister,' she called, her voice

muffled by a hand over the receiver, as if this were something I shouldn't hear.

As always Mike came to the phone out of breath, fresh from some feat of athletic fatherhood. When the boys were toddlers, he had enjoyed throwing them around the living room — *dwarf tossing*, he called it, a game that delighted all four of them. Now I imagined him in the backyard pitching Wiffle balls, the three boys taking turns swinging with an oversized plastic bat.

'Happy Easter,' I said. 'Please don't make me talk to Ma.'

'You're safe. They didn't come.' He sounded tense, distracted, in a hurry to get off the phone.

'On Easter? You're kidding. Is Dad okay?'

'Fine. The same, anyway.'

'Have you heard from Art?'

'No.' Just that one curt syllable, no elaboration. Another unsettling note.

'I've been trying to reach him since Wednesday. No one picks up at the rectory. I'm starting to worry.'

'Hang on a second.' Fumbling on his end, his footsteps on the stairs. Mike was taking the phone down to the basement — to get away from Abby, I assumed.

'Hey. Sorry.' I heard the refrigerator open and close, the pop and hiss of a fresh beer can. This, too, was unusual: Mike drinking on a Sunday night. At one time it would have been automatic, but that was before marriage and fatherhood, a long time ago.

'Mom was supposed to call you,' he said.

98

'About what? Is Art okay?'

Silence on his end.

'Mike, what the hell is going on?'

'Fuck,' Mike said (softly — his wife frowns on cursing). 'Okay, listen: Art's fucked. They're saying he — Jesus, I can't even say it. They say he molested a kid.'

It's hard to explain what went through my mind at that moment. The name: *Aidan*. And then a feeling like wind tearing through me, as through a bombed-out building; a great rush of air.

There wasn't much more to the conversation. The obvious questions from me — *What kid? Who says so?* — and Mike's edgy silence. 'Look,' he said finally. 'I don't know anything, and I don't want to know.' Only then did I understand that he actually believed it. Without hearing Art's side of the story, Mike believed this monstrous thing.

'He didn't do it,' I said.

I heard a door slam, a shrill cacophony of children's voices. *Daddy! Daddy!* My brother was needed, wanted elsewhere.

'Believe what you want,' he said. 'I got nothing more to say on this. Listen, I have to go.'

*   *   *

This exchange with Mike demands some clarification, a brief explanation as to how word travels in my family. I have said that Art and I were close, so how could he have withheld news of this magnitude? Why didn't my mother or

Mike pick up the phone? A person like Danny Yeager — a trained counselor, a member of the *helping professions* — might go a step further, and wonder: was I hurt or angry, or at least surprised, to be kept in the dark?

These questions will plague certain readers — those raised, I suspect, in a different style of family. Evasion comes naturally in my tribe, this loose jumble of McGann, Devine and Breen. The reasons for this are not so mysterious. My father is a man of shameful habits. My mother is lace-curtain Irish. She will settle for correctness, or the appearance of it; but in her heart she wants only to be good. The space between them is crisscrossed with silent bridges, built of half-truths and suppressions. The chasm beneath is deep and wide.

Those same bridges exist across the generations: my mother and her parents, my father and his. On both sides, we are a family of open secrets. When I was a child they enclosed my innocence like a tourniquet. Without knowing quite *how* I knew it, I understood what might be said, and what must be kept quiet. If from the outside the rules appeared arbitrary, from the inside they were perfectly clear.

Art's news was unspeakable, by him or by anyone. I didn't take this personally. If I felt excluded, injured and aggrieved, that bolus of emotion was at least familiar. It attends all my dealings with my family, and theirs with me. Every one of us limps from old wounds. In a perverse way, they entertain us. We poke each other's tender places with a stick.

That Easter Sunday Mike woke before dawn, an old Navy habit. In the basement he warmed up on the treadmill, then stretched out on the bench. I have witnessed this spectacle more than once, Mike grunting and huffing beneath a bar loaded with plates, his fair skin turning a rainbow of colors, pink to red to nearly purple. It seems a punishing way to spend one's first conscious minutes, and yet afterward he is weirdly invigorated. He bangs around the kitchen whistling and ravenous, scrambling egg whites, blending protein shakes, oblivious to any poor houseguest feigning sleep on the sofa bed below. He wolfs down his massive breakfast, and without even a cup of coffee he is ready to attack the day.

On Easter morning he showered, made French toast for the boys, helped Abby dress them for early Mass. Mike himself stayed behind to hide the Easter eggs in the yard. This was a tradition from Abby's childhood, not ours; but Mike had embraced it. Each year he looked forward to standing on the back porch with Ma and Dad, watching the boys race around the yard like excited puppies, the colored eggs magically appearing from behind rocks and flower pots, the dark corners of Abby's gazebo. 'It seems like a lot of bother,' Ma would say, though Mike understood that her disapproval was more general. The egg hunt, like all his wife's faults and failings, was a foreign custom, something Protestants did.

He was hiding the last egg when the telephone rang.

'Michael, I don't feel well. I'm not myself this morning,' Ma said, her voice indeed sounding sick and strange.

So for the first time since Ryan was born, Mike's boys celebrated Easter without their grandparents. Colored eggs were found and collected, a ham eaten, chocolate bunnies gored with small teeth marks and eventually gnawed down to nubs. Through it all my brother felt a creeping unease. Ma was then sixty-eight — not yet old, but neither could she be called young. His whole life she'd been immune to sickness, too mean even to catch a cold ('What germ would bother with *her*?' Clare Boyle used to say). Then, two years ago, she'd found a lump in her breast. Not cancer, thank God, but it had changed the way Mike looked at her. Suddenly she was no longer bulletproof, the indomitable Mary McGann.

In the afternoon he drove to our parents' house, to pick up the Easter baskets Ma had assembled for the boys. He enjoyed the ride, the roads empty of traffic. He didn't spend much time in Grantham anymore. Except for the occasional afternoon at the beach, Abby refused to visit. The house was small and cramped; the boys got restless there with nothing to do. 'There are five of us and only two of them,' she was fond of saying. 'If they want to see the boys, they can come to us.'

The neighborhood was bustling that day, families gathered for the holiday, Teare Street lined with cars. At the end of the block the Morrisons' windows blazed with light. Their front porch had become a staging area for strollers, grandchildren's bikes, an Igloo cooler, an extra case of beer. Mike drove slowly past the house, thinking he might recognize someone. Sure enough, Tim Morrison was getting out of his battered Ford truck, a magnetic sign on the driver's side door — MORRISON ELECTRIC *Serving the South Shore*. Mike rolled to a stop and lowered his window.

'Hey, man. Happy Easter.' They shook hands and Mike glanced quickly over Tim's shoulder, trying not to be obvious about it. It's a look I have witnessed many times, a charged sort of alertness. I can imagine Mike shuffling past the Morrisons' fifty years hence, drawn to that house by some ancient instinct, like an old dog with a vague memory of pleasure.

'Looks like a full house,' he said. 'Everybody make it this year?'

'All but one,' said Tim. 'She's at her in-laws'.'

'Too bad. When you see her, tell her I said hi.'

'I will,' said Tim, though they both knew he wouldn't. 'Hey, how's your ma?'

'Same as ever. You know Ma,' Mike said, slightly puzzled. Usually it was Dad people asked after. Ted McGann had been charming and convivial in his day, popular in the neighborhood. *Your dad's a character*, we were told throughout our childhoods. About our mother nobody said a word.

Mike gave him a wave and drove on, feeling foolish. *Everybody make it this year?* He'd never

103

had any self-control where Lisa Morrison was concerned. And now she was married to someone else, spending Easter with her own husband and kids. Better that he hadn't seen her, he decided. Better to remember the way she used to be.

He parked halfway down the block. Compared to the Morrisons', our parents' house was still as a tomb. A blue light glowed in their bedroom window. Dad spent whole days, now, staring at the TV screen.

Mike climbed the porch steps. When Ma came to the door he saw anguish in her face.

How exactly had she phrased it? 'They're going after Arthur.' And then: 'I was at the church this morning. They're saying terrible things about him. That he did something wrong.' Euphemisms for euphemisms, as though the usual terms — *molested, abused* — weren't vague enough.

And doesn't it say something about that particular moment, that spring in Boston, that Mike understood immediately what she meant? Sure, he read the paper. One priest, at St. Paul's in Hingham, had molested more than a hundred boys. In Mike's class at BC High, there'd been several boys from St. Paul's. Poring over the *Globe*, he had recalled their faces: Tom Downey, Michael Behan. He wondered — you had to — if they had been abused.

In the kitchen Ma put on the kettle. Grudgingly she gave up the details, as though she herself had been accused of a crime. There was a boy in the parish, eight years old; a boy

104

without a father. Arthur had been kind to him, taken him on outings. 'The mother is telling filthy stories,' Ma said, her mouth tight. 'She should be ashamed.'

Her mortification was palpable, her voice quavering, her color high. She blamed the newspapers, who'd brought up the ugly mess in the first place; the Cardinal, so cowed by the bad press that he'd turned on his own priests.

'Arthur gave his life to the Church,' said Ma, 'and what does he get in return?'

She wasn't looking for an answer, and Mike didn't offer one. He understood that she wanted an audience — loud agreement, righteous outrage. In Ma's eyes, Art was the victim. The Conlon boy she dismissed with a wave of her hand. 'There's something wrong with him. Only a disturbed child would invent a story like that.'

Mike was shocked by her callousness; shocked but not surprised. He had known it his whole life, and here was the proof: charged with the most despicable crime imaginable, Art was still a saint in her eyes. Her son the priest could do no wrong.

He got out of there as fast as he could. He wanted only to be alone in his truck, the stereo blasting. His mind could scarcely take it in. An eight-year-old boy: a year older than Ryan. Mike thought of his own son, boisterous, sweet-tempered, cheerfully nonverbal. Not if his life depended on it could Ryan invent such a lie.

And for a moment that was all Mike needed. He had never been an analytical thinker. As a cop, sailor, salesman, he had relied on instinct.

And he knew kids: disturbed or not, no eight-year-old boy would *pretend* to be abused.

His own brother.

Half brother, Mike thought. It was a term never used in our family, but in that moment it comforted Mike to think that whatever was wrong with Art, whatever diseased genes the guy carried, had come from Harry Breen. He'd always nursed a certain contempt for Art's father, a feeble loser who'd abandoned his wife and kid. Now he was grateful to the man for one thing: at least he'd given Art his name. In a day or two, when the story hit the papers, Mike's name, his kids' name, would not be tarnished. Art's parish was three towns over. Mike's friends and neighbors, the kids in Ryan's school, would never connect them to Father Breen.

Though in Grantham there would be no hiding it. Mike thought of Tim Morrison, for the first time in his life showing interest in Ma. Of course: Tim — and the whole Morrison clan — already knew.

He drove around for hours that night, knowing what was waiting for him at home. He knew exactly what Abby would make of this. That on some level she'd been waiting for — not *this*, not exactly, but something like it. To prove finally and forever that she'd been right all along.

He found her in the kitchen, packing Ryan's lunchbox. 'No Easter baskets?' she asked.

'Shit. I forgot.'

She gave him what he thought of as her Mom look: *Language!* 'Um, *okay*,' she said. 'But wasn't that the whole reason you went over there?'

For a moment Mike hesitated. *It's Easter*, he thought. *I'll tell her tomorrow.*

Another day wasn't going to change a thing.

*   *   *

He would see this later as a turning point, the moment when he stopped recognizing himself, the person he had always been. As I have said, deception is not in Mike's nature. He had no secrets from Abby, had never wanted any. He was simply unable to repeat what Ma had said.

Alone in his basement, he found himself reviewing his recent interactions with our brother. There weren't many, he realized. He saw Art mainly on holidays — a little apart, always, in his black garb; a little lost in the noisy throng of McGanns and Devines. Lately Mike had missed quite a few of these gatherings, which Abby attended only grudgingly. After an hour Mike felt her eyes on him. After two hours she began looking at her watch.

When had he last seen Art with no distractions: no bored, resentful wife, no kids tugging at his sleeve? He thought of a time years before, in the months leading up to his wedding, which Ma had initially refused to attend. Her objections were predictable, yet difficult to answer. Only Art had been able to appease her. He seemed not to mind that Abby had been raised Lutheran. For this Mike was grateful, if a little surprised.

Abby, Jesus. When she caught wind of this, he could say goodbye to peace.

Religion had always been the fault line between them, the crack in the seal. In the beginning she'd been amused by what she called Catholic superstitions — the Last Supper hanging in his mother's kitchen, the St. Christopher medal he wore around his neck. The medal was a confirmation gift from his godmother, Clare Boyle. It had sat in a drawer for years, until Mike was deployed to the Gulf in '91 and figured he needed all the help he could get.

As a kid, a young man, he'd considered religion irrelevant, a dull hobby like birdwatching or stamp collecting, the peculiar obsession of pious women like his mother. Yet he'd seen things, as a cop and in the Navy, that changed his thinking: the everyday cruelties and lewdness, aggression and vulgarity; the ODs and car crashes and barroom brawls. Human nature was volatile, perverse and treacherous. Religion was necessary the way marriage was necessary. People — male people in particular — were animals, dull-witted and violent. Left to themselves, they would fuck and fight and rip each other apart.

And so, every day since basic training, he had worn the medal. *Your lucky charm*, Abby called it, with unattractive sarcasm. Praying to saints she considered ridiculous. *How can they hear you? It's not like they're gods.* That first Christmas, wearing her engagement ring, she had joined his family at midnight Mass, but had refused to kneel for the Consecration. Mike was stunned. In all the time he'd known her, she'd never set foot in a church of any kind. Now, suddenly, her Protestantism was a matter of such deep conviction that she had to announce it to the whole congregation.

Back then Mike had made concessions, which he'd since come to view as mistakes. To please her parents they married at the Nelsons' church in Naperville, Illinois, a cold, empty building with a bare altar, the walls painted beige. Art had officiated alongside the minister — *concelebrants*, Mike explained to Ma, the word Art had used. Our parents drove out to Naperville the day before the wedding, sixteen hours in their little Escort. When they arrived, Mike was baffled to see Ma behind the wheel. 'I thought I'd pitch in with the driving,' she said. Later he realized that she'd driven the whole way, our mother who'd always been the passenger. It should have alarmed him; but at the time he'd scarcely noticed, absorbed in the commotion of his wedding day.

Now he'd been married eight years — happily, he thought, but how did you measure? He'd never been married to anyone else. And of course, it was useless to compare himself and Abby to his parents. By that standard, every marriage in America would look like bliss.

And yet some things *could* be measured. They lived in a good neighborhood, on a wide tree-lined street. Their house, a solid Colonial, was twice the size of his parents' cramped Cape. In a slow year he earned more than his father had in five, enough that Abby could stay at home with the boys. And compared to his previous jobs — security guard, sailor, beat cop — selling real estate was safe and cozy. No one was going to blow your head off for trying to sell them a house. Mike enjoyed the work: meeting new people, sharing an important milestone in their lives. He thought often of his former clients, raising their kids in the houses he'd sold them. It pleased him to know that, in some small way, he'd had a hand in their destinies. And really, in the life of a family — he knew this firsthand — the choice of a house was not so small. It meant something that his boys had large airy rooms, a grassy yard to play in; that he and Abby had the third floor to themselves, space and privacy to do what couples often stopped doing when the kids came. They agreed on the important things — sex, money, how to raise the boys. There was rarely anything to fight about, except religion and his family. In Mike's case, the two came intertwined. They were nearly the same thing.

At first he had chalked it up to simple difference. Before Abby, he'd dated local girls who shared his temper, his humor, his tastes and dislikes. All had been fond of our parents — of Dad, anyway, who sober could charm the birds out of the trees. Nobody had been fond of Ma — that would be asking too much — but Mike's girlfriends had accepted her. Lisa Morrison had even managed to make her laugh. In this way, as in all others, Abby was nothing like Lisa. At the beginning, and for a long time afterward, that had been part of her appeal.

* * *

Most marriages result from happy accidents. My brother and Abby are such a couple. I have heard Mike say (though not recently) that they met at exactly the right time. A year sooner he wouldn't have noticed her, so crazed and raw over Lisa Morrison that all other women seemed vague to him, slightly out of focus. Abby, of course, wouldn't have seen him at all. She wouldn't go near the places Mike favored, dark holes in Southie and Dorchester, by night loud with bar bands, by day filled with cops and firemen watching sports. But in the winter of 1993 Mike abandoned his locals. He'd resolved to make changes in his life — 'a course correction,' he told me by phone. For months he'd battled what he later understood was depression. Lisa Morrison had ditched him for the last time, and Mike had chased, and lost interest in, a string of girls — barflies mostly, good for a few weekends, nothing more. He grew tired of drinking, tired of chasing. Tired, to his astonishment, of being a cop. Desert Storm had messed with his head, left him dissatisfied and restless. Police work seemed increasingly pointless. There was no one he hated enough to harass, no one he valued enough to protect. The guys he worked with — the best part of the job, he'd always felt — began to grate on him. Their noisy camaraderie made him lonely. Our cousin Rich had gotten rich in real estate, and convinced Mike to study for a license. And a few months later, at his first closing, he met Abby.

111

Abigail Nelson, the seller's attorney: when they spoke by phone, Mike pictured a stout matron in bifocals and sensible shoes. At the closing he was startled to find her tall and shapely, dark hair in a ponytail like a high school cheerleader. He knew roughly how a closing worked, but was grateful at the way Abby took charge, passing around documents, collecting signatures with great dispatch. After the handshakes, the *thank yous* and *good lucks*, he found himself walking beside her, shoulder to shoulder, out into the cold. In high heels she was nearly his height, with marvelously long legs and feet to match. Once, laughing, he called them flippers, and learned that Abby was a girl who couldn't be teased. Later, meeting her family, he understood why. The Nelsons were serious people, Abby's father especially, a pediatrician who, to Mike's eye, had little feeling for kids. The details of Abby's childhood — the music lessons and summer camps, family vacations at the lake house in Door County — seemed to come from movies or television. Mike didn't know people who lived that way. It seemed in every way an improvement on our own family, who had never, in his memory, taken a trip together. We were latchkey kids before the word existed — like the Morrisons, the Pawlowskis, the Mullinses and Greers. Nobody considered this a problem (though we once set a small kitchen fire while heating a frozen pizza). It had never occurred to him that there was another way.

They'd been dating just a few months when Abby took a pregnancy test. A false alarm, it turned out, but for Mike the world had turned. However briefly, he had imagined himself a father, and Abby — unlike Lisa Morrison, or anyone else he'd dated — a mother. He'd tried on a life that fit him perfectly, comfortable right out of the box.

Their engagement stunned her parents, who'd already settled on one son-in-law — Abby's ex-fiancé, for whose medical residency she had moved to Boston two years before. The Nelsons had expected a doctor. Instead they got a loudmouthed ex-cop with, apparently, a harsh Boston accent, a thing Mike never knew he possessed. Worse still, their new son-in-law was Catholic. (*Very Catholic*, according to Abby's mother.) Mass on Sunday, fish on Friday. Catholic enough that his brother was a priest.

In the end it was Art who baptized their kids. As they debated the issue back and forth, Mike discovered a startling truth, that he couldn't have it any other way. Looking over the precipice of fatherhood, he thought — didn't everyone? — of his own childhood. The midnight Masses and Christmas pageants, the school years at St. Joe's and BC High. The priests who'd busted his balls, who'd coached his sports teams. Kindly nuns who'd mothered him better than Ma had, mean ones who'd bullied and later amused him, the ones he and I still told stories about. All that was best and sweetest in our childhood: he wanted the same for his own kids. And Abby, to his everlasting gratitude, seemed to grasp this.

At least he thought she had.

* ★ ★

The next morning he found her hunched over the breakfast table, the *Globe* beneath her elbow. She stared up at him balefully, her face pale, her neck splotched with red. She slid the paper toward him. SOUTH SHORE PRIEST OUSTED, ACCUSED OF ABUSE. One long column on the front page of the Metro section, just below the fold.

'Oh, Jesus.' Mike read quickly over her shoulder. 'They don't waste a minute.'

She stared at him, dumbstruck. 'You *knew* about this?'

'Ma told me last night. I know, I should have told you.' Mike ran a hand over his head, still wet from the shower. It's a gesture I have seen many times, my brother who broke the window, who dented Dad's bumper, confessing to his crimes. 'Sorry, Ab. I don't know what to say. I needed to think it through.'

A thump overhead, somewhere in the twins' room. 'Mom!' Jamie called. 'He's pushing!'

'No tattletales,' Mike called automatically.

They stared at each other unable to speak, bound by a pact they'd made years before and still lived by. They wouldn't let the kids hear them argue — not even now, not even over this.

'You've known him your whole life,' Abby said, her voice low. 'And you had no idea? How is that possible?'

'So this is my fault?'

She turned her attention to the newspaper, as though finished with him. As though nothing he

114

had to say could possibly interest her. 'I should have known,' she muttered.

'What is that supposed to mean?'

'Mike, think about it. The life they lead.'

'Who? Priests?' He felt his face heat. 'Art is guilty, automatically, just because he's a priest?'

Commotion on the stairs, loud laughter. One of the twins let out a delighted shriek.

Mike lowered his voice. 'They're all perverts? Is that what you're saying?'

'I wouldn't know,' she said coolly.

'Well, *I* know. They're not.'

'Fine,' she said. 'They're healthy, well-adjusted men of God. Except, wait.' She read: ''*The Boston Archdiocese has secretly settled sexual molestation cases involving at least seventy priests.*' Seventy, Mike! And those are only the ones who got caught. How do you explain that?'

'I can't,' he said, his heart racing. 'Look, I know it's bad. There's no excuse for it. Those perverts should rot in hell.' There was more he could have said. *I knew a kid. He was a friend of mine.* But why give her more ammunition? The goal was damage control.

'Ab, we're talking about my *brother*. And just because those other fucks are guilty — I *don't care*,' he said, interrupting her protests. 'I don't care about my fucken language. Just because those other fucks are guilty, it doesn't mean that Art is.'

'Fine,' Abby said again. 'You've known him your whole life. Could he have done this?'

Mike did not answer quickly.

'I don't know,' he finally said.

115

For the next few days he felt paralyzed, imprisoned by his thoughts. Never in his life had he given so much consideration to Art — who, as brothers went, had always been a disappointment. We grew up in a neighborhood teeming with brothers: the three Pawlowskis, the four Mullinses, the mighty Morrisons, six brothers strong. As a boy Mike had longed to run with such a pack. Tim Morrison was his own age; like him, stocky, red-cheeked and blond. *All* the Morrisons looked more like Mike than his own brother did. Which itself seemed a kind of sign.

As I have said, Art and I favor our mother, and maybe it was this resemblance that made Mike see him as slightly feminine, or at least not quite masculine: neither boy nor girl, but something in between. As a child he hadn't found this troubling. It was only later, as Mike approached adolescence, that Art — that priests in general — began to seem suspect. His schoolmates joked about Father John Ferry, the young assistant pastor who directed the altar boys: *Don't bend over in the vestry. Father Fairy is wicked queah.* How the priest acquired this reputation, Mike had no idea; it may have been nothing more than the man's last name. Certainly he'd never thought about it in a literal way — that Father Ferry was an actual homosexual, that he ever did or would lay a hand on a boy. It was just something to say, a way of being *pissah* — an imperative

116

that occupied him, and all his buddies, every hour of every day.

Still, the jokes raised a question. His whole life he'd had a certain feeling about Art, and for the first time he put words to it: was his brother gay? With the possible exception of Father Ferry, Mike had never met a homosexual. And because there was no way of knowing (short of asking Art, which was unimaginable), and because this was not a question he truly wished to have answered, he'd put the whole business out of his mind. Priests couldn't have sex anyway, he reasoned. Which made the whole question more or less irrelevant.

And there was this: for every Father Ferry, there was a Father Tony Kelso, the junior high basketball coach at St. Joe's. Though fiftyish and running to fat, Father Tony still carried himself like an athlete. His bulk, his gruffness, reminded the boys of their own fathers, the difference being that Father Tony actually liked them. He was quick with a joke, and didn't mind them talking smack; he could crack with the best of them. Father Tony was wicked pisser. You'd walk on your hands to make him laugh.

So priests could be manly, likable, admirable. Holy, even. His whole life Mike had believed it was so. He rejected Abby's smug conviction that any man who chose celibacy was an automatic nutcase. Sure, he couldn't imagine doing it himself. Certainly not when he was younger, when desire was like a medical condition, nearly disabling. (*No cure for it but marriage*, the joke went, and there was more than a grain of truth in

117

that.) Mike couldn't imagine performing surgery, either; but that didn't mean nobody else could. Some men could master the urge, God bless them. And those who couldn't had no business being priests.

Like everyone, he'd been shocked by the headlines, the cases where the worst had happened. The worst being cases like Andy Stasko — their sophomore year at Grantham High, Mike's best friend. Stasko was a city kid, with divorced parents. His mother had moved to Grantham to escape the busing and the riots. To Mike, still burning at his expulsion from BC High, Stasko seemed cooler than the Grantham guys. He understood later that they'd had certain things in common, their anger and their shame.

For a year they'd been inseparable. They met each night at the seawall to drink or smoke weed, joined sometimes by little Lisa Morrison from down the street. Unlike Mike or Lisa, Stasko always had money. Where he got it, Mike found out only later, on the night he and Stasko ended up in the back of a squad car. Mike got off with a lecture and, at home, a few belts from his dad. Stasko — with a record, a weapon and no Dick Brady to look out for him — was sent off to juvie. Looking back, Mike saw that Dick Brady had saved his life. A few years ago, when two angry misfits shot up Columbine High School in Colorado, Mike had felt a shiver of recognition. It wasn't hard to imagine. Under the right circumstances — or the wrong ones — Andy Stasko might have hatched a similar plan, and

118

taken Mike along for the ride.

For a long time, years, he forgot about Andy Stasko. Then, last fall, the name had appeared in the *Boston Herald*, one of the plaintiffs in a class-action lawsuit against a pedophile priest. The abuse had happened when Andy was in elementary school, before his mother moved to Grantham. Reading this, Mike remembered Andy's anger, raw and palpable. His gut told him that the allegations were true.

These thoughts went round and round in his head like laundry in the washer. At home, at work, there was no point in trying: he simply couldn't put it out of his mind. 'Go see your brother,' Ma urged. 'Hear his side of the story.' She'd written, on the back of an envelope, Art's new address, the apartment the Archdiocese had rented him. Mike still had the envelope — the return address was KeySpan, from Ma's gas bill. He'd shoved it into the Escalade's glove box, knowing he would not need it. The thought sickened him: to sit face-to-face with Art, forced to look at his hands, his mouth. Forced to imagine what they might have done to a child. Mike knew he couldn't stomach it. There had to be another way to get at the truth.

And when the truth came out, then what? Mike knew this much: if a priest, anyone, touched Ryan or the twins, he'd kill the guy with his bare hands. Even a lousy father — his own father, a useless drunk — would do that much. But the Conlon boy, like Andy Stasko,

119

had no father, a fact Mike couldn't forget. If Art had messed with the Conlon boy, who would stand up for the kid? Mike would protect his own family to the death. Should he do less for someone else's son?

Art spent Easter weekend alone. For several days he spoke to no one. He bought an inflatable mattress to sleep on, and spent an hour studying the manual to his new mobile phone. An actual bed, a regular telephone, would have seemed too permanent. At the post office he filled out a change-of-address form, checking the box marked *Temporary*. Again and again he told himself: *This too shall pass*.

Easter Sunday came. In churches and rectories it was a day of bustling activity; he'd never before noticed how quiet the streets were. He drove forty miles south to Providence, to a church he'd picked out of the Yellow Pages. The Mass was crowded; he recognized no one. He knelt in a rear pew long after the service had ended, his head bowed in prayer.

That afternoon he drove aimlessly, northward through New Hampshire. In Ogunquit, Maine, he ate a cup of chowder at a restaurant by the sea.

Back at Dover Court the lot was nearly empty. Art parked and got out of his car. A moment later a black Audi pulled in beside him. He recognized Chuck Farrell at the wheel.

'Jesus, these speed bumps,' Chuck called. 'Murder on the suspension.' He got out of his car and slammed the door.

'It does seem excessive,' said Art. 'Why so many?'

Chuck shrugged. 'Lot of kids around.' He nodded toward the playground, empty now. The day before it had been crowded with small visitors: weekend dads pushing them on swings, sitting back on benches to watch the older kids play. The men, as a group, had looked unpracticed at the whole business, unsure what to do with themselves, quite.

'Mine were here yesterday. Jesus, it was weird.' Chuck jangled his keys in his pocket. 'My son is three. He keeps asking when I'm coming home. His sister doesn't even ask. I gotta wonder what she knows.' He pointed. 'Her school is just over the hill, so this is pretty convenient. And their mother lives a mile away.'

'That's good,' said Art.

Chuck smiled ruefully. 'Good and bad. You have kids?'

It's a question I am asked myself, with surprising frequency — by friendly strangers who consider this a natural way of making conversation, a subject of universal interest, like the weather. *No*, I have learned, is a conversation ender. Which may explain (does it?) why Art — lonelier than he'd ever been in his life — responded as he did.

'A boy,' he said. 'Aidan. He's eight.'

Chuck nodded sympathetically. 'You get him on weekends?'

'Not exactly. His mother — ' Art broke off. 'It's hard to explain. It's been difficult.'

'Man, I hear that.'

'We were never married.' *Why am I saying these things?* Art wondered, his heart racing.

What is happening to me?

Chuck shrugged. 'Shouldn't make any difference, if you ask me. Your kid is your kid.' He glanced at his watch. 'You feel like grabbing a beer? That place down the street pours a decent pint.'

Art hesitated. His empty apartment awaited him like a tomb.

'I have an early morning tomorrow,' he said. 'Another time maybe?'

'Sure.' Chuck gave him a crooked grin. 'Breen, you're a better man than I. Have a good night.'

* * *

Later, alone in his apartment, Art thought of Chuck Farrell's offer. More than once he considered getting into his car and finding the bar down the street. *I was thirsty*, he'd say simply. *I changed my mind.* But his own lie — outrageous, perplexing even to himself — stood in the way. Perhaps a retraction was possible? He tested out the words in his head. *It isn't true what I said before, about Aidan. He's not my son.* But it wasn't the sort of thing you could take back.

He flicked on the television. The local news had just started. As he did every year, the Cardinal had celebrated Easter Mass at Holy Cross Cathedral. This time the TV cameras had been allowed inside.

'The Church is not a political institution, not a sociological institution,' his Eminence declaimed from the altar. 'It is a community of faith.'

123

Outside the protestors held signs. HOLD ON TO YOUR CHILDREN.

Art turned off the television. Absurdly, he felt a flash of sympathy for the Cardinal, who certainly hadn't expected such treatment when he left Missouri for Boston, a plum assignment for a dynamic young bishop. (In Church terms, anyone under sixty was young.) In Boston the old guard had viewed him with suspicion — his interest in ecumenism, his Harvard degree — but the new bishop seemed not to care. A year later he was named a Cardinal. He traveled to Cuba, and met with Castro. In Rome he was well connected, considered a contender — by those who believed such a thing was possible — to become the first American pope.

Art glanced at the clock. Six-thirty on Easter Sunday. People were at home with their families. Ma and Ted would be at Mike's house with their grandkids.

Fran Conlon, too, would be playing grandmother.

He dialed a Philadelphia number he knew by heart, relieved when Sheila — I — didn't answer the phone. He wasn't ready to explain his predicament, to say it aloud. Speaking of it would have made it real.

Again Art glanced at the clock. It was six hours later in Rome; Clem Fleury would be sleeping. He wasn't due back in Boston for several days.

Was there no one he could call just for the company? Just, simply, to pass the time?

Almost against his will, a name came to mind.

124

Rita Besson had been his parishioner at Our Mother of Sorrows, an apt coincidence. She was the most sorrowful mother he had ever known.

* * *

They'd met on what should have been a joyful occasion, the engagement of her only daughter. For Art, too, it was a disconsolate time. He'd been reassigned again, another wealthy suburban parish. With his fortieth birthday approaching, he was taking stock of his life. The loneliness of his days, his dwindling sense of purpose; his frustrations with the Archdiocesan bureaucracy: these, he learned, came with the cassock. They were simply part of being a priest.

Rita Besson's children were grown, her marriage long since dissolved. Her sole preoccupation, it seemed, was planning Celeste's wedding; and it was in this context that Father Breen became sucked into her orbit. She was a commanding woman, born into privilege, Miss Porter's and Wellesley. As the wife of a wealthy man, she had traveled the world. Now her husband had retired, sold his company and decamped to Florida, where he golfed and cavorted with a young live-in girlfriend. Rita had stayed in the marital home — she, and it, worth millions. What she did all day in the cavernous house was a mystery, though she was spotted often at fund-raisers for Catholic charities and on the society pages of the *Globe*.

She'd planned for Celeste a lavish wedding, no expense spared. *He can afford it*, she'd once

125

confided to Art, leading him to wonder about her motivations. Was the whole costly extravaganza intended as a financial punishment, a blow to the husband who'd left?

Rita's daughter seemed to harbor the same suspicion. Meeting with the young couple for Pre-Cana counseling, Art found Celeste lively and impetuous, and palpably angry. Her resentment didn't surprise him; he'd witnessed it often in children of divorce. That the Bessons weren't actually divorced, that Rita clung to their legal union, was one of many grievances Celeste bore against her. *A control freak*, Celeste called her. *I don't know how Dad lasted as long as he did*. Her fiancé, a small-town boy from Elkhart, Indiana, seemed bright and sincere. Art had said as much to Rita, earning him Celeste's undying gratitude. Rita, for whatever reason, put great stock in his opinion, and Art enjoyed the satisfaction of having brokered a temporary peace.

After the Pre-Cana sessions ended, he continued to counsel the bride's mother — on Sunday nights usually, often after some quarrel with Celeste. Mother and daughter argued ceaselessly — about dresses and menus, string quartets and wedding cakes. Art suspected that their rancor stemmed from a deeper source, that Celeste blamed Rita for driving her father away.

'That's ridiculous,' Rita snapped when he suggested this. The marriage had been shaky for years, and Alan's current girlfriend hadn't been his first. Wisely, Rita's sons had settled far away, in Vancouver and London; but Celeste, the baby, had stayed close by to torment her mother. This was Rita's assessment, and Art didn't entirely disagree. The young couple, usually reserved with each other, were in Rita's presence so affectionate that Art had to look away. The hand-holding and tender glances seemed to him a kind of performance. Celeste, clearly, wanted to show her mother how it was done.

He found this dynamic profoundly disturbing and tried, with probing questions, to address it in their counseling sessions: 'Has your parents' marriage affected your own views of the married state?' he asked Celeste, who guffawed and rolled her eyes.

Meanwhile Art and Rita became friends. They made a New Year's resolution to walk for exercise; each weekday afternoon they met at Wompatuck State Park. At her dinner parties he served as a stand-in husband, sitting at the head of the table, with Rita herself at the foot. They joked about their similar tastes. Art's years of traveling, his unusual education, had shaped him in ways that made him lonely: with other priests he had few common interests, and with his working-class family, none at all. With Rita he attended the theater and symphony. They swapped magazines, CDs and books. He didn't notice — though he should have — that their friendship had fueled the parish gossips. Because Rita was ten years older, and because he felt no attraction to her, Art had imagined himself protected. Of course, he was wrong.

Clement Fleury brought the rumors to his attention. *Be careful, Arthur. Appearances count.* Clem's parish, at that time, was halfway across the Archdiocese; who had apprised him about the goings-on at Sorrows? Not for the first time, Art was astonished by the way news traveled. Boston itself was a bustling metropolis, but the Boston Archdiocese might have been Elkhart, Indiana, a gossipy small town.

He'd been aware on some level that Rita had grown attached to him, that she'd turned to him to satisfy unmet emotional needs. Now he saw that he'd done the same. For the first time in his life he'd forged an intellectual connection with a woman. He looked forward to evenings at her lovely house in Weston, which was far more welcoming than the stiff rectory. They had even discussed traveling together: Rome, a city Art knew intimately; Paris, where Rita had lived as a student. Driving home that night, Art had felt uneasy. Surely Rita knew, as he did, that this was pure fantasy, inspired by the excellent pinot she'd brought up from her cellar, the warm glow of her fireplace on a cold Boston night. Later he saw that she'd been serious. To Rita, child of privilege, nothing was impossible. Her favorite expression was 'Why not?'

They buffered each other's solitude. How relieved he'd been, the night after Celeste's wedding, to take refuge in the air-conditioned comfort of Rita's house and watch a movie in the den. Over the years he'd come to dread the sacrament of matrimony. Watching from the altar as a young couple rushed down the aisle to start a new life together, he felt an overpowering loneliness. Now, for the first time, he had a partner in his melancholy.

'Rita,' he told her finally, 'we need to talk.' Delicately he explained the situation. Her reaction surprised him with its vehemence.

'You can't leave me,' she said. 'We're too good together.'

'We're not *together*,' he said gently. 'Rita. I'm a priest.'

'I could make you happy.'

He was aware, suddenly and uncomfortably, of their physical closeness, nearly shoulder to shoulder on the fine leather sofa where they'd watched *La strada* and *I vitelloni*; in films, as in all else, their tastes were remarkably congruent. He understood that she was offering herself to him, all that she was and all that she had. He had never felt drawn to her physically, and in that moment he felt a shudder of revulsion. Rita seemed to sense this. She drew back from him slightly, wearing a half smile.

'Why not?' she said. And then: 'Oh, I know. Your *vows*.'

He started to explain that diocesan priests weren't monks, that celibacy and obedience were solemn promises, not vows — a distinction laypeople seemed not to recognize. She stopped him midsentence.

'We could have a wonderful life,' she said, her hands spread as if to direct his attention to all that surrounded them: the handsome house, the walls lined with books he'd been meaning to read, Paris and Rome and countless more nights like this one, the deep sustaining comforts of food and wine and companionship and home.

It was a tantalizing prospect, and it came at a time, the early nineties, when his old classmates were leaving the priesthood in droves. His old friend Larry Person had left to marry — to Art, a shocking blow. Larry had knelt before him, asking his blessing, and Art had given it, his throat so swollen with emotion that he'd nearly choked on the words. Through the archdiocesan grapevine he'd heard a dozen similar stories. The stigma, if not precisely gone, was fading. These men, his friends, had abandoned neither faith nor church. They remained active in their parishes; some had families. They went on to lead, by all accounts, happy and purposeful and sanctified lives.

'Rita, I'm sorry,' he said, rising. 'I should go.'

That night he wrote a letter to the Vicar General requesting reassignment. In the fall he was sent to Sacred Heart. He no longer had any reason to drive through Weston, but he imagined Rita Besson was still there, in the handsome house her husband had bought, eight of its nine bedrooms still empty. Rita, like Art, still utterly alone.

Art had never, in my memory, taken a vacation. Now the empty weeks yawned before him. There were no Masses to say, no council meetings to attend, no catechism classes to visit.

A half mile from Dover Court he had spotted a public library. He drove there early Monday morning and sat poring over the *Globe*. From the first page of the Metro section his own face — many years younger — stared back, SOUTH SHORE PRIEST OUSTED, ACCUSED OF ABUSE.

The library was virtually empty at that hour. A young librarian sat at the reference desk, drinking her coffee. She, too, was reading the *Globe*.

He spent that morning at a local Honda dealership having a timing belt replaced. In the afternoon he parked near Kath Conlon's apartment in Dunster. He watched Aidan step out of the school bus and cross the street. He drove away when the boy was safely inside the door.

His datebook lists, for that week, a doctor's appointment, a dinner with Clem Fleury, a reminder to send Clare Boyle a birthday card. In his jacket pocket I found a dated ticket stub from Symphony Hall. For years Art had held season tickets, his Christmas present from Ma.

And maybe it was that night at the symphony, that guilty reminder of her love for him, that led

131

Art finally to her door. That conversation, so painful to both of them, is difficult to imagine. Even now Ma refuses to discuss it.

By then I hadn't heard from Art in ten days. I booked a flight and arranged a substitute to cover my classes. To Gail Hunter I offered no specifics. I simply told her that I had a family emergency in Boston.

Twilight was falling as my plane landed at Logan. I watched the shadows gather as the jet roared over Charlestown Navy Yard, the dark, orderly streets of Southie. Headlights glittered on the expressway, an endless stream of red taillights. The workday had ended, and all of Boston was sitting in traffic. Everyone was trying to get home.

The terminal was crowded at that hour, business travelers boarding the shuttles to New York and Washington, tired men in unfresh white shirts. I followed the signs to baggage claim. In past years one brother or the other would have met me at the gate, but new regulations had put an end to such welcomes.

Mike was waiting at the curb in a huge Cadillac Escalade, its chrome gleaming. He had always been meticulous about his cars. 'Sorry I'm late. Wicked traffic.' His tie was loose, his chinos rumpled, as though he'd worked a long day.

'You look good,' I told him. His blond hair was cut close, his face pink and unlined. He looked younger than he had in his twenties, when he'd worked the night shift and spent half his life in bars. Mike is built like a college athlete; at thirty-six he seemed to be still growing, taller and broader each time we met.

He gave my shoulder a rough squeeze, as close

as we would come to an embrace. Four years ago, at Gram's funeral, we had hugged briefly, awkwardly; it had seemed the correct thing to do. Now, with no older relatives present, such a gesture was out of the question. 'Don't be retarded,' one of us would have said, as we had so often in childhood. Then, as now, affection between siblings was *retahded* or *queah*.

We rode in silence, a slow merge onto the highway. The radio was tuned to an AM station, a voice I recognized from hundreds of Sox games.

'How's Ma?' I asked.

'How do you think? She's ashamed to leave the house.' Mike glanced in the rearview mirror, waved the other driver on.

'And Dad?'

'He can't remember what he had for breakfast. In other words, same old.' He grinned slyly. 'They'll be glad to see you still breathing, Mrs. Morrison and the rest. After all that chemo.'

I touched my hair, now long enough for a ponytail. Four years ago I'd shown up with a buzz cut. At Gram's funeral I'd been watched nervously. The neighbors had inquired after my health in hushed tones. *I have good days and bad days*, I told them somberly, and out the corner of my eye I saw Mike fall out laughing. The truth — that I'd lopped off my long hair for practical reasons, a summer of backpacking in Vietnam — would have seemed, on Teare Street, less credible. Who went to Vietnam on purpose?

'Fuck off,' I said. 'And anyway, they'll have enough to whisper about besides my shameful

134

haircut. Have you talked to Art?'

'No.'

A stony silence. I waited.

'Sorry, She. I got nothing else to say.'

★ ★ ★

It was full dark when we reached Grantham. Mike turned off Lisbon Ave. onto Teare Street. At the end of the block, in the Pawlowskis' front lawn, stood a knee-high Blessed Virgin framed in a cement archway. Years ago, every yard had had an identical statue, cast from the same mold. As kids we'd had a name for it, *Mary on the half shell*: the Virgin served up in her own neat container, like a littleneck clam.

At the front door I hesitated, my finger hovering over the bell.

'Don't be retarded.' Mike threw open the door. 'Ma! Sheila's here.'

The smell of the house hit me like vertigo: fried potatoes and onions, underneath it the clean, caustic odor of bleach. The parlor was dark and close, lit only by the television: the Sox were down, top of the fourth. One wall was covered with framed photographs. The Altar, Mike called it: a dozen Kodak moments Ma had chosen, plus a framed portrait of President Kennedy. As a child I'd assumed the man was a dead relative. Square-jawed and blue-eyed, he could easily pass for a McGann.

Mike put down my bag and kicked off his loafers, set them on the plastic runner. I bent to unlace my boots. It had been the rule for as long

135

as I could remember. I could still hear Ma's voice, rising slightly on the last word: *No shoes in the* **house***.*

'We fed her this evening,' Mike whispered. 'She won't bite.'

In the kitchen Ma was filling the kettle. On the table was her knitting basket and the *Grantham Tribune*, open to the obituaries — *the Irish sports page*, my father says.

'Hi, Ma.'

'Hello yourself.' Her mouth was freshly lipsticked, Chinese Red; her hair dyed the jet black of her youth. She looked older than the last time I'd seen her — she was at one of those peculiar junctures when four years makes a visible difference — but ours is apparently a face that ages well. In her late sixties she was a handsome woman and knew it, though she had long pretended indifference to such things.

I could sense her stiffening, but kissed her anyway, lightly, on the cheek. We have not been affectionate with each other in many years. As a little girl I delighted in sidling up close to her in church, slipping my small hand into the pocket of her coat. Now we are the same size exactly, our shoulders perfectly congruent, as though we were cast from the same mold. She had been to the hairdresser's. The smell still clung to her, perm solution and Aqua Net.

Mike opened the refrigerator and stared inside.

'There's shepherd's pie yet. It's still warm.' Ma took a casserole from the oven, seeming grateful for this bit of kitchen business. She is the sort of person who needs something to do. 'Your wife will have your head for spoiling your dinner. Though why anyone holds dinner until eight o'clock, I'll never know.'

'Ma, don't start.'

'I'm just saying.'

I watched them in wonderment: Ma serving the shepherd's pie, Mike poking around in the refrigerator as though he'd never left. In a way, he hadn't. Except for three years in the Navy, he'd never lived more than ten miles from this house.

'The flight was fine,' I said, though nobody had asked. 'Ahead of schedule, for once.'

'I don't know how you can get on a plane, after everything,' Ma said. 'I'll never fly again, I swear to God.'

You never flew before, I thought, but there was no point in saying it. No point in defending my own callousness, my apparent lack of feeling for the victims of terrorism, in getting on a plane.

Ma busied herself pouring the tea. 'It's our own fault for letting those people into this country.'

Those people — the faceless masses of nonwhite, non-Catholic, non-Irish. I kept quiet.

'Your father's downstairs watching the ball-game.'

'The TV is on in the parlor,' I pointed out.

'He likes to go back and forth. Don't ask me why.' Ma opened the door that led down to the basement. 'Ted! Mike and Sheila are here.' She sat, offered milk and sugar for the tea.

'I thought Art would be here,' I said.

A shadow passed over her face. 'The Archdiocese got him an apartment.'

'They kicked him out of the rectory?' I glanced over at Mike, hunched over his plate, impassively chewing. 'Can they do that?'

'It's church property,' he said.

'But he's lived there — what, ten years?'

Mike kept his eyes on his plate.

'It happened so fast,' said Ma. 'He doesn't know what hit him.'

A long silence. Finally Mike rose.

'I have to go. Abby will have dinner waiting. I might have to run around the block to work up an appetite.' He took his plate to the sink. 'Tell Dad I'll see him tomorrow.'

I watched him go. Without him, the energy in the room seemed to shift. Men did this: unconsciously perhaps, they drew the eye, directed all attention toward themselves. Was it just their size, their deep voices? I noticed that my chair, and my mother's, were tilted forty-five degrees to face Mike's.

'What's his problem?' I said.

'It's an uncomfortable situation. His own brother. He doesn't like to talk about it.' Ma rose to wash Mike's plate. I watched her lips move, counting to twelve. It was the way she'd taught me to wash dishes: eight strokes to the top of the plate, four strokes to the bottom. It was a fixation of hers, nearly a sickness. She couldn't allow a single dirty dish — a saucer, even a fork — to remain in the sink.

'It's a disgrace. One minute that girl is on the phone to Lake Street, telling tales. The next day

Arthur is out on the street.'

'What girl? Who is she?' I asked, though of course I already knew.

'A Conlon from Dorchester. Her mother was Arthur's housekeeper, a Kelly from St. Brendan's. Her father I don't know.'

'Art mentioned them,' I said carefully. 'Fran was concerned about her grandson, so Art spent some time with him.' This was how Art had framed it to me, at least at first: the whole business had been a favor to Fran. 'Ma, what is she saying? What exactly is he supposed to have done?'

'You'll have to ask Arthur about that.'

'I'd love to, but I can't reach him. I haven't heard a peep out of him. Ma, why couldn't he tell me himself?'

'He's ashamed, of course. And you're so far away.'

'Not now, Ma. Now I'm right here.'

Another silence.

'What did he tell you about the boy?'

Her mouth tightened. 'I don't know what you mean.'

'Just what I said, Ma. Jesus. Did Art talk about him?'

'I don't like what you're suggesting.'

'Oh, for God's sake. I'm not suggesting anything. Forget I asked.' I rose. 'I want to go see him in the morning. Okay if I borrow Dad's truck?'

'Sure, sure. He won't know the difference.' She eyed me uncertainly. 'Have you had dinner?'

'I grabbed something at the airport.'

'All right, then.' She blinked rapidly. 'About that boy.'

I waited.

'Arthur saw him quite a bit. The mother's car kept breaking down. Every weekend it seemed he was driving them somewhere. Shopping, or taking the boy to the movies.' Ma hesitated. 'At the time I didn't think anything of it, except that she was taking advantage of his kindness. It never occurred to me that it would look bad for him.' She wiped down the faucet, dried it with a towel, wrung out the dishcloth. 'Go down and say hello to your father. Keep him entertained while I have my bath.' Again she went to the basement door. 'Ted, Sheila's coming.'

The basement was my father's domain; to my knowledge Ma never ventured there, and for Dad this was surely part of its appeal. Ten years ago he'd laid the carpet and paneling, installed a suspended ceiling, bought a massive television. A bar ran along one end, good maple. He'd taken his time sanding and staining, to show off the grain of the wood. For years he'd described his plans in detail — usually with a glass in hand, held to his heart. *One day I'll have a proper bar in the house. Oak, I think, or maybe maple.* The day after he retired from Raytheon, he'd driven to the lumber yard.

Now he lay stretched out on his recliner, wearing work pants and a flannel shirt.

'Well, it's Sheila!' He got nimbly to his feet, and as always I was startled by how young he looked. His skin had lost its old yellowish cast; his pale blue eyes were lively as a child's. He is shorter than Mike, but otherwise the resemblance is startling. Dad is Mike in miniature.

He embraced me firmly. 'Such a good girl.'

I sat on the old sofa.

'What brings you to our house?' he asked, beaming.

'Art, Daddy. I've come to see Art.'

'Oh, very good.' He nodded energetically. 'Yes, he'll be glad to see you.'

I watched him intently. 'Have you seen him? How *is* Art?'

'Oh, very well. Fit as a fiddle, I'd say. He sends his love.' He turned his attention to the TV screen. It seemed too large for the room, too bright, too close. 'The Sox can't get a hit. Not for love nor money.'

I leaned over and kissed his cheek. 'You're a good girl,' he said, his eyes not leaving the screen.

Upstairs the house was quiet. Water rushing through the pipes, Ma running her bath. In an hour she'd be in bed, knitting in front of the TV — my parents have a set in every room — and I could rattle around the house in peace.

In the parlor I switched off the television. The divan was thirty years old, its scratchy brocade still covered with clear plastic, protected for some crisp, stain-free future. It seemed a bit optimistic, not a quality I have ever associated with my mother. More likely, the years had made the plastic invisible.

I stood a moment staring at the Altar. Twelve shots of the McGann family, the highlight reel: weddings and baptisms and First Communions, parochial school graduations, Art's ordination at St. John's. A photo of my father, arm in arm with his brother Leo. They stood on the deck of Leo's boat, the *Sweet Life*, each holding a can of beer. Except for the JFK portrait, it was the only photo not taken in a church.

I took my bag upstairs. My childhood room is ten feet square; it seemed roughly the size of Mike's Escalade. As a teenager I'd covered the walls with posters — Led Zeppelin, Bruce Springsteen. Now the walls were painted pink, a little girl's bedroom. *Your father's idea*, Ma had explained. Lace curtains covered the only window, lest any sunshine enter. Lace doilies lay on every flat surface, a slippery nuisance. Each time I came to visit, I gathered them up and stuffed them in a drawer.

I stretched out on the bed with my cell phone. 'Hey,' I said when Danny Yeager answered.

'You made it.'

'It was a breeze. The guy next to me kept buying me drinks.'

'Should I be jealous?'

'Very. He was my dad's age, at least. Viagra territory for sure.' I felt my eyes fill, and I realized that this was the reason I'd called.

'He looks good,' I said. 'His speech is fine, he's very pleasant and friendly, but after a few minutes you can tell he's faking it. He has no idea what he's talking about.'

'But he knew you, right? He recognized his own daughter?'

'I guess. It's hard to say. Ma is always coaching him. *Ted, Sheila's here.* That kind of thing.'

142

Silence on the other end. Poor Danny Yeager: fuck a girl twice, and look what you've gotten into. But he is a guidance counselor, after all. (What sane person would accept such a title? An open invitation to the distraught and disoriented, the wounded and the crazed.) And I was tired and hungover and too ragged even to feel ridiculous. I wanted only a familiar voice, someone who knew me. Not some earlier, larval version of myself, the soft simple creature who'd once slept in this bed; but the person I have grown into, whoever that is. I wanted someone to remind me who I am.

It's a Sunday afternoon, late summer, church behind me for another week. It's a Sunday afternoon, is not was, because here the past is present, with me always; it will not leave me alone, it doesn't know its place. We are riding in my father's car at noon or half past, the sun directly overhead, the black vinyl seat of the Pontiac Ventura sticky beneath my bare thighs. Route 3A is slow with traffic, the two-lane road that winds past the beach towns, fumes rising from the pavement, the air low and heavy, smelling of melting tar. I am thirteen, wearing denim cutoffs and a Red Sox T-shirt over the bikini I bought with my own money, that Ma has never seen and would not have let me buy. But the suit has been paid for and now worn, the sanitary adhesive strip removed from its crotch so that by law it cannot be returned.

Mike and I are in the backseat and we are riding past the town of Scituate — *the Irish Riviera* — where my uncle Leo and aunt Norma live on a dead-end street, the fine houses set far apart and heavily shaded with trees. We're riding to the marina where Leo keeps the *Sweet Life*, his forty-foot cabin cruiser. Long before it meant anything to me, I knew the phrase 'forty-foot cabin cruiser.' My uncle employs it often, as does my father, who enjoys telling people how he spends these Sundays.

144

He's done well, Leo, Dad says, holding his glass to his heart.

We will pile aboard the boat, Leo and Dad, then me and Mike and our cousins Brian and Richie and Ann Marie, except that Ann Marie hasn't come this time, which means that I will sit alone all afternoon being thirteen with no one to talk to, not even fat and boring Ann Marie. Ma and Aunt Norma will follow, carrying grocery sacks. My mother is famously nervous about the water, unhappy on, in or near it. Later I will understand what these afternoons cost her, the humming anxiety as she waits for the forty-foot cabin cruiser to return to the harbor, delivering herself and her children to dry land. Those fears live close to the surface. Beneath them is a deeper unease, also unspoken, a dread of what will happen later at home. Because even more than he loves Leo, my father loves Leo's life; and after these hours on the wide ocean, our snug house in Grantham will seem hopelessly constricting. My father, in his cups, will roar just to hear himself, to prove he is alive.

We motor out of the harbor with a noisy burst, belching diesel fumes — prompting dirty looks from the Scituate Yacht Club, genteel sailboaters who disdain our shiny fiberglass tub. My uncle Leo gives them the finger. He opens two beers from the cooler and passes one to my dad, standing beside him at the helm. They raise their cans in joyful salute. The word *cocksuckers* is lost in the engine noise.

Ma and Aunt Norma disappear below deck, to what Ma calls the kitchen until Norma corrects her: *the galley*. Norma wears her usual sailing costume, white Bermuda shorts and gold jewelry and navy-and-white striped tank top. Ma makes sandwiches as her own mother did: buttered bread, a single thin slice of ham. *We have more ham, you know*, Norma shouts over the engine. *No need to be chintzy. Leo likes a thick sandwich.* Watching, I dread my own womanhood, the day when I too will follow along carrying bags of groceries, my mission wherever I go to feed other people who take actual part in life while I am simply the catering staff. I hang back watching my mother take orders from Norma, whose freckled arms jiggle as she mixes green Kool-Aid. Everything — the table, the counters — vibrates with the engine, and Norma spills a little as she fills the plastic jug.

Then, suddenly, the noise stops. I climb the stairs to the deck where my uncle is dropping anchor. The men drain their cans of Pabst, crushing them to save space because the cardboard box on the floor is already half filled. They unbutton their shirts. My uncle's belly is round and hard like a melon. My father's arms are thick and brown, his chest lily-white. Both wear oval medals — St. Christopher, the patron saint of sailors — on silver chains.

I watch them jump overboard. *Into the drink!* Leo shouts. They are both excellent swimmers. My father dives beneath the surface and rises spitting a long stream of salt water, spurting like a whale. As a little girl I'd been delighted by this trick. Now it simply disgusts me, a mouthful of Boston Harbor effluent, untold molecules of

146

factory runoff, dioxin and urine and God knows what.

I stand back as Mike and Richie cannonball into the water with earsplitting whoops. Then I pull off my T-shirt and drop my shorts. As far as I can tell, sun on my skin is the only benefit of this lame family outing. I have built my tan all summer and am mortified by my relatives' pale freckled flesh.

My cousin Brian comes up behind me and reaches into the cooler, as he always does when Leo's back is turned. He is seventeen and adolescence has rendered him mute. But today, for the first time, Brian fishes out two cans. Miraculously, he also speaks. 'Catch,' he says, and I do, the wet can nearly slipping from my hands. 'Come on.'

I follow him to the rear of the boat, where he takes a pack of Camels from his pocket. I have smoked only once before, not inhaling. I glance nervously over my shoulder.

'Dad doesn't care.' Brian lights up. He wears a silver medal like his father's and mirrored sunglasses that hide his eyes.

I lean forward so he can light one for me. A breeze lifts my hair. 'Careful,' he says, holding it away from the flame.

It is the best moment of the afternoon, the summer, the entire year of being thirteen: the diesel breeze off the water, my cousin's bare chest and my own near nakednesss, his hand gentle where it holds my hair. I want it to last longer but there is my mother's voice cawing *Come and get 'em* and then a great mobilization of McGanns, Ma and Norma emerging from below deck, Dad and Leo and then the little boys scampering up the ladder, the boat rocking with their shifting weight.

Brian and I climb over to join the others. I stumble a little, and Brian reaches out a hand to steady me. *I'm drunk*, I whisper.

So are they, he says, and I am laughing with my handsome cousin who takes the bus into the city to go to BC High School, a thing I would love to do but can't because it's only for boys.

I accept a sandwich and a cup of Kool-Aid, ignoring Ma, who hisses at me: *Put on some clothes*. I'll hear about it later, but right now I feel good. Brian takes off his sunglasses and I feel him looking at my belly and my nipples hard from the cold. The fathers and the boys wait the required twenty minutes, then jump back *into the drink*. Ma accepts a beer and finally relaxes a little, and I go down to use the bathroom (*the head*, Norma corrects me). I want Brian to follow and he does, closing the door behind us. *Let me see them*, he says, and I don't understand and then I do.

They're still small, he says but kisses them anyway and when he puts my hand inside his shorts there is a funny kind of net inside them. *Swim trunks*, I think, and it is the last thought I will have, until the engine starts and my stomach lurches and I turn just in time to vomit green Kool-Aid into the toilet *the head*.

That night, his stomach already full of shepherd's pie, Mike sat down to dinner with his wife. He pulled into the driveway at the stroke of eight and found Abby at the kitchen sink, rinsing greens for salad. 'I just put the twins down,' she said. 'Jamie almost fell asleep in the bathtub. Ryan is out like a light.'

He watched her bang a drawer shut with her sleek denim hip. Three kids and she'd kept her figure, improved it even. She fed the family carefully, recipes clipped from *Prevention* magazine. His boys ate broccoli without complaint. At holidays this astonished our cousin Rich, whose kids lived on white bread and hot dogs and turned up their noses at anything else.

He helped her carry the plates to the dining room: the salad, a skinless chicken breast, the butternut squash he dreaded but pretended to like.

'How's Sheila?' Abby asked.

It is tempting, almost titillating, to imagine how others speak of us in our absence. In the case of my sister-in-law, it is unnerving to contemplate. My interactions with her have never been easy. On both sides there is a certain disquiet. Abby is beautiful, intelligent and self-possessed. She has never failed at anything as far as I can tell, and if that isn't enough to make you feel small and speechless, then you and I are different under the skin. And yet I jangle her, too, because Mike and I are closer than most siblings. We finish each other's sentences. Often enough, one of us will make the other laugh so hard and long that asphyxiation seems a real danger. It's a heady pleasure rare in adulthood, not unlike — I will say it — the shared breathlessness of rousingly successful coitus. Abby has been present when Mike and I fall out laughing, and her discomfort is so tangible that I suspect this has occurred to her, too.

'She's fine, I guess.'

'How did she look?'

'Better than last time. More hair.' He reached for pepper and salt.

'Your dad must have been happy to see her.'

Mike didn't respond. He sensed that she was baiting him. Abby knew that Dad, his mind gone from drink, did not recognize his own grandchildren, and that this pained Mike more than he would ever say. The old man stared blankly at the boys as though they were packages he hadn't ordered, but never failed to perk up at the mention of Sheila, who wanted nothing to do with the family, who visited only when a relative dropped dead (or, in Art's case, deserved to). *Ah, Sheila. Such a good girl.*

'I didn't see him,' said Mike. 'He was downstairs watching the game.'

They sat at the table. It was an unbreakable rule of Abby's: on weeknights, after the kids were in bed, she and Mike ate a civilized meal in the dining room, cloth napkins, soft jazz on the stereo. He appreciated this, found it relaxing. But some nights he missed eating with the boys. The squirming chaos, the occasional spilled milk, reminded him of our childhood, Ma barking orders, the two of us winding each other up, kicking under the table and dissolving sometimes in breathless laughter, for reasons he couldn't have named even at the time. This, to Mike, *was* family, the whole reason he'd wanted kids in the first place. Abby was an excellent mother, by every measure better than Ma had been. She rationed the boys' TV watching, doled out vitamins, kept track of their dental checkups, wrestled them into their baths. Yet Mike sometimes wondered: did Abby *enjoy* their children? Wasn't there more to being a parent than simply doing everything right?

He started in on his dinner, chewing slowly. The chicken was a little dry. He pictured Ma's shepherd's pie hardening in his stomach like cement.

'Don't you find it odd?' Abby asked. 'She hasn't come around in years. Now she hops on a plane for something like this.'

'Yeah, so? Art's her brother, too.'

'It's not as if they're close.'

Mike shrugged. 'Maybe they are.'

His wife closed one eye, her skeptical look. She was about to tell him, in delicate paraphrase, that he was full of shit.

'They have so much in common, right? I'll bet Sheila hasn't set foot in a church since our wedding.'

'Let's not start on that.'

'I wasn't.'

Upstairs a commotion started: crying, a shout. Lately Jamie was prone to nightmares.

'I'll go,' said Mike, springing from his chair.

Bless Jamie, he thought, grateful for the escape.

*   *   *

I have said already that Mike is a pragmatist. Having decided on a course of action, he proceeds without hesitation. I have never known him to second-guess himself, or to question his own motives. His energy is fearsome, his immunity to the modern illnesses: inertia, anxiety, ambivalence, regret.

The next morning, a Friday, he rose at dawn, hit the weight bench and ate breakfast with the kids. Abby joined them just as he was leaving, and he made sure the boys saw him kiss her goodbye. They were making an effort to keep things looking normal, though for several days they'd given each other wide berth. Abby went to bed soon after the boys did. By the time Mike came upstairs she was already asleep.

He took a back route to Dunster, avoiding the highway; at this hour the expressway would be a parking lot. He still had friends on the force, and had called in a favor. His old buddy Dan Flanagan had pulled Kath's RMV record. He hadn't asked why Mike wanted the address.

Naturally I have questioned Mike about his intentions that morning. What exactly was he hoping for when he went to Kath Conlon's apartment?

'I wanted to see the kid,' he said.

It's a fair answer — though, I suspect, an incomplete one. Mike believes in the basic honesty of children. In his view, no eight-year-old has mastered the cheap ruses of adulthood. When kids lie, they don't *want* to be believed; their deepest wish is to be known and understood. For my brother this is a point of faith: a child will tell the truth if he feels safe and accepted. All you have to do is gain his trust.

Fenno Street should have been bustling at that hour, and Mike did spot a few commuters, dog walkers, kids hiking to the bus stop. But he also saw young, able-bodied people drinking coffee on porches, smoking cigarettes on front steps. A pack of teenage boys in hooded sweatshirts lingered at the corner. It was what realtors called a *transitional neighborhood*, somewhere between welfare and respectable working class. Though in which direction it was moving — whether it was getting better or worse — was anybody's guess.

Mike parked at a discreet distance, two doors down, and scoped out the house, a run-down three-decker as shabby as (but no worse than) any other on the block. The first-floor shades were drawn. On the front porch were two plastic chairs, a plastic table, a yellow toboggan. An old Buick was parked out front — late eighties vintage, he'd guess, with a landau top. A bigger gas hog than his Escalade: ten miles to the gallon, if you were lucky. Then again, if you were truly lucky, you wouldn't be driving such a car.

It was astonishing what you could learn about people from the way they lived. Mike saw it every day, walking through strangers' houses. Their furniture and keepsakes, their personal photographs; what they kept in the refrigerator, the hall closet, the medicine chest. This apartment, for example. If only he could see inside it, he would know a great deal about Kathleen Conlon and her son.

He turned his attention to the house across the street. Twelve Fenno was a small Cape, its clapboards painted yellow. The windows and doors cried out for replacement. The roof would last another year. Mike had rarely shown a house in such condition, but he'd gone out of his way to get this one. The property was listed with one of their branch offices, and the agent, Teri Pappas, was about to take maternity leave. She'd been mystified by his interest. *Number twelve? Sure, take it. They're asking three hundred. In their dreams.*

Mike got out of his Escalade and glanced up and down the street. It was trash day; at each address, a few plastic recycling bins sat at the curb. He strolled casually toward the three-decker. A single bin sat on the sidewalk, full of empty bottles, bargain brands of whiskey and gin.

A drinker, then.

For a second his mind raced, pondering the implications. If the mother was a drunk, could her word be trusted? On the other hand, the child of such a mother would be doubly vulnerable, unprotected from any predator that came along. She hadn't filed criminal charges, a fact that nagged at him. Did that make the accusation less credible? Or was she simply hoping to spare the kid the trauma of a trial? In her place, would he have done the same thing?

At that moment a girl came out of the first-floor apartment, a recycling bin in one hand, in the other a bag of trash. 'Aidan!' she called. 'Come on already!' She was small and slender, her hair streaked an improbable shade of blond. She wore a raspberry-colored tracksuit and was loaded down with a pocketbook, a tote bag and a backpack that looked weirdly familiar. It was, Mike realized, the same Batman pack Ryan carried.

'Gimme that,' Mike called, approaching her. He took the bin in one hand, the trash in the other, and swung them easily to the curb.

'Thanks.' The girl eyed him warily. 'Aidan!' she called, unlocking the Buick. 'I'm going to be late again.'

A boy appeared on the porch, pale and skinny, his dark hair shaggy. Mike felt something catch in his throat.

'I can't find my backpack.' The boy's voice was low and troubled, almost comically distressed. A worrier, then, like Mike's Jamie: the kind of kid who sees disaster everywhere. He was small for eight. Ryan had been that size in kindergarten, the tallest boy in his class.

'I've got it, sweetie. Let's go.'

The kid scrambled down the steps and went around to the passenger side. To Mike's surprise, he went straight for the front seat. His own kids always sat in back, in case of accident: a child lighter than seventy pounds could be crushed if an airbag deployed. Of course, this old clunker wouldn't even *have* airbags. While Mike's boys rode around town in Abby's brand-new Explorer, sturdy as a Sherman tank, Aidan Conlon was living a more dangerous life.

Mike turned and headed back to his Escalade, but not before getting a good look inside the recycling bin marked CONLON. Yogurt cups, a milk carton, soda and shampoo bottles. A plastic jug labeled 'Juicy Juice.'

What happened next was, simply, a stroke of luck.

'I forgot my lunch,' the boy said suddenly.

'Jesus, Aidan.' The girl set her pocketbook on the Buick's roof and handed him her keys. 'Lock the door after you. Can you do that?'

Mike watched the boy scamper up the porch steps.

'I have twins that age,' he called to the girl. 'I swear to God, it takes us half an hour to get out of the house.' He unlocked his truck and took a stack of signs — SOUTH SHORE REALTY — from the backseat.

He was surprised when she came toward him, arms folded across her chest. 'Who's selling?' she asked, eyeing the signs. Her lips were glossy pink, the same color as the tracksuit. She looked very young.

'Number twelve,' he said, pointing. 'You interested?'

'Maybe. What are they asking?' She smelled of cigarettes and fruity perfume. The top of her head was level with his shoulder. He looked down at the dark roots of her hair.

'Two-fifty. But I'd consider that a suggestion. I'm Mike, by the way.' He handed her a business card from his pocket. 'Open house tomorrow, four to six. Stop by, if you want.'

'Maybe I will,' she said.

When I knocked at Art's door it opened quickly, as though he'd been waiting behind it. He looked gaunt and stricken, distinctly unwell. He was unshaven, his chin bristling with silver. The last time I'd seen him, in Philadelphia, he'd looked fit and suntanned. In six months he'd aged ten years. He was dressed in lay clothing, dark pants and a checked shirt, but hadn't quite gotten the hang of it. His trousers were the kind he'd always worn, made of slick black fabric. The kind worn only by priests.

'You found me,' he said.

'The banners helped.' NOW RENTING: the bright green vinyl flapping in the wind. As always when I came back to Boston, I was struck by the touches of green everywhere. Was this some kind of marketing strategy? In my parents' neighborhood, parked behind Ma's Escort, the Morrison Electric truck was plastered with shamrock decals, an unsubtle appeal to the Irish-American consumer: We're for you.

Briefly we embraced, the A-frame hug, leaning forward from the waist. 'Art, are you okay?'

He gave me a crooked smile, as though there were no short answer to that question, and waved me inside. The room was too large for his few possessions. Against one wall was a worn futon. At the far end sat an armchair and a

158

portable television, huddled together as if for warmth.

'Have you seen Mike?' he asked.

I nodded.

'I haven't heard from him. Not since all this happened.'

'I know,' I said. 'I gave him shit for it.'

Art looked down at his hands. 'He has kids, Sheila. I understand.'

'He also has a brother. For Christ's sake.' I unzipped my jacket and tossed it on the floor. 'Art, what the hell happened?'

He spoke haltingly, as if each word pained him. 'That boy I told you about. Fran Conlon's grandson.'

I forced myself to meet his eyes.

'He got very attached to me,' Art said carefully. 'I guess he was looking for a father.'

'Where *is* his father?'

'Gone. They never married. They were very young.' Art's face was flushed, his lips trembling with some high emotion. 'It was Kathleen who made the accusation. That I — ' His voice broke. 'That I touched him. It isn't true,' he added, almost as an afterthought. 'You know that, right?'

There was only one possible response.

'Of course,' I said quickly. 'But *why* is she saying this? I don't understand.'

'I have no idea.' Art made a tour of the room. He seemed unable to stand still. 'The boy — Aidan — has had a rough time. Out in California he was in foster care for a while. Kath had a problem with drugs. Methamphetamine.

159

But she went through a rehab program, and she seemed to be doing well.' He stood at the window, opening and closing the blinds. 'God, this is so mortifying. That anybody would believe I could do this. Sheila, it makes me sick even to say it. I hate saying these things to you.'

His back was to me, his neck flushed from collar to hairline.

'I know you,' I said simply. 'Nobody who knows you could ever believe this.' Except our own brother, I thought but didn't say.

The words hung between us as though I'd spoken them. There was an awkward pause.

'So what happens now?' I asked.

'An investigation, apparently. They didn't tell me much.' Art ran a hand through his hair — a long, delicate hand, strangely like my own. 'I just want to tell my side of the story. So far nobody's even asked.' He smiled grimly. 'Sitting there in the Cardinal's office, do you know what my first thought was? *How am I ever going to tell Ma?*'

'How did you?'

'I didn't.' He sat and crossed his legs; the shiny fabric made a scratching noise. 'You know she always comes to my Masses on holidays. Well, she showed up Easter Sunday and there was a substitute. Apparently the parishioners were already whispering.' He reached into his breast pocket as if for a cigarette, then remembered he no longer smoked. 'When I finally worked up the nerve to go over there — well, I've never seen her in such a state. 'What's the matter, Arthur? Are you sick? You won't believe what people are saying.' And I had to tell her — ' His voice broke

160

again. 'Sheila, it was the hardest thing I've ever had to do.'

I tried to imagine it. Art was the pride of Ma's life. I'd heard her say it more than once, not caring that her other children were listening: *He's the only thing I ever did right.*

'Poor Ma,' I said, and for once I meant it. None of my own sins — the divorce, my estrangement from the church, my failure to bear children — could have wounded her this gravely. Art had much, much farther to fall.

'Do you have a lawyer?' I asked.

'They said I don't need one.'

'They?'

'Bishop Gilman. Anyway, I don't want one.' Art spread his empty hands. 'I have nothing to hide.'

'But you have to defend yourself.'

'It's out of my hands,' he said mildly. 'What will be, will be.'

I stared at him in disbelief. Was this Christlike pacifism, or simple fatalism? Had Art's years in the priesthood robbed him of his spine? Later I would understand the reasons, that his passivity was more than simple habit; but at that moment I wanted to shake him.

'Get down off your cross,' I said.

* * *

I have always admired Art's calm temperament; in our hotheaded family it seemed almost saintly, evidence of a more evolved nature. But at that moment — with his reputation in tatters, his

161

life's work collapsing around him — I found it maddening. For the first time in years I thought of Father Frank Lynch, Art's first pastor. Was *this* the reason the old priest had tormented him? Had Art infuriated him in exactly this way?

I met Father Lynch only once, when I was home from college on spring break. While my classmates were flouting the Commandments in Fort Lauderdale, I'd been summoned back to Boston for a family gathering, a fiftieth birthday party for Aunt Clare Boyle. Art had no wheels — he had occasional use of the parish sedan — so I'd stopped by in Ma's car to give him a lift.

The pastor himself answered the door. I'd heard so much about him that it was like meeting a celebrity, and Frank Lynch lived up to the part. He was charming and surprisingly handsome — a fact that Art, in all his grousing, had neglected to mention. I remember piercing blue eyes, a full head of silver-gray hair. It sounds strange to say that a priest flirted with me, but he did, and skillfully, as though he'd had a lifetime of practice.

I knew from Art that Father Lynch was a bully. Later I found out that he was also a crook. His first Christmas at Holy Redeemer, Art had made a shocking discovery: the parish's entire holiday collection found its way into the priest's bank account. At one time, apparently, all pastors had done likewise. The practice had since fallen out of favor, but Lynch was old-school.

When Art told me this, I thought of my father and men like him, working hard for hourly wages; the shamed husbands of pious wives. How much of Dad's small Christmas bonus did Ma sneak into the collection basket?

You have to tell someone, I said to Art. *A bishop, someone.*

Oh, Sheila. He seemed touched by my innocence. *They already know.*

★ ★ ★

I remembered those words as Art and I rolled up to Sacred Heart in my father's truck. We went in through the back door, carrying empty boxes. 'Thanks for doing this,' he said. 'The locksmith is coming on Monday. It's my last chance.' Of course, nobody really *believed* he'd break into the rectory, he'd explained. *Pro forma tantum.*

I followed him through a dark basement, past a washer and dryer, a hot-water heater. We went up a rickety staircase into the silent kitchen.

'Nothing we need to worry about in here,' said Art. 'None of it is mine. A couple coffee mugs, maybe. The rest was here when I came.'

I thought of my own tiny kitchen, crammed with small treasures I'd acquired here and there, and imagined living as Art did, for ten years eating off the parish's dishes. Nothing in the world belonged to him, not even the rug beneath his feet.

We went into the parlor, filled with heavy furniture: an old-fashioned divan with a curved back, two stiff armchairs with ornately carved legs. Above the mantelpiece was a framed portrait of the Sacred Heart. Some forgotten part of me was still Catholic enough to be affected by these trappings, to feel chastened and respectful and curiously mute.

'It's like a cave in here,' I complained, parting the curtains. In a moment I saw why. The window behind them was made of stained glass.

'*Ex umbra in solem*,' Art said, switching on a lamp. 'On a sunny day it's beautiful. Of course, we haven't had a sunny day in weeks.'

I stared at the window. It was a biblical scene I recognized, the raising of Lazarus. Christ standing before the tomb, hands outstretched. The sisters, Mary and Martha, gazing in wonderment. Lazarus reaching toward them, surrounded by a golden light.

We divided the house by rooms. Art took the first floor, leaving me the bedroom and upstairs bath.

'Are you sure you want me going through your things?' I asked.

'Why not?' said Art. Then, in a flat voice I recognized, the voice Ma used when she was joking: 'I keep the crack pipes and Uzis downstairs.'

Art's bedroom was small and square, crammed with the same sort of dark, claw-footed furniture as downstairs: dresser, night-stand, a high, stiff, twin bed. A faded Oriental rug covered the floor. There were layers of curtains at the windows, brocade drapes over lace panels. All of it was depressingly familiar: my mother's taste. It occurred to me, not for the first time, that she'd spent too many years in the orbit of priests.

The narrow closet was stuffed with black sport

164

jackets, black shirts, black pants. I took them from their hangers and laid them on the bed.

'Art,' I called down the stairs. 'The comforter is yours, right?'

'Correct,' he said.

I marveled to think we were shouting in the rectory. There was still enough parochial school in me to make me sweat.

The fat down comforter filled an entire bag. I was cheered by the sight of it, glad my brother had this one bit of luxury in his life, at the end of the day a soft place to land.

Under the bed I found a stack of record albums: the Who, the Doors, *Sergeant Pepper*, music popular in Art's seminary days. I know, from a few misguided attempts at dating older men, that this is not unusual. It may be unfair to say that an entire generation is besotted with the music of its youth, but that is how it seems.

Behind the records were several Thom McAn boxes, identically marked: WNGTP BLK 10 WIDE. I opened each one briefly. No sense in moving empty boxes across town.

The first box was full of paper: a Christmas card, some receipts, ticket stubs from Boston theaters, the American Repertory, the Publick. A paper program, professionally engraved: *Father Dennis Rickard, A Fiftieth Jubilee*.

The second box was heavier. Inside were bundles of cards, bound with rubber bands. Prayer cards, the sort given out at funerals: *Eternal rest grant unto him, O Lord*.

I opened another box. On top, seeming to grant me permission, was by sheer stupid chance a photo of myself — in costume for a college theater production of *The Merchant of Venice*, smiling at curtain call, hand in hand with my castmates. Taken twenty years ago: my face rounder then, my eyes bright. How ridiculous I looked in my elaborate wig and makeup. How happy, and ridiculous, and young.

More photos. Myself and Art arm in arm, in long wool coats and mufflers, standing before the marquee at the Helen Hayes Theatre. Teenage Mike in graduation cap and gown, the blond fringe of his mullet visible beneath his mortarboard. An unfocused shot of my parents, Dad smiling, Ma with the fierce, tight-lipped look she always wore when approached by a camera: *Get that thing away from me.*

I closed the lid and gathered up a tower of boxes, piled to my chin. As I got to my feet the topmost one tumbled over, scattering more photos to the ground. Scooping them up, I noticed the same two faces in every shot, a young woman and a little boy. At the bottom of the pile were the ones I have already mentioned, taken at Nantasket Beach.

What can a photograph mean? It seems to me, now, that it's not so much the image itself as the fact that it was kept. In my own bedroom closet are three large boxes I labeled — late one night, in a dark mood — PLUTONIUM. They are filled with my own keepsakes and very heavy, decades of living distilled down to a few potent sentiments: tenderness, longing, regret.

I studied the photos until I heard footsteps on the stairs. Quickly I swept them into the box and shoved it under the bed.

'I shoved all your Johnny Cash gear into trash bags,' I called. 'Is that a sin?'

Art appeared in the doorway and looked around the room. 'I feel like a fugitive. Like the Angel of Death is passing over.' Then, seeing my blank look: 'The Israelites, remember?'

I frowned. Had I really spent twelve years in parochial school? Twelve solid years of religion classes — fifty minutes, five days a week. What I had retained would fit on an index card.

Art glanced around the room. 'I guess we can load up the truck. All set here?'

I remembered the box of photos under the bed. I imagined it smoldering like hot coals.

'I'll be down in a minute,' I said.

The open house was poorly attended. The first hour brought plenty of foot traffic, but no serious buyers. It was easy to spot the difference. This crowd was mainly snoops and gossips, curious to see the inside of a neighbor's house. Nobody looked at the fact sheet Mike had piled near the entrance. Some hadn't even bothered to go upstairs.

Periodically he glanced out the front door, looking for signs of life at Kath Conlon's. The little boy resembled her distinctly, once you got past his dark hair. Her natural color, probably. Mike had always dated blondes, though he realized now that most had been fake. Even Lisa Morrison did something to her hair — highlights, something — though as a kid she'd been a towhead like her brothers. Abby had been his first brunette, a fact that had seemed significant.

'Open house today,' he'd told her over breakfast. He let himself sound irritated, as though he resented working on a Saturday afternoon.

'Where?' she asked.

Just making conversation, probably, but the question had made his heart race. Before he knew it, he'd made up a fake address in Quincy. The lie had rolled off his tongue smooth as butter. He hadn't lied in many years, not since Lisa.

Back then he'd had plenty to lie about. After hours, a drink in his hand, he'd been confident and aggressive. Having a girlfriend wasn't the same as being married. Cheating was a relative term. Of course, if Lisa had opened her legs for some guy, he would have screamed bloody murder. They were both suspicious, wildly jealous. They drank too much and were young. Every few months Lisa would catch him in a lie, or think she had. He'd complain that she didn't trust him, genuinely outraged. The breakup would last a month or two, until he spotted her at the Claddagh or the Banshee with some guy's hands all over her. One asshole kissing the tattoo Mike had bought her, the tiny heart on the back of her wrist. Mike had thrown a punch that time (usually he didn't). At the end of the night Lisa went home with him.

It seemed they'd go on that way forever, fighting in public, making up in private. He'd known her so long that their togetherness seemed inevitable. It still astonished him, sometimes, that they'd made their lives with other people, that she'd given birth to kids that weren't his.

'Hey, what are they asking?'

Mike turned. A young couple had just come in, the girl obviously pregnant.

'It's listed at three hundred, but I'd consider that a suggestion.' Mike grinned. 'They're pretty motivated to sell.'

'We're just looking,' said the guy — Hispanic maybe, just a kid.

169

Mike had learned not to hover. 'No problem,' he said easily. 'Any questions, give a shout.'

He stepped out onto the porch. The sky was clearing; it was the first dry weekend in a month, the first clean breath of spring. Across the street there was still no sign of the girl.

He wanted only to talk to her: to hear her story, to watch her as she said the words. As a cop he'd learned that every liar had a tell. *The hands*, he'd told Dan Flanagan one night, when they were off duty and getting loaded at the Banshee. *They can't keep their hands still. I just keep an eye on their hands.*

It was Flanagan who gave him the nickname. The Polygraph. He was always needling Mike, giving him shit; but Mike liked the name and took it to heart. He'd been right often enough to be proud of his instincts. It was harder with strangers, of course. He could be fooled — anyone could — by a stranger. But once he got to know them, Mike could always spot the tell.

⋆ ⋆ ⋆

By three-thirty the house was empty. He gave it another ten minutes, then began closing windows. Finally he locked the doors.

Outside the girl was sitting on her porch, eyes closed, basking in the afternoon sun. She was barefoot, in jeans and a tank top, bra straps showing. You couldn't miss it, a bright purple bra.

'Hey,' he called. 'You didn't stop over.'

She opened one eye, turned her head slightly, like a preening cat.

Mike crossed the street and approached the porch. 'Jesus, you must be freezing. It's not *that* warm.'

The girl smiled. 'I like the sun.'

'I can show you the house another time.' He reached up, offered his hand. 'I'm Mike, by the way.'

'Kath.' Her hand was small and cold, surprisingly strong.

'Some night this week, maybe.'

'I'm not ready to buy yet. Another month, I think.'

'What, you planning to win the lottery?'

Kath shrugged. 'You never know.'

'Well, you should take a look. I doubt it'll be on the market in a month. It's a hell of a good deal.'

She scrabbled in her purse for a cigarette, menthol light. Her nail polish was chipped. Then, on her left wrist, he saw it: a heart-shaped tattoo.

Mike felt as though he'd been slapped, blood rushing to heat his face. In the exact same spot, yet. What were the odds?

He said, 'I knew someone who had a tattoo like that.'

'Oh, yeah?' She examined it as though she'd forgotten it was there. 'I've had that one forever. This one I just got.' She bent forward and pulled up her pant leg. A green vine curled around her anklebone.

Mike leaned forward to examine it. He caught

a whiff of fragrance on her skin, fruity and sweetly synthetic, a smell not found in nature. Candy, he thought.

'Nice,' he said. 'Got any more?'

'None I can show.'

At that moment a car pulled up in front of the house, a beat-up Camaro with a mangled bumper. The windows were down, rap music blaring. At the wheel sat a guy in sunglasses. Mike got a good look at him, dark hair, goatee, skinny arm hanging out the window. A real dirtbag. As if sensing his gaze, the driver rolled up the window.

'I gotta go.' Kath slipped on a pair of clogs, grabbed her leather jacket and purse. Her shoes were loud on the rickety steps.

'How about tomorrow morning?' Mike said, a last effort.

She frowned. 'I might not be — around. In the evening maybe.'

'Sure,' Mike said.

He watched her get into the car, lean over to speak to the driver. The car squealed away from the curb.

★   ★   ★

He'd bought Lisa the tattoo on her nineteenth birthday. With their fake IDs they'd stopped first at a bar in Providence. *Make sure I'm good and loaded*, she said. It was as close as he'd ever come to seeing her afraid. He understood later that this was why he'd loved her. Lisa had always been fearless. Being with

172

her had made him brave.

For half an hour the guy had worked on her — a bald freak with a pierced eyebrow, his own arms covered with tattoos. Drunk himself, Mike sat beside her, their thighs touching. Together they watched the pulsing needle, the blood welling up from Lisa's skin. Lisa in a short denim skirt, her bare thigh warm under his hand.

He hadn't fucked her yet, not properly, though there had been some awkward groping years before. Back then she'd been Tim Morrison's baby sister, a skinny little thing, and there wasn't much to grope. She'd grown up since then, had more boyfriends than Mike cared to think of. He suspected she could teach him a few things. Later that night he'd find out it was true.

'Your turn,' she said when it was finished.

'No fucken way.' He had broken his nose playing hockey, dislocated a shoulder in jayvee football. He could handle pain if necessary, but he wasn't stupid enough to go looking for it.

There would be other tattoos, less visible. A detailed crucifix high on one shoulder; a bird at the base of her spine, its wings spread wide. A tiny flower blooming deep inside her left hipbone, a spot so private that even a bikini would hide it. That was a night Mike would remember forever, Lisa lying on the table, naked from the waist down. The same bald guy leaning over her, close enough to smell her. *When he's finished*, Mike thought, *I'll beat the shit out of him*. The thought was strangely arousing. He'd taken Lisa home and fucked her senseless. He

173

had never been so turned on in his life.

He imagined her now, in the careless nudity of marriage: Lisa stepping out of the shower, her husband shaving at the sink. The pattern Mike would never forget, heart bird cross flower, her secret punctuation. Did her husband know who'd paid for the marks on her body? That it was Mike McGann who'd sat beside her, grasping her thigh, watching the needle do its work?

★　★　★

He drove away from Dunster feeling restless. Saturday night, the first weekend of spring weather. The beachfront bars were filled, bands playing. Kath Conlon had been wearing perfume. Where was her kid on a Saturday night while she was riding around in some guy's Camaro? The driver had closed his window when he caught Mike looking. Something about that was unsettling. It gave him a bad feeling.

Accidentally maybe, he zoomed past his exit on the highway. He wasn't ready to go home. Instead he took the back way into Grantham. Abby would be expecting him, but then she was always expecting him. As he parked behind Ma's Escort, he turned off his cell phone.

The house was dead quiet inside. 'Ma?' he called.

He heard noises below, the creaking of the stairs. The basement door opened. 'Hello, there,' Dad said.

'Hey. Where's Ma?'

Dad hesitated only a moment. 'Having her hair fixed,' he said pleasantly. 'You know women and their hair.'

Mike glanced at the clock: six-thirty on a Saturday night. Probably she had gone to the evening Mass. She would leave Ted alone for an hour, not longer. For one hour he could manage on his own.

'What about Sheila?' said Mike. 'Don't tell me Ma dragged her to church.'

'Not a word against your sister. She's a good girl. I'm having a Coke,' he announced. 'Want one? There's cold ones in the fridge.'

'I'm good. I have to get going.'

'All right, then. Happy trails.'

It was, on balance, as satisfying a conversation as they'd had in many years.

Where were you during the storm?

In Boston it was the question for a generation. Ma and Clare Boyle remembered Pearl Harbor, Art the Kennedy assassination. Mike McGann remembered the storm.

It came early in February, a frigid Monday. Schools let out early, and to a boy like Mike — big for twelve, strong and tireless — the frigid air smelled of money. He imagined the sky bursting open like a piñata, a shower of five-dollar bills falling from heaven.

At home he suited up in his ski jacket and trousers. He went from door to door knocking, a shovel over his shoulder, but there were no takers. The snow was falling fast, the wind howling. No one was ready to think about shoveling. The storm had just begun.

Inside he stripped off his jacket. Ma was staring at the television. 'Your sister called,' she said.

Ever loyal, Mike feigned ignorance. 'Oh, yeah? Where is she?' He knew that the high school had closed at noon, that I had gone to my boyfriend's.

'At Paul Donovan's, of course. She claims Lisbon Ave. is flooded. So she's gotten herself stranded at his house, at least until the tide goes out. I guess that's what she wanted.'

Ma was no fool.

'Holy shit,' Mike said, glancing at the television, aerial footage of a massive pileup in Canton. Two tractor-trailers had jack-knifed on the highway; traffic had backed up five miles in each direction. No one knew, yet, that it would take a full week to clear the wreckage, the thousands of abandoned cars buried in the snow.

'Watch your language,' Ma said automatically, her eyes not leaving the screen.

'Where's Dad?' Mike asked.

Ma blinked rapidly. She had already called Raytheon. Ted McGann had left for the day. On his way home, a secretary told her; but his wife knew better.

'He could be anywhere,' Ma said.

* * *

They ate a late supper, leftover stew from Sunday. Ma had planned a meat loaf, but for just the two it was hardly worth the trouble.

'I'll make your father a sandwich when he comes in,' she said.

Mike watched her lips move as she washed the dishes — counting or praying, who could tell? Finally she called his uncle Leo, trying to sound casual. *Have you seen your brother, then?*

Leo had not.

'I don't know what to do,' she told Mike, her voice barely a whisper. 'I suppose I could call Arthur.'

'*Art?*' He looked at her as though she'd lost her mind. Art tucked away in his rectory in cozy West Roxbury, the other side of the universe; Art who'd be useless even if he were here. 'For God's sake, Ma. What's Art going to do about it?'

He put on his jacket and went out to the porch. The sky was dark and moonless. He walked down Teare Street into a wall of wind. His footsteps were silent, muffled by the snow. The sidewalk had disappeared, though it hardly seemed to matter. There were no cars in sight.

He went back into the house. 'Power's out across the street,' he called. 'At least we still have power.'

At that moment the lights went out.

Ma found candles in the breakfront and wedged them into bottles; Mike had found a few of Ted's empties in the trash. In the kitchen they fired up the gas stove. Most of the neighbors had switched over to electric, but remodeling a kitchen was expensive. Ma was glad, now, that they'd put it off a year.

As she refilled the kettle, they heard a knock at the front door. Dick Brady, the town cop, had arrived by snowmobile. He came in stamping the snow from his feet.

'For Christ's sake, Mary. What are you still doing here?' The block was being evacuated, he told her. A shelter had opened at Grantham High.

'Ted hasn't come home,' Ma said.

'Yeah, well, there's plenty are stranded. Did you see that mess in Canton?'

'He left work early,' said Ma. 'I called and checked.'

'Oh, Jesus.' Dick Brady took off his hat and

ran a hand over his crew cut. 'How long has he been out?'

'I called at two. He'd already left, they said.'

Dick Brady looked at his watch. Mike could see him calculating. How much could a man drink in four, six, eight hours? If the man were Ted McGann, the answer was ominous.

'Everything's closed on Lisbon Ave. Theoretically,' he said with an elaborate shrug. 'I can keep an eye out for him, but we need to get you out of here. I can take you right now on the snowmobile.'

'I can't go,' Ma said.

Dick Brady looked ready to slap her. The National Guard was posted at the town line, he said; no one was allowed in or out. Wherever Ted was, he'd have to stay there. 'You'll freeze to death waiting for him,' he said.

'We have the gas stove.'

'You're in the flood zone, woman. The surge is fifteen feet. It's coming over the wall.'

'I said no.' Ma's color was high, her voice vibrating. 'He won't know where to find us.' She didn't say — she didn't have to — that Ted would need looking after, that he'd be in no shape to take care of himself.

'My God, you're impossible. I'll come back in the morning to check on you.' He gave Mike a stern look. 'Keep an eye on her, if she'll let you. And no wandering out. There's a curfew on.'

Ma followed him to the door and closed it behind him — quickly, to keep the heat in. From the window Mike watched the lights of the

179

snowmobile disappear down the road. Then he put on his jacket.

'I'm going out,' he said.

★ ★ ★

He made his way through the dark, looking for the sidewalk, trying to keep his boots dry. Sheila was right: Lisbon Ave. was underwater. Mike stared, confused. High tide had been hours ago; why hadn't the water receded? It seemed to be coming in from both sides, the ocean and the bay meeting in the middle of the street.

He turned down a side street and walked into the wind, head down, fists clenched in his pockets. All the streetlights were out. He raised his head periodically to get his bearings. The familiar landscape had gone white and strange.

He cut down an alley and rejoined Lisbon Ave. The west end of town had power. A few lights glowed in the distance — at the Black Sheep and Fagan's, Dad's locals. Mike quickened his pace.

He went into Fagan's. Music was playing; a small crowd had assembled, but his father was not among them. The indoor heat burned his cheeks.

At the bar was a bald man Mike recognized from church. 'That's Ted McGann's kid,' he said, squinting drunkenly. 'What are you doing here?'

'Have you seen my dad?' Mike said.

'He was here this afternoon,' said the bartender. 'I cut him off hours ago.'

'He was heading home,' the bald man said.

'What time was that?'

The men exchanged glances.

'He could've gone next door,' the bald man said. 'They would have served him there.'

Mike went back out into the cold. The Sheep was three doors down, a smaller, darker bar with a green awning hanging askew, clanging in the wind like the rigging of a ship. A neon sign glowed in the small window: OPEN. But when Mike tried it, the door was locked.

The windows were crusted with ice. Mike peered inside. The room was empty, the lights on. He could make out a figure moving behind the bar.

Mike pounded the window with his fist.

The man looked up, startled. He came to the door.

'We're closed!' he shouted into the wind. 'What's the matter, kid? You stranded?'

'Have you seen Ted McGann?'

The man stepped back and waved Mike inside. The air was harsh and smoky. The Sheep smelled just like Fagan's. He wondered if all of them smelled the same, and how his father could stand it. Why he'd want to spend half his life in a place that smelled like this.

'He left a while ago. He was feeling no pain, so I took his keys.' The man ducked behind the bar and handed them over. Mike recognized Dad's key ring, the miniature Red Sox hat. 'He's probably home waiting for you.'

'Thanks,' Mike said.

He went back into the cold. Lisbon Ave. was

181

lined with strange shapes, abandoned cars that had been buried by the snowplows. Mike fingered the keys in his pocket. Any one of them might have been Dad's.

It was a ten-minute walk back to the house, twenty minutes if the wind shifted, thirty if you were slowed by drink. And Ted might have gone down a side street to avoid the flooding, or taken a wrong turn. It would have been easy to do: the streets dark and shadowy, the familiar landmarks covered in snow.

Mike himself had been drunk only once, when Tim Morrison stole a six-pack from the fridge in his dad's garage. Afterward, he'd looked at his own father differently. He had seen, plenty of times, Ted stumbling, puking, lost in his own storm. Now that he'd felt it for himself, he understood it was more pleasant from the inside.

He made his way down the flooded avenue, sticking close to the sidewalk. The water was above his ankles, deeper in the middle of the road. Home was a straight shot down Lisbon Ave. Ted, in his cups, would have taken the most direct route.

He'd walked maybe fifty yards, half a football field, when he spotted a dark figure stretched out on a snowbank. He recognized his father's green parka.

Mike knelt beside him and brushed the snow from his cheeks.

★   ★   ★

That long trek home — Dad leaning on him heavily, out of his head and barely walking — will stay with Mike forever. He speaks of it only rarely, when he himself is in his cups. They found Ma in the kitchen asleep in a chair, rosary beads in her hand. Not for the first time and not for the last, she'd sat up waiting for an errant husband, certain that this one, too, had disappeared for good.

The next morning the front door wouldn't open. Outside was a solid wall of snow. Mike went upstairs and opened his bedroom window; he dropped easily to the porch roof and rolled onto a snowbank. The sky was vivid blue, the sun blinding. He walked down Teare Street toward the beachfront. The seawall had broken into pieces like the wreckage of an earthquake. He heard, but couldn't see, helicopters flying overhead.

The beach was littered with frozen lobsters. He grabbed one in each hand and headed for home.

In the kitchen the radio was playing: the power had come back on. A man with a deep voice was reading the weather. *Mostly sunny this afternoon, with a high near ninety. Humidity is at 90 percent.*

'What's he fucken saying?' Mike gasped, out of breath.

For once Ma didn't tell him to watch his language, a shift they both noticed. He had located our drunk father passed out in a snowbank and saved him from freezing to death. It was a kind of adulthood.

183

'They're reading the forecast from last summer,' Ma said. 'To take our minds off it, I guess.'

After thirty-three hours, the snow stopped. As Ted McGann lay upstairs sleeping, Ma boiled lobsters and melted butter. She and Mike sat in the kitchen cracking tails and claws, remembering the dog days of August, the ninety-degree heat.

When our father was first diagnosed, the neurologist gave us a fact sheet. Certain behaviors were to be expected: Meager content in conversation. Lack of insight about his condition. Confabulation. A short attention span. Reading it, Mike and I exchanged crooked smiles. It wasn't necessary, it wasn't constructive or kind, to point out that this had described our father for years. He had always been forgetful, scornful of introspection, a teller of tales. Now he lied to fill in the gaps, the hours or days he had forgotten. It is — well, sobering — to wonder how much of Ted McGann's famous personality was simply end-stage alcoholism: tiny holes in the hippocampus, slowly growing; the bleak signs of neuronal loss.

It is an enduring shock to all who know him that my father is now sober. For twenty years Ma begged for this, prayed for it; she made his drinking the central drama of her life, and his. Each day after Mass she lit a candle for his recovery. Over the years she said countless novenas and rosaries, her Hail Marys flooding the heavens like so much junk mail. She saved her sweet talk for the Virgin. With Dad she swapped insults and epithets. There were marital dust-ups that attracted the police, ultimatums that led to AA meetings and, in the early 1980s, the Pioneer Pledge. There may have been more than four DUI arrests, two cars totaled, three bouts of alcohol poisoning; those are merely the official totals, the ones to which Ma will admit. Other incidents defy categorization. I am thinking of the old Chevy that Dad abandoned one night on a street in Hyde Park, in the direct path of the commuter rail. An alert conductor spotted it just in time; my father, passed out cold on the sidewalk, woke to squealing brakes. Less dramatic were the everyday mishaps, the falls and blackouts and finally, hospitalizations: for seizures, hepatitis, pneumonia, a bleeding ulcer, several concussions, a broken collarbone.

It is a litany of ruin.

The fortunate among you will find this implausible. How could one human being survive so many calamities? A man less hardy or bullheaded, or simply less addicted, might have taken any one of them as a sign.

But what all these miseries could not effect, simple atrophy in the end accomplished. Ted McGann forgot. After his last hospitalization, for a bout of acute encephalitis, my father was docile as a child. I can't explain how it happened, only how it appeared: that after years of thinking of little else, the man simply forgot to drink.

He spent two weeks in South Shore Hospital in a state of near oblivion; and when he woke, it was as though he'd taken a trip around the world and lost most of his luggage along the way. Heavy bags they were, packed with thirty years of indignities, rages, brawls and indiscretions. The injustice of it is hard to fathom: the shameful scenes we will never forget, he is spared the pain of remembering. It is perhaps the final irony of a life filled with them: everyone on Teare Street can tell a Ted McGann story, except Ted McGann.

My father who roared like a lion is now silenced, diminished. After years of resenting him, Ma became his caretaker. She lost the man she married, the best and the worst of him. And yet for her there is relief in it. She'll never admit it, but I know this is so.

Sobriety came too late to save him, though for a time his doctors held out hope. Twice a month Ma took him for injections, intramuscular thiamine; but after a year it was clear that there was no point. His memory hadn't improved at all (though, as the doctors pointed out, it hadn't worsened). The patient's oldest memories were intact; he simply couldn't make new ones. He remembered his boyhood, his dead parents, his years in the Navy. He recognized his wife and children, but not his daughter-in-law or grand-kids. By the time Abby joined the family, my father's memory was like a doctor refusing new patients. The rolls, it seemed, were already filled.

In Mike's neighborhood nobody parks on the street. It is the oldest section of a very old town whose proportions predate the automobile. Each large house has a tiny garage behind it, built more or less as an afterthought, a tight fit for the hulking vehicles modern suburbanites drive. When I arrived I noticed Abby's Explorer parked in the back alley, as wide as the garage and nearly as long.

She answered my knock with twinkling eyes, a smile in her voice. I could hear it through the closed door: *Ryan, you're being silly!* Her smile died when she saw my face through the screen.

'Oh. Sheila. Hiy.'

She hesitated a moment before manners kicked in. I could see her calculating: however objectionable, I was her husband's sister, and she hadn't seen me in four years. She was thus obliged to invite me in.

'Mike's not home yet. He's out showing a house.'

'I called his office. They said he was on his way home.'

'Oh. Okay. Well, you're welcome to wait,' she said, in a tone that meant I was anything but.

'Where are the boys?' I said, making an effort. 'I'd love to see them.'

'I'd rather not disturb them. They're doing homework.'

It was a Saturday night. Ryan was in second grade, the twins in kindergarten.

In the kitchen we drank iced tea, unsweetened. The minutes ticked by. 'Your parents must be glad to see you,' Abby said.

'I haven't seen much of them, actually. I'm staying at Art's apartment.'

The mask fell. 'He has an apartment?'

'Temporarily. Until this mess gets straightened out.'

A screen door slammed at the rear of the house.

'That's Mike,' said Abby, with audible relief. She slipped out from behind the table. 'Excuse me, Sheila. I need to go check on the boys.'

★ ★ ★

Before the wedding I'd met Abby just once, a brief hello at a crowded family gathering. From the first they seemed mismatched, but that may have been my own bias. I had loved Lisa Morrison like a devilish little sister; I'd never imagined Mike marrying anyone else. Abigail Nelson: it was a name to which I could attach nothing, no private jokes or shared laughter, no memory of hijinks. If Mike had married Lisa, there would have been no pricy flight to Chicago, no rental car I couldn't afford. The wedding Mass would have been held at St. Dymphna's in Grantham, the church crowded with friends.

What did my brother see in Abby? It's a question I still can't answer. Equally mysterious:

what did she see in him?

They married in June, a summer weekend packed with festivities. The event unfolded according to its own daft logic, inexorably, like a madwoman's dream. By someone's insistence — Mike's, I guess, though it's hard to imagine him caring — I was included in the wedding party, along with five of Abby's sorority sisters from Northwestern, slender, lovely girls who seemed comfortable in the strapless gowns she'd chosen, all rustling silk and glossy hair and velvet skin. Each came packaged with a boyfriend or husband, and these men filled out the wedding party. Mike's cop buddies, one by one, had sent their regrets, and so a best man was assigned to him: Abby's younger brother, Robert Jr.

We were seated together at the interminable rehearsal dinner — at the far end of a long table, the two forgotten siblings. Abby, I assume, placed us there; she'd planned the weekend like an invading general, and such a detail couldn't have escaped her notice. More than once I have pondered this fact, though I know it's a weak defense for what happened next.

Robby and I drank a great deal at dinner, a fact that went unnoticed; we were seated so far down the noisy table that we could have been plotting to bomb the Sears Tower for all anyone knew. We continued later at the hotel bar. I blushed when the bartender asked to see his license. Robby was old enough to drink legally, but just barely. He'd flunked out of Lake Forest and now caddied at his parents' golf course. I had known a few Robbies at Villanova: sweet,

190

cherished boys unfazed by failure; blessedly blind to their own inadequacies, having been their whole lives guided, flattered and loved.

He was handsome, I remember, tall and dark-haired, with absurdly long eyelashes. In my drunken state he reminded me of someone, though to save my life I couldn't say whom. I was newly divorced, and wore the scars like jewelry. In bed he was curiously passive, less experienced, perhaps, than I'd imagined. Then again, I was nine years older. Nine years of boyfriends and love affairs and a failed marriage will teach you a few tricks.

We spent several hours in Robby's room — noisily, I was later told; for a posh hotel its walls were surprisingly thin. Somewhere in the course of our couplings, it came to me in a flash. Robby resembled no man I'd ever known. In the dim light he looked strikingly like his sister.

Suddenly everything seemed distorted, reversed as in a mirror, the world flipped around backward. We finished; I dressed quickly.

'Robby,' I whispered. 'I have to go.'

I crept out quietly, shoes in my hand. Who saw me leave his room? What sort of person would feel it necessary to mention such a thing to Abby? I never found out, and after that weekend I never saw Robby again. I've wondered, often, what became of him. Did he ever finish college? Does he still live and golf in Naperville, with someone else's flunky son to carry his clubs? I wonder, too, what became of me. Am I still that wounded and vindictive girl who wanted to put things even? To make myself known to this

Abigail Nelson, who had taken my brother. To show her just how easily I could take hers.

★ ★ ★

Mike came into the kitchen whistling, his tie loose. When he saw me he looked stricken, as if caught in some misdeed. 'What are you doing here?'

'I came to say goodbye. I'm heading back tomorrow. I need to get back to school.'

Mike nodded.

'There's nothing more I can do here,' I said, as though I had done anything at all. 'Art can take me to the airport. He's got nothing else to do.'

'All right, then.'

We stared at each other a long moment.

'I have to know,' Mike said slowly, 'whether or not he did it.'

'Well, he didn't. Now you know.'

'Not good enough. I need proof.'

'Good luck with that. What are you going to do, dust the kid for fingerprints?' I felt my pulse quicken. 'Sorry, Mike, but sooner or later you have to decide what you believe.' It was a thing I'd always known but until recently had forgotten: that faith is a decision. In its most basic form, it is a choice.

'You're worse than Ma,' Mike said. 'She'd never believe he was guilty. Not if he knelt and confessed at her feet. But you — ' He glared at me. 'If he did it, you'd forgive him.'

I could not deny this.

'You're not my only brother,' I said.

* * *

I have gone over this conversation many times in my head, my recollection colored, no doubt, by what I later discovered. When I replay it now, I see something in Mike's face, furtive and oblique, stubborn as a closed fist.

This isn't just hindsight. As I drove away from his house that day, I remember thinking that my brother had a secret.

On Sunday morning Mike and Abby took the boys to Mass, followed by Bickford's pancakes, a rare treat. 'They'll be sugared up for hours,' Abby protested, but Mike secretly loved Bickford's and joined in their wheedling.

'I'll take them to the slides after,' he said. 'I'll wear them out, I promise.'

It was that rare thing in New England, a balmy afternoon in springtime. At Abby's insistence he coated the boys in sunscreen, but forgot to cover himself. Driving back to the house he caught a glimpse of himself in the rearview mirror, his nose and cheeks red, even the part in his hair.

'Sunburns give you cancer,' Jamie told him as they crossed the lawn. 'Mom said so.'

Cancer, Mike thought. *Jesus, Abby. He's five.*

They found Abby sitting at the kitchen table reading the paper.

'It's never going to end,' she said through her teeth.

Mike felt a flash of panic. 'Another one?'

Jamie glanced from his mother to his father.

'Don't worry, buddy.' Mike gave his shoulder a squeeze. 'Mom's mad at the president.'

It was parental shorthand, code for any adult ranting about the state of the world, any argument too abstract for a child to comprehend. Until recently it had been roughly accurate, but now Abby liked the president a lot

194

more than she used to, and liked Mike's relatives a lot less.

'Go play in your room,' Mike said.

He read over Abby's shoulder, the front page of the Local section. He was careful not to touch her. Outrage rose from her like fumes.

A PARISH DIVIDED

Beneath the headline were two photographs. The first showed Art with the parish council. The second was a familiar portrait, identical to the framed one that hung on Ma's Altar: young Father Breen in his Roman collar, at his seminary graduation, half a lifetime ago.

The reporter had done her homework. Nearly a dozen parishioners were quoted. Some were angry, some defensive, some merely confused.

They're making an example of him, said Donald Burke, a local attorney and father of two. They've been covering up these crimes for years. Now they're using Father Art to send a message, that they're not letting this happen anymore.

'Jesus,' Mike said finally. 'Poor Ma.'

Abby looked at him as though he'd belched or farted. 'That's all you have to say?'

'What else do you want?'

'It's all about the *parish*,' she said, exasperated. 'Losing their priest at Easter, and so on. As if you'd want a pedophile on the altar at Easter! Honestly, what's the matter with people?'

Mike looked again at the paper. 'Well, some of

195

them don't believe it,' he pointed out — reasonably, he thought. 'Some of them think he's innocent.'

'Some people don't *think* at all.'

Stupid brainwashed Catholics, he could hear her thinking. She didn't say it — not this time — but Mike heard it all the same.

'Did you notice that they barely mention the child who was molested?'

'They can't mention him,' Mike said. He read: ' — *whose name is being withheld to protect the privacy of the family.*'

'Well, of course! If it were Ryan who'd been abused, would you want his name in the papers?'

'Of course not. My point is — ' He stopped. There was no hope of reasoning with her when she was like this, no fucking hope.

'Honey, stop. You're just winding yourself up.' He took away the paper, folded it closed. 'I know you're upset. But this has nothing to do with us.'

Something in her face changed. 'Oh, really? We have three children, last time I checked. Three *boys*, Mike. Do you really want to raise them in this kind of church?'

'Don't start,' Mike said. 'We already decided that, remember? When we had them baptized.'

'I gave in,' she said. 'I shouldn't have. That was my mistake. I'm serious,' she added, somewhat unnecessarily. Abby was always serious.

He inhaled deeply, staying cool. 'Maybe so, but what's done is done. They're baptized. End of story.'

Abby closed one eye.

'Wait a minute. We have *options* here. Just

196

because we made one bad decision — ' She broke off. 'What I'm saying is, let's not go any further down that road than we already have.'

It took him a moment to grasp her meaning.

'Oh, not *that*.' He felt his pulse. 'Jesus, Ab, it's next month. He's been preparing since September. It's a big deal for a kid.' (Was it really? He didn't know, could scarcely remember his own First Communion. But they had *agreed*.)

'Please. He doesn't even understand it.'

'Sure he does,' said Mike.

'In Communion we consume the Body and Blood of Christ,' she recited. 'I know: I've been quizzing him for weeks. He can regurgitate what *Sister* says' — she spat the word angrily — 'but he has no clue what it means.'

Nobody does, Mike could have said, but it wouldn't have helped his case. He'd been taught in childhood that transubstantiation was a mystery he would never understand and shouldn't expect to, an article of faith. Mike accepted this explanation. He still received Communion every Sunday, usually — he had to admit — giving it little thought.

'You knew the deal when we got married,' he said, keeping his voice calm. 'The kids are Catholic. When they grow up, if they want to, they can choose something else. Abby, look at me.' He waited until she did. 'We agreed on this.'

'*We didn't know then*.' She stood, her eyes flashing. 'If I'd had any idea that this was happening — priests molesting kids! And Mike, they all knew about it. The Cardinal, all of them. Your *Church*.' The words seem to be choking

197

her. 'If I had any idea it was so corrupt, so *morally bankrupt* — no way would I have agreed to raise my kids Catholic. No way in hell.'

Mike took his keys from the table. 'Ryan is making his First Communion,' he said. 'You can be there or not. That's up to you.'

That Sunday evening, after dropping me at the airport, Art went on a mysterious errand. Months later I would learn that, in clear violation of Bishop Gilman's orders, he stopped at Fran Conlon's duplex.

She looked stricken when she answered the door.

'Father, what are you doing here?' Her voice a whisper. She looked over his shoulder, up and down the street, as though afraid of being seen.

'I had to come.' His eyes scanned her face, half afraid of what they'd find there. Fran's broad, open face, her blue eyes that hid nothing. Why wouldn't she look at him? Did she believe what they'd said?

'Can I come in?'

'That isn't a good idea. Aidan's here,' she lied.

(*I confessed it the very next day*, she told me later. *Can you imagine? Lying to a priest.*)

At the name Art's pulse quickened. 'Aidan? Where? Inside?'

'He's playing in the backyard. He spent the night.'

'Can I see him? Forget I said that,' he said, seeing her expression. 'I just want to know — is he all right? Does he understand any of this?'

'I don't know what he understands.'

An awkward silence. Down the street a screen

199

door opened, a dog barked. Again Fran glanced over his shoulder.

'This is a terrible idea, Father. You shouldn't have come here. If anybody found out — ' She paused. 'I'm not to have any contact with you.'

'Who says so?'

'Kathleen's lawyer.'

He took a moment to digest this.

'You look awful, Father.' She eyed him anxiously. 'You've lost weight. I hate to think what you're eating.'

'Not much.'

She smiled then, the Fran smile. They stared at each other a long moment.

'For Pete's sake,' she said.

He nodded in agreement. That about covers it, he thought.

'I'll go,' he said quietly. 'But first I want to tell you myself. I want you to hear it from me. I never laid a hand on Aidan. Not in a million years would I hurt that child.'

★ ★ ★

It was nearly dark when Art returned to Divorce Court. The parking lot was dead at that hour. He approached the empty playground. The slide and climbing bars cast odd shadows in the floodlights; the swings blew, creaking, in the wind. At the foot of the slide lay a child-size Red Sox cap, like the one Aidan wore. Art picked it up and tucked it into his pocket.

Furtively he crossed the parking lot. He had never stolen anything in his life. At the front door he stopped short.

A handbill had been taped to the front door.

The flyer was laser-printed, lettered in bold capitals:

HAVE YOU SEEN THIS MAN?

The photo had been cribbed from the newspaper, Art with the parish council, his face circled in fat black marker.

This ACCUSED SEX OFFENDER is living at Dover Court!!!

Father Arthur Breen, a priest at Sacred Heart Church, has been accused of molesting an 8-year-old boy.

DO YOU HAVE KIDS?

DO YOU WANT THEM HAVING CONTACT WITH A SUSPECTED PEDOPHILE?

Keep them away from THIS MAN.

The sun was setting as Mike ambled across Dot Ave. For the first time in years he'd spent an entire Sunday afternoon at the Banshee, bullshitting with the bartender and watching the Sox beat the Orioles, feeling that particular guilt that comes from spending a sunny afternoon in a gloomy bar. Even more than the drink, baseball had the power to soothe him. It was only at the commercial breaks that he remembered his degenerate brother, his angry wife. When the game ended he paid the bartender, his steepest tab in years. Then he drove across town to Dunster, where he had a house to show.

He drove with the windows open, enjoying the asphalt breeze. The day had finished hot and muggy. It happened a few times each spring: summer making a surprise appearance, like an actor who'd rushed his entrance. Mike didn't mind the heat. It felt good to sweat, and yet, as he parked at the curb, he felt suddenly gamy. He hadn't showered after the playground, hadn't even changed his shirt.

He parked on Fenno Street and got out of the truck, feeling the alcohol. He hadn't driven drunk in years. *Stupid*, he thought, but the thought was fleeting. He climbed the steps to Kath Conlon's porch. The two plastic chairs sat facing each other, as though someone had stretched out there. Beside them, on a table, was a bottle of nail polish. A cigarette burned in an ashtray like the climax of a magic trick, the pretty assistant vanished in a puff of smoke.

The front door was open. Mike tapped at the screen door and peered inside. The apartment was nearly dark. An electric fan hummed in one window. 'Anybody home?' he called.

Kath came to the door in a tank top and denim cutoffs, a bottle of beer in her hand. She looked stunned to see him. 'Jesus, you scared me.' The purple bra again, a strap wandering over her bare shoulder. Absently she tucked it back into place.

'Sorry,' Mike said.

'Open this, will you?' She pushed open the screen door and handed him the bottle, as though she'd been expecting him. As though they had known each other for years.

He took the bottle and gave it a twist.

'That one's yours,' she said, blowing on her nails. 'Have a seat, okay? I'll be right back.'

Mike sat on one of the plastic chairs and waited. He took a long cold slug of beer and thought, *This is exactly what I need.*

'Jesus, it's hot.' Kath stepped onto the porch, a beer bottle pressed to her forehead. Her feet were bare and suntanned. She sat and blew on her nails.

Mike watched her, amused. His wife never wore nail polish. *It looks cheap,* she said, and Mike had to agree. When he saw a woman with long red nails, he instantly imagined her hand on his dick.

'You shouldn't leave that burning,' he said as

Kath dragged on her cigarette.

'Oh no?'

Mike reached for the nail polish. 'This stuff is wicked flammable. It says so on the bottle, in tiny fucken print.' He felt warm and loose. The expletive rolled pleasingly off his tongue. DO NOT USE NEAR OPEN FLAME.

'That's what you do when you're not selling houses? Read the tiny fucken print on nail polish?'

Mike grinned. He'd forgotten the pleasure of being teased by a girl, a flush from deep inside.

'You got sun,' Kath said.

'I took my kids to the playground.'

'Twins, right?'

'Plus one. Michael and Jamie are five. Ryan is seven.' Mike took a long pull on his beer. 'How old is yours?' he asked casually.

'Nine in August. He's already planning his birthday. He wants to go to Six Flags. It's all I hear about.'

Mike groaned. 'Jesus, I hate that place.'

'You hate it now. But when you were nine? It was awesome.'

'It was Riverside then. But I never went. My folks took us to Paragon.' Mike grinned. 'You're too young to remember that. I'm an old man, you know. Pushing forty.'

'No way.' She looked genuinely surprised, and for some reason this pleased him immensely. He could remember feeling, not long ago, as she did: that forty was a foreign country, one he had no desire to visit.

'Okay, thirty-six. Class of eighty-five,' he said.

204

'How about you? You went to Dunster?'

'Dot High.' She took a drag on her cigarette. 'You?'

'BC High,' he said automatically — the answer he gave to colleagues, to clients. He saw that she was not impressed.

'Actually, they kicked me out,' he admitted. 'I graduated from Grantham.'

Something in her face changed. 'I know a guy from Grantham. He's older, though.'

'Try me,' he said. 'I was a cop there. I knew the whole fucken town.'

'I knew it! You look like a cop. Anyway, he didn't go to school there. He's a priest.'

Mike felt a sudden jolt. *Don't blow it*, he told himself, watching her closely. 'You hang out with priests, do you?'

'My mother does. She works at Sacred Heart. Practically lives there. She lives for that shit.'

'Mine, too. Hey, whatever gets them through the day, you know?' Mike reached for the medal at his neck, a nervous habit. His own tell, probably, the antsy way he raced St. Christopher back and forth on his chain. 'So who's this priest?'

'Nobody,' she said abruptly. 'I bet you go to church. I can just tell.'

Mike shrugged. 'I got kids, you know? We do it for them.' As he said it he realized his mistake. He had lapsed into the marital *we*.

There was a long silence. Mike could sense the moment fading. In a second his chance would be lost.

'Come on. Let me show you the house.' He

patted his pocket. 'I got the keys right here.'

'You always show houses loaded?'

I'm not loaded, he started to say, but stopped himself. There was no reason to deny it. This girl wasn't Abby. Not even close.

'Whenever possible,' he said.

She laughed then, filling him with relief and something else, a strange ache. It was Lisa Morrison's laugh, smoky and sweet. 'Yeah, well, you're wasting your time with me. Like I said, I don't have the money yet.'

'*Yet?* What are you going to do, knock over a liquor store?'

'Human trafficking,' she said, rising. 'You want another one?'

Mike held up his empty bottle and followed her inside. The apartment was dark and stifling, loud with fans. He stumbled briefly over a wheeled something, a child's toy.

'Turn on a light, will you? I can't see a thing.'

'It's cooler this way.'

She led him by the hand.

★ ★ ★

It was hard to say, in retrospect, when Kath Conlon slipped out of focus. In the glare of the porch light he saw her clearly, but in the dark apartment things became confused. For the first moments he was conscious of pretending; later it truly was Lisa Morrison he followed into the dim kitchen, her small hand in his. He felt boozy and heated, drifting out of time.

In the kitchen he held her shoulders. A single

206

bulb burned over the sink. The refrigerator was decorated with childish drawings, alphabet magnets. In one corner was a Halloween photo, the kid in his Batman costume, held up by the letter *A*.

'Where's your boy tonight?' Mike asked, suddenly remembering.

'Asleep,' she said. 'He's sick. I gave him Benadryl.'

They stood a long moment staring at each other. A lick of sweat ran down his back.

'Hot as fuck in here,' he said. 'You need an air conditioner.'

Kath opened the refrigerator, took out two more beers. 'There's one in the basement.'

'What's it doing in the basement? I'm sweating my nuts off.'

That laugh again. 'I can't get it up the stairs, idiot. It's fucken huge.'

'How heavy can it be?'

Again she took his hand, led him down a rickety staircase. The basement was unfinished, a cellar really, smelling of damp.

'There,' she said, pointing.

'That? It's not so big. Not for a strapping lass like yourself.' He grasped her arm then, the small, hard biceps fitting easily in his hand. She looked up at him, laughing, laughing. Her eyes — hers or Lisa's, what did it matter? — were level with his throat.

'Okay. Here goes.' He bent and grasped the thing, lifting with his legs.

'Careful,' she said.

'Nothing to it,' he said easily, though it was

heavier than he'd expected. 'Lead the way.'

He staggered upstairs and through the kitchen, down a dark hallway. The bedroom was shadowy. He spotted a window and propped the thing on the sill.

'Not there,' she said. 'I don't want it blowing in my face all night. Here.' She bent to unplug one of the fans, the denim shorts climbing her thighs.

'Hurry up, will you? This fucker is heavy.'

She struggled a moment with the screen. Finally Mike bent and set the thing in the window.

'It's not going to fall out and crush my car?'

Mike glanced out the window, at the lime-green Buick parked at the curb. 'If you're lucky.'

'Fuck you,' she said.

'Okay. The moment of truth.' He wiped his hands on his pants and looked for an outlet. They waited, a shared breath.

Nothing happened.

'Wait.' Mike fumbled briefly with the controls, and a moment later the thing rumbled to life. Kath squealed, gripped his arm. Her nails were red against his skin.

'Hallelujah,' she breathed, and it was a kind of celebration that brought their bodies together. A high-five, a loose embrace. She fell against him laughing. He lifted her — after the air conditioner, light as a child — into his arms.

Their mouths had barely touched when he heard a small voice behind him.

'What happened?'

He set her down. Aidan was standing in the doorway in short pajamas, squinting in the half light.

'It's okay, sweetie.' Kath went to him, ran a hand through his shaggy hair. 'We were putting in the air conditioner. We made too much noise.'

'It's hot,' the boy wailed.

'I know, baby. But come and feel.' She walked him to the window and held out his hand. 'See? It's cooling off now. You can sleep in here with me.' She turned to pull back the quilt from the bed.

'I need to put him down,' she murmured. She glanced quickly at Mike, but did not meet his eyes.

'Sure. I should be going, anyway,' he mumbled, heading for the door.

'Thanks for bringing that thing upstairs,' she said. 'You saved us.'

'No problem,' Mike said.

Donald Burke ran his law practice downtown, from a fine old house in the center of Quincy. A receptionist showed Art into the inner office. Attorney Burke sat behind a cluttered desk, a portly man with a leonine head.

'Thanks for seeing me,' Art said briskly.

'I'm glad you called,' said Burke. 'Marilyn has been concerned. The parish council called an emergency meeting. The discussion was quite heated, from what I understand.'

'Thanks for what you said to the newspaper. Excuse me,' Art said, and coughed deeply.

Burke drew back, startled. Art felt contaminated and contagious, the carrier of some dreaded disease.

'Your support means a lot,' he said, recovering. 'Frankly, it's why I came.'

As he told the story, Burke listened without comment. He made a few notes on a yellow pad.

'Where are you living now, Father?'

'They put me in an apartment complex in Braintree. Actually, that's partly why I'm here.' He took the folded flyer from his pocket and slid it across the desk. 'Somebody posted this yesterday. Apparently they saw the article in the paper.'

'Apparently,' Burke said dryly.

'Can they do that?' Art demanded. 'Isn't it . . . slander or something?'

'This is written communication, so technically it's libel. But only if it isn't true.' He took

210

reading glasses from his pocket. 'This is worded very carefully. Notice how they don't come out and say you actually *did* anything. Just that you've been accused.'

Art leaned forward in his chair. 'My question, I guess, is this. If you were me — if you were accused of something like this — what would you do?'

Did he imagine it, or did Donald Burke flinch for an instant, a shudder of revulsion? *I'm not you,* Art imagined him thinking. *I would never be you.*

But when he spoke his tone was neutral. 'Let me contact the Archdiocese on your behalf. Inquire about the state of their investigation. It won't change anything in the short term, but at least they'll know you have counsel.'

'So you'll represent me?' Art smiled grimly. 'A lot of people aren't going to like it. Marilyn's going to be very unpopular with the council.'

Burke chuckled. 'From what I understand, that's hardly a new situation.'

'I have some savings,' Art said. 'I can't pay you much, though.'

'You can pay me ten dollars. I'd happily do it for nothing, but some nominal sum has to change hands.' Burke rose. 'We'll never forget what you did for Caitlin. You're a good priest, and there aren't many left.' He offered his hand. 'Take care of that cough, Father. Let me get on the phone to Lake Street. I'll be in touch.'

'What about the posters?' Art demanded.

'If I were you,' said Burke, 'I would take them down.'

211

At some point temporary becomes forever. There was a moment thirty years ago when Ma bought her first tube of Chinese Red, a day during the Nixon presidency when she covered the new sofa in vinyl, telling herself *Just for now*.

By my last count, forty-eight priests have been expunged from the clergy directory of the Boston Archdiocese. The most egregious offenders, like the Street Priest, have been defrocked and brought to trial; but most were simply taken out of service. In another era they would have been quietly reassigned to unsuspecting new parishes, shuffled like jokers in a deck. Now public pressure has put that game to an end, and the accused are barred immediately from their rectories. Their official status is *Suspended*, and the term seems apt: left to swing over a precipice, dangled by an invisible hand.

How long would my brother be left hanging? Limbo, don't forget, is a Catholic invention. It's a shocking bit of doctrine, cruel and whimsical even by Church standards. I was an infant myself when the Church got rid of Limbo, and like many people I still wonder what became of all those babies, the countless infant souls consigned there over the centuries, for the unforgivable crime of dying before they could be baptized. Have their sentences been commuted?

The Church has never been quick about correcting its mistakes.

MAY

'Suffer the little ones to come to me.'

At the pulpit the priest paused for effect. He was the pastor at Mike and Abby's parish. I don't recall his name, only his voice, a lovely tenor with the barest ghost of a brogue. Our small family sat shoulder to shoulder in a single pew, Clare Boyle on the end, then Ma and me. Mike was beside me, and beyond him the twins, Michael and Jamie, their shiny blond heads like an ad for some children's shampoo. Ahead of us, in the front row, sat the First Communion class. They had entered in an orderly procession, like a miniature Moonie wedding: the boys squirming in dark suits, the girls eerily poised in their white dresses and veils.

It was a balmy morning, the second Sunday in May, sunlight streaming through the stained glass: Jesus with his lambs, his loaves and fishes, in colors bright and clear as lollipops. Like many parishes, Mike's had scheduled First Communion on Mother's Day — for me, two birds with one stone. I had driven up from Philadelphia for a long weekend — my second visit in a month, a lifetime record. I could tolerate my family in little sips, but this was a toxic — perhaps lethal — dose.

'Our Lord Jesus Christ,' the priest continued, 'had a special love for children.' Around me a sea of heads, Ma's and Clare's included, bowed slightly. They were Catholics of a certain age, taught in childhood to show reverence for the Holy Name. *Our Lord Jesus Christ.*

The priest extended his arms. His robes today were pale blue, Marian colors for May. He repeated: 'Suffer the little ones to come to me.'

I felt a sudden chill.

It was a rote sermon, delivered, with slight variations, at every First Communion Mass I'd ever attended — at my own probably, some thirty years before. And yet that spring, in the Boston Archdiocese, the words had a sinister new meaning. I looked around at the congregation mostly staring into space. Kids fidgeted. A few fathers fiddled with camcorders. Only Mike seemed troubled. I felt him stiffen next to me. Cautiously I stole a glance at his face. He gave me a warning look.

Already we'd been sitting there for nearly an hour. Ma always arrived thirty minutes early, to say a rosary and frown at the latecomers.

Some people will be late for their own funerals, she'd whispered. To which Mike responded: *Beats being early.*

'Suffer the little ones to come to me.' The first time he said it I caught my breath.

★   ★   ★

My parents' house holds ten comfortably, twenty in a pinch. For the party Ma expected twice that many. 'We'll be fine as long as the weather holds,' she said as we laid the buffet. 'Keep the little demons out of the house.' The kids

218

congregated in the backyard, Ma's brothers in the parlor around the television, where she'd pass through periodically to sweep away their empties and offer cold replacements. The basement belonged traditionally to the McGann men: Dad and Leo, Richie and Brian and Mike. In the kitchen the women would gather, chiming in occasionally when Clare Boyle paused for a breath.

The buffet was a slapdash affair: deviled eggs, a platter of cold cuts for sandwich-making, a supermarket cake with Crisco frosting, hastily decorated — *God Bless Ryan* — in sugary yellow script. There was a potato salad slick with mayonnaise, a relish tray of cut vegetables. A big basket of Clare Boyle's soda bread was the one respectable touch. I laid out paper plates and napkins and an assortment of cookies, also store-bought. 'The boy is used to better,' Ma murmured, a comment that could be taken two ways. A backhanded compliment, an appreciation of Abby's domestic skills? Or an observation, probably true, that Ryan was a spoiled brat?

Once, years ago, I visited Mike and Abby at Christmas. Usually I plan more successfully, retaining, if possible, a boyfriend through those trying weeks, a human shield for under the mistletoe. That year it was not possible, and so I found myself driving back to Massachusetts for the holiday. I can still remember the fragrant wreath on Mike's front door, the tree festooned with salt dough cookies and garlands of popcorn. I felt trapped

219

in a holiday photo spread for some glossy magazine, a showcase for Abby's domestic wizardry. Ma's First Communion buffet was pathetic by comparison, though in fairness, she'd been given short notice. Mike had called the night before with news of Abby's migraine, and Ma had done her best.

I left her to fuss with the cookies. In the kitchen Clare Boyle was stuffing celery with cream cheese. I offered her more tea from the pot.

'I've had enough of Mary's tea. You could skate across it,' Clare said, looking into her cup. 'A pity about the boy's mother. A headache, is it?'

I glanced out the window. In the backyard Mike was putting up a volleyball net, spiking, with more force than necessary, an aluminum endpost into the ground.

'A migraine,' I said.

Her eyebrows shot up. 'Interesting how you can plan them the day before.'

Clare Boyle is my godmother and Mike's, the great friend of my mother's life. As far as I can tell, she's the only friend Ma has ever kept, though they harp on each other like squabbling sisters. By all accounts they have done this since they were teenagers. I have seen pictures of Clare in those days, a doe-eyed beauty. That she never married is considered a mystery. According to Ma the boys found her too forward, a claim seconded by Henry Devine and Leo McGann, for whom, it is said, she nurses a fondness to this day. My uncles are old men now, and it is vaguely repulsive to hear them congratulate each other on their prescience, as if they'd somehow foreseen that Clare's voluptuous figure would triple in size. Clare today is a big woman, the largest I have ever seen walking — or, indeed, outside the pages of a supermarket tabloid. Her exact weight is a matter of some speculation. She hasn't seen a doctor in many years. My mother — herself no fan of doctors — calls Clare a walking time bomb; yet her health so far as been unexceptional. Until a few years ago she even managed to drive, though how she fit behind the wheel of her old Chevy is anybody's guess.

For Ma, Clare's weight is a project of sorts, filling a void in her life now that my father is officially irreparable. (Perhaps he was always so, but now that the diagnosis is definitive, she needs someone else to fix.) At the beauty parlor she tears pages from magazines: low-calorie recipes, exercises that can be done by anyone, no matter how decrepit, safely in a chair. In return Clare gives her books borrowed from the library: *The Co-Dependent Marriage*, *Adult Children of Alcoholics*. They take positive joy in each other's failures, and yet each is the other's staunchest defender. When we joke behind Ma's back, Clare will laugh wickedly; but she lets us know, sharply, when we have gone too far.

That day Clare seemed, as always, in possession of secrets. A woman who moves only when necessary, she had stationed herself at the kitchen table, an oracle to be visited.

'Sheila, don't be a ninny. Abby doesn't have a headache. She's in a snit about Arthur. She and

Michael had words.' She arranged the celery on a tray. 'I'm surprised he didn't tell you. You two were always thick as thieves.'

'We haven't talked much lately.'

Clare leaned in avidly, smelling gossip. 'Mary said you'd had a falling-out. Because of Arthur, she said.'

I wondered what else Ma had told her.

'Art's my brother, too,' I said. 'I can't turn my back on him.'

'That's true, I suppose. Still, Michael has a point. It's revolting business. These priests,' she said, disgust in her voice.

Clare is known for her disdain of the clergy, a sentiment proportionate to — and probably inflamed by — my mother's blind devotion. Yet her coolness toward Art predates the seminary. It reaches all the way back to his baptism, when Ma and Harry Breen chose a Breen cousin and his wife to be the baby's godparents. It was a slight Clare never forgot, compounded when the couple died a few months later in an auto accident, leaving Art with no godparents at all. Apparently Ma learned her lesson, because it was Clare who stood for both me and Mike. I have seen photos of each baptism. At mine she is shapely still, standing arm in arm with my godfather, Jackie Devine. Three years later, her waist considerably thicker, she stands holding the infant Mike, staring adoringly at Leo McGann.

'I'll give Arthur the benefit of the doubt,' said Clare. 'Priests used to help out with children all the time, the CYO and that. Nobody saw any harm in it.' She opened a tin of Danish butter cookies and nibbled one daintily, her favorite treat.

'Father Fergus, I remember, was a great one for children,' she continued. 'He was Mary's uncle. You won't remember him, but Arthur will.'

The doorbell rang.

'That'll be Leo and Norma. I understand they have a new Cadillac.' Clare lowered her voice. 'As if the old one had a scratch on it. Sheila, go have a look.'

I went to the window. The new Eldorado looked like all Leo's cars, more or less: the landlubber version of the *Sweet Life*, another big, shiny boat.

Clare smiled broadly so I could check her teeth for lipstick.

'All clear,' I said.

'Thank you, dear. Now go and let them in. And bring Leo back to say hello.'

I headed into the dining room, nearly colliding with Ma, who was loaded down with empty bottles. 'Leo and Norma are here,' she whispered, glancing at the sad buffet. 'I didn't think they'd come.'

Her embarrassment was palpable, and I remembered how, as a girl, I'd been forced to write thank-you notes for my aunt's ten-dollar birthday checks, even though Norma's own kids never acknowledged gifts. *Prove you're better,* Ma liked to say.

I squeezed past a cluster of Devines, my uncles in their cups and growing louder, in a cloud of cigarette smoke.

223

'My dad was in the Coast Guard during the war,' Uncle Jackie told his audience. 'He was guarding the coast all those years, and we never lost any coast.'

I opened the front door.

'Sheila! What a surprise. We were so happy to see you in church.' Norma hugged me briefly, a perfumed formality.

'Hi kid,' Leo said, kissing my cheek.

It was a version of them I had never seen, these two icons of my childhood, now in their old age. Norma was pear-shaped and improbably blond, her hairline dotted with age spots. Leo was square as a dishwasher, with a bristly white crew cut. His beefy neck strained against the collar of his shirt. I felt Ma watching me from across the room, her anxiety and mistrust. Four years ago, at Gram's funeral, Norma had been surprised to see me without my husband. By then I'd been divorced for several years, and I realized with a kind of shock that Ma had kept it secret. *We split up*, I told Norma, knowing that Ma would never forgive me for it. And, indeed, she hasn't.

'We can't stay,' said Norma. 'We want to stop and visit Mammy.' Incredibly, Norma's own mother was still living, at ninety-nine, at a nursing home in Milton.

I ushered them into the room. Trailing behind them was a lanky, curly-haired boy I recognized, or thought I did, from some past life. My heart did a little skip.

'You remember Jeffrey,' said Norma. 'Brian's oldest.'

The kid stared at the floor, a dead ringer for the boy I remembered that afternoon on the deck of the *Sweet Life*, Brian McGann in his mirrored sunglasses.

'He's a senior at BC High,' said Norma. 'He's going to be a Double Eagle like his dad.'

'Where *is* Brian?' I asked, flustered.

Norma pointed across the room, to a man I'd walked past without noticing. He was tall and red-faced, in chinos and a golf shirt. Except for a fringe of curly hair above the ears, his head was smooth as plastic.

'Oh, *Brian*,' I said, flustered. 'Hello.'

My cousin gave me a bashful wave.

* * *

Mike sat on the back porch watching the clouds move, an open beer in his hand. The sky changed fast in Grantham. As a teenager, lifeguarding on Massasoit Beach, he had learned to recognize a storm head rolling in, to clear the water of swimmers before the first thunderclap. The signs were unmistakable, if you paid attention. If you kept an eye out.

The backyard volleyball game was in full swing, dominated by the bigger kids: his cousin Brian's boys, little Julie Devine, who was no longer so little, a tall, raw-boned girl who spiked the ball with surprising force. Though two heads shorter, Ryan held his own with the older cousins. It was good for him, probably, a lesson in sportsmanship. The kid was stronger and faster than any boy his own age, used to excelling

225

at every game he played. The twins were less successful. Mike watched as little Michael took a turn serving, almost, but not quite, clearing the net. Jamie had lost interest entirely. He'd wandered off after Richie's girls, Meg and Sarah McGann.

Mike took a long pull on his beer. It was a relief, it was, to sit out here playing referee for the kids, safe from adult questions. Under different circumstances he'd be in the basement with the McGanns: Ted chuckling at Leo's stories, chiming in here and there with a memory from childhood, a scrap of the past he could actually recall. Leo's was one face he always recognized, and for long moments Ted would seem nearly intact, the person he used to be. But today Mike was avoiding the house entirely, the endless prying questions. *A migraine, is it? She must be heartbroken about missing his Communion. I hope you took lots of pictures.* In fact he'd taken no pictures at all. He wanted nothing to remind Ryan, years from now, that his mother had boycotted his First Communion, no mementos of this endless, humiliating day,

Until it happened Mike wouldn't have believed it. For all the arguing, the anger, he was certain Abby would relent in the end. But last night she'd been immovable. She would have no part of the ceremony, nor the party afterward. She would not set foot in a Catholic church again.

Tell Ryan Mommy is sick, she said. *I don't care about the others. Tell them whatever you want.*

226

She had ruined the day for him, for everyone. Mike hadn't even been watching when Ryan knelt to receive the Host. His thoughts were elsewhere — across town in Dunster, where he had left a piece of himself. While his son received the sacrament, Mike's thoughts were in Kath Conlon's bedroom.

Five weeks — he'd counted — had passed since that night. He hadn't seen her again, though for days afterward it was all he could think of: the girl in his arms, their chests pressing, for a brief moment her small, firm ass in his hands. But he hadn't gone back, not even to show Twelve Fenno, though two potential buyers had called about the house. His original plan — to question the boy, to determine Art's guilt or innocence — had not been abandoned, just deferred. The problem was Kath Conlon, his hunger to see her. He could question Aidan later, he reasoned — at some point in the future, when his hunger had abated. But more than a month had passed, and he was still starved.

'There you are.' The screen door opened and his uncle Leo appeared, with two cold bottles. 'I brought reinforcements.'

They watched as Julie Devine spiked the ball over the net, her team erupting in childish shrieks.

'Jesus,' Leo said, covering his ears. 'I should have brought the whole case.'

'Thanks.' Mike pulled up a webbed lawn chair. 'Have a seat.' Leo, he realized, was the only relative he could bear seeing, the only one who wouldn't ask questions. When it came to First Communions, or family gossip, or marital discord, Leo simply didn't give a shit.

He sat heavily in the flimsy chair. 'Thought I'd find your dad out here with you.'

'He's in the basement,' Mike said. It pained him to think of it, the old man hiding out from the crowd, his home invaded by people who'd become strangers, dozens of faces he ought to recognize but didn't. Ted was yet another victim of Abby's selfishness. Had that even crossed her mind?

'I was just down there,' said Leo. 'The game was on, but no Ted.'

'He could be upstairs, I guess. In one of the bedrooms.' Mike rose, an uneasy feeling in his stomach. 'Let's have a look.'

He led the way through the crowded kitchen, brushing off hugs and kisses and surprised greetings. ('Well, it's Michael! We've been looking all over for you.') Leo followed behind him like hired muscle. They cut through the living room, where the Devine uncles sat staring at the television ('Have a seat, Mikey! Sox are up, top of the third.'), and climbed the stairs.

Both bedrooms were empty.

'I already checked his room,' said Leo. 'Thought maybe he was taking a nap.'

Mike hurried down the stairs. He spotted Ma on her way to the kitchen. 'Have you seen Dad?' he asked in a low voice.

'He's not downstairs?'

'Nope. We checked the bedrooms. He must have wandered off.' Mike gave her shoulder a squeeze. 'I'm going to take a walk down the street.'

'I'll come with you.' Leo wheezing slightly, the emphysema he wouldn't admit to.

'Nah, you have a seat. Check the score for me.' Mike grabbed his jacket and headed out the front door, cursing Abby with every step.

★ ★ ★

As I stood blushing and stammering, making awkward small talk with Brian McGann, a second car had pulled into Teare Street and parked behind Leo's Cadillac. The driver sat a long moment before getting out of the car. He carried a bouquet of flowers, a stuffed bear for Ryan, a strawberry tart in a white bakery box. In years past he would have come empty-handed, as priests did, as though their mere presence were a gift.

Art stood a moment on the sidewalk, listening to seagulls, a siren in the distance, children's squeals from the backyard. A storm was coming, and he had no umbrella; but no matter. He would head straight for the kitchen to greet Ma, his sole reason for coming, the one person who wanted him here. He would hand over his gifts, wish her a happy Mother's Day, and be back in his car before the rain started.

A voice called to him from across the street. 'Hello, Father!'

He turned. A white-haired man waved from the Pawlowskis' front porch.

'Hi, Bern,' he called. Then he stopped a

229

moment, looked again. The man on the porch wasn't Bernie Pawlowski, but Ted McGann.

'Ted?' he called, crossing the street. 'What are you doing over there?'

'Lovely day, isn't it? I thought I'd enjoy the weather before the rain comes.' He eyed Art, his three odd packages. 'Sit with me, Father.'

'Here?' Art glanced uncomfortably at the window overlooking the porch. The Pawlowskis' van, to his relief, was gone from its carport. 'Why don't we go across the street and join the party?'

'It's a bit noisy for me,' Ted said. 'I'm not one for a crowd.'

Art sat, wondering how much of the family Ted actually recognized. Were they all strangers to him now?

Ted nodded pleasantly. 'What brings you to the neighborhood, Father?'

Art's hand went automatically to his throat. He hadn't worn his collar in weeks. Yet even without it, Ted remembered. The thought moved him nearly to tears.

'I came for the party,' Art said. 'It's Mother's Day, and the boy's First Communion.' He patted the stuffed toy. 'I brought this for him.'

Ted stared at him, frowning slightly. A flicker of something — confusion? insight? — crossed his face.

'The boy,' said Ted. 'I've been meaning to talk with you about that, Father. What you're doing with that boy — it isn't right.'

Art stared at him, dumbfounded.

'You stay away from Arthur,' said Ted. 'I mean it, Fergus. He's a good boy. It isn't right.'

230

The rain had come. I heard the first drops landing, halting, uncertain. Sitting on the vinyl-covered couch next to Dick Devine, I saw Mike come down the stairs into the living room, Leo behind him, red-faced and breathless. Mike spoke briefly to Ma, his hand on her shoulder. I felt a wash of alarm. You didn't touch Ma for no reason.

Something was very wrong.

I watched Mike leave through the front door, then waited a moment as all eyes returned to the screen. Pedro delivered a blistering pitch, to loud applause, and I slipped out through the front door.

Mike was standing on the sidewalk, hands on his hips, glaring at something across the street. Raindrops bounced off his broad shoulders: he was Superman deflecting bullets. I followed his gaze to the Pawlowskis' porch swing, where Dad was sitting. Beside him, holding a bouquet of flowers, stood our brother Art.

Mike crossed the street in a few steps, a loose athlete's jog. I ran after him.

'Mike, take it easy,' I said.

He bounded up the porch steps. 'What are you doing here?' he said through his teeth.

Art extended his hand, as though offering the flowers. 'Mike, I — '

'My kid's First Communion. What the fuck were you thinking? We've got a houseful of *kids* over there.'

'Ma asked me to come,' Art said softly. 'I was

231

just going to stay a minute. It's Mother's Day.'

Mike laid a hand on Ted's shoulder. 'You okay, Dad?'

'Fine, fine,' said Dad, his eyes darting. 'Don't blame Fergus. I've had a talk with him.'

Fergus. It was a name I hadn't heard in years. Now I'd heard it twice in one day.

'Dad, come on,' I said, taking his hand.

Mike stared evenly at Art. 'Give your flowers to Ma,' he said. 'Then get the fuck out of here.' He turned and crossed the street to his Escalade, fumbling in his pocket for his keys.

'Where are you going?' I called after him.

'I've had enough.'

'You're leaving?'

'Take the boys home, will you?' Mike called over his shoulder. 'Can you do that for me?' He got into the truck and slammed the door.

From the Pawlowskis' front yard, the Blessed Mother watched from her container, Mary on the Half Shell. Raindrops slipped down her face.

It was pouring by the time Mike arrived in Dunster. He paused at a stoplight and lowered the window. Rain hit the sidewalk, a thousand rubber bands snapping. At four in the afternoon, the sky was dark as dusk.

This is a terrible mistake, he thought. He understood it in a factual way, the way he knew baseball stats, the catechism he'd memorized. It was all just information, all equally irrelevant to him now.

He drove past houses, a gas station, a drugstore. Braking, shifting, signaling. He felt himself falling. Of course Kath Conlon might not be at home, or might have company: Mother's Day, her mom visiting. A boyfriend, even — the dirtbag in the Camaro. Aidan might have a playdate, neighborhood kids watching a video in the living room. Aidan himself might answer the door.

Perversely, these thoughts cheered him. He could still turn back. There was still hope for his marriage, his family, his future. Hope even for his soul.

Lightning, a clap of thunder. And when he turned the corner onto Fenno Street, Kath Conlon was sitting alone on her porch.

I have heard two accounts of what happened next, what was said and what transpired between my brother and Kath Conlon. Their stories are remarkably congruent, differing in one particular only: the time elapsed between the rain-loud porch and Kath's bedroom, dim at that hour, its bed unmade, its bureau laden with female clutter, their clothing scattered across the bare floor. In one version the thing happened immediately, wordlessly. Both had been waiting for this, only this. That is Mike's account, and in his eyes, I am sure, it's perfectly true.

The basic facts Kath does not dispute, but her version is informed by events in her own life, which she explained to me later.

Of these events Mike knew nothing at all.

Take, for example, the morning of their first meeting, the Friday after Easter: Kath running late, struggling to get Aidan out the door. He is a slow-moving child, indecisive and pondering: if he finishes the Cocoa Puffs today, there will be only corn flakes tomorrow, and so on. That morning Kath's hurry has a nervous edge. She has an appointment with a man named Ron Shapiro at an office in downtown Boston. She has nothing decent to wear, even if she'd gone to the laundromat. (She hadn't.) She isn't sure what the right clothes would be, only that she isn't wearing them.

'Aidan, come on already!'

And when she nudges open the front door with her hip, her hands full with the trash and recycling, a strange man is standing on the sidewalk. Out of nowhere he appears and relieves her of her burdens, deposits them effortlessly at the curb. She registers, in order, that he is large, polite and well dressed: white shirt, striped tie, nice shoes. But his hair is very short, like a cop's or a soldier's, and this is an immediate turnoff. After Jack Strecker military men do not impress her, and cops have caused her nothing but grief. So, no cops for her. No thanks.

Her life is complicated enough. At that moment, for instance, Kevin Vick lies passed out in her bed, sleeping off whatever he did before he turned up on her doorstep in the middle of the night. He is not her boyfriend; he is a complication. They sleep together as chastely as children, because Kevin isn't interested in fucking. Isn't interested in anything these days except her lawsuit, and getting high.

These things interest her, too, more than a little, more than she'd like. It's a game they play sometimes, late at night: what they will do when the money comes. 'When,' Kevin insists, 'not *if.*' He believes in the power of positive thinking, though his own life isn't much of an advertisement so far.

He has plans for Kath's money. They will buy a boat and live on it — no neighbors, no rent to pay. In winter they will pull up anchor and sail south. That Kevin has never actually piloted a boat is a point neither mentions. They don't say, either, what Kath knows for certain: that Kevin can't be trusted with a hundred bucks, never mind a hundred thousand. That when it comes to money he is a human vacuum, any spare change instantly disappearing into his veins or up his nose.

But Kath has her own plans, beginning with her boss. She will tell him to go fuck himself. Twice now, the office empty, Chris Winter has put his hands on her. 'Just playing,' he says, but Kath knows better. She's at a low point in her life, but not *that* low. She isn't about to blow some AA loser just to keep her shitty job. She will buy a little house for her and Aidan, a place from which they can't be expelled when a boyfriend is tweaking or evicted or ships out to Okinawa. She imagines a yard for Aidan to play in, her own washer and dryer. An address in Dunster, to keep Aidan in his new public school, with the teacher he likes. This is all she needs.

The little Cape across the street would satisfy her completely, and it is the yellow house she thinks of as she fingers Mike's business card: *South Shore Realty. Michael J. McGann.* She drops Aidan at school and begins the long crawl up the Expressway, chewing her cuticles, ruining her manicure, glancing periodically at the dashboard clock. Her appointment with Ron Shapiro is at nine o'clock. *Nine* A.M.? Kevin repeated when she relayed this information. *Are you crazy?* It hadn't occurred to her that she had a choice in the matter, that it was no different from scheduling a haircut: *Nine isn't good for me. How about ten?* Her last lawyer had been

236

court-appointed. Locked up with nothing else to do, she had met with him whenever he said.

She reminds herself, often, that she is no longer a criminal. Her affirmations are taped to the bathroom mirror. 'I am lovable and capable. Let go and let God.'

Let God what? says Kevin. *What the fuck does that mean?*

He laughs at them — more AA bullshit — but Kath leaves the affirmations on the mirror, just as she kept going to meetings even after deciding a few beers wouldn't hurt her. She was a tweaker, not a drunk; one had nothing to do with the other. For some people, maybe; but for her they had never been the same thing.

She is twenty minutes late for the appointment. Last time she'd managed to park on the street. This time she drives twice around the block looking for a space and empties her wallet, finally, to park in the garage.

Ron Shapiro has a new receptionist. The last one was stout and friendly. This one is Kath's age, and wears a skirt and stockings. Her nails are perfect, French tips. 'May I help you?' she asks, eyeing Kath's Skechers and tracksuit.

Kath thinks, *I am lovable and capable.*

She thinks, *Fuck you, bitch.*

After all her hurry Ron Shapiro keeps her waiting. Kath sits and flips through an old *Time* magazine. The waiting room is empty, which surprises her. Ron Shapiro moves fast, talks fast, like a very busy man. She has met him only once before, also in this office. Kevin saw his name in the newspaper when the stories started. *That,* he said, *is our guy.*

She wishes she'd brought somebody with her, but who? Kevin, Aidan? Her mother?

And strangely she finds herself thinking of the man she just met: his cop's haircut, his crisp shirt and tie. Michael J. McGann would know how to talk to a lawyer. They would get down to business after a manly handshake.

She barely remembers the drive home — high on what Ron Shapiro had said, as high as if she'd scored. He had apologized for his lateness and offered coffee, served by French Tips. *I've been in touch with the Canon lawyer. The ball is in their court now. You have an excellent case, Miss Conlon. All we have to do is wait.*

That afternoon she walks past the yellow Cape, goes around to the back door and peers through the window. She sees a cute kitchen with an island, like her mother's; a sunny window where she could grow plants, vegetables maybe: tomatoes, peppers. She hates vegetables but would eat them if she lived in this house.

So when Mike McGann returns she is ready. She has banished Kevin for the weekend. In spite of his big talk, in the business of adult life he is essentially a fuckup: Kath's age, twenty-seven, and he's never even had a bank account. Buying a house, she knows, is complicated: there are endless forms to fill, building inspections, taxes to pay. It is way beyond Kevin's capacity. Beyond hers, too, probably, but she is determined to try.

That afternoon she has a few beers to even her out, to give her courage. Aidan is sick again, a sinus infection, and the prescription is expensive. She has signed up for MassHealth but the ID cards haven't yet arrived in the mail. The Benadryl, at least, will put him to sleep. All day long he's been dancing on her nerves.

She has just gotten him down when Mike McGann knocks at her door. She is surprised, embarrassed. She didn't plan to greet him with a beer in her hand. She expected him in a shirt and tie, a suit maybe. In his grimy T-shirt he is like a big boy, the athletes she remembers from high school but was too shy, then, to talk to. But Mike McGann is easy, friendly. He talks about his kids. They sit on her porch chatting like two parents. She has been a stripper, a drug addict. Men do not speak to her this way.

She doesn't have to ask him; he *offers*. Kevin, the lazy fuck, has been promising for weeks, though he isn't much stronger than Kath, with his stringy arms, his junkie's chest. Mike McGann lifts the air conditioner as if it were a toy, and she thinks about how smoothly some people move through the world, breezing through tasks she finds so crushingly difficult, as if they were nothing at all.

Watching him, she feels a little buzzed. Drunk, even. Drunk maybe, but not wasted; and as she watches Mike McGann she thinks of her father, a strong man, dead so long now that he seldom crosses her mind. Her father has been gone fifteen years, and she hasn't known a strong man since.

Help me, she thinks, and Mike does. He lifts her into his arms.

And then it begins, the waiting. Days pass, then weeks. He doesn't come back to show her the house. He doesn't stop by, or call. From across the street the sign taunts her, South Shore Realty. Across the bottom is his name, Michael J. McGann.

She lets three days pass before calling the number. A machine answers. 'I'm interested in seeing the yellow house on Fenno Street. In Dunster,' Kath says carefully, the speech she rehearsed. She doesn't leave her name, only her number. Surely he will recognize her voice.

He doesn't call.

And so she stops, actually stops, thinking of him. Then Mother's Day comes and Aidan is at his grandmother's house, a present to one of them, Kath isn't sure which. She is sitting on the porch listening to the thunder, about to light a cigarette, when his Escalade rolls up to the curb.

* * *

I often imagine how strangers make love. It's not a hobby so much as an idle habit, nearly unconscious, a way of passing time on the train. Yet when it comes to my own family I am more reticent, so we will give Mike and Kath a few moments of privacy, and rejoin them when the deed is done.

I imagine them lying there silent, their skin cooling, rain beating out a pattern against the windowpanes. The windows open, a breeze

240

blowing the smell of wet asphalt, the white curtains dark with damp. In the gray light, her face turned slightly away, she could have been Lisa Morrison: the sharp clavicle, the curve of her hip. Familiar marks had been displaced, new ones added. Mike had found the heart, the cross, but no bird, no flower. The room was quiet but for their breathing, slowing now, as though a fever had broken.

Kath rose on one elbow and reached for her cigarettes, and Mike felt a momentary jolt. Abby had never smoked in her life. After so many years with her, only her, he'd forgotten how different women could be. He watched Kath light up, as in an old movie — what everyone used to do, he supposed, afterward.

'How long have you smoked?'

'Too long.' She inhaled deeply. 'I quit when I was pregnant. I never should have started again.'

'Why did you?'

Kath shrugged. 'Life is hard enough, you know?'

'Smoking makes it easier?'

'Quitting makes it harder.' She waved the smoke away from him. 'Sorry. Anyway, who wants to live forever? It would suck to be old.'

Mike recalled the scene on the neighbor's front porch, his father lost, confused and distraught. It seemed a long time ago.

He traced with his finger the tiny butterfly at her hip.

'You like them,' she said. 'But you don't have any.'

'I like them on girls. I knew someone,' he

241

began, then stopped. 'It was a long time ago.'

'Let me guess. She broke your heart.'

'Every goddamn day.' He took the cigarette from her hand and took a long drag. 'We grew up together. I knew her brothers.'

'She was your first?'

'The first time I got it right.' He'd forgotten this part, how sex could shake things loose, the secrets tumbling out. He and Abby had shared their secrets long ago — at least, all the ones they were going to reveal. Now there was nothing left to tell.

Kath said, 'I was twelve my first time.'

'*Twelve?*' He stared at her, aghast. He had a clear image of her at twelve, her body unpierced, unmarked. He was suddenly, powerfully grateful that he didn't have a daughter. 'Jesus. How old was the guy?'

'He was a sophomore. So fifteen, I guess.'

'Did you like it?'

'It was over fast.' She stubbed out the cigarette 'It was just — nothing, you know? I didn't see what the big deal was.'

She stretched out on her back. There was a horizontal scar low on her belly, surgically precise. Until then Mike hadn't seen it; too much down there competing for his attention. He traced it gently with his finger and felt her flinch, as though he'd touched a tender place.

'Aidan,' he said.

'I was in labor forever. They lost his heartbeat. I was by myself, and it was too late for the epidural. I was freaking out.'

Mike stroked her belly, the shining stud in her

navel. The room had darkened, dusk falling. In the dim light he could ask her anything.

'Where was his father?'

'No father. Virgin birth.' She exhaled. 'You just popped my cherry.'

'Funny girl.'

She gave him the cigarette. 'He was a sailor. When he shipped out he had no idea I was pregnant. Not that it would have mattered.'

Mike remembered a few close calls of his own, with Lisa and with others. How easily it could have happened: a kid of his gone unclaimed, out in the world alone.

'It would have mattered,' he said.

'Maybe. Who knows?' Kath shrugged. 'I made the, you know, appointment. I kept putting it off. I figured I'm never going to do this again, so I just wanted to be pregnant for a while. To see what it was like.'

'And what was it like?'

She lay a hand on her belly. 'Weird. I talked to him all day long. It sounds queer, I know, but I liked it. How I was never alone.' She grinned. 'I love that fucken kid. I quit smoking for him.'

'But you started up again.'

'The minute they cut the cord.'

And Mike thought — he couldn't help it — of his own sons' births, the nurse placing the scissor in his hand.

'You shouldn't have been alone,' he said.

Kath rolled her eyes then, the tart reply forming on lips: *Yeah, whatever.* But when he pulled her close she let him, and they were off again.

HAVE YOU SEEN THIS MAN?

I stood a moment reading over the man's shoulder. He turned to face me, a tall red-haired guy in a Boston College sweatshirt.

'What's this?' I demanded. 'This garbage you're posting.'

'You haven't heard? We've got one of these pedophile priests living in this building.'

'You don't know what you're talking about,' I said, my voice trembling. 'It's just an accusation. Nothing has been proven.'

He gave me a withering look. 'You have kids?'

I shook my head.

'Well, I do. And this piece of shit lives right across the hall from me.'

'This is slander, libel.' I knew there was a difference, but what was it exactly? 'Both, maybe. Anyway it isn't true.'

'Believe what you want.' He turned away and headed out the front door.

Believe what you want. Not long ago, my brother Mike had told me the same thing.

I waited until the front door closed behind him. Then I tore down the flyer and tossed it, crumpled, into the trash.

★　★　★

'That was a terrible mistake,' said Art.

We were sitting in his living room, which now resembled that of a poor graduate student. He'd accumulated a few possessions since my last visit. Books — church history, theology, a smattering of popular novels — sat on improvised shelves, made of bricks and boards. The room smelled of throat lozenges, Halls Mentho-Lyptus, which Art sucked constantly. I stretched out on the lumpy futon, opposite his one chair.

'Ma wanted you there,' I said.

He had stayed just a few minutes, per Mike's orders; yet his appearance had finished off the party. The aunts — Norma McGann, Patti Devine — had greeted him in hushed tones: *Hello Father*, hesitating just slightly on the second word. What to call him now that he wore no collar, just a sport shirt and pressed chinos, like an ordinary man?

The other ordinary men, McGanns and Devines alike, had avoided him entirely. My cousins Brian and Richie hustled their wives out the back door, breaking up the volleyball game as they collected the kids. *Thanks for everything*, they called over their shoulders, giving Ma a wave. I helped Clare Boyle clean up, then took my nephews home to their mother. Oddly, Abby didn't ask where Mike was. She refused the foil-wrapped cake Ma had sent. *No, thank you. I don't eat that sort of thing.*

'At least now I know for sure,' said Art. 'Mike hates me. Not that there was any doubt.'

'There's no point in talking to him now,' I

245

said. 'Seriously. I wouldn't even try, until your name is cleared.'

Something in Art's face shifted.

'I got a call from Don Burke on Friday,' he said. 'My lawyer.'

'You have a lawyer?'

Art ignored the question. 'It looks like the Archdiocese wants to settle.'

I stared at him.

'Nothing's official yet, but they asked if I'd be willing. We wouldn't have to go to court. The whole thing could be over in a matter of weeks.' Then, seeing my expression: 'This is good news, Sheila. I'm going out of my mind here. I need to go back to work.'

'You'd get your parish back?'

'Well, no. They'd reassign me to an administrative post. It's not my first choice, I'll admit,' he added hastily. 'But at this point I'll take anything. I just want this to be over.'

'An 'administrative post'?'

Art took a deep breath. 'One of the stipulations is that I couldn't have contact with children.'

'But isn't that like saying you're guilty?'

I will admit, I can be dense in these matters. There was a long pause.

'Jesus, Art! I thought you wanted to clear your name.'

'Honestly, I don't think that's possible. The Archdiocese hasn't investigated anything, and I don't think they intend to. They'd rather throw money at the problem and make it go away.'

'That doesn't bother you?'

'Of course it does. But in this case, that money could do a lot of good. That boy — ' Art stared at his hands. 'Aidan and his mother have nothing. She has no skills, no training. She can barely earn a living. This is a chance for the Church to do some real good.'

'At your expense?' I glared at him. 'A settlement isn't charity, Art. You'd be selling off your good name.'

'Which isn't worth a dime now anyway.' He reached for my hand, a gesture that surprised me. 'I'm not young, Sheila. I've had a wonderful ministry, a wonderful life. This girl has everything ahead of her. She's made some mistakes, big ones, the kind you can't undo without somebody's help.' He hesitated. 'She's a tough person. In a way she reminds me of Ma.'

At the time I found this comment mystifying. Later, meeting Kath Conlon, I would understand that she reminded Art of a different Ma, a woman I had never met: Mary Breen who'd raised him alone, in a time when this was a curiosity and a shame. I had seen her in a photograph. Her short skirt, her black hair loose; a man sitting beside her, his arm slung round her shoulders, a cigarette in his hand. Out late at the dances, she had met a fellow who amused her. He knew how to have a good time, this Ted McGann.

'I don't get it,' I said. 'Why do you care what happens to her? She ruined your reputation. Ruined your *life*.'

Art did not contradict this.

'You'd have to say you did it.' I stared at him a

long moment, my stomach churning with dread.

'Go ahead and ask,' he said, reading my face. 'You've never asked me. Go ahead and ask.'

I would not.

'I didn't,' he said. 'But trust me, plenty of priests have. The Church hasn't begun to pay the damage.'

There was something in the way he said it: *Trust me*. An agitation in his voice, his trembling hands. I guessed a moment before he told me.

Fergus was a priest, our mother's uncle. To his face she called him *Uncle Father*. Arthur had been taught to do the same.

Uncle Father was small for a man, with coppery hair and a craggy freckled face and bright green eyes that danced and twinkled and widened dramatically when he was telling a story, which he was usually doing. It was the sort of animated face found on clowns, the actors on television pretending to be Buffalo Bob or Clarabell the Clown. Adults whose sole purpose in life was the entertainment of children.

To Arthur, at eight or nine or ten, Fergus was the only adult in the world who actually seemed young. Yet years later, looking at the man's tombstone, he saw that Fergus was born in 1901. That he'd been fifty years old when Arthur was born.

Uncle Father had a car, a Ford Crestline. He came every Saturday afternoon to drive Mary and Arthur to Star Market. He walked ahead of them as they filled the carriage with heavy items, sacks of potatoes even, not to worry, because Uncle Father would drive them home and carry their bundles up the stairs.

They lived in a third-floor apartment in a loud part of Jamaica Plain. They were lucky to have the third floor, 'above the noise,' his mother said. Imagine having eight Sullivans above you, including a father and grown sons in the roofing trade, who wore heavy work boots all day and all night.

When the carriage was full Fergus would push it to the checkout and pay for everything. *Thank you, Uncle Father,* Mary would whisper. He answered, *Dear girl, don't mention it.* It was a thing adults always said, but Fergus seemed to mean it. He was flummoxed by her gratitude, blushing and stammering. Awkwardly he patted her hand.

They drove home in his magnificent car, which smelled of hair oil and chewing gum, Wrigley's Double Mint. Arthur preferred Juicy Fruit, which tasted nothing like fruit and was not even fruit-colored, but was delectably sweet for a minute or two. Occasionally Fergus would surprise him with it, an entire pack of Juicy Fruit all to himself. Arthur rode alone in the back seat, wide enough that an adult could stretch full-length across it. He knew for a fact that this was so.

At the apartment they unloaded the groceries. Arthur and his mother made a show of helping, each carrying a carton of eggs or a loaf of bread, but it was Fergus who hauled the heavy bundles up the three flights of stairs. Anyone they happened on — Mrs. McCready, one or two small Sullivans — would step aside to let them pass, looking chastened and impressed. *Good morning, Father. How are you, Father?* On any other day Mrs. McCready would ignore his mother entirely. Francis Sullivan would smack Arthur in the back of the head, but not if Uncle

Father was present. There were things even Sullivans didn't do in the presence of a priest.

Later, the groceries unloaded, his mother would start dinner. Other nights they ate soup and potatoes only, but on Saturday nights she served lamb to the priest. Uncle Father would watch her briefly, jangling his keys in his pocket.

Why don't I take the boy for a ride? he'd say, as though the thought had just occurred to him. *Give you a bit of a break.*

Oh, that would be lovely, his mother would say in the same tone, pleased and surprised, as though he hadn't made the same offer just last week.

Arthur would follow him down to the street, in plain sight of the neighbors. Imagining, always, that someone would appear and stop them, his father perhaps. *No need, Father Egan. Arthur can stay here with me.*

Of course, this never happened. His father had gone away shortly after Arthur was born. To work in Florida, his mother said. To build railroads in California. His father was a train conductor, an engineer. He had gone back to Ireland to look after his grandparents. To run a farm. To raise sheep. All these explanations, and more, had been offered to Arthur. He could choose from among them whichever he liked, like drawing a card from a deck. Was any one of them true? It didn't matter. It mattered only that Harry Breen did not return, that he never once appeared as Uncle Father led his boy down the stairs.

They would drive down South Street in Uncle

Father's car, Arthur now in the front seat, looking out over the long hood. Uncle Father would be silent, as though he'd used up all his conversation on Arthur's mother.

He would park the car at Forest Hills Cemetery, and if the weather was fine they would have a walk. Uncle Father would point out gravestones of particular importance — a bishop, a general, governors of Massachusetts — as though some dead people were more interesting than other dead people. Arthur would read each inscription; to distract himself he'd do the arithmetic: dead at age sixty, age forty, age ninety-two. One boy had died at eight, his own age. For a moment Arthur envied him, this boy who'd escaped from the world, beyond anyone's reach.

In the car the heater would be running, the rosary beads hanging from the mirror. There was a card on the dashboard that let Uncle Father park anywhere, a yellow card printed with the word CLERGY and a small black cross.

You must be tired from all the walking, he'd say. *Lie down and have a rest.*

And Arthur, following instructions, stretched out on the back seat, the black wool of Uncle Father's trousers scratchy beneath his cheek. Flutes and fiddles on the radio, a raucous *céilí*. For the rest of his life Arthur would cringe at the sound.

Afterward they would go to Brigham's. Arthur would ask for three scoops, more than he could possibly eat. There was Fudge Ripple with chocolate jimmies, a multicolored sherbet called Rainbow that was pink and blue and yellow and seemed to have three distinct exotic flavors until his mother told him it was simply vanilla with food coloring added and then it tasted all the same.

Uncle Father got a vanilla cone and drove home with one hand — jolly now, his good humor restored. *I've ruined my appetite*, he'd say, patting his belly. *Don't tell your mother. She'll have our heads.*

At home the lamb would be cooking. Arthur would smell it in the stairwell, even in the street. The waste of it shamed him. Lamb was expensive and delicious and he was not hungry, would choke it down as if it were poison, knowing he would not have lamb again until next Saturday when he would again not be hungry. He could have cried from shame.

His mother would pour two glasses of Jameson's: half a tumbler for Uncle Father, a smaller glass for herself. When her glass was nearly empty Arthur would ask to be excused. The emptier her glass, the likelier she'd say yes. In the parlor he would sink into Saturday television, a western if he was lucky. He lay on the rug on his belly, feeling perfectly invisible, below the adults' line of vision. The soft front parts of him protected and hidden, pressed safely into the floor.

Were there a dozen such Saturdays? A hundred? Fifty? Three? Truly, he had no idea. He has tried to remember a first time, a first walk in the cemetery, a first *little rest* in the backseat of the car. Did Fergus plan it beforehand, or did it happen spontaneously? How exactly does such an idea occur to a man?

He has even wondered — is it possible? — if he, a boy of seven, started it himself.

I'm tired from all the walking. I need a little rest.

He has seen the affectionate nature of children. Is it possible that he curled up next to his uncle, lay his head in the priest's lap? Though clearly it was Uncle Father's doing, the thing that happened next. Prompted, perhaps, by simple pressure, the warm weight of a child's head in his lap.

Don't tell your mother. She'll have our heads.

Of course, he had never told.

★　★　★

Saturdays and more Saturdays. It seemed that nothing could stop it. And then, miraculously, something did.

His whole life his mother had been prone to nightmares. She dreamed, always, that she was drowning. As a boy Arthur often heard her cry out in her sleep. Then he would creep out to the living room, where Mary slept on the pullout couch, and climb in beside her. *Don't worry,* is what he'd say. *It's just that dream.*

So when something woke him one night, he was not alarmed. He padded barefoot into the hallway and stopped short. The bathroom door was open, a man standing at the toilet, pissing through the opening in his boxer shorts. Arthur

254

stood staring at the arc of urine, clattering loudly into the bowl.

The man saw him then. *Jesus Christ! You scared me, kid.* He gave himself a shake. *Your mother's still asleep. Go back to bed.*

When Arthur woke the next morning, the man was in the kitchen reading the newspaper. His mother stood at the counter fixing tea and toast.

Arthur, this is Ted. She was already dressed, which surprised him. Usually she ate breakfast in her housecoat. Today her hair was combed, her mouth flushed red as it often was on a Saturday morning, when she'd been out late the night before.

Hi, kid. Have a seat. I won't bite.

After that, a change in their living arrangements. Mary took over Arthur's bedroom, and it was Arthur who slept on the pull-out couch. The bedroom door had always been propped open with a doorstop, a brick wrapped in green velvet. Now the velvet doorstop disappeared, and his mother's door was kept closed.

★   ★   ★

Ted visited on Friday nights, and sometimes Saturdays. He was always gone by morning. Sometimes Arthur woke as he was crossing the living room, shoes in his hand.

Each Friday night Arthur watched his mother dress and put on lipstick. He didn't ask where she was going, or when she would return. He'd be awakened later when she and Ted came in, on tiptoe, and disappeared into Mary's room. They were quiet, but always he heard noises. Murmurs, a stifled laugh.

Spring came, then summer. On a Saturday afternoon in July, Ted McGann appeared at the door. Arthur was lying on the parlor floor staring at the television. *Turn that thing off*, his mother called. *Ted is taking us to the beach.*

She said it shyly, her cheeks flaming. For months, since that one awkward breakfast, they had both pretended there was no Ted, no man creeping out of her bedroom at dawn, his car parked discreetly down the block to avoid alerting Mrs. Sullivan. Now Ted was here in daylight, decently dressed in Bermuda shorts and a madras shirt, for a wholesome outing in the sunshine.

Arthur had seen Ted's car from the window, in the half-light of early morning, peeling away from the curb. Now, for the first time, he climbed inside it, a gleaming white Impala with a broad backseat. Art sat close behind Ma, as if for protection. Beside him were a pile of beach towels, a Styrofoam cooler, and the picnic basket she had packed.

Ted drove fast, the windows down, the jangling piano of Jerry Lee Lewis bursting from the radio. To Arthur, who just a few moments before had lain in the dark parlor watching *Brave Stallion*, the wind and sun and loud music were strange and wonderful and nearly too much. He felt as though he'd been abducted, swept away by a stranger into a normal boy's life.

They parked among a sea of cars. *Gimme a hand, kid*, Ted said, and Arthur took one handle of the cooler. It was very heavy, but he didn't say so, having intuited, somehow, that it was important not to complain.

They made a long trek down the beach, looking for a secluded spot. Drinking was prohibited on the beach, but the town cops knew Ted and would give him a pass if he was discreet. Finally they set down the cooler and spread out the blankets. Mary stepped out of her dress. Underneath she wore a two-piece bathing suit, navy blue — not a bikini, not in those years; but brief shorts and a matching bra. Ted gave a low whistle. *That right there was worth the trip.*

He stripped off his shirt. His chest and shoulders were thick and muscled. A green tattoo covered his left biceps.

Whaddaya say, kid?

Go on, his mother said.

Arthur stared at her, astonished. His whole life she had kept him away from lakes, beaches, the town swimming pool. She herself would wade in up to her ankles, no more.

Reluctantly he followed Ted to the shoreline. Ted broke into a run, crashing into the surf. *What's the matter?* he called. *It ain't that cold.* In a single graceful motion he dove beneath the surface. Then his slick head emerged smooth as a seal's. He exhaled with a burst, a plume of seawater shooting from his mouth, and Arthur remembered him standing at the toilet, the great noisy arc of wet.

He stood at the water's edge up to his knees, watching his mother's lover shoot through the water, his muscled arms slicing like a propeller.

Ted stopped, turned, yelled something unintelligible. *What's the matter with you? Grow a set of balls, for Christ's sake.* He might have said something else entirely, but that is what Arthur heard.

He's so little, his mother said later. She and Ted sat in the kitchen, a raft of empties on the table between them. She spoke softly, but Arthur — lying in the dark parlor room, staring at the television — heard every word.

Maybe he's past the age, she said. *There was no one around to teach him. Heaven knows I couldn't.*

I've seen you at my brother's house. You won't even look at the aquarium.

It makes me nervous, she said.

Arthur listened, then, as Ma told a story he had heard many times, the story of his grandfather. This hurt him in a way that was nearly breathtaking; until then the tale had been theirs alone. His grandfather, also named Arthur, had drowned while fishing for lobster. Mary was twelve years old when he died, his boat lost in a storm. He was the third Devine to die of drowning, and finally the family had learned its lesson. *I won't go near the water,* she said. *Arthur will be just the same.*

At this Ted snorted. At Arthur's age he'd helped Leo steal their uncle's cape dory; the two boys had sailed to Plymouth and back in the leaky old tub. No radio in it, no Coast Guard to bail them out if they ran into trouble. They were boys, and figured it out for themselves.

Oh, Ted, Mary said. *He isn't like you.*

258

And Arthur, listening, knew that it was true. He was not, would never be, anything like Ted McGann. Ted unafraid, rushing into the surf with fierce pleasure. Ted, a man.

★ ★ ★

'He terrified me.' Deliberately Art lit a cigarette. It was his sixth or seventh, I had lost count. Halfway though his story he'd disappeared into the kitchen. He'd come back with an ashtray and a fresh pack of Marlboros, his secret stash.

'And yet in the end it was Ted who saved me. After they got married, Fergus stopped coming around. I always wondered if Ted said something to him. And then tonight, on the porch — ' His eyes welled. 'Ted called me Fergus. He was confused, Sheila. And he told Fergus to leave Arthur alone.'

'My dad knew?' It was the first I had spoken. My jaw ached. For twenty minutes, more, my teeth had been clenched. 'Not Ma?'

Art stared at the floor.

'She must have! I mean, wouldn't Dad have told her?'

Art closed his eyes. He looked, suddenly, exhausted. 'I doubt it. Can you imagine that conversation? Imagine Ted saying such a thing.'

'She should have known. She should have done something.'

'Sheila, it doesn't matter now. I don't even know why I'm telling you this. It was so long ago.' Art looked, suddenly, at the cigarette in his hand, as though someone else had put it there.

'I'm sorry,' he said, butting it in the ashtray. 'I know you hate these things.'

I had the urge to reach for his hand, but didn't. As I have said, we are not a demonstrative family, and even when he is your brother, there is something strange about touching a priest.

We said our goodbyes at the door. I had a long drive ahead of me. I have thought a great deal about what I might have said next. *You're my brother, Art. Whatever you did or didn't do, I will always love you.* All that I might have said and didn't.

'Thank you, Sheila,' he said. And to my astonishment he kissed my cheek.

As I left the lobby, I saw that Art's neighbor had been busy: another flyer was posted on the front door.

HAVE YOU SEEN THIS MAN?

I stood a moment, deliberating. In the end I left it there, fluttering a little in the wind.

I drove back to Philadelphia through a dense fog. The sudden rain had cooled the air and left the ground steaming. At times the road disappeared completely. Still I ignored the speed limit. I drove as if someone were chasing me.

I thought back to the story I'd coaxed out of Clare Boyle: the day Harry Breen vanished, leaving Ma and Art behind. Art's revelation had given it a whole new meaning. The story had fascinated me for all the wrong reasons. I'd been so preoccupied with the man who wasn't there — the ghostly Harry Breen — that a far more important character had escaped my notice.

Fergus was a great one for children.

When Harry didn't come home, Ma had phoned her uncle. And for years afterward — until she remarried — it was Fergus who'd looked after her and Art.

There is a vast body of scientific literature devoted to those who molest children, an entire field of psychology of which, until recently, I was completely ignorant. Yet somehow — newspapers? osmosis? — I had absorbed one fact: that victims often repeat the pattern. Molested in childhood, they grow up to do the same.

Art had been molested.

This one fact changed (didn't it?) the shape of things.

For the first time, I let myself believe it.

Suddenly it seemed not just likely, but probable, that the worst was true.

As moral beings we despise the predator; we feel compassion for the victim. Conscience and humanity demand this much. But when it comes to a man like my brother, nothing — nothing — is clear.

Art, and others like him: grown men maimed in childhood, infected by a repellent desire — and, like vampires in a horror movie, powerfully driven to infect. In a single evening Art was transformed before my eyes, not once but twice. I saw him as both predator and prey. I found myself thinking back — I couldn't help it — over his history. He'd been a youth minister at St. Rose of Lima. He had worked with altar boys.

And so by some instinct that now seems cowardly, I withdrew from him. I didn't do it consciously — at least, there is no single moment when I recall thinking, Art is a pedophile; therefore, I will have nothing to do with him. I simply returned to my life in Philadelphia with unusual gratitude: for my friends and colleagues, my familiar apartment and even my squirrelly students, in those fitful last weeks when spring is bursting forth and it seems ridiculous, utterly, to confine the young indoors. I took pleasure in my daily routines, the glorious weather. I joined a weekly game of Ultimate Frisbee. I had the diversion of Danny Yeager in my bed.

Meanwhile, back in Boston, my brothers moved inexorably along their courses, like locomotives in an algebra problem: two trains moving at different speeds, their tracks about to intersect.

Kath woke the next morning in a state of dazed wonder. It is a sensation I have experienced myself, a frank amazement when my cynicism is confounded. When, defying all precedent, the thing I most desire actually appears.

She woke before the alarm, a thing that seldom happened. After years of night work, in a temperate climate, winter mornings in Boston had seemed a bleak punishment. Father Art had told her, once, how certain monks rose in the night to pray, interrupting their sleep as a kind of penance; and Kath recalled this every single morning as she dragged herself from bed to dress in the dark in a cold apartment and drive a shitty car through bad weather to a job she despised. But now spring had arrived, and by 6 A.M. the bedroom was filled with a golden light. In the kitchen she switched on the Weather Channel and caught the tail end of the forecast: *Winds light and variable. Ceiling unlimited.*

She made a cup of tea and drank it on the porch, like a woman in a TV commercial for laxatives or antidepressants, a calm and centered adult enjoying the morning's quiet pleasures. She did not smoke a cigarette.

I am lovable and capable.

She finished her tea and took the cup inside. As if seeing it for the first time, she noticed the clutter and chaos of the apartment, the

263

overflowing ashtrays, the piles of junk mail and unpaid bills, the Batman action figures littering the floor. After work she would run the vacuum. She would buy a plant for the windowsill.

In the bedroom Kevin Vick lay tangled in the sheets. He'd let himself in with his key, crawled in beside her and passed out cold in the bed she'd shared, just hours before, with Mike McGann. In the morning light he looked ragged, blemished, his arms bruised.

'Hey,' she said. When he didn't move she gave his shoulder a shake. 'Kevin. You need to go.'

He didn't take it well. There was whining protest — *Jesus, what time is it?* Then grumbling. Then, finally, genuine anger when he realized Kath didn't mean just this morning. She meant for all time.

Luckily he was still half asleep, even more crippled by the morning than Kath usually was. She gathered his things: toothbrush, razor, a rank pair of sneakers from under the bed. In the front pocket of his jeans she found the key chain she'd bought him — a pewter charm attached, shaped like a tiny mug of Guinness. (Kevin who lived nowhere, who owned nothing: what was he doing with all these keys?)

Carefully, minding her nails, she slipped her key off the ring.

'Where am I supposed to go?' he said.

'Your mother's. I don't know. Wherever you used to go.'

It wasn't her problem to solve; it was Kevin's. Let God fix him. After repeating the words for months, she finally understood what they meant.

Let go and let God.

She was driving Aidan to school when her cell phone rang. 'It's me,' said Mike McGann, his voice warm and rough, like something she could wrap herself in. They made plans for later. He had afternoon showings in Quincy, and one in Dunster. If he finished early, he would swing by the apartment.

'Who was that?' Aidan asked when she hung up.

'That was Mike,' she told him. 'Mommy's new friend.'

* * *

Of Mike's affair with Kath Conlon I know very little. In sexual matters there is an instinctual reserve between a brother and a sister, a shyness that I suppose serves an evolutionary purpose. Mike claims he saw her — a vaguer euphemism cannot be imagined — just a few times, in the evening after work. He found it surprisingly easy to arrange. *I have a showing later. I'll grab dinner out.* It was a plausible excuse — spring is every realtor's busy season. And when he sold, in rapid recession, two pricy houses that had lingered on the market for months, it was as if some external force had intervened to corroborate his alibi. In his deluded state, it seemed a kind of sign. Each time he left Kath's bed, he took a quick shower and drove across town just as the rush hour traffic eased. He arrived in time to kiss the boys good night.

My whole life I have held my brother in a

265

certain regard, and it unnerves me to imagine him going home to Abby on those nights. He insists that she suspected nothing, but in this, I'm fairly certain, he has underestimated her. I speak from experience when I say it's hard not to notice a husband's hair damp from an evening shower, smelling of unfamiliar shampoo.

It isn't clear to me, as I recount these details, where Mike's heart lay. He maintains to this day that Aidan Conlon was never far from his thoughts; that what happened with the boy's mother was an accident, an unforeseen complication. He swears that he never wavered in his original intent: to know Aidan, to hear his story. To find out once and for all whether the unthinkable could be true.

⋆ ⋆ ⋆

That week or the following, Mike no longer remembers, he showed Kath the house at Twelve Fenno. 'Bring Aidan,' he said, a suggestion that delighted her. Unlike any of her previous boyfriends, he wanted to spend time with her son.

I imagine the three of them walking through the little Cape, Mike skipping the usual sales pitch, letting Kath move at her own pace, opening closets and drawers. Anyone watching would think them a small family, and I wonder if Kath herself pictured Mike's clothes in the double closet, his shaving things in the renovated bathroom with its his-and-hers sinks. Aidan, for his part, loved the snug rear bedroom with its gables and skylight, the small backyard with a cement birdbath in one corner — long unused, filled with dirt and leaves. Kath was pleased when Mike took him outside to examine it. He was good with kids, that much was clear. She thought fleetingly of his three boys waiting for him at home. For just a moment she craved a cigarette, an urge she resisted. She hadn't smoked in six days.

She was alone in the kitchen, trying to figure out the convection oven, when her cell phone rang. It was Kevin Vick, talking fast. She knew instantly that he had scored.

'I was at your house,' he said. 'Your car was there. Where the fuck were you?'

'None of your business. I'm out.'

He inhaled wetly, the cokehead's sniffle. The sound triggered something in her. Her mind tried to forget, but her body still remembered. Sour and delicious, that burning postnasal drip; whatever was left of the drug sliding down the back of her throat.

'You scored,' she said.

'Yeah. Great shit, too.'

For just a moment she hesitated, hating herself. Then she heard Mike's voice at the back door.

'I'm hanging up now,' she said. 'I told you. Leave me alone.'

She turned off her phone and stowed it in her purse.

'Can we get a feeder?' Aidan demanded, bursting through the door.

'As many as you want,' Kath said.

267

She led him by the hand as Mike turned off the lights and locked the doors. It was nearly Aidan's bedtime. In half an hour she and Mike would be alone.

But to her surprise he headed straight for his truck, kissing her briefly at the curb. 'I'll call you,' he said.

★ ★ ★

Mike drove away in a bewildered state. Walking through the house with Kath had affected him powerfully, in ways he couldn't have predicted. Over the years he'd encountered every sort of difficult client, the critical, the demanding; but Kath was openly delighted by the modest little Cape. There was something touching in her simple enthusiasm, her palpable longing for a home. His own boys would have roared through the empty rooms like hyperactive banshees, but Aidan had stayed close to Kath, reaching often for her hand. Mike watched them intently. Kath was an affectionate mother, a spontaneous kisser and hugger, but her mood could shift in an instant: tender one moment; then impatient, sardonic, profane. *Slow down*, she'd yelled when Aidan raced down the staircase. *You want to wind up paralyzed? You'll break your fucken neck*. Minus the expletive, it was a comment that would have rolled easily off our own mother's tongue. Abby, of course, would never say such a thing.

And that, really, was the source of Mike's

confusion, the reason his instincts contradicted themselves. Was Aidan a normal, well-adjusted kid with a loving, responsible mother? It depended entirely on how you defined those things. By Abby's standards, the kid's home life was catastrophic — *dysfunctional* was the word she liked to use. But was her way the only right way? What made her the authority on such things?

In the end, a single moment troubled him. When he took Aidan's hand and led him into the backyard, Kath had stayed behind to examine the appliances, opening the dishwasher and the side-by-side fridge. Everything about that seemed wrong.

If her son had been molested, would she let him walk off hand in hand, even for a minute, with a strange man?

★ ★ ★

That long Memorial Day weekend passed in a blur. He was a realtor and a father. He was always driving somewhere. There were open houses, two each on Saturday and Sunday; T-ball practice, a birthday party. For three days Mike's Escalade criss-crossed the South Shore, idled in suburban weekend traffic. Periodically Kath's number popped up on his cell phone.

'Who keeps calling?' Jamie demanded from the backseat.

'Nobody,' Mike said.

It would have been easy enough to return her calls, but Mike didn't. He was still brooding over

269

that moment, her blithe disregard when he took Aidan's hand.

On Sunday morning, Abby made a great show of sleeping in — *Mom's morning off,* she called it — and so it was Mike who fed the boys and got them into their church clothes. Shepherding them out the front door, he noticed — it was hard to miss — a familiar car disappear down the street. In his neighborhood, a fifteen-year-old Buick Regal was as conspicuous as a hearse.

He knew, then, that trouble was coming. He'd have known it sooner, had he checked the messages she'd left on his cell phone.

Hey, how's it going? It's Thursday night. Give me a call.

And then:

Hey, it's Friday. Happy long weekend! Aidan's at my mom's, so stop by if you want.

And then:

Saturday night. Where are you, anyway? I mean, what the fuck?

★   ★   ★

On Memorial Day Mike showed a house in Milton, a handsome old Victorian on a wide tree-lined street. The seller was asking eight hundred, but in this neighborhood it could easily go higher. The open house was crowded with prosperous-looking buyers. Mike expected an offer by the end of the day.

He was standing on the front porch talking to the Weinbergs, a young orthodontist and his wife, when he saw the Buick out of the corner of his eye. Kath stepped out of the car and left the engine idling. Aidan waved from the front seat.

'Hey,' she called from the sidewalk, shading her eyes. Kath in blue jeans and a bikini top, the nicotine patch on her shoulder, her jeweled navel flashing in the sun. 'We're on our way to the beach. I thought we'd stop by.'

The orthodontist's wife gave her a smile. Her eyes went from Kath to the Buick. 'Is this your family?' she asked Mike.

He did not answer the question.

'The roof is two years old,' he told Dr. Weinberg. 'They're thirty-year shingles, which means fifteen. Even still, you're good for a while.' He shook the man's hand. 'Sleep on it if you need to, but don't sleep in. It'll go fast. Any questions, give me a call.'

He gave them a wave as they got into their car, a shiny Lexus. The wife gave Kath a piercing look.

'What are you doing here?' Mike demanded, his voice hushed.

'I was in the neighborhood.'

It was a winding, dead-end street miles from the highway, even farther from the beach. The sort of place nobody passed through.

'All right. Fine. Your secretary gave me the address.'

'Did you drive past my house this morning?' Mike could barely contain his anger. His boys had noticed the car.

(*It's a bomber*, Ryan said, laughing.
I love it, Jamie said.)

Kath frowned. 'Maybe. How the fuck do I

271

know? You never told me where you live.'

'Kath.' Mike ran a hand over his head. 'This is not cool.'

'No shit. I haven't heard from you since, like, Wednesday.'

'I'm sorry. It's been a crazy few days.'

'Aidan's staying at my mom's tonight.'

Mike glanced at his watch. 'I have another showing after this. In Quincy. I'm not sure how long it'll run.'

There was an awkward silence.

'Are you mad at me?' she asked.

'Jesus, no,' he said, an edge in his voice. 'But I can't just drop everything every time you call. This isn't easy for me. I have responsibilities.'

A woman came out of the house then, a tall blonde in a flowing sundress. Mike treated her to the full wattage of his smile.

'What can I do for you?' he asked.

★ ★ ★

Kath slept poorly that night, worry gnawing at her stomach, a creeping dread. The feeling was all too familiar. It had visited her periodically since the age of twelve, the year her father died, the year she'd undressed for a sophomore: the horrible knowledge that she had surrendered too much, that she had given herself away. The last time — the worst time — had nearly killed her; and except for Kevin (who didn't count), she had sworn off men entirely. Then she met Mike McGann.

The holiday weekend had come and gone, and

272

except for three miserable minutes on the sidewalk, there had been no Mike. She'd stood by like an idiot as he chatted with the well-dressed couple, smiling his salesman's smile. He'd looked through her as though she were invisible. Nothing for her to do but wait there, her cheeks flaming, as Mike shook the man's hand.

Are you mad at me?

She hated herself for asking the question, for caring one way or another. She had not gone looking for Mike McGann. He had come to her. He'd inserted himself into her life and turned it sideways. She'd been fine on her own, just fine.

She lay awake a long time, thinking. As always, her worries seemed larger at night. *It happens to us all*, Father Art had once told her. *The dark night of the soul.* The black sadness that sometimes engulfed her: he hadn't tried to advise her, or talk her out of it. He simply saw her anguish and pronounced it normal, and this had comforted her. Father Art at her kitchen table, before everything had gone so horribly wrong. It seemed very long ago.

The next morning she slept through the alarm. She skipped breakfast and snapped at Aidan: 'Jesus Christ, kid. Can you get a move on?' On the way to work she bought a pack of Newports. Her cell phone she placed squarely on her desk. All morning long she glanced at it periodically. *Ring, you motherfucker. Can't you just fucking ring?*

At lunchtime she got a salad from the deli but couldn't choke it down. She contemplated the unopened pack of Newports. She wasn't supposed to smoke in the office, but Chris Winter wouldn't know the difference. He had gone out in one of the trucks.

Her cell phone rang.

'Hey,' she said, breathless. 'About fucken time.'

'Miss Conlon?'

It took her a moment to understand that it wasn't Mike McGann calling to apologize. *I'm sorry I didn't call. I miss you. Can I see you later?*

A woman's voice said, 'Please hold for Ron Shapiro.'

★ ★ ★

What will you do when the money comes?

'The Archdiocese wants to settle,' said Shapiro, talking fast. 'It isn't a fortune, but it's a healthy number. Miss Conlon, I believe we have won.'

Kath sat a moment, dazed. She lit a celebratory cigarette. She'd imagined this moment so thoroughly that her next move required no thought. But Chris Winter wouldn't return for at least an hour. She was denied the pleasure of telling him to fuck himself. Instead she simply walked out the door.

It was a high bright day, the sky vivid blue. *Ceiling unlimited.* She got into her car and drove.

For eight years, Phyllis Gruber has been my brother's secretary. She remembers that Monday in vivid detail. First, Mike was in a foul mood, a rare occurrence. As soon as he walked in the door she'd been treated to a scolding: 'Yesterday, that showing in Milton: what were you thinking, giving out the address?'

The question confounded her. She'd been told again and again that every caller was a potential buyer. The goal, always, was to get them in the door.

In all the time she'd worked for Mike McGann, his personal and professional lives had seemed refreshingly uncomplicated. She had never been asked to lie. Now, clearly, something had shifted. Phyllis understood this at one o'clock that afternoon, when the girl walked through the door.

'Where's Mike McGann?' she demanded.

Phyllis eyed her short skirt, her tattooed arm and leg. 'Can I ask what this is in reference to?'

The girl seemed agitated, restless. 'He showed me a house the other day. Twelve Fenno Street.'

'I'll see if he's in,' Phyllis said.

Mike's office was in the rear corner, just opposite a small kitchen. As always, his door was open. Phyllis knocked lightly at the door frame.

'There's a — young lady here to see you,' she said carefully.

Mike gave her a blank look.

'She says you showed her a house. Twelve Fenno.'

(*No poker player, your brother, she told me later. I knew right away.*)

Phyllis showed the girl in. When Mike's door closed, she busied herself in the kitchen. She made coffee and wiped the counters. She checked the supply of creamer and tea. The girl's voice, she could have heard in New Hampshire. Mike spoke more softly, at least at first.

I imagine Kath looking around the office, which I suppose impressed her. It impressed me the first time I saw it, the big picture window, family photos arranged on the heavy oak desk. On the wall were two framed certificates. For two years in a row, Mike had been South Shore Realty's Salesperson of the Year.

'I tried to call, but your phone is turned off,' she said. 'I couldn't wait.'

'Kath, what the fuck? Are you crazy?' His skin turning colors — pink, red, purple — as though he were bench-pressing his own weight. 'You can't be coming to my office like this.'

'It's okay.' Kath grinned. The astonishing news welled up inside her, but she was determined to take her time. She had learned to make the good things last: sex, drugs, the sweet pleasures you never had enough of. Kevin used to laugh at her, the way she rationed her happiness — trying to stretch the moment, like a little girl with a treat.

'I'm a customer, remember? You're going to

sell me a house.' She took a framed photo from his desk and examined it for a moment. 'They're beautiful,' she said. What she meant was *She's beautiful*: Abby with her long dark hair, her dazzling smile, Mike's ring on her finger. Mike's two babies in her arms.

He took the photo from her hands. 'You need to go.'

'Wait a minute. I'm ready to, you know. Make an offer, or whatever.' The news expanding inside her, so big she could scarcely contain it. I'm rich, she thought.

Mike eyed her suspiciously. 'What's the matter with you? Are you high or something?'

She flinched as though he'd slapped her.

'Look, I thought we understood each other.' He ran a hand over his head. 'You know my situation. For Christ's sake, I have a *family*. I can't have you following me around like this.'

Her temper flared then. '*Following* you? Are you fucken kidding me?'

I have a family, too, she thought. I have Aidan. I am lovable and whatever.

'Keep your voice down.'

'Don't tell me what to do.' She stared at him, hurt and stunned. She had good news, the best news of her life. She just wanted to *tell* him. How had it gone so horribly wrong?

'I came here to talk to you,' she said, choking on the words. 'You think you know everything about me? You don't know a fucken thing.'

★   ★   ★

277

'She stormed out of here,' Phyllis told me later. From the window she'd watched the girl get into a dilapidated old Buick. She sat there for several minutes, smoking. Then she made a call on a cell phone.

Aidan stood on the sidewalk, waiting. The sky had darkened; wind ruffled his T-shirt. He had forgotten his sweatshirt, his rain jacket. One by one the yellow buses pulled away from the curb.

All right, all right, I'll come and get you. His mother had been crabby that morning, but she had promised to pick him up. He'd told her a hundred times how he hated the school bus — loud and crowded, the rear seats occupied, always, by fifth graders, Jordan Dailey and his friends. When Aidan climbed aboard they erupted in fart noises, four boys farting for all they were worth. Jordan Dailey's farts were always the loudest; he was the ringleader. Without him, Aidan felt, the other boys would leave him alone. In March Jordan had been absent for a week, taken skiing by his parents, and without him the farts seemed halfhearted. Then Jordan returned, farting louder than ever, a paper tag hanging from the zipper of his jacket. A lift ticket, it was called, for riding the ski lift.

Father Art had promised, once, to take him skiing. But winter had come and gone. Aidan didn't care about skiing, not really. But he'd have liked a lift ticket for his jacket.

At his old school ski jackets weren't allowed, which would have solved the problem. No blue jeans, no sneakers. You didn't have to worry about wearing the wrong kind. But his old school cost money, and his mother couldn't afford it. Talking about it made her feel bad. That was how his grandmother had explained it: *The less said, the better*. So Aidan said nothing at all.

He missed the old school: Sister Paula, his friend David Chilicki. More than anything or anybody, he missed Father Art. A few times he had seen the priest's car parked in his neighborhood, Father Art at the wheel reading a newspaper.

He hadn't told his mother.

Aidan watched his bus depart, the last to pull away from the curb. Through the rear window he could see Jordan Dailey shouting, his arms flailing. Jordan Dailey farting at someone else.

A raindrop fell, then another. Aidan watched the teachers leave through the back door. His teacher, Ms. Bilback, wore a long raincoat. She crossed the street with the others, to the parking lot behind the school.

It wasn't the first time his mother had forgotten. At his old school she forgot him all the time. There it didn't matter: he simply went next door to the rectory. 'Homework first,' said Father Art, leading him into the office. Later they had milk and peanut butter cookies. They watched *Dora the Explorer* on TV.

Aidan crossed the street and started walking. Down the street was the hospital, where the city bus stopped. He had taken the city bus before, with his grandmother always. He had never taken it by himself. Each bus, he'd noticed, had a different number. His grandmother's bus was number 6.

At the plastic shelter he stood and waited. Buses came and went. The 19 came first, then the 46; then the 11, then the 4. Aidan stood at the curb, watching people get on buses. Gradually the sky darkened.

He was all alone.

Finally a bus pulled up; its doors opened. The driver looked at him and smiled, a black man with a shiny bald head.

'Which bus are you waiting for, son?'

'Number 6.'

'The six don't stop here. That's a different route. You want to go to Dunster, you could take the nineteen.'

'Thank you,' Aidan said.

The rain started. Aidan waited under the shelter for Bus 19. When it finally arrived he got on board. He had a dollar in his pocket, two nickels and a penny. When he handed it to the driver she shook her head.

Aidan felt his eyes tearing.

'Oh, Jesus. Get in,' she said.

He sat on the bus a long time, staring out the window, watching for something familiar: his street, the corner store, his playground, his house. Again and again the bus stopped. Passengers got on and got off: a fat lady, a lady with a baby, an old man with a cane, a girl with giant boobs. A bearded man talked to himself loudly, his mouth jerking. He caught Aidan looking at him.

'What did I do now?' the man demanded.

Aidan looked away.

Finally the bus pulled into a garage. The driver

turned off the engine and turned on the lights. 'What are you still doing here?' she called over her shoulder. Only two people were left on the bus, Aidan and the man who talked to himself.

'I want to go to Dunster,' Aidan said.

'Dunster is inbound. You got on the outbound.' The driver turned around in her seat and started the engine. 'Don't worry, we going back out in a couple minutes. You set tight. I'll get you there.'

* * *

In the dark Aidan crossed the street to his house. His mother's car was gone, the front door closed, the windows dark. He took the key from under the mat and unlocked the front door. 'Mom?' he called, though he could see that she wasn't home.

He put on dry clothes and switched on the TV. The kids' shows were over, the news starting. Still it was better than a quiet house.

In the kitchen he rifled through the cupboards, thinking of the cookies at the rectory, two Nutter Butters on a plate, a third one if he asked. His mother sometimes bought Oreos, but the cookies never lasted. She and Aidan ate them together in front of the TV, the whole bag in one night.

In the refrigerator he found beer and Coke, orange cheese slices in plastic wrappers. There was ketchup and mustard and mayonnaise. He poured himself some Coke and ate a slice of cheese in front of the television.

The news ended; a program began.

At the commercial he went into the kitchen and called his grandmother. He let it ring a long time. His grandmother was slow, her knees hurt her.

Nobody answered the phone.

He remembered, then, that she had gone for the day, away on a bus trip. She wouldn't be back until late.

He ate another slice of cheese.

There was one other phone number he knew by heart, but he didn't call it. He was not to speak to Father Art.

There was a knock at the door.

Mike left the office early that day. 'I have a showing,' he told Phyllis, avoiding her eyes. He wondered how much she had heard.

He drove to Quincy in a panic. Be cool, he told himself. There was no reason to think Kath would go to his wife. (Except the look on her face when she stared at Abby's photo. Except that she knew exactly where he lived.)

Please God, Mike thought, Mike who prayed rarely. Don't let this happen. He understood that he'd brought it on himself, that in every way he deserved it. He had betrayed his wife, his family. He had a great deal to lose.

Abby's Explorer was parked in the driveway. He looked up and down the street, but there was no lime-green Buick, thank God.

He parked and went in through the back door. In the kitchen Abby was unloading the dish-washer. 'You're home early,' she said. 'What happened?'

'Hey.' He came up behind her, kissing her neck. The clean smell of his wife, no cigarettes, perfume or alcohol. Just shampoo, soap and skin. 'I skipped out. I wanted to have dinner with the boys.'

'I thought you had a showing.'

'Not tonight.' He watched her move around the kitchen, stacking plates in the cupboard, sorting the clean silverware into its drawer. 'Ab, I'm sorry.'

'For what?'

Mike felt his face coloring. 'It's been crazy lately. I haven't been around much. It isn't fair to the boys. Or to you.' He reached for the medal hanging at his throat. St. Christopher raced back and forth on his chain.

To anyone who knows Mike as I do, his guilt would have been obvious. And Abby — it pains me a little to say it, but Abby surely knows him better.

She closed one eye.

I'll be different, he wanted to say. *I promise*. A criminal's mistake: the guilty always said too much.

'Where are the boys?' he said instead.

'Ryan's room, last time I checked.'

Mike climbed the stairs, relief flooding him. Life could return to normal now. There would be no more lying. He would have nothing else to lie about.

He would never see her again. Unquestionably, it was the right decision: for a guy in his shoes, an affair, *any* affair, was madness. And Kath Conlon — he saw it clearly now — was an unstable unit. Crazier, even, than Lisa Morrison; she was a midnight fistfight. Years ago he'd had the stamina for it — the passionate theatrics, the angry tussles and pulsing reconciliations. Okay: he'd gotten off on it. But no more.

He had failed in his mission. His questions about Art had gone unanswered. In all probability they would remain so; but at the moment it seemed a secondary concern. He had risked too much, a fact painfully evident. He had far too much to lose.

The boys were sprawled on the floor in Ryan's room, hunched over a board game.

'Daddy!' Michael called, rushing toward him.

Mike swept the boy into his arms. Ryan looked up from the game and grinned crookedly. Mike gave him a high-five. Lately Ryan had dodged his parents' caresses; he was getting too old for hugging. Mike was grateful that the twins still clung to him.

'Where's Jamie?' he asked.

'In his room,' said Michael. 'He's mad. He hates losing.'

Mike looked down at Ryan, who simply shrugged. 'Whatever,' he said, his new favorite word.

Mike put down Michael and headed down the hall. 'Hey, James?' he called. 'What's up, dude?'

Jamie lay on his bed, staring out the window.

'Your brothers said you were mad.'

'Nah,' said Jamie. 'Just bored.'

Mike sat on the bed and stroked his son's hair.

'You guys have a birthday this month,' he said. 'Any special requests?'

'Binoculars,' Jamie said without hesitation. 'We used them in school. They're cool.'

'Oh, yeah? What do you want to look at?'

'Birds,' Jamie said.

★　★　★

'I never wanted to see her again,' Mike told me later, and I believe him. Certainly the facts support his claim. That afternoon he'd left a

286

message for Teri Pappas. He would unload Twelve Fenno, hand the listing to another office. Kath would have no excuse to bother him again.

So why, after the boys and Abby were asleep, did Mike grab his keys and jacket, get into his Escalade and drive the eight miles to Dunster?

He found it difficult to explain.

All evening long he'd replayed the memory, Kath storming out of his office. *You think you know everything about me. You don't know a fucken thing.* Tires squealing, the Buick peeling out of the parking lot. Where had she gone in that agitated state? If he'd known her better — if he'd known her *at all* — he might have been able to guess. Her mother's? A bar? Home to her son?

'I had a bad feeling,' Mike said.

★   ★   ★

He glanced up and down Fenno Street. Kath's windows were dark, her car nowhere to be seen. He was driving past the house when a light came on in the kitchen.

He parked and climbed the steps to her porch.

'Kath!' he called, knocking. 'It's Mike. Can I come in?'

He waited a moment, then went around to the back. The kitchen window was now dark.

Again he knocked at the front door. 'Look, I know you're in there. Open the door, will you?'

He waited a moment. Finally the door opened slightly. Aidan peered out through the crack.

'Aidan. Are you okay?'

'I'm not supposed to open the door.'

'That's good, buddy.' Mike peered over the boy's head into the living room. 'Listen, I need to talk to your mom.'

'She isn't here.' Aidan opened the door another inch. He wore Batman pajamas like the ones Ryan had outgrown.

'Where is she?'

'I don't know.'

'You're here by yourself?'

Aidan nodded.

'For how long?'

'I don't know. A long time.' The boy was near tears. 'She was supposed to pick me up. I took the wrong bus. I got lost.'

'Have you had dinner?'

The boy shook his head.

'Listen, I know you're not supposed to,' Mike said, 'but just this once, I need you to let me in. I want to help find your mom, okay?'

Aidan opened the door.

★ ★ ★

They sat at the kitchen table. In the cupboard Mike found peanut butter and saltines.

Aidan ate ravenously. He didn't know where his mother was. With Kevin maybe?

'Who's Kevin?' Mike asked.

'Her other friend,' Aidan said.

His grandmother wasn't home, he explained. She had gone on the bus to play the slot machines. His face wrinkled; again he seemed ready to cry. He'd wanted to go along, but she wouldn't let him. She said it wasn't for kids.

288

Foxwoods Casino, Mike thought: a two-hour bus ride to backwoods Connecticut. 'Grandma's right. It's not for kids.'

He rose and paced. On the side of the fridge he found a business card attached with a magnet. 'What's Winter Towing?'

'Mom's work,' Aidan said.

Mike called the number. 'I'm looking for Kathleen Conlon,' he told the guy who answered.

'Me, too. Crazy bitch ran out of here in the middle of the day.'

Mike glanced at the clock. 'What time was that?'

'After lunch. One o'clock maybe.'

'Any idea where she went?'

'I could give a shit. When you find her, tell her not to come back.'

Mike hung up the phone. From work she'd driven straight to his office. Where she went next was anyone's guess.

'Is there somebody else I can call?' he asked Aidan. 'An aunt or an uncle maybe?'

'My uncle Denny lives in New Hampshire.'

'You know his number?'

Aidan shook his head.

'Think, Aidan. There's got to be someone.'

Aidan chewed thoughtfully. His pajamas were dusted with cracker crumbs.

'Maybe,' he said slowly, 'we could call the priest.'

Father Art had taken him to the beach, helped him with his homework. Twice they had gone to the movies. They'd eaten popcorn and Goobers for dinner. It was a long time ago.

More recently, Father Art had bought him a toboggan for Christmas, left it on the front porch tied with a bow. One time he'd promised: as soon as it snowed, they'd go sledding in the park. But the priest had never come.

'Why not?' Mike could feel his heart hammering.

'Mom's mad at him. They had a fight.' Aidan looked down at his plate. 'I'm not supposed to talk about him.'

The priest was a bad man who hurt children. At this Mike nodded silently. It's what he would have told his own kids. How else did you warn an eight-year-old? For Christ's sake, what more could you say?

'Did he ever . . . hurt you?' Mike watched him closely.

'He was my friend,' Aidan said.

★   ★   ★

Mike was sitting in the kitchen with an open beer when Kath burst in through the back door.

'What the fuck?' Her face was very pale, her makeup smeared. Somewhere she'd acquired a grimy sweatshirt. A man's sweatshirt, too big for her; it nearly covered her brief skirt. 'What are you doing here?'

Feeding your kid, Mike thought. *Putting him*

290

to bed. 'I came to check on Aidan,' he said.

'Oh, Jesus. Is he okay?' She threw down her pocketbook and headed for his bedroom.

'He's fine.' Mike put out a hand to stop her. A mistake.

'Get your fucken hands off me,' she growled, her eyes wild.

He saw, then, that she was on something. He would have to handle her carefully. He'd seen plenty of times how these things escalated. One false move and he'd end up in a squad car, jailed on a domestic. Good luck explaining *that* to Abby.

'Sorry,' he said evenly. 'The kid's had a long day, you know? He's beat.'

Kath nodded, mollified.

'Here. I just opened it.' He offered her the beer from his hand.

She took a long pull. 'I was supposed to pick him up,' she confessed, her speech thick. 'I dead forgot.' She sat heavily at the table. 'I'm a shitty mother. That's what you think, right?'

Mike ignored the question. He sat across from her. 'Kath, about before. In my office. I'm sorry.'

She stared at him sullenly.

'I — wasn't expecting you, you know? You caught me off guard.'

'I had good news,' she said. 'The best. I have money coming. I can buy that house.' She scrabbled in her purse for a cigarette. 'I'm suing that fucken priest. My lawyer called. They're going to pay.'

Mike chose his words carefully. 'The priest. You mean Father Breen.'

Kath eyed him warily. 'What do you know about it?'

'I was talking to Aidan. About what happened. He said you told him not to talk about it.'

Kath shrugged. 'Yeah, well, what's the fucken point? What's done is done. I just want him to forget it ever happened.'

'Forget *what*? That priest. What did he do?'

Mike reached across the table for her hand.

★ ★ ★

I can picture them in her tiny kitchen, Kath riding the tide of the last few hours, the dark back room of a bar in Southie, the owner a friend of Kevin's, a guy she vaguely knew. They'd been waiting for her with a full bag, Kevin showing unusual restraint. Fourteen months clean, and she couldn't get it into her fast enough.

Home, she thought as the wave broke inside her. I'm home.

By the time she remembered Aidan it was too late, dark outside. Well, she wasn't the first mother to forget her child; probably it happened all the time. The school would have called somebody, her mother maybe. Problem solved.

She thought, Whatever is going to happen has already happened. It was a comforting thought. There was no point in moving now, though she would soon. In a minute, she thought. And then time did what it always did, ticked away boringly. Time was petty and unforgiving, humorless and joyless. In her mind it resembled Sister Gertrudis, her eighth-grade teacher. Fuck time.

She'd crept in through the back door and closed it quietly behind her. With any luck her mother would be asleep on the couch. Instead she'd found Mike McGann in her kitchen, wide awake, waiting for her. She'd have been less surprised to find the house on fire. His face was achingly familiar, like someone she knew from another life, an old friend lost or dead: Jack Strecker, her father maybe. Was it just that afternoon that she'd stormed out of his office? It seemed very long ago.

She needed a moment to get her bearings. But Mike McGann wouldn't let her. He was large and loud and had surprised her. He was asking about Aidan.

He reached across the table for her hand.

'I didn't think anything at first,' she said slowly. 'He was nice to Aidan. To both of us. I thought it was good for him. A father figure, or whatever.'

Mike frowned. 'And? All that time he was — molesting your kid?'

'No. I don't know. It happened later.' She looked down at her hand, safe inside his. 'We could — I don't know. You really want to hear this?'

'I do,' he said somberly, as though he'd just married her.

Kath stared at their entwined hands.

★ ★ ★

It was the end of summer, the last week of August. In a few days school would start. Aidan's birthday fell on a Thursday. He'd clamored for a day at the shore. Kath's car was in the shop — the alternator, they said — and so it was Father Art who drove them to Nantasket Beach, paid for lunch and ice cream and gas and parking. He gave them quarters for the arcade, Kath and Aidan both, like a father spoiling his children. When did a day at the beach get so expensive? With kids everything cost a fortune. But Father Art had been happy to pay.

The beach had been swarming with kids — school out, the fine weather; whole families camped out under umbrellas, eating from coolers, enjoying the sun. (Who were all these people, she'd wondered: these dads throwing Frisbees; these mothers scolding and doling out snacks? It was a weekday, for godssakes; didn't people *work*?) Kath had taken her place among them, stretched out on her blanket. She'd spent the afternoon flipping through magazines, dozing in the sun. And it was a relief, not worrying about Aidan every blessed minute. Father Art was happy to look after him. For a day she was like other women, who had husbands to help them. For that one day, she could take a break.

'I must have been asleep when it happened,' she told Mike. She hadn't actually seen it herself.

The priest had taken Aidan swimming in the ocean. High tide then, a dangerous current. Aidan had been afraid. He had clung to the priest as they swam and frolicked, and the priest had pressed up against him. The current was rough, the water empty of swimmers. Alone in

294

the surf he'd reached into Aidan's swim trunks. He'd made Aidan reach into his. Father Art had touched her son out in the open, in front of God and everybody. And Kath had lain there sleeping, not fifty feet away.

Mike McGann was looking at her strangely. 'You never reported it,' he said. 'You could have called the police.'

'I fucken hate cops.'

There was a long silence.

'So it happened just that once?' Mike said slowly. 'That one time in the water?'

'Yeah, I guess. Isn't that enough?'

He released her hand quickly, as though it burned him. 'I have to go,' he said.

What thoughts ran through Mike's head as he roared across the South Shore, flouting local speed limits, racing up the ramp to the empty interstate on the first dark hour of a Tuesday morning? He'd found the KeySpan envelope in his glove box, Art's address written in Ma's neat hand.

His brother was afraid of the water. More than afraid: Art was terrified. Mike himself was a fearless swimmer, a skilled surfer. His whole life he had viewed his brother with disdain. In all his years as a lifeguard he had never seen anyone so pathetic: a grown man skittish even while wading, who jumped back like a little girl if the water rose above his ankles.

Art swimming at high tide, clutching a fifty-pound child?

Art groping the boy while the surf rose around his shoulders?

He had done *nothing of the kind*.

Mike drove fiercely that night, the rage nearly blinding him. It had taken all he had to walk out of Kath Conlon's apartment. He could have shaken her, strangled her, killed her with his bare hands. Never in his life had he exercised such self-control.

You're a fucken liar. He hadn't said it, didn't need to. Kath Conlon no longer mattered. She wasn't worth his time.

Green highway signs flew past. Grantham, Weymouth, Abington, Braintree — a maze of suburbs Mike navigated without thinking. For eight years he had sold real estate; he carried in his head a detailed street map of the entire South Shore.

Dover Court was silent when he arrived, the front lawn illuminated by floodlights, the parking lot bright as day. Mike pulled into a visitor's space in front of the office. As he approached the A building he saw the flyer posted on the front door.

HAVE YOU SEEN THIS MAN?

Art's face circled in fat black marker, subtle as a bull's-eye.

'Motherfucker,' Mike muttered.

He jogged up the stairs to Art's apartment, his shoes loud on the metal rungs. He didn't care if he woke the whole building. He knocked at Art's door.

I'm sorry, man. Can you ever forgive me?

He knocked again, glanced at his watch. Art was asleep, had to be. Where did a priest go at one in the morning?

'Art. Open up.'

Across the hall a door opened. A big red-haired guy stood there in a bathrobe, squinting. 'Keep it down, will you?'

'I'm looking for your neighbor,' said Mike. 'Have you seen him?'

'He's gone,' the guy said.

'Gone where?'

297

He shrugged. 'The hospital, I guess. The ambulance came a couple hours ago.'

'*Ambulance?*' Mike stared in disbelief. 'What happened?'

'Beats me,' the man said.

Mike ran a hand over his head. 'Can you at least tell me what hospital?'

The guy tightened the belt of his robe. 'I could give a shit. Fucking degenerate. Liar, too. I hope he dies, you want to know the truth.'

Mike felt the rage fill him like liquid, flowing into every corner. 'That's my brother,' he said evenly.

'Congratulations. You must be proud.'

He was a big man, nearly Mike's size, but groggy and unprepared. Mike charged like a bull.

★　★　★

The emergency room was busy for a Monday night. Two lone women on opposite ends of the waiting room, domestics probably. An old man waiting, reading a newspaper. A Muslim woman in a headscarf, holding a fussy baby. She looked up periodically to scold three little girls who chased each other around the room.

Mike approached the reception desk, clutching his right hand. The soreness was deeply satisfying. He hadn't hit anyone in years.

Behind the desk sat a large black woman in a colorful smock. She eyed Mike's hand. 'Your name, please.'

'Mike McGann. But I'm not here for myself.

This is nothing.' He shoved the bruised hand into his pocket. 'My brother came in on an ambulance. Arthur Breen.'

'Have a seat, please.'

'Can you just tell me — '

'Have a seat, sir.'

Mike felt a hand on his back.

'Hey. McGann, right?'

Mike turned. The guy was his own age, vaguely familiar. He wore the standard EMT uniform, black pants and blue shirt, and a name tag: KELLY. He offered his hand.

'Been a few years, man. I heard you left the force. How you been?'

'Hey, Kelly.' Mike glanced over his shoulder. The black woman had left the desk. 'Help me out here. My brother came in on an ambo. South side of Braintree. His name is Art Breen.'

Kelly's eyebrows shot up. 'That was your brother?'

'Yeah,' Mike said warily, remembering the headlines, Art's face in the newspaper: DO YOU KNOW THIS MAN?

'Dude, I brought him in. An OD. Some kind of pills. We couldn't find a bottle.'

Overdose? *Art?* Mike stared at him, not comprehending. 'Are you sure?'

'He wasn't breathing,' said Kelly. 'I had to intubate.'

Mike thought: This is not possible.

'A priest was there with him,' said Kelly. 'We defibbed and got here as quick as we could.'

'OD,' Mike said. 'Are you sure? It couldn't have been — a heart attack, or something?' He

299

lowered his voice. 'He's been under a lot of stress.'

If Kelly caught his meaning, he gave no indication. 'Look, I'm not saying it was intentional. Some kind of drug interaction, maybe. Was he taking any medication?'

'Art? He's in perfect health, far as I know.'

Kelly frowned. 'This is kind of weird. When I opened his shirt, I saw marks on his chest.'

'Marks,' Mike repeated. 'Tattoos?'

'Nah. Some kind of medical marking. For surgery, maybe. Was he in the hospital recently?'

'Mr. McGann.'

Mike turned. The black woman stood at the desk.

Kelly offered Mike his hand. 'Good luck, man. I hope he pulls through.'

Me, too, Mike thought.

Benedicamus Domino.
  Deo Gratias.

Art had risen early that morning, an old habit. For weeks he'd slept poorly, wandering through the days in a trance of exhaustion. Yet even in that state, his internal clock was unforgiving. His eyes snapped open at six o'clock without fail.

He longed for sleep the way a man longs for a woman, a yearning that would not abate, a need unsatisfied by prayer. For most of his life he'd been spared both hungers. He had slept easily. He had not longed. He understood, too late, that he had lived in a blessed state, innocence or ignorance; a state to which he would gladly return.

But time, the engine of the physical world, moved in one direction only; there was no reversing it. Would he have done so, if it were possible? Would he have given back the last year of his life, his *annus mirabilis*, its exhilaration and sweetness? Were the piercing joys at least equal to the dark miseries, despair and shame?

It was a frivolous question, predicated on fantasy. Time would not change course, not for anyone. Certainly not for Arthur Breen.

★　★　★

2002

27 MONDAY

28 TUESDAY

29 WEDNESDAY

May 30–June 2

A
B
C
D
E
F
G
H
I
J
K
L
M
N
O
P
Q
R
S
T
U
V
W
X
Y
Z

THURSDAY **30**

FRIDAY **31**

1 SATURDAY

SUNDAY **2**

He began that day in his usual fashion, at the public library. According to a librarian I asked, he was waiting in the parking lot each morning when the place opened at nine. She couldn't tell me which books he checked out, just that he spent hours poring over foreign newspapers, French and Italian.

'That stuck in my mind. I was glad to see someone read them,' she said.

No *Globe*, then, for my brother; no *Herald*. No lurid headlines condemning the Cardinal, the Archdiocese, the dozens of priest in disgrace. I imagine him at the long table beneath the sunny window, hunched over the *Corriere della Sera*, his reading glasses sliding down his nose. Art taking a last look at the world, the parts of it he loved the most.

He left the library at ten-thirty. Where he went next, I can't say. The final pages in his datebook were left blank, as though even that small discipline were no longer worth the effort. It was only later, at the hospital, that I sorted through the worn black leather wallet I'd given him one Christmas and found the appointment card.

VILLAGE RADIATION ONCOLOGY

Arthur is expected at *1pm*

May 18

In event of cancellation kindly give 24 hours' notice.

The laws protecting patient confidentiality are stricter than I'd realized. To my surprise, they apply even after the patient is dead. I was unable to extract any information from his doctor. What I know, I learned from a pamphlet I found in Art's briefcase. *Small-Cell Carcinoma and You: The ins and out of combined modality treatment.*

On its front cover was a color photograph of a middle-aged couple, bathed in sunlight, walking hand in hand down a country lane. A stock image, but not, I think, randomly chosen. The photo had been taken in autumn. A few golden leaves shimmered on the trees, but most had already fallen to the ground.

I know from the receptionist that Art kept his appointment. Later he drove across town to Dunster, parked and waited. At three-thirty the yellow school bus discharged its passengers at the corner of Fenno Street. Art recognized several of the children — it wasn't the first time he'd watched them debark. But that day, Aidan didn't come.

At some point that afternoon he drove back to his apartment. He poured himself a glass of Scotch and sat down to his final task. As he wrote, the prayer ran through him like music playing inside him. He was not the one praying. He was simply a vessel — once hollow, now filled with prayer.

Let not your heart be troubled.

If you abide in me, and my words abide in you, you shall ask what you will, and it shall be done unto you.

Abide in me, and I in you.

Abide in me.

My brother was buried on the first of June — cold for late spring, damp and blustery, the air redolent of sea. In twenty-five years of ministry he'd performed hundreds of funerals. He had preached eulogies and counseled widows, said blessings, held hands. But of all those he'd comforted, not one showed up on that blustery Saturday when Father Breen was committed to the earth.

The church was nearly empty that morning — Sacred Heart, the church he had left in disgrace. The interim priest had declined to officiate, and so it was Clement Fleury who stood on the altar and pronounced the holy words — not the usual Mass of Christian Burial but the old Latin Mass, what Father Fleury called the Extraordinary Rite. Whether Art wished this explicitly, I can't say. Father Fleury may have done it to please my mother, or simply to please himself.

This funeral Mass, its licitness or illicitness, had for days been Ma's great preoccupation. Shocked, rent by grief, she became fixated on the words to be said over Arthur's body. By long tradition, a funeral Mass was refused in cases of suicide; but apparently the Church is not as obdurate as she once was. Rome now accepts the modern understanding of depression as an illness. In the space of a month my brother had

306

lost his job and his home; he'd been diagnosed with a deadly form of cancer. In many people, even one of these blows might trigger a clinical depression.

This was how Clement Fleury explained it to Ma. Still she was not convinced. At her insistence, Art's obituary was unusually specific. She personally called the editor of the Irish sports page. *Died at home, of lung cancer.* She'd insisted that he read it back to her, to make sure this detail was not omitted. She wasn't taking any chances.

★ ★ ★

Requiem æternam dona eis, Domine; et lux perpetua luceat eis.

Father Fleury, old-school, still wore black vestments for funerals. His voice echoed in the empty space, his fine tenor climbing the steeple all the way to heaven. If any human voice could, Father Fleury's would reach the ear of God.

Our family clustered in the front pews: Ma and Clare Boyle on either side of me, behind us Mike and his boys. By unspoken agreement we'd left Dad at home in front of the television, to be soothed by his usual morning programs: *Wheel of Fortune, Judge Judy.* His hostility to the Church predated his affliction, and there was no sense in winding him up.

Across the aisle sat two full rows of Devines. Uncle Dick and Uncle Jackie had pooled their resources, as it were, and offered up their sons as pallbearers. Say what you will about Ma's family, they are unfailingly loyal. Whatever they felt about Art's public disgrace, his alleged transgressions, they would not disown him at the end.

A small cluster of parishioners sat in the rear pews, at a respectful distance from the family. I recognized Attorney Burke, his wife and their daughter Caitlin, her eyes rimmed with red; Fran Conlon in her lavender coat. (She apologized for it later: it wasn't right for a funeral, but she didn't own a black one.) We stood in numb silence as the four young Devines brought in the box, which Ma had chosen from a catalog at Galvin Brothers Funeral Home. It was — if such a thing can be said to exist — a lovely coffin: gray with a nacreous sheen, like the inside of a seashell. The Devine boys placed it on its stand, head pointing toward the altar, a special distinction reserved for priests.

Out the corner of my eye I saw Clare Boyle crane her neck. 'Where's Leo?' she whispered.

I stared at her in disbelief. Apparently even the Oracle has her blind spots: after all these years she'd failed to grasp the basic architecture of our family. *Of course* Norma and Leo would not be seen at Art's funeral; *of course* Brian and Richie McGann had refused to bear his coffin. In death, as in life, Art was no McGann.

Requiem æternam dona eis, Domine; et lux perpetua luceat eis.

I inched closer to my mother. For the first time in thirty years, I slid my hand into her coat pocket.

Her fingers intertwined with mine. Our hands

308

were exactly the same size. It was like holding my own hand.

★ ★ ★

After the Mass we processed to the cemetery. I rode in the hearse with Ma and Art. In one hand she held the ticket stub I'd found in her pocket.

We rode shoulder to shoulder, hands still entwined. She did not meet my eyes as she told her story, the last evening she had spent with Art.

His invitation had come out of the blue, a gift fallen from heaven: Symphony Hall, the Boston Pops. Art had bought the tickets without telling her, a late Mother's Day gift. Anticipating her objections, he'd arranged for Clare Boyle to sit with my father. Ma would be free for the entire evening, her first night out in years.

As she spoke, I pictured her in dark lipstick, the green dress she'd bought, years ago, for Mike's wedding. On Arthur's arm she entered Symphony Hall, to his eye and mine the most beautiful building in Boston. He'd heard dozens of concerts there, and yet the place never failed to affect him. Each time he walked down the aisle to his seat, he was filled with a kind of awe he'd felt only in churches. That night Ma felt it, too.

'Fancy,' she whispered as they took their seats.

On the program that night was a premiere of a new violin concerto Art was keen to hear. Ma had no interest in classical music, but when the soloists stood she couldn't believe her eyes.

309

'They were ladies,' she told me, still sounding amazed.

The show ended, Ma and Arthur walked out into the spring evening, the air balmy and redolent of blossoms. Arm in arm they walked a few blocks, to a little bistro Art knew. He'd reserved the table under Ma's name, but he needn't have worried. Without his collar he wasn't recognized. In all the years he'd come to Symphony Hall, he had never encountered another priest.

For Ma it was the height of luxury: dinner downtown with her favorite son, at ten o'clock yet. For forty years she'd lived by Ted McGann's timetable — his shifts at the factory, the evening festivities from which she'd long been excluded, the nightly circuit of bars up and down the South Shore. Now Dad no longer goes out at night. He no longer notices time one way or the other, and yet Ma adheres to the old schedule: dinner cooked, served and eaten, the dishes washed and the kitchen sanitized, in time for the local news at six.

At the restaurant Arthur ordered mussels — Ma's favorite, though I have never known her to cook them at home. (Dad's interest in fish begins and ends with the Friday fry-up; I have never seen him touch shellfish of any kind.) With dinner she drank a pint of Guinness, another rare pleasure. She hadn't had a pint in donkey's years, had avoided the stuff entirely after Ted got bad. For years you couldn't have a sip in his presence; it wasn't worth the grief. I witnessed these arguments many times as a child: if Ma drank one, Dad considered it permission to finish the case.

The evening, for Ma, was magical. She will live on the memory forever, and I know that this was Art's intention. It was his way of saying goodbye.

★ ★ ★

The rain stopped just as we pulled in to the cemetery, but the sky couldn't be trusted. We assembled at the graveside beneath a dark green tent. It was an uncommonly sturdy model, chosen with Grantham burials in mind. The Galvin brothers manned it with the rough expertise of sailors, rushing to tie down a corner flap threatening to go airborne, leaving us mourners — a pitifully small group now — unprotected from the rain.

In nomine Patris, et Filii, et Spiritus Sancti. Father Fleury had changed out of his vestments, into clericals and a black balmacaan.

I glanced over Ma's shoulder, to see if any stragglers had joined us. To see for certain if the girl was gone. When the hearse parked at the foot of the hill, I'd glimpsed a young woman in blue jeans standing alone under the tent, gazing down into the empty hole. Art's headstone — Ma had chosen it a few days before — was already in place: FATHER ARTHUR HAROLD BREEN, GOD'S SERVANT. His grave set like a fancy banquet, waiting for the guest of honor to arrive.

The girl stood there a moment, smoking. Her hair — tousled, bottle-blond — whipped in the

311

wind. Then, spotting the hearse, she had hurried away, toward a lime-green Buick Regal parked at the crest of the hill. If Ma knew who she was, she gave no indication. She stared deliberately out the window, in the opposite direction, as if the girl were beneath her notice.

The girl's car started loudly, its radio blasting. I saw her arm flick a cigarette out the window. Then the Buick — scarcely smaller than our hearse — rolled slowly down the hill.

Now, conceding to the weather, Father Fleury sang an abbreviated blessing. *Recto tono*, plain chant: each syllable on the same note, a graceful lilt at the end of the phrase.

There was a long silence.

'Arthur's family invites all of you to join them at their home for coffee and refreshments,' he said softly. He sounded a bit abashed, like a Pavarotti obliged to interrupt his performance to point out the fire exits and toilets.

Another clap of thunder urged the mourners toward their cars, until only Ma and I stood at the grave site. I stared at Art's lovely container, delicate as a jewel box. It seemed a shame to put it in the ground. I imagined my brother inside it, dressed in his white alb, chasuble and stole. To my great relief we'd been spared what locals called *the viewing*. This is standard practice within my tribe, the Irish Catholic diaspora of Greater Boston: interminable hours at Galvin Brothers, the corpse primped and displayed like a hunter's trophy, ready to receive visitors. Ma had decided against it, fearing that someone would make a scene: a reporter, an angry parishioner, embittered Catholic activists from Voice of the Faithful. Or, just as devastatingly, that no one would show up at all.

I watched her approach the coffin and lay her hand gently upon it. Her eyes were tightly closed, as though she feared what she might see.

'Take your time,' I whispered. 'I'll meet you in the car.'

The Galvin brothers stood by at a respectful distance, hands clasped at groin level, the Adam pose. They are gentle bachelors, kind and self-effacing, alike as twins. The older Galvin had been a schoolmate of Leo McGann's, though if he noticed Leo's absence, or my father's, he gave no indication.

'About ready, then?'

'My mother needs a few more minutes.'

'Of course. No rush, dear.'

The *dear* was unconscious, nearly automatic; yet for some reason it made my throat ache. At that moment I couldn't bear even that small kindness. I turned away, blinking back tears.

Another gust of wind. The hearse waited at the bottom of the hill and I hurried toward it, holding down my skirt. It was the same dress I'd worn four years ago to Gram's wake, so distinctly funereal that it seemed logical to leave it hanging in my old bedroom closet in Grantham, to be worn again when the next relative died. It is an unspeakable thought, the dark actuarial calculation performed by those of us with aging parents, as one by one they falter and fail. Guiltily we wonder who will be next. For many years Dad had seemed the likeliest candidate. In those days, a late-night phone call could set my heart racing — the Massachusetts Staties surely, having pulled his remains from flaming wreckage, unwrapped his truck from around a tree. Dad is safe now, but Clare Boyle is ripe for a heart attack, and Leo's lungs won't last forever. As that whole generation shuffles toward the grave, who would have imagined that Art would be the next to go?

As I neared the hearse, I saw a woman struggling down the path, a stout white-haired person in a lavender coat.

'Fran,' I called.

She turned. 'Oh, Sheila. God help us.' Her eyes were swollen, her face streaked with tears.

'Watch your step.' I caught up with her and gave her my arm to lean on. 'It's slippery from the rain.'

We walked in silence for a few moments. I felt raindrops like pinpricks through the back of my dress.

'I'm surprised to see you here,' I said finally.

'I had to come. Father was good to me. To the whole parish. He was a good priest.' She lowered her voice. 'No matter what anybody says.'

Anybody. I wondered if she'd seen Kath earlier, hurrying away from the gravesite. My heart was racing. I had to ask.

'You don't believe it?'

'I don't know what to believe.' Fran stopped a moment to catch her breath. I saw that her chin was trembling. 'She's my own daughter. But Father was my friend.'

314

By local standards, Art's wake was a tame affair. This is natural enough, given the circumstances of his death and the nature of his occupation; still, it seemed an inadequate sendoff. Ma had put out a bottle of Jameson's, and a case of beer chilled in the refrigerator. I saw later that neither had been touched. In the basement my father watched the Sox lose to the Yankees. It was agreed that Mike would sit with him, a security measure that was probably unnecessary. The arrangement was fine by me. Since landing in Grantham I had avoided Mike completely; honestly, I couldn't stand to look at him. ('Get away from me,' I hissed when he tried to talk to me outside the church.) It seemed correct that he spend Art's wake confined to the basement. And judging by his hangdog look, Mike seemed to agree.

Ma sat in a corner with Father Fleury, who spoke to her in a low voice. Devines came and went; Mike's old buddy Tim Morrison. Clare Boyle held court in the kitchen. I poured coffee and offered sandwiches. Mike's boys had been left at home with Abby. There were no children in sight.

The day passed in a blur of condolences. Only two conversations stick in my mind. I was standing on the porch, saying goodbye to Tim Morrison, when an unfamiliar car parked at the curb. I stopped in mid-sentence to stare. On Teare Street, a Mercedes sedan was as exotic as a unicycle.

A well-dressed couple stepped out. Donald Burke introduced himself first. His wife excused herself delicately, and I saw that he wanted to speak to me alone.

'Thank you for coming,' I said. 'For all you did for my brother.' The words came out a bit awkwardly. In truth, I didn't know how to feel about this man. Had he encouraged Art to settle the lawsuit, to confess to the unspeakable? Did he really believe my brother was guilty?

Burke seemed to read my mind. 'I'm not sure how much I helped him. I would have defended him at trial, if it had come to that.' He hesitated, as if there was more he wanted to say. But attorneys, like doctors, keep the secrets of the dead.

'So what happens now?'

'As far as the court is concerned, Father's death has no bearing on anything. The settlement will go forward as planned. He was very conscientious about putting his affairs in order.'

I stared at him. 'You knew he was ill?'

'I had a hunch. Not from anything he told me, though.' Burke paused. 'He was a private guy.'

I said goodbye and left him on the porch. Inside, his wife was standing before the Altar, studying our family photos. 'You must be Sheila,' she said.

'Thank you for coming,' I said for the tenth or

twentieth time; the phrase had become automatic. Marilyn looked surprised.

'I had to,' she said simply. 'What they did to your brother was disgraceful. He was a wonderful priest.' She pressed my hand. 'My daughter adored him. I don't know how she made it through the funeral. She's very upset.'

She told me, then, a story I'd never heard. Caitlin Burke was fifteen when, riding her bicycle to the Y, she was struck by an SUV, a distracted driver talking on a cell phone. She spent two weeks in the hospital with a broken pelvis, another month in rehab.

'I'd just gone back to work, and I hated to leave her there. But Father sat with her every afternoon.' Marilyn paused. 'Cait was a picky eater — still is — so Father sneaked in egg rolls at lunchtime. He didn't miss a single day.'

'He never told me that,' I said.

'He wouldn't. He was very humble.' She said it in full voice, as though she wanted everyone to hear. 'He had no idea how much good he did.'

*   ★   ★

That evening, still in my funeral clothes, I met Clement Fleury at a bar he'd suggested. He was waiting when I arrived, a tall, somber man in his seventies, his blue eyes sharp, his wavy hair still more blond than gray. He'd abandoned his shiny black suit for a turtleneck and sport jacket — Italian, I think, and beautifully tailored, the fabric soft and fine. It suited him. In clericals he'd resembled an actor in costume, Richard

317

Chamberlain in *The Thorn Birds* (a film Ma had forbidden us to watch, deeming it both blasphemous and salacious). Even in his old age, Father Fleury is, like Richard Chamberlain, a bit too handsome for a priest.

I spotted him first, and stood a moment watching him. He might have been an aging movie actor or a wealthy European tourist, hopelessly lost in the Boston suburbs. The illusion was shattered the moment he spoke.

'Sheila,' he said, rising. 'It's good of you to meet me. I know this is a bit out of the way.' The gentle voice, the precise, pedantic diction: suddenly Clement Fleury exuded an ineffable priestliness, as though the Roman collar were tattooed on his skin.

'For you, too. Isn't your parish in — Wellesley?' Weston, Wayland, West Newton? One of Boston's posh western suburbs: W for Wealth.

'I like to avoid the local watering holes.' His voice — resonant, unabraded — seemed to belong to a much younger man.

'I guess it looks bad,' I said. 'Meeting a woman.'

He shrugged. 'Meeting a woman, meeting a man. God forbid, meeting a child. I'm a priest, my dear. In the current climate, any human interaction is suspect.'

I sat beside him and ordered a Guinness. He'd started without me, tipping back a short glass — gin or maybe vodka, I didn't ask. By my lights he had earned a drink, or several. It was Father Fleury who'd found my brother slumped at the kitchen table in his apartment at Dover Court.

On that table were an overflowing ashtray and a glass smelling of whiskey, with which Art had washed down the pills.

'You knew he was sick,' I said.

He nodded. Art hadn't *felt* ill, not yet; but for several months the slightest exertion had left him breathless. His cough sent shivers up Fran Conlon's spine. Once, while sorting the laundry, she'd noticed blood in his handkerchief. It was Fran who'd pestered him to see his doctor: *Go in for a checkup, Father. Get your tires kicked.*

'Why didn't he tell us?' I demanded.

'He felt the family had suffered enough.'

Art had seen his internist the day after Easter, a routine checkup he'd postponed several times. Over the next few weeks, more appointments followed. Tests were performed: X rays, CT scan, MRI, bronchoscopy. Later, as I studied his datebook, I would note a succession of doctors' names. Their specialties I gleaned from the Yellow Pages: pulmonology, oncology, radiology. The tumor was in the mediastinal region of his left lung, inoperable.

'The treatment would have been ghastly,' Father Fleury said.

I'd gathered this already, from *Small-Cell Carcinoma and You*. The drugs would be injected three days in a row, the cycle repeated every three weeks. I'd done the math: Art was facing a half year of chemotherapy. In addition, for the first month, his chest would be blasted with radiation: fifteen minutes, five days a week, to specific areas on both sides of the thorax. The oncologist would have explained this in some

319

detail, as the nurse marked Art's skin with a felt-tip pen.

'I could have come back here to help him,' I said. 'I could have taken a leave of absence from school.'

Father Fleury gave me a look of gentle rebuke, and I thought of the generations of schoolboys shamed into learning by that look.

'Arthur wouldn't have permitted that. It's the last thing he would have wanted — to be a burden to you.'

As the treatments went on, Art would have grown weaker. He'd have been unable to drive himself to the clinic. In his briefcase, along with the pamphlet, I'd found a business card:

THE CARE SHUTTLE

A free service for patients on the South Shore.

Our clients generally live alone. No family, I'd been told, by the woman who answered the phone there. *You'd be amazed how many people are alone in the world.*

Was this how Art had seen himself? I thought again of the pamphlet: the middle-aged couple walking hand in hand down a road I couldn't imagine walking at all, never mind alone.

'My mother would have helped. And our brother Mike lives in Quincy.' Even as I said it, I

320

felt foolish. This man had known my brother nearly forty years; I was still in diapers when he'd taught Art to decline verbs at St. John's. Clement Fleury had been Art's teacher, confessor, spiritual advisor and confidant. He probably knew more about my family than I did.

'Michael,' he said. 'Yes. Arthur spoke of him a great deal.'

There was a long silence.

'So Art couldn't face the treatment,' I said.

'This particular cancer has a high rate of recurrence.' He stared into his drink. 'Arthur might have endured months of treatment only to have it come back in a year.'

'So he was going to die anyway?'

'My dear, we're all going to die.'

We sat in silence, drinking. My mind hummed with questions I couldn't bring myself to speak. For Art's particular cancer, chemo and radiation are given together, and their side effects — what the pamphlet called 'Ins and Outs' — are amplified. Nausea, difficulty swallowing, inflamm- ation of the lungs. Diarrhea, kidney malfunctions, infections, crushing fatigue. Weight loss, hair loss, hearing loss. Other losses, too, beyond the scope of the pamphlet: loss of dignity, purpose, heart and hope. Though Art had perhaps already lost those things.

'You saw him before he died,' I said. 'I saw it in his datebook. You had dinner the night before.'

'Yes,' he said softly. 'We'd been trying for some time to get together. I was in Rome for Easter and ended up staying longer than I'd planned.' His voice trailed off. 'I knew Arthur's situation,

321

of course. We spoke often by phone. I should have come back immediately when the Cardinal suspended him. That was my mistake.'

'That night,' I said. 'How was he?'

'You're asking if I saw it coming? No, I didn't. Though perhaps I should have.' He drained his glass. 'He'd been despondent for some time, as I'm sure you know. But that night he was different, animated. Strange as it sounds, he seemed happy.' He closed his eyes as though trying to visualize it. 'I suppose he'd already made his decision.'

I stared into my glass. This was what I wanted to hear: that Art's decision had been firm, immutable. That there was nothing I could have done to stop him. And yet, that final morning, he'd kept his appointment at the clinic, as though living still interested him. As though he might, still, change his mind.

My throat ached with unshed tears.

'It's a sin, isn't it? Suicide. Even in a case like this.'

To my surprise, the answer mattered a great deal.

The priest covered my hand with his. 'It's true that despair is a very serious sin, the most serious of all. The Church defines it as losing all hope of salvation. But I don't believe Arthur felt that way. He was at peace with his God, and with his death. His faith was very strong.'

He signaled the bartender and pointed to his glass.

'As Catholics we believe it is wrong to hasten natural death under any circumstances. Of course Arthur knew that. Though in my view, that's between your brother and God.'

We watched the bartender fill his glass.

'After our dinner together, I felt uneasy. I tried to call him the next day, several times, but he didn't answer. That's why I went to his apartment. On some level, I suppose, I knew.'

He'd found Art's door locked, the rental office closed. When he called the after-hours emergency number, Mrunal Patel came and opened the door. Father Fleury gave my brother the Last Rites. He looked for and found Art's briefcase, which contained his wallet, cell phone and health insurance card. When the ambulance arrived, he followed it to the hospital, and from the emergency room called my mother and me. The next day, the briefcase and its contents were given to us at the hospital. A nurse had placed it in a clear plastic bag, along with the clothes Art was wearing when he died.

'You were very dear to Arthur,' said Father Fleury. 'You and Michael both, but you especially. You believed in his innocence. It meant everything to him.'

The words burned into me. *I didn't*, I wanted to say. *I doubted him in the end.*

He reached into his jacket and handed me a bright green envelope. 'I found this in Arthur's apartment. I took it before the police came. I imagine that's a crime of some sort.'

'What is it?'

Again the rebuking look. Father Fleury did not suffer fools. 'A letter, I assume.'

The envelope had been recycled — Art's own

name crossed out, 'Sheila' scrawled above it in black marker, in my brother's jagged hand. Unsealed: I wondered, for a moment, if Father Fleury had opened it.

His face was inscrutable. 'It's addressed to you,' he said, as if reading my thoughts.

That night I lay awake in my girlhood room, waiting for morning. At dawn I drove across town to Dunster. In my handbag, folded in half, was the green envelope.

I had trouble finding the address. I haven't lived on the South Shore in twenty years, and I'd never had any reason to spend time in Dunster. Fenno Street is only four blocks long, a narrow after-thought running between two busy avenues. The neighborhood was dead that Sunday morning, Kath and her neighbors sleeping off the weekend. I knocked several times at the front door, but no one answered. Relieved, I drove away.

That night I flew back to Philadelphia, where my presence was required at graduation. Weeks would pass before I returned to Fenno Street, on a rainy Friday afternoon — the summer solstice, the longest day of the year. The house looked abandoned and a little sinister. Shades — not Venetian blinds, but flimsy sheets of white vinyl — were pulled all the way to the sills. I would have driven away again, had I not spotted the lime-green Buick parked at the end of the block, as if wanting nothing to do with that house.

I crossed the street in the rain and climbed the porch steps; finding no bell, I knocked firmly at the door. Instantly I saw movement at a window, the vinyl shade quivering, as though someone were peeking from behind it.

The door opened a crack.

'Kathleen Conlon?'

She threw the door open, squaring her shoulders, a scrawny thing in jeans and a tank top. I was struck by her smallness — her arms were thin as a child's — and her swagger. Kath Conlon came out swinging.

'Look,' she said, 'I fucken paid him. What does he want from me, blood?'

'No, it's nothing like that — '

'I have a lawyer. Tell Finn I'll sue him for harassment. Ever heard of tenants' rights? I have a kid, for Christ's sake. What's he going to do, put us out in the street?' Her speech was fast, a little garbled, her eyes shifting rapidly. I was no expert, but even I could see that she was high.

I have since learned a few things about crystal meth — according to Art and her mother, Kath's drug of choice. A few of its effects — wild energy, aggressiveness, paranoia — resemble those of cocaine, a drug nearly ubiquitous on college campuses in the 1980s, where my nodding acquaintance with it began and ended. But a meth high, I'm told, is trippier. Hallucinations are common, visual and auditory. Danny Yeager, the school guidance counselor — I didn't yet call him my boyfriend — had attended grad school in Iowa. He'd interned at a substance-abuse clinic at a time when meth labs were exploding, literally, across the Midwest: in rural Kansas and Nebraska, trailers and motel rooms bursting into flames.

Kath Conlon stared at me, her toe tapping manically. Her skin was very pale, her chin studded with acne. Her lower jaw slid back and forth as though something slippery were caught between her teeth. And yes, Danny Yeager: she was tense, agitated. Frankly, she seemed terrified, though I don't believe she was delusional. Flip Finn, I later learned, really *was* trying to evict her. She hadn't paid rent in several months.

'I don't want your money. I saw you that day at the cemetery. You knew my brother. Father Breen.'

It's impossible to describe what came over her face at that moment. Her jaws stilled; her eyes softened. For a moment I thought she was going to cry.

'He was your brother?' she said softly. 'How did you find me?'

'I talked to your mother.' A stiff wind blew across the porch, sweeping rain against my back. 'Hey, I'm getting soaked out here. Can I come in?'

Kath hesitated a moment. Then she took a step back and let me inside.

The dark living room was a shambles: clothing piled everywhere, toys and magazines littering the floor. The television had been unplugged and sat in a corner facing the wall, as though being punished for bad behavior. In the center of the room, crumbling plaster had been swept into a pile. I glanced around looking for its source and saw a jagged hole in the wall, the approximate size of a man's fist.

I followed her into the kitchen, where she moved some clutter from the table — beer cans, a pizza box — and offered me a seat. Kath lit a cigarette and stood with her back to the counter, also littered with trash. I remember empty soda bottles, wrappers from Oreos and frozen burritos, crumpled cigarette packs. A KFC bucket filled, inexplicably, with dirt, as though something were planted inside it. She stood before this display defensively, I thought, her skinny arms crossed over her chest.

'We have to be quiet,' she said in a low voice. 'My boyfriend is sleeping.'

'Kevin?'

'You know him?' Her eyes darted anxiously. 'Jesus, how much did that old bag tell you?'

It took me a moment to understand that the *old bag* was her frantic mother — kindly, heartbroken Fran.

'Art told me,' I said. 'I'm Sheila, by the way. My brother talked about you.'

'He never told me he was sick.' She blinked rapidly. 'The paper said he had cancer.'

'Yes,' I said.

'But he quit smoking! He *quit*!' For a moment she sounded like a child, stunned by the injustice, howling in outrage and disbelief.

'He smoked for thirty years,' I said softly. 'My whole life, practically. I can't remember a time when he didn't smoke.'

I watched her closely.

'Actually,' I went on, 'I was amazed when he quit. He did it for Aidan, you know. He didn't want to smoke around your son.'

328

Kath dragged fiercely on her cigarette, her eyes welling with tears.

'Where *is* Aidan?'

'My mother's.' She inhaled sharply. 'Is it true that he offed himself?'

I flinched.

'Yes,' I said.

'Jesus, no.' Her eyes rolled heavenward; all at once tears rolled down her face. For a moment she looked as young as one of my students, a teenager reprimanded by a teacher, crushed by a boyfriend. For some reason this enraged me.

'OxyContin,' I said pitilessly. She wanted details, I had details. 'He took a whole fistful. When they found him he was already blue.'

'He kept them?'

I stared at her, mystified. 'What are you talking about?'

'They were mine. He took them from me, and I guess he kept them. It was my fault,' she moaned. 'What I said about him and Aidan.'

Time seemed to slow then, or maybe it was my imagination. I had to ask.

'Why did you do it? How could you say those things?'

Kath's eyes darted around the room. I had the distinct sense that she was seeing something I wasn't. 'It was Kevin's idea. He saw those stories in the paper.'

I heard movement in the next room, the bedsprings creaking. 'Kath?' a man's voice called.

Her face froze. 'Oh, Jesus. That's him. You better go.' She butted her cigarette in the sink.

'Wait a minute — '

'He's sick, all right? He's in a shitty mood.'

Are you safe here? I wanted to ask. *Are you in danger?* For a split second I reacted just as my brothers had. I wanted to take care of her.

'Please,' she whispered. 'Just go.' Hastily she unlocked the back door.

I rose to go, peering briefly into the sink. One of its basins had become a cigarette graveyard, a damp, fetid mound of butts. I reached into my handbag for the green envelope.

'He asked me to give this to you.' I handed over the envelope. 'He loved you.'

She took it from my hands, wiping her nose with her bare arm. She mumbled something unintelligible.

It might have been 'I loved him, too.'

The green envelope contained two letters. One was addressed to me. Judging by the handwriting — still firm and decisive — I'd guess Art wrote this one first.

You were a rare child, and are a rare woman. Never fear the part of you that is extraordinary. You are God's child still.

There was more, of course; but they were my brother's last words to me, and I am not willing to share them. It's enough to say that the letter was full of regrets and blessings, and one final request.

Sheila, I know you'll do this for me. There's nobody else I can ask.

The other, longer letter — truly a lost gospel — was addressed to Kath.

In the lobby at Dover Court is a large brass mailbox, thirty-six steps — I have counted — from Art's front door. How easy it would have been, even in a drugged stupor, to walk from apartment to elevator to lobby and back again, to entrust to the United States Postal Service this final, critical task.

Instead Art placed Kath's letter, and mine, in the green envelope. Both unsealed. I believe he meant for me to read them both, and that is what I did.

The human heart: its expansions and contractions, its electrics and hydraulics, the warm tides that move and fill it. For years Art had studied it from a safe distance, from many perspectives — the engaged couples appearing at his rectory; the middle-aged spouses seeking counsel; the widows and widowers numb with grief or relief. Father Breen listened in fascination and revulsion, in envy and pity. He dispensed canned wisdom, a little scripture. He sent them on their way with a prayer.

For years he had shrunk from their moist human anguish. Their needs were troubling symptoms, of an illness to which he was blessedly immune. It was a secret he'd carried since childhood: sexual need, that most primal instinct, was simply beyond him, a drive he had never felt.

Could he love as other men loved?

His whole life he'd been haunted by the question. He'd concluded, finally, that he was broken — the mechanism frozen by disuse or by something more sinister, the trauma he'd suffered as a child. He was not insensible to beauty. The Cindy Clays of the world, its lilac-scented females, were a pleasure to behold. But his response was aesthetic rather than erotic: a weak mimicry of desire, a cool appreciation of what would move another man, a normal man, to his core. Other men could be gripped by this yearning, ruled by it, ruined by it. From a distance Art had seen the grim consequences. Through marriages and families it scorched a devastated trail.

There was celibacy, and there was chastity. At seminary he'd learned they were two different things. A celibate priest had no sexual contact with anybody. But what about his private thoughts, what he did when he was alone? Chastity, it was explained, was a loftier goal: perfect self-containment, complete purity in thought, word and deed. After urging the boys to mind their *vessels*, Father Koval had acknowledged that chastity was a tall order, a level of mastery few men could ever attain. Hearing this, young Arthur Breen had felt a certain smugness: he would be one of the exalted few. In those years his frigidity had seemed a rare talent, a gift like his celibacy; it was the original gift that made the other possible. He'd imagined it, even, a kind of superpower, like flying or X-ray vision — an ability denied to ordinary men.

Later he was ashamed of his hubris. First year of seminary, the *Confessions* of St. Augustine: *To abstain from sin when one cannot sin is to be forsaken by sin, not to forsake it.* Gradually he came to see himself as stunted, maimed like the poor *castrati*, their manhood stolen. Not extraordinary, but less, much less, than ordinary.

Could he love as other men loved?

The doubt was always with him, buried like some dark evidence. As though asking the question were itself a crime.

333

Years ago, his anxieties had come to the surface. He was stationed, then, at St. Rose of Lima, and made daily visits to the parish school. When a fifth-grade teacher was hospitalized with pneumonia, Art took over her classroom, teaching religion and music. A male teacher was a novelty at St. Rose, and the children idolized him — the boys especially, after so many years of being minded by nuns.

They were the happiest months of his ministry. Teaching satisfied him deeply: the affection of his small pupils, the camaraderie of the faculty lounge. His colleagues welcomed him. A pretty math teacher named April Horner even flirted a little, and Art allowed himself this small diversion. There was nothing in the Rule against having an attractive friend.

For the first time in his adult life, he took a hard look at his future. To his surprise he saw not a single road, but a maze of highways, interconnecting. There was no telling where they might lead. Alone, late at night, he imagined a different life at St. Rose, not as a priest but as a lay teacher. His own apartment, April Horner his girlfriend. (Was he attracted to her? The question plagued him. He'd been willing — almost — to find out.)

Then, halfway through the school year, he saw a news report on television: a preschool in California, its entire staff marched away in handcuffs. A whole team of Ferguses, apparently, with daily access to children. Quickly Art turned off the television, as though the image burned his eyes.

The events of his childhood had never left him. Instead the memory had grown watery, indistinct, like something he'd dreamed. *Abused, molested*: these were not terms he used, even to himself. When he recalled those Saturday afternoons — which wasn't often — he had no vocabulary to describe what had happened. His uncle's name, *Fergus*, became shorthand for the act.

Now, suddenly, the story was everywhere: newspapers, magazines. Wherever he turned, a psychologist was discussing *pedophilia*. Undoubtedly he'd heard the term before, but never with such numbing frequency. Again and again he heard the assertion — made with *ex cathedra* assurance — that abuse begot abusers. That a child who'd been molested would grow up to do the same. In psychological circles this was apparently common knowledge, but to Art it was a shattering discovery. His potential career as teacher, his new life at St. Rose: he saw them, suddenly, through different eyes. His fondness for his pupils, the comfort and delight he took in their company: what dark needs drove him to crave their attention?

Children and women, women and children. He spurned them, now, for corollary reasons: he feared being drawn to one, and feeling nothing for the other. In pastoral life, both were easy to avoid. He hid behind his cassock and his confessional. The altar boys he entrusted to colleagues. The schoolchildren he left strictly to the nuns.

This system served him even as it isolated him — until that spring day in 2001, when Kath Conlon appeared at his rectory with her son.

★ ★ ★

They swept into his life like weather, a sudden nor'easter: the beginning of his *annus mirabilis*.

Year of wonders.

'Father, I want you to meet someone. This is my daughter, Kathleen.'

The morning was balmy, almost summerlike; yet as they stood at his office window, watching the boy rushed by seagulls, he had sensed her shivering beside him. Her eyes were bloodshot, her complexion ashen. From his time among the homeless of the South End, he remembered the signs of intoxication. He saw instantly that she was high.

'Are you all right?' he asked softly.

Her eyes darted toward him, then away. 'Yeah. Fine. Why?'

'Does Fran know you're using?'

'I'm *not*.' She glanced furtively out the window. 'Jesus, it's nothing. I ran into someone at a party. Are you going to tell her?'

'Give me one reason I shouldn't.'

'She'll call the cops. I just got off probation. They could take my kid.'

In the kitchen the screen door slammed. Fran's heavy tread on the linoleum, Aidan scampering ahead.

'Please,' Kath whispered.

'I'm watching you,' Art said.

336

From the first she had tested him: all that the cassock demanded, and all that it forbade. For years he'd complained to Clem Fleury that he felt irrelevant — at weddings and funerals, a bit player in black clericals; a droll little penguin at council meetings and bingo games. Now he found himself in a genuine moral quandary. What he did next, or failed to do, would have tangible consequences — for Kath and her son, for Fran and for himself.

Your daughter is on drugs, he might have said as Fran entered the room.

Instead he stepped up and took the boy's hand.

He kept his promise: he watched her. Whenever possible he watched her son. That day, leading Aidan across the schoolyard, Art had plied him with gentle questions. Did his mother stay up late? Sleep all day? Did she disappear into the bathroom for long stretches, locking the door behind her?

'She used to,' Aidan admitted. 'Not no more.'

'Not *any* more.' For reasons he couldn't have explained, the grammatical error delighted him. And Art, who hadn't touched a child in many years, tousled the boy's hair.

It amazed him, in retrospect, how quickly he'd become enmeshed in their lives. With much huffing and puffing he moved their furniture into the new apartment he'd found for her — in a safe neighborhood, a cheap but decent part of Dunster. Importantly, it was on the bus line to

Dorchester, so that when her Buick died she'd have a way to work. She had bought the car over Art's objections. When the timing belt went, it was Art who paid to have it replaced.

While her car was in the shop, he got into the habit of driving Aidan home from the rectory in the evenings. Tuesday and Friday nights, while Kath attended AA meetings, Art read to the boy and put him to bed. Then he made a discreet inspection of the apartment. He opened drawers and cupboards, inventoried the medicine chest. He knew roughly what to look for: needles, spoons, rolling papers. Though what exactly he'd do if he found them, he had no idea.

For Aidan, he told himself as he crept into Kath's bedroom. The bed was neatly made with a flowered quilt. As he pulled back the sheet and felt under the mattress, a memory came to him unbidden, his mother folding her nightgown and tucking it beneath the pillow. A pure flash of his own boyhood, forgotten these forty years.

Under Kath's pillow he found a silky black camisole. His cheeks flaming, he replaced it and remade the bed.

The dresser top was littered with perfumes and lotions, a lighted mirror for makeup. It was an item he associated with actresses, chorus girls. He remembered that she had been a dancer. In San Diego, in rooms full of strange men, she had taken off her clothes.

That night they sat in her kitchen drinking coffee. Like Art she was a night owl, immune to the effects of caffeine.

'What was it like?' he asked her. 'The first time you did it.'

'Cold,' she said.

Aha, he thought. His attempts to counsel her had so far been fruitless. He had found her impermeable, hard-shelled like a crab. Now — at long last — he detected remorse.

'Cold in what way?' he asked gently, intending to draw her out. It would be therapeutic, he felt. Probably she'd never spoken about what she'd suffered, the soul-chilling anomie.

She had done a tryout for the club's owner, brought with her a tape of a song she liked. An old one; maybe he'd remember it. Had he ever listened to Luna Sky?

'No,' Art said.

Anyway. It was late afternoon, summertime. Outside the sun was blazing, but the club was fucken freezing. Only the stage was warm, like being under a French fry lamp. Kath was always glad to step out on stage, glad to be in the light.

Against his will Art pictured it, her slim body swaying and writhing. I shouldn't be listening to this, he thought. But he was determined, still, to counsel her, to prove himself equal to the task.

'But wasn't it — demeaning? To be ogled by strangers. Men who don't know you, or care about you.' He had never felt less equipped to counsel anyone. Had never felt more acutely what he was: a middle-aged epicene, a castrato, a prig.

Kath eyed him irritably. 'Oh, Jesus. What are you, my father?'

Had he ever been misread so completely? Art

was both offended and relieved. Never in his life had he felt less fatherly. Yet, in this instance, it was far better to be misconstrued.

★　★　★

Long evenings at her kitchen table, the boy asleep in the next room. After that one attempt, he did not ask about her past. Instead he focused on the future. What sort of life did she want for her and Aidan? Had she considered continuing her education? What did she believe God wanted for her?

Her responses were frustratingly opaque. By nature or necessity she refused self-examination. 'I don't think about that shit. That stuff,' she corrected herself. 'I live in the moment, you know? At AA they tell you to take one day at a time.'

Art tried a different tack: What did she want for Aidan?

'To be somebody,' she said promptly. Not like herself or her older brothers — one a prison guard at Walpole, the other chronically unemployed. She grinned slyly. 'Maybe he could be a priest.'

Was she mocking him?

'Is that something you would want for him?' he asked cautiously.

'Why not?' she said. 'He's smart, like you.'

'Me?' Pleasure flooded him like liquid filling a glass.

'You're the smartest person I know.' She smiled then, a genuine smile, free of mockery.

340

She had a lovely smile.

'It isn't an easy life,' he said softly. He'd been careful, always, to keep himself out of their conversations. Through pointed questions he had controlled the dialogue. Kath hadn't minded, or perhaps hadn't noticed. She had never asked a single question about him.

'It's a solitary life.' He chose his words carefully, consciously avoiding the word *lonely*. 'It demands a certain temperament. I suppose it helps to be a loner.'

'Is that what you are?'

'At one time I thought so. Now I'm not so sure.' He looked down into his cup. 'It gets harder with age. Priests make a great many sacrifices. I'm very aware of all I have missed.'

'Like what?' said Kath, her eyes serious. For once she wasn't teasing him.

He looked around the apartment, Aidan's drawings on the refrigerator, his small shoes and Kath's sandals lined up neatly at the door. 'I'll never have what you have. A family. I would have liked that.' He had never said the words aloud. As he did, he realized they were true.

'You would have been a great father,' she said. 'Aidan loves you.'

They sat there a long moment. But for Art the silence was charged with emotion. He wondered if Kath felt it, too. How did anyone know, ever, what another person was feeling? As a priest he had rarely wondered. Laypeople — he saw it now — lived much more complicated lives.

Art said, 'I love him, too.'

And after that night something shifted. More and more he found himself confiding in her.

One night Kath asked him, 'Have you ever been in love?'

'I love God,' Art said, his heart racing. 'I try to love all my parishioners. And of course I love my mother and my brother and my sister. But, no. Not in the way you mean.' He hesitated. 'I've often wondered if I'm capable of it.'

Another confession he'd never before made, words he'd never said aloud.

'That must sound ridiculous to you,' he said quickly. 'A man of my age. I suppose you've been in love many times.'

Her eyes narrowed. 'Are you calling me a slut?'

'No! I only meant — '

'Relax,' she said, grinning. 'I'm just messing with you.'

He hesitated a moment, paralyzed with embarrassment. Then, out of sheer nervousness, he laughed. What a relief, that laughter! What a blessed release.

'I've never been in love, either.' Her voice was small, her eyes shining. For a moment she looked no older than Aidan.

'Not with Aidan's father?' Art had never mentioned the man before; he'd never felt he had the right.

'I liked him,' she said slowly. 'At the beginning anyway. He seemed different. He never came to the club. He hated that I worked there.'

'That's understandable. I suppose I'd feel the same way.' Art hesitated. 'You know, as a man.'

'He wanted me to quit. And I did, for a while. I did everything he wanted. He hated my friends, so I stopped seeing them. He wanted us to move far way. We had to, he said, because every guy in San Diego had seen my tits.'

Art's face burned. Thank God, thank God for the dark.

'I was like a prisoner in that apartment,' said Kath. 'He wouldn't let me go anywhere alone. The sick thing is, I liked it at first. I thought he was protecting me.'

'Maybe he was,' said Art.

'Oh yeah?' She eyed him levelly. 'Like when he used to lock me in the apartment before he went to work?'

'On purpose?' Art said, aghast. 'Dear God. Did you call the police?'

Kath snorted. 'With what we were into? No way was I calling the cops.'

Art stared in disbelief.

'I had to get out of there. So I ran away.' She paused. 'I had a friend in L.A., a girl I used to dance with. When I found out I was pregnant, I stayed with her right up to the end. I didn't want him seeing me that way.'

'You never told him?' Art said. 'About Aidan?'

'Nope. He shipped out, and I went back to San Diego. Six weeks after Aidan came, I went back to work.'

Again the visions: Kath dancing. Art pushed them out of his head.

'You're embarrassed,' she said.

'Not at all.'

'Liar.' She grinned.

'Okay, a little embarrassed.'

A long silence.

'But I'm wondering, too. Being a mother — ' He broke off. 'Didn't you consider some other kind of work?'

'Like what? Brain surgery?' She shifted in her chair. 'I had a kid to support. How else was I going to make that kind of money? Eight hundred a night?'

'That much?' Art said, astounded. 'For dancing?'

She explained it then: the VIP room in the back, the curtained booths where customers paid extra for private dances. *Lap dances*. He was too embarrassed to ask what exactly that entailed. Later, alone in bed, a hundred questions filled his mind. What did Kath wear while lap dancing? Was the man's lap clothed, or exposed? If his life depended on it, he could not have worked up the nerve to ask.

Night after night in the dim kitchen. The confidences exchanged. Then one Thursday Kath came home late. For nearly two hours Art waited. Finally, at just before midnight, he heard her car at the curb.

'Where were you?' he demanded. 'I was worried.'

'I had a meeting.'

'Hours ago. Where have you been?'

'I ran into an old friend. We stopped out to hear a band.'

'You went to a bar.'

Her smile faded. 'I'm not using,' she said flatly. 'I haven't touched the stuff in donkey's years.'

Donkey's years. It was what his own mother — our mother — might have said. Art thought of the old apartment in Jamaica Plain, high above the neighborhood noise, Mrs. Ruocco's grandchildren, the boisterous Sullivans. His childhood before Ted McGann had muscled into their lives. Ma tired, always, from the long shifts at Raytheon, but still dressing for the dances on a Friday night, her hair in rollers, a cigarette burning in an ashtray. Ma had been just like Kath Conlon: just that avid, and lonely, and young.

★ ★ ★

Summer came. With school ended, Aidan spent whole days at the rectory, a fact noticed and commented upon. Once, at a council meeting, Kay Cleary made a snide comment about *Father Breen's kindergarten.* Art ignored the jibe. For the first time he understood that summer vacation was a hardship for working parents, a fact that had never occurred to him. It made him wonder what else he'd failed to notice, just how blind he'd been to the difficulties of his people's lives.

'I wish I could go with you,' Kath often said when he planned their excursions. And finally, on the last Thursday of August, she did. *It's my kid's birthday,* she told Chris Winter, who gave her the day off. To join Art and Aidan for an afternoon at Nantasket Beach.

They set out after lunch, with a cooler full of drinks and snacks. Art had bought a pair of swim trunks for the occasion. At the back of his closet he'd found a pair of flip-flops, a garish Hawaiian shirt he'd bought on a dare in Miami, where he'd traveled one year for a pastoral conference. For a man who dressed always in black, this bright getup felt like a costume, a kind of reverse camouflage.

At Nantasket Beach they parked and unloaded the car. Driving east into the bright sun, he'd been dogged by a creeping sense of déjà vu, but it wasn't until Kath called to Aidan — *Help Father with the cooler!* — that he recognized the scene from his own childhood. How strange, how disorienting, to find himself in the man's seat, driving, when in his mind he was still the little boy.

The morning was bright, the beach crowded. Kath spread out the flowered quilt she'd taken from her bed. She kicked off her sandals and squealed delightedly as she dug her toes into the sand. Toes small and plump like a child's, the nails painted metallic blue.

She pulled her T-shirt over her head, a moment Art had anticipated. He'd rehearsed in his mind the proper way to react. Turning away slightly, feigning some busyness with the umbrella Fran had insisted they bring, he sensed rather than saw her breasts and bare belly, her shoulders and thighs. The individual parts were much as he'd pictured them, and yet he was unprepared for the effect in aggregate.

346

(Ted McGann whistling: *That right there was worth the trip.*)

When at last her back was turned, he allowed himself to study this neutral part of her, the long, smooth plane of it, the slight indentations on either side of her lower spine. He slipped off his shirt. On the crowded beach he was like any middle-aged man in swim trunks; no one could see that he had prised away the cold cataphract of the priesthood, the invisible armor that had imprisoned him for years.

Art sat quickly, his duffel bag in his lap. At that moment Aidan ran to him squealing. 'Can I? Iggy used to let me.'

(Iggy, he'd told Art, had been Mom's friend in San Diego. But she didn't like him anymore.)

Nimbly he straddled Art's shoulders. 'Take me for a ride!'

Kath laughed silently, a trick of the wind: a stiff breeze blowing the sound out to sea.

Art had never been so close to a woman wearing so little. That the woman was beautiful and dear to him, that he'd told her things he'd never told a living soul: this would have been more than enough even without the dreamlike echo of another moment, equally potent. For it seemed to him, the whole day long, that both reels were rolling at once, his boyhood and manhood, the indelible past and achingly tangible present. The boy he'd been and the man he was; the woman he couldn't look at and the child clambering over him.

The afternoon was rife with such moments. It seemed to him, later, that in those hours he lived many lives. He watched Aidan race up and down the beach like a crazed gerbil, Kath preening like a cat, dozing in the sun. Once, twice, she rose and stretched, strolled languidly in the direction of the bathhouse. 'I'll be back in a minute,' she said.

Art watched her go, grateful for his mirrored sunglasses. All day long he'd felt it. Now it struck with full force.

What a man feels.

At one time the choice had seemed binary: he could become a man, or become a priest. He'd felt, for various reasons, that he had a better shot at the latter. And it wasn't entirely welcome news — he wasn't entirely overjoyed — to discover he was both.

★   ★   ★

They ate fried clams for dinner, then packed up the car. Stuck in beach traffic, they amused themselves with the radio. Art's was preset to the classic rock station, a fact that delighted Kath.

'What did you expect?' he asked. 'Gregorian chant?'

A bright patter of talk and commercials; then came the first familiar strains of strings and piano.

'Oh,' said Kath. 'I love this song.'

A little shyly at first, Art sang along: *Yesterday, all my troubles seemed so far away.* He stole a sideways glance, expecting an ironic smirk. Kath stared at him in wonderment.

'Wow,' she said. 'You can sing.'

'All priests sing.'

'Not like that.' Kath eyed him shyly. 'You could have been — I don't know, a Beatle or something.'

Art burst into laughter.

'I'm serious,' she said. 'You could have been a star.'

She leaned forward and fiddled with the dial. 'Enough with the sad songs.' She dialed past a jazz station, country, NPR. 'All right, rock star. How about this?'

'Piece of cake.' And in his best falsetto he began:

In the still of the night I hear the wolf
    howl honey
Sniffing around your door

It wasn't anything Father Dowd would have applauded; it wasn't singing, it was howling. Art had spent a thousand hours alone in the car cutting up with the radio. Never in his life had he imagined doing it for an audience. Kath clapped delightedly. And at the ripe age of fifty Art learned what other males discovered at puberty, the reason teenage boys join bands in the first place.

★　★　★

It was nearly dark when they turned on to Fenno Street. Art parked in front of the house. Aidan snored softly in the backseat.

'I can't believe he slept through that,' said Art.

349

'He's used to it. I play music all the time.' Kath looked over her shoulder. 'I hate to wake him.'

'Let me,' Art said, getting out of the car.

He reached into the backseat and took the boy in his arms. Aidan stirred, mumbled, settled against him. I am touching a child, Art thought, but the thought did not alarm him. He was part of the universe of caring adults; he was no Fergus. In a moment of rare clarity he understood the difference.

Moment of grace.

He carried the boy inside to his bed. 'You get him settled,' he whispered to Kath. 'I'll unpack the car.'

Outside he opened the trunk; he took out the kite, the sandy blanket, Kath's quilted bag. As he lifted it a bottle rolled out, amber plastic. Squinting, he held it close to the dim trunk light. Without his glasses he could scarcely make out the label: **Althea Ferguson Oxycodone 10 MG Take as needed for pain.**

He waited for Kath in the kitchen.

'Who is Althea Ferguson?'

She stared at him blankly.

'A friend of yours?' Art produced the bottle from his pocket. 'I suppose she must be, since her medication was in your bag.'

Kath's face closed. 'You went through my stuff?'

'I did not. It rolled out of your bag.' He stared at her, waiting. 'Well?'

'Yeah. Althea. I picked up her medicine for her. So what?'

350

'I've known a few Altheas in my life. Not one of them was younger than eighty. You have many friends that age?'

She did not respond.

'Kathleen?'

'All right. Fine. It's Oxy.'

'I know exactly what it is.' He had seen a news report on television: Hillbilly heroin, they called it. Addicts crushed the pills, then smoked or injected it. Pharmacies wouldn't keep it in stock, for fear of being robbed.

'Where did you get this?' he demanded.

'Some guy at the beach. I didn't go looking for it.'

He thought of her walking off toward the bathhouse, not once but twice. He'd been so distracted by her body that he'd never guessed she was going to score drugs.

'So a total stranger just offered you a bottle of OxyContin?'

'He wasn't a stranger. I knew him in high school, okay?' She met Art's gaze. 'I was different then. I'd do anything.'

'Did you pay for this?'

The smirk returned. A contemptuous look, he thought, disdainful of his ignorance. 'I never pay.'

He saw that she was boasting, daring him to wonder what she'd done instead, what favors she'd offered as payment. Hoping, through shock and titillation, to distract him. But Art would not be deterred.

'Have you taken these before?'

'No,' Kath said.

His mind raced. She had betrayed his trust, probably not for the first time. If she wasn't using now — *if!* — she would be soon enough. He thought of the boy asleep in his arms, Aidan at the mercy of a drug-addled mother. An intolerable situation; he would not tolerate it. But what, exactly, could he do? The drug was not illegal; was there any point in calling the police? He thought fleetingly of his brother, who still had friends on the force. Mike would know what to do.

'I'm sorry,' she said in a low voice. 'I wasn't going to get high. I don't even like that shit. It's like being dead, except you're awake for it.'

'So what were you planning to do with it?'

'What do you think?' She didn't add *you idiot*, but her tone implied it. 'There's, what, ten of them? I could get fifty bucks a pill.'

He stared at her stupefied. 'Kathleen, have you lost your mind?'

'Yeah. Maybe.' She did not flinch from his gaze. 'I'm behind on the rent, okay? And there's Aidan's tuition. School starts next week.'

'I told you, I'll take care of that.'

'Then how come I keep getting bills in the mail?'

Art flushed. For months, now, he'd postponed the conversation with Father Money. *My housekeeper's daughter. No, she's not a parishioner. And she hasn't been paying a dime.*

'Forget about tuition,' he said. 'I promise. I'll find a way.'

'It's more than that. It's everything. No matter what I do, I'm always behind. And it's *never going to get better.'* To his shock, her eyes filled with tears. 'I'm doing everything right, you know? I'm working. I'm not using.'

'I know,' Art said.

'I can't keep this up,' she said, her voice ragged. 'You don't get it. It's *too fucken hard.'*

Her shoulders shook with sobs. He took her into his arms.

★   ★   ★

What happened next should not have happened. Having happened, it is not for a sister to know. And yet I believe Art wanted me to know it. He wanted somebody to understand.

He kissed her hungrily, as if for nourishment. Later it would seem to him an act of cannibalism; the law he violated seemed nearly that ancient. But that night he was beyond reason, a man too long starved.

'Help me,' he whispered. 'I don't know what to do.'

It wasn't precisely true. After the first moments instinct took over, itself a revelation; it was an instinct he'd doubted he possessed. A lifetime's doubt and anguish dispelled — was it possible? — in a matter of minutes. Less than an hour had passed since he'd parked the car on Fenno Street. In that hour three lives were changed forever: his own and Kathleen's, but Aidan's, too, in ways he couldn't have foreseen and wouldn't have believed if he had.

He made love to her. This was my brother's transgression. He made love to a woman, and in so doing abandoned all he had promised and all he believed. Afterward, creeping out of Kath Conlon's apartment, conspicuous as a traffic cone in the ridiculous Hawaiian shirt, he wore his crime like a brand.

He had broken his covenant. He wasn't the first priest to fall, as Clem Fleury would remind him later. One needn't reach as far back as Alexander VI, the Renaissance pope who'd fathered eight children. Of Art's own graduating class at St. John's, two had already left the priesthood. How many others had lapsed in secret? It was impossible to know.

But the sin itself — it was that, too, a sin as well as a promise broken — wasn't the worst of it. He had taken advantage of a distraught and damaged young woman who trusted him, a girl who'd placed herself, and her child, in his care. Like so many men before him, he had exploited her weakness. He was no better — in fact much worse — than the men in San Diego buying lap dances in the dark, curtained booths. Her whole life Kath Conlon had been desired by men, used and discarded. It was a fraternity Art never imagined he'd join.

At long last the question was answered. Arthur Breen could love as other men loved. In the end, he was no more and no less than a man.

★   ★   ★

Days passed. Art didn't see her, didn't call. He explained to Fran that he'd be spending the Labor Day weekend with his sister, me, in

354

Philadelphia. Aidan could spend the days, as usual, at the rectory, in his grandmother's care.

That visit — the first time Art had shown up in Philly without warning — caught me completely off guard. I was amused by this burst of midlife spontaneity, glad to see him roll up in his battered Honda. (Diocesan priests take no vow of poverty, as many people believe; they are simply underpaid.) We rented him a bike and spent an afternoon cycling in Pennypack Park. Art's breathlessness, after thirty years of smoking, concerned but did not surprise me. I remember thinking, Thank God he finally quit. I can't recall him coughing, but I suppose that came later. He wouldn't be diagnosed for another eight months.

His mood that weekend was peculiar, a reckless gaiety I found alarming. We drank pots of strong coffee. Art seemed antsy and distracted, dying for a cigarette. Only alcohol seemed to calm him. That Saturday night, sitting on my roof to escape the heat, we opened a bottle of wine and made plans for the following day, an outdoor arts festival in New Hope. Art asked me — jokingly, I thought — the time of the morning Mass.

'There's a church down the street,' I said. 'It might be Catholic. Wake me up when you get back.'

I laughed, but Art didn't.

'Don't you miss it?' he said.

'What, church?'

'Faith.'

He eyed me intently, waiting. Amazingly, it

355

was a conversation we'd never had.

'I wonder if I could live without it,' he said. 'I don't think I could.'

He spoke softly, his voice vibrating with emotion. I refilled his glass.

'I'm not like you, Art. I'm not sure I ever had it.'

'You did. I remember.' And then: 'Your closet.'

At this I flushed red. At age ten I'd set up a secret altar in my bedroom closet, an idea I'd cribbed from a book: in *Little Women*, the youngest of the March sisters had done the same. My own altar was a footstool laid with rosary beads and a porcelain Virgin Mary, First Communion gifts from Clare Boyle. I sat there each morning saying a rosary — even at my size, kneeling was impossible in the cramped space. I remember feeling strangely elated as I prayed in secret, as though this were a forbidden activity. In fact it was anything but — Ma would have been overjoyed to see me with rosary beads, which was precisely the reason I hid them. Only when I prayed in secret did the prayer belong to me.

'You knew about that?' Nearly thirty years later, the memory was still embarrassing. I worried what it said about me. At best it seemed to point to some intrinsic foolishness, a deep-seated eccentricity that lurked within me still.

'Ma told me,' said Art. 'I thought it was extraordinary.'

'I thought nobody knew.' I drained my glass, longing to be drunker. Longing, suddenly, for

Art to disappear, or to disappear myself.

How I wish, now, that we had continued that conversation. Instead, eager for escape, I dragged Art on a pub crawl. In Manayunk the crowds were noisy and lively, and Art drank a great deal. I know now that he was thinking of Kath Conlon, trying by the time-tested method to obliterate all thought of her. I imagine her waiting for him back in Dunster, in a state of high anxiety: picking up Aidan at the rectory every night, willing the phone to ring. My heart aches for her. I am, myself, no stranger to this waiting, the charged and terrible uncertainty that follows the surrender to passion — this dangling in limbo, waiting, waiting for a man to call. It's a pale shadow, I suspect, of what Kath Conlon must have felt that weekend. Like me she is descended from a long line of Catholic daughters: virgins cast from the same mold, fired in the same oven. My own faith is a relic kept under glass, a holy curiosity like the bones of a saint. But whatever apostasy I may now affect, I blanch at the very thought of

(it is nearly unspeakable)

going to bed with a priest.

* * *

They never discussed what had happened between them. For Kath this was only briefly surprising, as her experience in this arena is vast. I am speaking not just of sex, but of heartbreak and disappointment, a long series of nocturnal lovers scattering like roaches in the light. And yet nothing in her barbed history had cut her so sharply. Of all her wounds this was the deepest, one that may never heal.

The ironies here are too many to count. To Art, especially, they should have been obvious, Art who too had been wronged by a priest.

I don't mean to equate their affair — if that is what it was — with that earlier horror. Of course they are not the same. Art and Kath were both adults (though it's possible to argue that one was as inexperienced as a child, the other as reckless and raw). And yet there's no denying that these events generated a tidal wave of confusion and shame, and neither party was much of a swimmer. My brother drove back from Philly with a raging hangover, fighting Labor Day traffic. That Tuesday morning was the first day of school. At the rectory Art watched from his bedroom window, waiting for the boy to appear.

Later he found out that Aidan hadn't enrolled at Sacred Heart. At his mother's request, Sister Ursula had sent his transcript to the Dunster public schools.

Had I known that weekend what I have since discovered, I'd have turned Art away from my doorstep. *Go back to Dunster. Talk to her.* But I didn't, and he didn't; and his silence, more than anything, made Kath vulnerable to dark imaginings. In the end she cast him, as women will, in the most sinister light. He cared nothing for her; he blamed her for seducing him. Or — worse — he didn't blame her at all. She was nothing to him, interchangeable with any number of female parishioners he'd hit on, lonely fucked-up women

358

so desperate for male attention that they'd do it with anyone, even a priest.

Art's silence was his great failure. In the Church's eyes it doesn't compare in magnitude to the sin of bedding Kath Conlon, but I am a woman, scarred in my own ways, and to me it is nearly as great. Because I am not Kath, I can forgive him. I understand that he ran from her not because the act had meant so little to him, but because it had meant so much. That night he'd glimpsed, however briefly, a sweetly exalted human happiness he'd only read about, Art who'd spent his whole life reading about apparitions. In those few moments he knew genuine tenderness, given and received. He experienced grace. If it sounds like heresy, I am far past caring: for my brother, making love to Kath was a reflection of divine love, a brief flash of God alive in the world.

If Art had been able to speak, this is what he would have told her.

By now you, reader, know Kath as well as I do. What she would have made of such a profession is impossible to say. Yet the consequences couldn't have been grimmer than what eventually did happen. Kath's shame and agitation hardened into anger. And months later, when Kevin Vick spotted a headline in the paper and had a wild idea, her anger found, at last, its object.

'Sure,' she said. 'Why not?'

Because I loved him, I have tried to imagine a different outcome for my brother: Art turning away from his life's work, the solemn promises he'd made; Art making a sharp detour — *banging a Uey* — to build a new life with Kath and her son. I have wished for him the only sort of happiness my secular mind can conceive of, the kind created by and between human beings who love. Art, himself, longed for this. On the night he made love to Kath Conlon, and in the weeks and months that followed, he dreamed of a home with her and Aidan, the family they might make. Ever passive, my brother waited. He prayed for guidance, for clarity. He sought counsel from Clement Fleury. Summer faded into fall.

What stopped him, in the end, were not the obvious obstacles: that Kath was young enough to be his daughter; as unsuited to him, intellectually and emotionally, as any woman on earth. His spiritual commitments; the covenant he'd made: even these, in the end, were beside the point.

That winter he came down with his usual bronchitis, the worst he'd ever suffered. Even after his fever broke, his deep cough would not resolve. Beginning in spring his datebook is filled with medical appointments: weeks apart, and then with accelerating frequency.

What stopped him, in the end, was what stops everybody. He simply ran out of time.

The day after Art's funeral, I drove my father's truck to Dover Court. I didn't have to do this, not yet. Art's rent was paid through the end of October; so objectively there was no hurry. And yet I felt drawn to the spot where my brother had ended his life. I am Irish enough to believe that the dying leave some bit of themselves behind, some animate residue that does not linger. I didn't want to wait too long.

The apartment was eerily quiet. For the second time I packed Art's clothes in boxes. A book, covered in library plastic, lay open beside his air mattress — one he'd read many times, Umberto Eco's *The Name of the Rose*. He had turned to it again, in extremis. I imagined him reading late at night, unable to lose himself in sleep.

The kitchen was tidy and nearly empty. A few clean dishes — a spoon, a saucer — had been set on a towel to dry. In the refrigerator I found instant coffee and canned soup. Art may not have known that these items don't require refrigeration. I have never known anyone less adept in the kitchen. His whole adult life there'd been someone to feed him: the invisible nuns who staffed the refectory at St. John's; kindly women like Fran Conlon who considered it a privilege to serve a priest.

The oven door was open a crack. Inside I

found a sheaf of takeout menus: pizza, grinders, Chinese. The oven was electric, so presumably this was not a fire hazard. Still: the *oven*? For a moment I forgot that my brother was gone, that there was no longer anyone left to scold.

'Art!' I said out loud. 'For God's sake.'

At that moment I heard a sharp knock, a male voice calling my name.

For an instant I froze. Silly girl, I thought, and went to the door.

My brother Mike stood in the hallway, dressed for work. At the funeral we had barely spoken; he was occupied with his boys, and I with my grief.

I opened the door a crack. 'What do you want?'

I'd noticed at the funeral that he'd lost weight. For the first time Mike seemed to be shrinking rather than expanding. His chinos hung on him. His hairline was receding. He looked diminished and tired, a middle-aged man.

'Ma said you'd be here.' He looked over my shoulder into the apartment, the floor littered with the empty boxes I'd brought. 'You should have told me. I could have helped.'

'I didn't think you'd want to.'

'Okay. I deserve that.' Mike took the box from my hands. 'Show me where to start.'

We packed in silence, the books Art had collected over many years, in Boston and in Rome. 'The last time I saw him — ' Mike began.

'Stop. I don't want to hear it.'

'Sheila, please.' He looked stricken. 'You were there. At Mom's.'

I thought of Mike stomping up the Pawlowskis'

362

porch stairs, hurling invective. Mike ready to tear our brother in two.

'For the rest of my life I've got to live with that,' he said. 'Art died thinking I hated him. That his own brother believed he was a pedophile.'

He wanted comfort, and I wouldn't give it. I had no sympathy for him.

'Well, he was right,' I said. 'You do.'

'Not anymore.'

I stared at him.

'I — saw her. The kid's mother.' How to convey the look that passed over his face? Even now it is difficult to describe.

'What do you mean, you saw her?'

'Nobody knows this,' he said. 'Nobody can. Abby would kill me. I'd lose everything.'

And then he told me what I've just told you.

'She's a liar,' Mike finished. 'She made the whole thing up. The hell she put that kid through, and for what? A little money.'

'Not exactly,' I said.

I didn't tell him Art's secret, not then. One day soon he will read these pages, and he will understand.

★ ★ ★

I parked the truck on Teare Street and unloaded the boxes. Art's books would be stored at my parents' house. His furniture had gone back to the St. Vincent de Paul Society.

Ma helped me carry the boxes into the parlor. I stopped a moment at the Altar and touched my

363

parents' wedding picture in its dark wooden frame.

'Who married you and Dad?' I asked.

Ma looked startled by the question. 'Father Cronin. Do you remember him?' She set a box of books on the floor. 'He was at St. Dymphna's for years. He passed away when you were small.'

'Not your uncle Fergus?' I turned to her. 'Ma, why not?'

'Your father never liked him,' she said.

I stared at her until she turned away, to straighten by a millimeter the photograph I'd disturbed.

'You'd have to ask him. I never understood it, myself. Fergus was good to me and Arthur. He looked after us all those years.'

Did you know, Ma? For God's sake, did you wonder? If I were a different person, I might have asked her. But I am her daughter, and the words wouldn't come.

Ma laid a hand on one of the boxes. 'Someday I'll go through Arthur's things. Not just yet, though.'

Again our eyes met.

'Don't wait too long,' I said.

'He loved her.'

I meet Father Fleury for breakfast at a diner near the highway. He is dressed this time in black clericals, and the waitress serves him shyly. A Catholic girl, I can tell immediately. She will not meet his eyes.

'Yes,' he says.

He leans back courteously as the waitress sets the plate before him. One poached egg, a stewed tomato. My stack of pancakes looks massive by comparison. The waitress sets down syrup and a side of bacon and refills my cup.

'I blame myself, in a sense. I didn't realize until it was too late.' He tears open a pink packet and stirs saccharine into his cup. 'He'd put himself in a dangerous situation. The girl had grown very attached to him.' He hesitates. 'And, of course, there was the boy.'

A long silence.

'I know about Fergus. What he did to my brother. Art told me before he died.'

We stare out the window into the parking lot, where a young mother wrestles her toddler into a car seat.

'He was afraid to be around kids,' I said.

'He'd always been tentative with children.' Father Fleury stares into his cup. 'I knew his reasons, of course. It seemed to me that he was unnecessarily cautious, but perhaps not. Perhaps

365

he knew better than I did.'

Was he attracted to them? I don't ask the question; I know that Father Fleury won't answer it. And maybe I'm not as brave as I pretend to be. Maybe, deep down, I don't want to know.

'The girl was troubled,' he says. 'I think in some way that was part of her appeal. Arthur wanted to save her. Priests are particularly vulnerable to that sort of thing.'

'He was lonely.'

'We all are.' He smiles faintly, a handsome man still, and for a second I can see the young priest he once was, Richard Chamberlain at the height of his film star looks. Women — men too — would have been drawn to him. Had he ever stumbled as Art had? Had he too transgressed?

'Is that the problem? You're all *lonely?*'

I sound angry, and I am. The week of my brother's death, a new scandal exploded in the Boston Archdiocese: another boy molested, another priest accused. Holy Mother, like my own, has been a negligent parent. She has failed to protect those in her care. Like many people, I have wondered: is celibacy to blame? That renunciation of human closeness, of our deepest instincts: is it, in the end, simply too much to ask? Good men — sound, healthy men — can't make the sacrifice, or don't want to; has Holy Mother settled for the unsound and unhealthy? Has the Church, ever pragmatic, made do with what is left?

Father Fleury clears his throat. 'Priestly celibacy is a recent invention, at least in Church

366

terms.' His diction turns scholarly, pedantic, and I am treated to a history lesson I don't want. Of the Apostles, only Paul was unmarried. I listen politely through the fourth century, the councils of Elvira, Nicaea and Carthage. Finally I interrupt with what, in my mind, is the only question that matters.

'Can the Church continue this way?'

He gives me an indulgent smile.

'The Church can always continue,' he says.

Two years have passed since that heartrending spring. My grief at losing my brother is compounded by the knowledge of what Art himself had lost. In the last year of his life, he made a seismic discovery: his own capacity for intimate connection and love. Given a few more years, he might have had another chance, with a different woman, one who saw all that was dear in him and loved him in return.

Of course, that is my own fantasy. Art, had he lived, might have done nothing of the kind. But that I wish it for him, with such fervor, shines a light on my own longings. It raises sharp questions about my own life, constructed, as Art's was, to preserve my solitude. Except for the one brief, doomed experiment, I have, like Art, made my life alone.

Like my brother, I have feared the water. I dove in once but quickly retreated, fearing I would drown. As many fears do, this one dates to childhood. For as long as I can remember, I've watched Ma flail against the current, refusing to let go of my father, the dead weight she was towing to shore.

Those storms in Grantham, the chaos of our household: Ma screeching like a seagull, Ted McGann roaring like the wind. The wild destruction followed by hasty repairs, and finally, an eerie calm. When I grew up and finally had a say in the matter, I moved inland, a decision I have not much regretted. Until now.

I have mourned Art's death and his lonely life, and yet my own is no less lonely. His solitude, at least, was in the service of something larger, a spiritual path designed, centuries ago, to bring him closer to God. My own isolation has taken me nowhere. It has merely kept me dry.

Last fall, shocking all who know me, I bought a house with Danny Yeager. On Christmas Eve we welcomed our first foster child, a boy named David, who has himself weathered some storms. He is the same age as Aidan Conlon — the age Art was, more or less, when Ted McGann came into his life.

For all that my father destroyed, he performed that one great kindness: he saved my brother from Fergus. He may not remember it now, but Art never forgot it, and neither will I.

This summer I will bring Danny and David to Grantham for a visit, though the very idea makes Ma squirm. It troubles her that Danny and I aren't married. As ever, her rectitude remains a wall between us. I can't quite square it with the wild girl she once was, the *céilí* dancer, the hoyden of Dudley Street. I never knew that girl, but Art did. As he explained to me one hot summer night, drinking wine on my roof in Philly: only after remarrying did Ma become so fiercely virtuous. Like her cleaning and her counting, her strictness quells a terrible fear inside her. When Harry Breen left, the earth slid out from under her. God would spare her another catastrophe if she were very, very good. If she did everything right.

★　★　★

We all continue. My parents have graduated into their seventies and manage as old people do, eased along by the gentle routines of age. Ma has scaled back her church activities — the bake sales and Catholic Daughters — and now works part-time cleaning a Catholic nursing home two towns over, less for the modest paycheck than for the regular respite from caring for my father. On those afternoons Clare Boyle comes to sit with Dad, who maintains his sunny demeanor even when the Sox are down. Grantham remains the windiest town in Massachusetts, but inside my parents' house the gusts have calmed. My father's equanimity is made possible by forgetting. His mind is like the Etch A Sketch toy I cherished as a child. With each new day his memory is wiped clean.

Mike lives, as before, in the comfortable house in Quincy. In recent months I have visited him there several times. Abby hasn't warmed to my presence so much as weathered it. She is pregnant again, with my fourth nephew; and her physical miseries occupy all her attention. Her animus toward me is overshadowed by her queasy stomach and aching back.

Mike seems delighted at the prospect of another son, a new addition to his band of brothers. *The team is shaping up*, he often says.

Of the boys, only Jamie has failed to blossom as an athlete. To Abby's horror, he expressed a brief interest in becoming an altar server (the term *altar boy* has been retired, having acquired a dark connotation, and serving Mass is now a co-ed activity). He is my favorite nephew, a quick, birdlike boy curiously unlike his fraternal twin, the beefy Michael. Now and then, when I catch Jamie singing, my eyes meet Mike's, and nothing is or can be said.

Mike never saw Kath Conlon again. Those weeks — that spring's peculiar intrigue, its nervy dance — belong in his mind to another life. He has something of our father's gift for forgetting, though Dad's blankness is neurological and Mike's is a skill, honed by practice and sheer stubborn will. And yet this faculty occasionally fails him. From time to time, when he sneaks out for a pint at the Banshee, he will glimpse a blond-haired girl, pierced or tattooed, and for just a moment he'll remember the girls who once led him through life by a wire, a vivid and pulsating strand.

Kath reminded him of Lisa Morrison, and that resemblance drew him. When he thinks of her at all, this is how he explains it to himself. It's true more often than we realize: each new love is built from the wreckage of the loves that came before. In Kath, Mike saw Lisa; in Art's eyes, she resembled our mother. I can't look at Mike's face without seeing Dad's. Art, to Ma, was the living ghost of Harry Breen. We love those who fit the peculiar voids within us, our hollow wounds. We love to fill the

371

spaces the old loves left behind.

Kath's apartment on Fenno Street now stands empty, Flip Finn having succeeded, finally, in evicting her. He'd been appalled by the condition of the apartment, mystified by the slips of paper taped to the bathroom mirror.

Let go and let God.

Meanwhile the house across the street, Twelve Fenno, sold at a handsome profit, at nearly 20 percent above the asking price. I know this because Mike sold it. For the fourth year running, he is South Shore Realty's Salesperson of the Year.

To Mike — to most people who have ever known her — Kath Conlon has disappeared completely. It is an addict's trick, this vanishing act, this dizzying plunge through a dim portal into a dark and beguiling parallel world. She lives now with Kevin Vick — I know this from Fran — in a rented apartment in Dorchester, her dream of home ownership temporarily suspended. Ron Shapiro's fee took an unexpected bite out of the settlement money; and of what remained, 80 percent will be held in trust until Aidan's eighteenth birthday. Kath's 20 percent is long gone.

Aidan, I'm told, spends most of his time at Fran's.

Back in Philadelphia, I monitor the newspapers. Every few months there is a new development, often reduced to a single paragraph: accusations and legal actions, charges pressed and much more rarely, charges dropped. In each case I wonder how much the paper doesn't tell. Is every story as complicated as Art's was, as replete with human anguish?

The journalist's craft is, to me, a mystery. My own story is written not for strangers, but for the flock Art loved and served. I want them to understand why he wouldn't defend himself. Though he hadn't touched Aidan Conlon, in his own eyes he was not blameless. He was simply guilty of a different crime.

I write for Kath Conlon, and for Aidan.

For my nephews Ryan, Jamie and Michael, who will soon forget that they ever had an uncle.

And though they may not forgive me for it, I write for my mother and Mike. If they don't wish to know certain truths about themselves and each other, they should at least know, too late, the son and brother we have lost.

(What Ma knew, and what she didn't. The question will haunt me the rest of my life.)

Ex umbra in solem.

I write to open the curtains, and let in the sun.

★   ★   ★

I write to expiate my own failing.

My brother had been molested, and that was not his fault. And yet I took it as evidence of his guilt; in effect, I condemned him for it. I live with that shame.

The adult who preys on children is, to the rest of us, a frightening enigma. Of their inner lives we know little, and a little knowledge is more dangerous than none. While it is true that most pedophiles were themselves victims, it turns out

373

that the correlation is weaker in the other direction. Not all victims grow up to be predators. My brother — I am now certain — did not.

I don't pretend to know what desires haunted him. Whose fantasies, after all, can bear the light of day? If my brother looked at Aidan Conlon, even once, with sexual longing, I will never know it, and for this I am grateful. I have learned all I can know, and all I wish to. As all of us will eventually do, Art took some secrets to his grave.

What matters, in the end, is this: if Art was plagued by dark compulsions, he didn't act on them. I know this, and Kath Conlon, lost in the shadows, knows it, too.

Was my brother tempted? I can imagine it. I can imagine Art a swimmer caught in the current, fighting his way to shore.

★ ★ ★

Father Fleury is right: the Church continues. That December, nearly five months after Art's death, the Cardinal slipped quietly out of town. A protest had been planned for that Sunday, outside Holy Cross Cathedral: when the Cardinal arrived to celebrate Mass, angry Catholics would demand his resignation. For many months, Voice of the Faithful had clamored for him to go.

Under cover of night he fled Boston, the capital of Catholic America. Like Arthur Breen, like all the other priests abruptly barred from their rectories, His Eminence traveled light.

From The Residence where he'd lived for eighteen years, he took only a small suitcase of clothes.

The source of these details — my Deep Throat — is Father Gary Moriconi. He was no friend to my brother, and yet he is now eager to help me. His long loyalty to the powerful has dissipated overnight, as though he understands that his secrets will soon lose their value. He is like a trader in foreign currencies who hears rumors of a coup.

The secrets are many, and he takes pleasure in the telling. A coat closet in the Cardinal's office had a hidden back entrance. At His Eminence's request, his secretary often lurked there during meetings, taking notes.

'Imagine that — a priest hiding in a closet,' says Father Gary, with a gentle flutter of the eyelids.

In a stage whisper he tells me of His Eminence's famous antipathy for another prominent Cardinal. The two could scarcely conceal their dislike. Father Gary is an excellent mimic; he demonstrates the nervous way they shuffled their feet in each other's presence, two Princes of the Church pawing the ground like a couple of ornery bulls.

He describes in some detail the Cardinal's final days in Boston, holed up in The Residence like Hitler in his bunker. His Eminence slept poorly. Most nights a faint blue light showed through the windows of his office, the Cardinal at his computer monitoring the press coverage, surrounded, like a Third World dictator, by portraits of himself. Threats were a daily occurrence. The reception desk at the Chancery was enclosed in bulletproof glass. A panic button under the desk would sound an alarm in the Cardinal's office and Bishop Gilman's. The rest of the staff would have to take their chances. Father Gary pointed out, rather sourly, that there was no general alarm.

Vigor in Arduis.

That winter, the Street Priest, long defrocked, was stabbed to death in his prison cell at Walpole. An investigation followed, but no charges were ever filed. Nearly a dozen inmates took credit for the crime.

News of his death, I am sure, reached the Cardinal. He is now the Archpriest — the first American ever to hold the title — at Santa Maria Maggiore, that exquisite jewel box.

My brother said, often, that it was the most beautiful church in Rome.

Acknowledgments

I would like to thank the Anderson Center, the Ucross Foundation and the Baltic Centre for Writers and Translators, where portions of this book were written.

Paul Dinter, author of the excellent memoir *The Other Side of the Altar* (FSG, 2003), taught me a great deal about life in the priesthood. Patrick Lamb, Michael Schiavone, Michael Rezendes and Dr. Donald Yee also shared generously of their expertise.

Through the *annus terribilis*, Jack Shapiro kept me alive.

Peter Nichols and Marjorie Brasem were loving and supportive early readers. Dan Pope and Dorian Karchmar worked their usual magic. Geir Angell Øygarden appeared just in time.

Juliette Shapland has helped my books find readers around the world. And Claire Wachtel, Jonathan Burnham and Michael Morrison have given my work a marvelous home. Again and always, I am grateful.

We do hope that you have enjoyed reading this large print book.

Did you know that all of our titles are available for purchase?

We publish a wide range of high quality large print books including:

Romances, Mysteries, Classics
General Fiction
Non Fiction and Westerns

Special interest titles available in large print are:

The Little Oxford Dictionary
Music Book
Song Book
Hymn Book
Service Book

Also available from us courtesy of Oxford University Press:

Young Readers' Dictionary
(large print edition)
Young Readers' Thesaurus
(large print edition)

For further information or a free brochure, please contact us at:

Ulverscroft Large Print Books Ltd.,
The Green, Bradgate Road, Anstey,
Leicester, LE7 7FU, England.
Tel: (00 44) 0116 236 4325
Fax: (00 44) 0116 234 0205

Other titles published by
The House of Ulverscroft:

BAKER TOWERS

Jennifer Haigh

Stanley Novak is a Polish immigrant who moves to Bakerton and finds work in the booming local mine. The Novaks live on Polish Hill, with immigrants from all over Europe, chasing the American Dream. The eldest child, George, is drafted to the Pacific when America joins the war. Dorothy finds it hard to cope with her desk job in Washington. Joyce must hold the family together, aware of the life that she could have had. Sandy swans through life with his movie-star looks. And Lucy, the youngest, must find her own path in the shadow of her formidable siblings.

COME THIS WAY HOME

Liz Lyons

It's a stormy Irish summer, and the three Miller sisters are gathering at their beautiful, but shabby old family home, Tobar Lodge. Gina, middle sister and single mum, is doing her best to keep the country house afloat by playing host to summer visitors. Eldest, Lottie, is home to lick her wounds after her latest romantic adventure has ended in disaster once again. Rachel, the youngest, has led a more charmed life, but this time is bringing back a family who are struggling after the collapse of her husband's business. Family and strangers meet and collide, and as the holiday season draws to a close a long-hidden secret comes to light. All are forced to look at what home and family really mean to them.